THE ATLANTIS PLAGUE

THE ORIGIN MYSTERY
BOOK TWO

ALSO BY A.G. RIDDLE

The Long Winter

COMPLETED TRILOGY

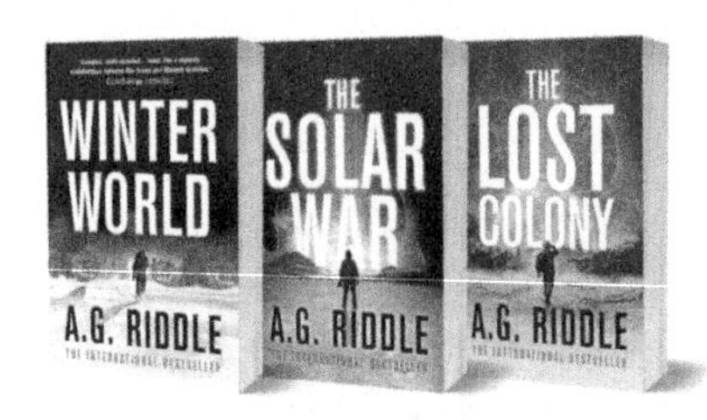

The Extinction Files

COMPLETED DUOLOGY

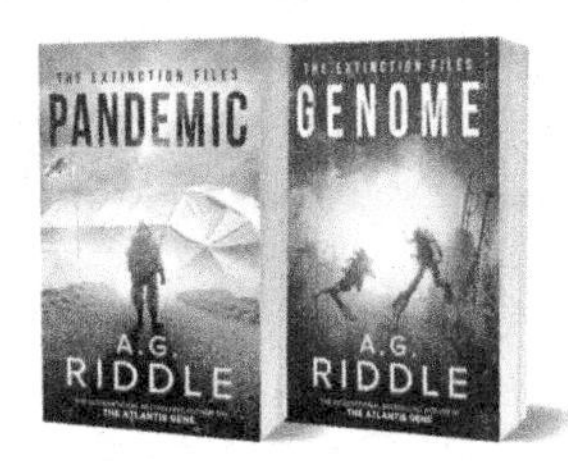

Departure

SEE MORE AT: AGRiddle.com

THE ATLANTIS PLAGUE

THE ORIGIN MYSTERY

BOOK TWO

A.G. RIDDLE

LEGION BOOKS

Published in North America by Legion Books.

Published in print in the UK and Commonwealth countries by Head of Zeus.

ISBN // 978-1-940026-07-7 // HARDCOVER
ISBN // 978-1-940026-03-9 // PAPERBACK
ISBN // 978-1-940026-02-2 // E-BOOK

THIRD EDITION (3.7.4)

For the intrepid souls who take a chance on unknown authors.

THE ATLANTIS PLAGUE

THE ORIGIN MYSTERY
BOOK TWO

PROLOGUE

70,000 Years Ago
Near Present-Day Somalia

THE SCIENTIST OPENED her eyes and shook her head, trying to clear it. The ship had rushed her awakening sequence. *Why?* The awakening process usually happened more gradually, unless... The thick fog in her tube dissipated a bit, and she saw a flashing red light on the wall—an alarm.

The tube opened, and cold air rushed in around her, biting at her skin and scattering the last wisps of white fog. The scientist stepped out onto the frigid metal floor and stumbled to the control panel. Sparkling waves of green and white light, like a water fountain made of colorful fireflies, sprang up from the panel and engulfed her hand. She wiggled her fingers, and the wall display reacted. Yes—the ten-thousand-year hibernation had ended five hundred years early. She glanced at the two empty tubes behind her, then at the last tube, which held her companion. It was already starting the awakening sequence. She worked her fingers quickly, hoping to stop the process, but it was too late.

His tube hissed opened. "What happened?"

"I'm not sure."

She brought up a map of the world and a series of statistics. "We have a population alert. Maybe an extinction event."

"Source?"

She panned the map to a small island surrounded by a massive plume of black smoke. "A supervolcano near the equator. Global temperatures have plummeted."

"Affected subspecies?" her companion asked as he stepped out of his tube and hobbled over to the control station.

"Just one. 8472. On the central continent."

"That's disappointing," he said. "They were very promising."

"Yes, they were." The scientist pushed up from the console, now able to stand on her own. "I'd like to check it out."

Her companion gave her a questioning look.

"Just to take some samples."

Four hours later, the scientists had moved the massive ship halfway across the small world. In the ship's decontamination chamber, the scientist snapped the last buckles on her suit, secured her helmet, then stood and waited for the door to open.

She activated the speaker in her helmet. "Audio check."

"Audio confirmed," her partner said. "Also receiving video. You're cleared for departure."

The doors parted, revealing a white sandy beach. Twenty feet in, the beach was covered in a thick blanket of ash that stretched to a rocky ridge.

The scientist glanced up at the darkened, ash-filled sky. The remaining ash in the atmosphere would fall eventually, and the sunlight would return, but by then, it would be too late for many of the planet's inhabitants, including subspecies 8472.

The scientist trudged to the top of the ridge and looked back at the massive black ship, beached like an oversized mechanical whale. The world was dark and still, like many of the pre-life planets she had studied.

"Last recorded life signs are just beyond the ridge, bearing two-five degrees."

"Copy," the scientist said as she turned slightly and set out at a brisk pace.

Up ahead, she saw a massive cave, surrounded by a rocky area covered in more ash than the beach. She continued her march to the cave, but the going was slower. Her boots slid against the ash and rock, as if she were walking on glass covered in shredded feathers.

Just before she reached the mouth of the cave, she felt something else under her boot, neither ash nor rock. Flesh and bone. A leg. The scientist stepped back and allowed the display in her helmet to adjust.

"Are you seeing this?" she asked.

"Yes. Enhancing your display."

The scene came into focus. There were dozens of them: bodies, stacked on top of each other all the way to the opening of the cave. The emaciated, black corpses blended seamlessly with the rock below them and the ash that had fallen upon them, forming ridges and lumps that looked more like the aboveground roots of a massive tree.

To the scientist's surprise, the bodies were intact. "Extraordinary. No signs of cannibalism. These survivors knew each other. They could have been members of a tribe with a shared moral code. I think they marched here, to the sea, seeking shelter and food."

Her colleague switched her display to infrared, confirming they were all dead. His unspoken message was clear: get on with it.

She bent and withdrew a small cylinder. "Collecting a sample now." She held the cylinder to the closest body and waited for it to collect the DNA sample. When it finished, she stood and spoke in a formal tone. "*Alpha Lander*, Expedition Science Log, Official Entry: Preliminary observations confirm that subspecies 8472 has experienced an extinction-level event. Suspected cause is a supervolcano and subsequent volcanic winter. Species evolved approximately 130,000 local years before log date. Attempting to collect sample from last known survivor."

She turned and walked into the cave. The lights on each side of her helmet flashed on, revealing the scene inside. Bodies lay clumped together at the walls, but the infrared display showed no signs of life. The scientist wandered further into the cave. Several meters in, the bodies stopped. She glanced down. Tracks. Were they recent? She waded deeper into the cave.

On her helmet display, a faint sliver of crimson peeked out from the rock wall. Life signs. She rounded the turn, and the dark red spread into a glow of amber, orange, blues and greens. A survivor.

The scientist tapped quickly at her palm controls, switching to normal view. The survivor was female. Her ribs protruded unnaturally, stretching her black skin as if they could rip through with every shallow breath she drew. Below the ribs, the abdomen wasn't as sunken as the scientist would have expected. She activated the infrared again and confirmed her suspicion. The female was pregnant.

The scientist reached for another sample cylinder but stopped abruptly. Behind her, she heard a sound—footsteps, heavy, like feet dragging on the rock.

She turned her head just in time to see a massive male survivor stumble into the cramped space. He was almost twenty percent taller than the average height of the other male bodies she had seen and more broad-shouldered. The tribe's chief? His ribs protruded grotesquely, worse than the female's. He held a forearm up, shielding his eyes from the lights that shone from the scientist's helmet. He lurched toward the scientist. He had something in his hand. The scientist reached for her stun baton and staggered backward, away from the female, but the massive man kept coming. The scientist activated the baton, but just before the male reached her, he veered away, collapsing against the wall at the female's side. He handed her the item in his hand—a mottled, rotten clump of flesh. She bit into it wildly, and he let his head fall back against the rock wall as his eyes closed.

The scientist fought to control her breathing.

Her partner's voice inside her helmet was crisp, urgent. "Alpha Lander One, I'm reading abnormal vitals. Are you in danger?"

The scientist tapped hastily on her palm control, disabling the suit's sensors and video feed. "Negative, Lander Two." She paused. "Possible suit malfunction. Proceeding to collect samples from last known survivors of subspecies 8472."

She withdrew a cylinder, knelt beside the large male, and placed the cylinder inside the elbow of his right arm. The second it made contact, the male lifted his other arm toward her. He placed his hand on the scientist's forearm, gripping gently, the only embrace the dying man could manage. Beside him, the female had finished the meal of rotten flesh, likely her last, and looked on through nearly lifeless eyes.

The sample cylinder beeped full once, then again, but the scientist didn't draw it away. She sat there, frozen. Something was happening to her. Then the male's hand slipped off her forearm, and his head rolled back against the wall. Before the scientist knew what was happening, she had hoisted the male up, slung him over her shoulder, and placed the female on her other shoulder. The suit's exoskeleton easily supported the weight, but once she cleared the cave, keeping her balance was more difficult on the ash-covered rocky ridge.

Ten minutes later, she crossed the beach, and the doors of the ship parted. Inside the ship, she placed the bodies on two rolling stretchers, shed her suit, and quickly moved the survivors to an operating room. She looked over her shoulder, then focused on the workstation. She ran several simulations and began adjusting the algorithms.

Behind her, a voice called out, "What are you doing?"

She whipped around, startled. She hadn't heard the door open. Her companion stood in the doorway, surveying the room. Confusion, then alarm spread across his face. "Are you—"

"I'm..." Her mind raced. She said the only thing she could. "I'm conducting an experiment."

PART I

SECRETS

1

Orchid District
Marbella, Spain

DR. KATE WARNER watched the woman convulse and strain against the straps of the makeshift operating table. The seizures grew more violent, and blood flowed from her mouth and ears.

There was nothing Kate could do for the woman, and that bothered her more than anything. Even during medical school and her residency, Kate had never gotten used to seeing a patient die. She hoped she never would.

She stepped forward, gripped the woman's left hand, and stood there until the shaking stopped. The woman blew out her last breath as her head rolled to the side.

The room fell silent except for the pitter-patter of blood falling from the table, splattering on the plastic below. The entire room was wrapped in heavy sheet plastic. The room was the closest thing the resort had to an operating room—a massage room in the spa building. Kate used the table where wealthy tourists had been pampered three months before to conduct experiments she still didn't understand.

Above her, the low whine of an electric motor broke the silence as the tiny video camera panned away from the woman to face Kate, prompting her, saying: file your report.

Kate jerked her mask down and gently placed the woman's hand on her abdomen. "Atlantis Plague Trial Alpha-493: Result Negative. Subject Marbella-2918." Kate eyed the woman, trying to think of a name. They refused to name the subjects, but Kate made up a name for every one of them. It wasn't like they could punish her for it. Maybe they thought withholding the names would make her job easier. It didn't. No one deserved to be a number or to die without a name.

Kate cleared her throat. "Subject's name is Marie Romero. Time of death: 15:14 local time. Suspected cause of death... Cause of death is the same as the last thirty people on this table."

Kate pulled her rubber gloves off with a loud crack and tossed them on the plastic-covered floor next to the growing pool of blood. She turned and reached for the door.

The speakers in the ceiling crackled to life.

"You need to do an autopsy."

Kate glared at the camera. "Do it yourself."

"Please, Kate."

They had kept Kate almost completely in the dark, but she knew one thing: they needed her. She was immune to the Atlantis Plague, the perfect person to carry out their trials. She had gone along for weeks now, since Martin Grey, her adoptive father, had brought her here. Gradually, she had begun demanding answers. There were always promises, but the revelations never came.

She cleared her throat and spoke with more force. "I'm done for the day." She pulled the door open.

"Stop. I know you want answers. Just take the sample, and we'll talk."

Kate inspected the metal cart that waited outside the room, just as it had thirty times before. A single thought ran through her mind: leverage. She took the blood draw kit, returned to Marie, and inserted the needle into the crook of her arm. It always took longer after the heart had stopped.

When the tube was full, she withdrew the needle, walked back to the cart, and placed the tube in the centrifuge. A few minutes passed while the tube spun. Behind her, the speakers called out an order. She knew what it was. She eyed the centrifuge as it came to a stop. She grabbed the tube, tucked it in her pocket, and walked down the hall.

She usually looked in on the boys after she finished work, but today she needed to do something else first. She entered her tiny room and plopped down on the "bed." The room was almost like a jail cell: no windows, nothing on the walls, and a steel-frame cot with a mattress from the Middle Ages. She assumed it had previously housed a member of the cleaning staff. Kate considered it to be barely humane.

She bent over and began feeling around in the darkness under the cot. Finally, she grasped the bottle of vodka and brought it out. She grabbed a paper cup from the bedside table, blew out the dust, poured a sailor-sized gulp, and turned the bottom up.

She set the bottle down and stretched out on the bed. She extended her arm past her head and punched the button to turn the old radio on. It was her only source of information on the outside world, but what she heard she hardly believed.

The radio reports described a world that had been saved from the Atlantis Plague by a miracle drug: Orchid. In the wake of the global outbreak, industrialized nations had closed their borders and declared martial law. She had never heard how many had died from the pandemic. The surviving population, however many there were, had been herded into Orchid Districts—massive camps where the people clung to life and took their daily dose of Orchid, a drug that kept the plague at bay but never fully cured it.

Kate had spent the last ten years doing clinical research, most recently focused on finding a cure for autism. Drugs weren't developed overnight, no matter how much money was spent or how urgent the need. Orchid had to be a lie. And if it was, what was the world outside really like?

She had only seen glimpses. Three weeks ago, Martin had saved her and two of the boys in her autism trial from certain death in a massive structure buried under the Bay of Gibraltar. Kate and the boys had escaped to the Gibraltar structure—what she now believed to be the lost city of Atlantis—from a similar complex two miles below the surface of Antarctica. Her biological father, Patrick Pierce, had covered their retreat in Gibraltar by exploding two nuclear bombs, destroying the ancient ruin and spewing debris into the straits, almost closing them. Martin had spirited them away in a short-range submersible just minutes before the blasts. The sub barely had enough power to navigate the debris field and reach Marbella, Spain—a resort town roughly fifty miles up the coast from Gibraltar. They had abandoned the sub in the marina and entered Marbella under the cover of night. Martin had said it would only be temporary, and Kate hadn't taken any notice of her surroundings. She knew they had entered a guarded complex, and she and the two boys had been confined to the spa building since.

Martin had told Kate that she could contribute to the research being done here—trying to find a cure for the Atlantis Plague. But since her arrival, she had rarely seen him or anyone else, save for the handlers who brought food and instructions for her work.

She turned the tube around in her hand, wondering why it was so important to them and when they would come for it. And who would come for it.

She looked over at the clock. The afternoon update would come on soon. She never missed it. She told herself she wanted to know what was happening out there, but the truth was more simple. What she really wanted to hear was news of one person: David Vale. But that report never came, and it probably wouldn't. There were two ways out of the tombs in Antarctica—through the ice entrance there in Antarctica or via the portal to Gibraltar. Her father had closed the Gibraltar exit permanently, and the Immari army was waiting in Antarctica. They would never let David live. Kate tried to push the thought away as the radio announcer came on.

You're listening to the BBC, the voice of human triumph on this, the 78th day of the Atlantis Plague. In this hour, we bring you three special reports. First, a group of four offshore oil rig operators who survived three days at sea without food to reach safety and salvation in the Orchid District of Corpus Christi, Texas. Second, a special report from Hugo Gordon, who visited the massive Orchid production facility outside Dresden, Germany and dispels vicious rumors that production of the plague-fighting drug is slowing. We end the hour with a roundtable discussion featuring four distinguished members of the royal society who predict a cure could come in weeks, not months.

But first, reports of courage and perseverance from Southern Brazil, where freedom fighters won a decisive victory yesterday against guerrilla forces from Immari-controlled Argentina...

2

Centers for Disease Control and Prevention (CDC)
Atlanta, Georgia

Dr. Paul Brenner rubbed his eyelids as he sat down at his computer. He hadn't slept in twenty hours. His brain was fried, and it was affecting his work. Intellectually, he knew he needed rest, but he couldn't bring himself to stop. The computer screen flashed to life, and he decided he would check his messages, then allow himself a one-hour nap—tops.

1 NEW MESSAGE

He grabbed his mouse and clicked it, feeling a new surge of energy...

FROM: Marbella (OD-108)
SUBJECT: Alpha-493 Results (Subject MB-2918)

The message contained no text, only a video that instantly began playing. Dr. Kate Warner filled his screen, and Paul fidgeted in his chair. She was gorgeous. For some reason, just seeing her made him nervous.

Atlantis Plague, Trial Alpha-493... result negative.

When the video ended, Paul picked up the phone. "Set up a conference—All of them—Yes, now."

Fifteen minutes later, he sat at the end of a conference table, staring at the twelve screens in front of him, each filled with the face of a different researcher at a different site around the world.

Paul stood. "I just received the results of Trial Alpha-493. Negative. I—"

The scientists erupted with questions and incriminations. Eleven weeks ago, in the wake of the outbreak, this group had been clinical, civil... focused.

Now the prevailing feeling was fear. And it was warranted.

3

Orchid District
Marbella, Spain

IT WAS THE SAME DREAM, and that pleased Kate to no end. She almost felt as though she could control it now, like a video she could rewind and relive at will. It was the only thing that brought her joy anymore.

She lay in a bed in Gibraltar, on the second floor of a villa just steps from the shore. A cool breeze blew through the open doors to the veranda, pushing the thin, white linen curtains into the room, then letting them fall back to the wall. The breeze seemed to drift in and retreat in sync with the waves below and with her long, slow breaths there in the bed. It was a perfect moment, all things in harmony, as if the entire world were a single heart, beating as one.

She lay on her back, staring at the ceiling, not daring to close her eyes. David was asleep beside her, on his stomach. His muscular arm rested haphazardly across her stomach, covering most of the large scar there. She wanted to touch his arm, but she wouldn't risk it—or any act that could end the dream.

She felt the arm move slightly. The subtle motion seemed to shatter the scene, like an earthquake shaking, then bringing down the walls and ceiling. The room shuddered one last time and faded to black, to the dark, cramped "cell" she occupied in Marbella. The soft comfort of the queen bed was gone, and she lay again on the harsh mattress of the narrow cot. But... the arm was still there. Not David's. A different arm. It was moving, reaching across her stomach. Kate froze. The hand wrapped around her, patted her pocket, then fumbled for her closed hand, trying to get the tube. She grabbed the thief's wrist and twisted it as hard as she could.

A man screamed in pain as Kate stood, jerked the chain on the light above, and stared down at...

Martin.

"So they sent you."

Her adoptive father struggled to get back to his feet. He was well past sixty, and the last few months had taken a toll on him physically. He looked haggard, but his voice was still soft, grandfatherly. "You know, you can be overly dramatic sometimes, Kate."

"I'm not the one breaking into people's rooms and patting them down in the dark." She held the tube up. "Why do you need this? What's going on here?"

Martin rubbed his wrist and squinted at her, as if the single light bulb swinging in the room were blinding him. He turned, grabbed a sack off the small table in the corner, and handed it to her. "Put this on."

Kate turned it over. It wasn't a sack at all—it was a floppy white sun hat. Martin must have taken it from the remains of one of the Marbellan vacationers. "Why?" Kate asked.

"Can't you just trust me?"

"Apparently I can't." She motioned to the bed.

Martin's voice was flat, cold, and matter of fact. "It's to hide your face. There are guards outside this building, and if they see you, they'll take you into custody or worse, shoot you on sight." He walked out of the room.

Kate hesitated a moment, then followed him, clutching the hat at her side. "Wait. Why would they shoot *me*? Where are you taking me?"

"You want some answers?"

"Yes." She hesitated. "But I want to check on the boys before we go."

Martin eyed her, then nodded.

Kate cracked the door to the boys' small room and found them doing what they spent ninety-nine percent of their time doing: writing on the walls. For most seven- and eight-year-old boys, the scribblings would have been dinosaurs and soldiers, but Adi and Surya had created an almost wall-to-wall tapestry of equations and math symbols.

The two Indonesian children still displayed so many of the hallmark characteristics of autism. They were completely consumed with their work; neither noticed Kate enter the room. Adi was balancing on a chair he had placed on one of the desks, reaching up, writing on one of the last empty places on the wall.

Kate rushed to him and pulled him off the chair. He waved the pencil in the air and protested in words Kate couldn't make out. She moved the chair back to its rightful place: in front of the desk, not on top of it.

She squatted down and held Adi by the shoulders. "Adi, I've told you: do not stack furniture and stand on it."

"We're out of room."

She turned to Martin. "Get them something to write on."

He looked at her incredulously.

"I'm serious."

He left, and Kate again focused on the boys. "Are you hungry?"

"They brought sandwiches earlier."

"What are you working on?"

"Can't tell you, Kate."

Kate nodded seriously. "Right. Top secret."

Martin returned and handed her two yellow legal pads.

Kate reached over and took Surya by the arm to make sure she had his attention. She held up the pads. "From now on, you write on these, understand?"

Both boys nodded and took the pads. They flipped through them, inspecting each page for marks. When they were satisfied, they wandered back to their desks, climbed in the chairs, and resumed working quietly.

Kate and Martin retreated from the room without another word. Martin led Kate down the hall. "Do you think it's wise to let them go on like that?" Martin asked.

"They don't show it, but they're scared. And confused. They enjoy math, and it takes their minds off things."

"Yes, but is it healthy to let them obsess like that? Doesn't it make them worse off?"

Kate stopped walking. "Worse off than what?"

"Now, Kate—"

"The world's most successful people are simply obsessed with something—something the world needs. The boys have found something productive that they love. That's good for them."

"I only meant... that it would be disruptive for them if we had to move them."

"Are we moving them?"

Martin sighed and looked away. "Put your hat on." He led her down another hallway and swiped a key card at the door at the end. He swung it open, and the rays of sunlight almost blinded Kate. She threw her arm up and tried to keep up with Martin.

Slowly, the scene came into focus. They had exited a one-story building right on the coast, at the edge of the resort compound. To her right, three whitewashed resort towers rose high above the lush tropical trees and previously well-maintained grounds. The glitzy hotel towers struck a harsh contrast to the twenty-foot tall chain-link fence topped with barbed wire that lined the development. In the light of day, this place looked like a resort that had been made into a prison. Were the fences to keep people in—or out? Or both?

With each passing step, the strong odor that hung in the air seemed to grow more pungent. What was it? Sickness? Death? Maybe but there was something else. Kate scanned the grounds near the bases of the towers, searching for the source. A series of long white tents covered tables where people worked with knives, processing something. Fish. That was the smell but only part of it.

"Where are we?"

"The Marbella Orchid Ghetto."

"An Orchid District?"

"The people inside call it a ghetto but yes."

Kate jogged to catch up. She held her hat in place. Seeing this place and the fences had instantly made her take Martin's words more seriously.

She glanced back at the spa building they had exited. Its walls and roof were covered in a dull, gray sheeting. Lead was Kate's first thought, but it looked so odd—the small, gray, lead-encased building by the coast, sitting in the shadow of the gleaming white towers.

As they moved along the path, Kate caught more glimpses of the camp. In every building, on every floor, there were a few people standing, looking out the sliding glass doors, but there wasn't a single person on a balcony. Then she saw why: a jagged silver scar ran the length of the metal frame of every door. They had been welded shut.

"Where are you taking me?"

Martin motioned to the single-story building ahead. "To the hospital." The "hospital" had clearly been a large beachside restaurant on the resort grounds.

At the other end of the camp, beyond the white towers, a convoy of loud diesel trucks roared to the gate and stopped. Kate paused to watch them. The trucks were old, and they hid their cargo behind flopping green canvases pulled over the ridges of their spines. The lead driver shouted to the guards, and the chain-link gate parted to let the trucks pass.

Kate noticed blue flags hanging from the guard towers on each side of the gate. At first she thought it was the UN flag—it was light blue with a white design in the middle. But the white design in the center wasn't a white globe surrounded by olive branches. It was an orchid. The white petals were symmetrical, but the red pattern that spread out from the center was uneven, like rays of sunlight peeking out from behind a darkened moon during a solar eclipse.

The trucks pulled to a stop just beyond the gate and soldiers began dragging people out—men, women, and even a few children. Each person's hands were bound, and many struggled with the guards, shouting in Spanish.

"They're rounding up survivors," Martin whispered, as if they could hear him from this distance. "It's illegal to be caught outside."

"Why?" Another thought struck Kate. "There are survivors —who aren't taking Orchid?"

"Yes. But... they aren't what we expected. You'll see." He led her the rest of the way to the restaurant, and after a few words with the guard, they passed inside—into a plastic-lined decontamination chamber. Sprinkler nozzles at the top and sides opened and sprayed them down with a mist that stung slightly. For the second time, Kate was glad to have the hat. In the corner of the plastic chamber, the red miniature traffic light changed from red to green, and Martin pushed through the flaps. He paused just outside the threshold. "You won't need the hat. Everyone here knows who you are."

As Kate pulled the hat from her head, she got her first full view of the large room—what had been the dining room. She could barely believe the scene that spread out before her. "What is this?"

Martin spoke softly. "The world isn't what they describe on the radio. This is the true shape of the Atlantis Plague."

4

Two Miles Below Immari Operations Base *Prism*
Antarctica

David Vale couldn't stop looking at his dead body. It lay there in the corridor, in a pool of his blood, his eyes still open, staring at the ceiling above. Another body lay across him—that of his killer, Dorian Sloane. Sloane's body was a mangled mess; David's final bullets had hit Sloane at close range. Occasionally, a piece of the carnage would peel off the ceiling, like a slowly disintegrating piñata.

David looked away from the scene. The glass tube that held him was less than three feet wide, and the thick wisps of white fog that floated through it made it feel even smaller. He glanced down the length of the giant chamber, at the miles of other tubes stacked from the floor to a ceiling so high he couldn't see the end. The fog was thicker in those tubes, hiding the inhabitants. The only person he could see stood in the tube across from him. Sloane. Unlike David, he never looked around. Sloane simply stared straight at David, hate in his eyes, his only movement the occasional flexing of his jaw muscles.

David briefly looked into his killer's glaring eyes, then resumed studying his tube for the hundredth time. His CIA training didn't cover anything like this: how to escape from a hibernation tube in a two-million-year-old structure two miles below the surface of Antarctica. There was that class on escaping from tubes in one-million-year-old structures, but he had missed that day. David smiled at his own lame joke. Whatever he was, he hadn't lost his memories—or his sense of humor. As the thought faded, he remembered Sloane's constant stare, and David let the smile slip away, hoping the fog had hidden it from his enemy.

David felt another pair of eyes on him. He looked up and down the chamber. It was empty, but David was sure there had been someone there. He tried to lean forward, straining to see deeper into the corridor with the dead bodies. Nothing. As he panned around, something alarmed him—Sloane. He wasn't staring at David. David followed Sloane's gaze into the vast chamber. Between their tubes, a man stood. At least, he looked like a man. Had he come from outside or inside the structure? Was he an Atlantean? Whatever he was, he was tall, easily over six feet, and dressed in a crisp black suit that looked like a military uniform. His skin was white, almost translucent, and he was clean-shaven. His only hair was a thick shock of white atop his head, which might have been a little oversized for his body.

The man stood there for a moment, looking from David to Sloane and back again, as if he were a betting man, touring the stables, sizing up two thoroughbreds before a big race.

Then a rhythmic noise cut the silence and began echoing through the chamber: naked feet slapping the metal floor. David's eyes followed the sound. Sloane. He was out. He hobbled as best he could toward the dead bodies—and the guns beside them. David looked back at the Atlantean just as his own tube slid open. David leapt free, stumbled on his barely responsive legs, and then trudged forward. Sloane was already halfway to the guns.

5

Orchid District
Marbella, Spain

THE MAKESHIFT HOSPITAL wing was divided into two sections, and Kate had trouble understanding what she saw. In the middle of the room, small beds stretched out, one after another, like an army field hospital. People lay moaning and convulsing, some dying, others drifting in and out of consciousness.

Martin began marching deeper into the room. "This plague is different from the outbreak in 1918."

The first outbreak Martin was referring to was the Spanish flu pandemic that swept the globe in 1918, killing an estimated fifty million people and infecting one billion. Kate and David had discovered what Martin and his Immari employers had known for almost a hundred years: that the plague had been unleashed by an ancient artifact her father had helped extract from the Atlantis structure in Gibraltar.

Kate's mind raced with questions, but as she surveyed the rows of beds and the dying, all she could manage was, "Why are they dying? I thought Orchid stopped the progression of the plague."

"It does. But we're seeing a collapse in efficacy. We estimate that within a month, everyone will become unresponsive to Orchid. Some of the dying volunteer for the trials. Those are the people you've seen."

Kate walked closer to one of the beds, surveying the people, wondering... "What happens when Orchid fails?"

"Without Orchid, almost ninety percent of those infected die within seventy-two hours."

Kate couldn't believe it. The numbers had to be wrong. "Impossible. The mortality rate in 1918—"

"Was much lower, true. That's one way this plague is different. We realized the other differences when we began seeing the survivors." Martin stopped and nodded toward a series of semi-enclosed cells along the dining-room wall. To Kate, the people inside seemed healthy, but most huddled together, not looking out. There was something very wrong with them, but she couldn't quite place it. She took a step toward them.

Martin caught her arm. "Don't approach them. These survivors seem to essentially... devolve. It's like their brain wiring gets scrambled. It's worse for some than others, but it's a regressive state."

"This happens to all survivors?"

"No. Roughly half suffer this sort of de-evolution."

"And the other half?" Kate almost dreaded the answer.

"Follow me."

Martin briefly conversed with a guard at the end of the room, and when he stepped aside, they passed into a smaller dining room. The windows had been boarded up, and every inch of the room was divided into large cells, save for a narrow walkway down the middle.

Martin didn't step further into the room. "These are the other survivors—the ones that have caused trouble in the camp."

The cramped room must have held a hundred or more survivors, but it was dead silent. No one moved. Each stood and stared at Kate and Martin with cold, dispassionate eyes.

Martin continued in a low tone. "There aren't any dramatic physical changes. None that we've seen. But they experience a change in brain wiring as well. They get smarter. Like the devolving, the effects are variable, but some individuals exhibit problem-solving abilities that are off the charts. Some get a bit stronger. And there's another theme: empathy and compassion seem to wane. Again, it varies, but all survivors seem to suffer a collapse in social function."

As if on cue, the crowds on both sides of the room parted, revealing red letters on the walls behind them. They had written the words in blood.

Orchid can't stop Darwin.

Orchid can't stop Evolution.

Orchid can't stop The Plague.

On the other side of the room, another survivor had written:

The Atlantis Plague = Evolution = Human Destiny.

In the next cell, the letters read:

Evolution is inevitable.

Only fools fight fate.

"We're not just fighting the plague," Martin whispered. "We're fighting the survivors who don't want a cure, who see this as either humanity's next step or a completely new beginning."

Kate just stood there, unsure what to say.

Martin turned and led Kate out of the room, back out into the main hospital room, and through another exit, into what must have been the kitchen but was now a lab. A half dozen scientists sat on stools, working with equipment that sat on top of the steel tables. They all glanced up at her, and one by one they stopped their work and began gawking and conversing in hushed tones. Martin wrapped an arm around her and called over his shoulder, "Carry on," as he ushered Kate quickly through the kitchen. He stopped abruptly at a door in the narrow hall behind the kitchen. He keyed a code into a small panel, and the door popped open with a hiss. They stepped inside, and the moment the door sealed shut, he held out his hand. "The sample."

Kate fingered the plastic tube in her pocket. He was only giving her half the story—just enough to get what he wanted. She rocked back on her heels. "Why are the plague effects different this time? Why isn't it happening like it did in 1918?"

Martin paced away from her and collapsed into a chair at a worn, wooden desk. This must have been the restaurant manager's office. It had a small window that looked out onto the grounds. The desk was covered with equipment that Kate didn't recognize. Six large computer screens hung on the wall, displaying maps and charts and scrolling endless lines of text, like a stock market news ticker.

Martin rubbed his temples, then shuffled a few papers. "The plague is different because we're different. The human genome hasn't changed much, but our brains operate very differently than they did a hundred years ago. We process information faster. We spend our days reading email, watching TV, devouring information on the internet, glued to our smartphones. We know lifestyle, diet, and even stress can affect gene activation, and that has a direct effect on how pathogens influence us. This moment in our development is exactly what whoever designed the Atlantis Plague has been waiting for. It's like the plague was engineered for this moment in time, for the human brain to reach a maturation point where it could be used."

"Use it for what?"

"That's the question, Kate. We don't know the answer, but

we have some clues. As you've seen, we know that the Atlantis Plague operates primarily on brain wiring. For a small group of survivors, it seems to strengthen brain wiring. For the remaining survivors, it scrambles it. It kills the rest—apparently those it has no use for. The plague is changing humanity at the genetic level—effectively bioforming us into some desired outcome."

"Do you know what genes the plague targets?"

"No but we're close. Our working theory is that the Atlantis Plague is simply a genetic update that attempts to manipulate the Atlantis Gene. It's trying to complete the change in brain wiring that started seventy thousand years ago with the introduction of the Atlantis Gene—the first Great Leap Forward. But we don't know what the endgame is. Is it a second Great Leap Forward—forcing us to advance—or is it a great step backward—a large-scale reversal in human evolution?"

Kate tried to digest this. Through the window, a massive fight broke out on the grounds near the closest tower. A line of people scattered, and a group rushed the guards. Kate thought it was the same group who had been brought in earlier, but she couldn't tell.

Martin glanced out the window briefly and focused on Kate again. "Riots are common, especially when a new group is brought in." He held out a hand. "I really do need that sample, Kate."

Kate scanned the room again—the equipment, the screens, the charts on the wall... "This is your trial, isn't it? You're the voice in the room. I've been working for you."

"We all work for somebody—"

"I told you I wanted answers."

"The answer is yes. This is my trial."

"Why? Why lie to me?" Kate said, unable to hide the hurt in her voice. "I would have helped you."

"I know, but you would have had questions. I've dreaded this day—telling you the truth, telling you what I've done, telling you the state of the world. I wanted to shelter you from it, for... just a bit longer." Martin looked away from her, and in that moment, he looked so much older.

"Orchid. It's a lie, isn't it?"

"No. Orchid is real. It stops the plague, but it only buys us time, and it's failing. We're having production problems, and people are losing hope."

"You couldn't have developed it overnight," Kate said.

"We didn't. Orchid was our backup plan—your father's backup plan, actually. He made us assume that a plague would be unleashed and forced us to search for a cure in case it ever occurred. We worked on it for decades, but we didn't make any real progress until we found a cure for HIV."

"Wait, there's a cure for HIV?"

"I'll tell you everything, Kate, I swear it. But I need the sample. And I need you to go back to your room. The SAS team is coming for you tomorrow. They'll take you to England, to safety."

"What? I'm not going anywhere. I want to help."

"And you can. But I need to know that you're safe."

"Safe from what?" Kate asked.

"The Immari. They've moved troops into the Mediterranean."

The radio reports Kate had heard mostly talked of Immari forces being defeated in third-world countries. She hadn't given much thought to them. "The Immari are a threat?"

"Absolutely. They've taken over most of the southern hemisphere."

"You can't be serious—"

"I am." Martin shook his head. "You don't understand. When the Atlantis Plague hit, over a billion people were infected within twenty-four hours. The governments that didn't topple overnight declared martial law. Then the Immari started mopping up the world. They offered a novel solution: a society of survivors—but only the rapidly evolving ones, what they call 'the chosen.' They started with the southern hemisphere, with high-population nations near Antarctica. They control Argentina, Chile, South Africa, and a dozen others."

"What—"

"They're building an army for the invasion in Antarctica."

Kate stared at him. It couldn't be. The BBC reports were so positive. Subconsciously, she pulled the tube from her pocket and handed it to him.

Martin took the tube and swiveled around in the chair. He hit a button on a thermos-like container with a small readout and what looked like a satellite phone attached to the side. The top of the container opened, and Martin dropped the plastic tube inside.

Through the window, the fighting in the camp grew more intense.

"What are you doing?" Kate asked.

"Uploading our results to the network." He looked at her over his shoulder. "We're one of several sites. I think we're close, Kate."

Explosions in the camp filled the small window, and Kate could feel the rush of heat, even through the wall. Martin punched the keyboard, and the screens switched to a view of the camp, then the coast. A group of black helicopters filled the screen. Martin stood a split second before the building shook, throwing Kate to the ground. Her ears rang, and she felt Martin jump on top of her, sheltering her from the rubble falling from the ceiling.

6

Two Miles Below Immari Operations Base *Prism*
Antarctica

DORIAN HAD ALMOST REACHED the dead bodies—and the guns—in the corridor beyond the cavernous chamber. Behind him, he heard David's bare feet pounding the floor. Dorian was about to jump when David tackled him, sending Dorian face first into the floor. A shrill wail filled the space as his skin slid across the cold floor.

They came to rest in the drying pool of blood around the dead bodies—their dead bodies. Dorian got the jump on his pursuer. He lifted his blood-soaked body just far enough off the floor to throw an elbow into David's face.

David reeled back, and Dorian seized the opening. He twisted and threw David off of him, then scrambled for the pistol lying six feet away. He had to reach it; it was his only chance. Though Dorian would never admit it aloud, David was easily one of the best hand-to-hand fighters he had ever seen. This was a fight to the death, and without the pistol, Dorian knew he would lose.

Dorian felt David's fingernails dig into the back of his thigh the instant before the fist slammed into his lower back. Pain radiated from his back into his abdomen and swept up his chest. Waves of nausea engulfed him. Dorian gagged as the second blow struck higher up, in the middle of his back, directly on his spine. The pain rushing over him almost subsided as he lost sensation in his legs. He collapsed to the floor as David crawled on top of him, preparing to finish him with a blow to the back of the head.

Dorian set his palms on the bloody floor, and with every ounce of strength he could muster, he pushed up, throwing his head back. He connected squarely with David's chin, knocking him off balance.

Dorian collapsed back to the floor and commando-crawled on his elbows, dragging his body through the blood. He had the gun, and he flipped over just as David landed on top of him. Dorian raised the gun, but David grabbed his wrists. Out of the corner of his eye, Dorian saw the Atlantean pace closer. He stared dispassionately, like a spectator at a dog fight who hadn't bet on this round.

Dorian tried to think—he had to regain the advantage somehow. He released the tension in his arms and let them fall quickly to the ground. David lunged forward but held his grip. Dorian twisted the gun in his right hand, pointed it at the Atlantean, and pulled the trigger.

David released Dorian's left hand and grabbed desperately for the gun with his right. Dorian formed a straight wedge with his left hand and drove it into David's upper abs, paralyzing his diaphragm. David gasped for air and rocked back. Dorian broke David's grip, raised the gun, and shot him once in the head.

Then he turned the gun and shot the Atlantean until the magazine was empty.

7

Two Miles Below Immari Operations Base *Prism*
Antarctica

THE ATLANTEAN STARED at Dorian with a look of mild amusement. Dorian's bullets had gone right through him. Dorian's eyes went to the other pistol in the chamber.

"Want to try another gun, Dorian? Go ahead. I'll wait. I've got all the time in the world."

Dorian froze. This thing knew his name. And it wasn't afraid.

The Atlantean stepped closer to Dorian. He stood in the pool of blood, but not a single drop stuck to his feet. "I know what you came here to do, Dorian." He stared at Dorian, not blinking. "You came down here to save your father and kill your enemy—to make your world safe. You've just killed your only enemy down here."

Dorian tore his gaze from the monster and scanned the room for something, anything he could use. Sensation had returned to his legs, and he stood and staggered backward, away from the

Atlantean, never taking his eyes off him. The Atlantean fixed Dorian with a smile but made no effort to move.

I have to get out, Dorian thought. His mind raced. *What do I need? An environmental suit.* His father had worn Dorian's suit out. Kate's suit had been damaged, but maybe he could repair it. The suits the children had worn would be too small for him, but perhaps he could use some of the material to patch Kate's suit. He only needed protection from the cold for a few minutes—just long enough to get to the surface and order the attack.

He turned and darted down the corridor, but the doors slammed shut in front of him and all around him, sealing every exit.

The Atlantean materialized in front of Dorian. "You can go when I say you can go, Dorian."

Dorian stared at him, a mix of defiance and shock on his face.

"What's it going to be, Dorian? The easy way or the hard way?" He waited, and when Dorian didn't respond, he nodded dispassionately. "So be it."

Dorian felt the air drain from the room like a vacuum. All sound faded, and a sharp punch hit him in the chest. He opened his mouth and tried in vain to suck a breath. He fell to his knees. Spots dotted his vision. The floor raced up as he fell into darkness.

8

Orchid District
Marbella, Spain

KATE ROLLED Martin off of her and quickly inspected him, assessing his wounds. Blood flowed from a gash at the back of his head. Kate thought he probably had a mild concussion, but to her surprise, he squinted, blinked several times, and leapt up. He scanned the room, and Kate followed his gaze. Most of the computers and equipment on the table had been destroyed.

Martin stepped to a cupboard and took out a satellite phone and two handguns. He held one out to Kate.

"The Immari will try to close the camp," Martin said as he began filling a backpack. He briefly inspected the thermos-like device from the desk, then stuffed it in the pack, along with several notebooks and a computer. "They've been taking islands in the Mediterranean, testing the perimeter, seeing if the Orchid Nations can or would fight them."

"Can they?"

The building had stabilized, and Kate wanted to treat

Martin's head wound, but he was scurrying around the room too fast.

"No. The Orchid Alliance is barely hanging on. All their resources—military included—are devoted to Orchid production. Help isn't coming. We need to get out." He set an egg-shaped device on the table and twisted the top. It began ticking.

Kate tried to focus. Martin was destroying the office. They weren't coming back here. She immediately thought of the spa building and the boys. "We need to get Adi and Surya."

"Kate, we don't have time. We'll come back for them—with the SAS troops who are on their way."

"I'm not leaving them. I won't," Kate said with a finality she knew Martin would recognize. He had adopted Kate when she was six, right after her biological father had disappeared, and Martin knew her well enough to know there would be no room for compromise.

He shook his head, a look somewhere between bewilderment and disbelief. "Fine but you better be ready to use that." He motioned to the gun. Then he punched the key code to exit the office, paused just long enough to let Kate come out, then keyed a code on the outside to lock the door.

The hallway was filled with smoke, and where the hallway met the kitchen, a fire raged, and screams called out in the smoky space. "Is there another exit—"

"No. The decon chamber is the only way," Martin said as he stepped in front of her. He held up his gun. "We'll run. Shoot anyone—*anyone*—who tries to stop you."

Kate glanced down at the gun, and at that moment, fear gripped her. She wondered if she could actually shoot someone. Martin grabbed the gun and pulled the slide back. "It's not complicated. Just point and squeeze." He turned and dashed toward the smoke- and fire-filled kitchen.

9

Two Miles Below Immari Operations Base *Prism*
Antarctica

Dorian strained to see the blurry shape. He couldn't take a deep breath—only a shallow, ragged breath that made him feel like he was drowning. His body hurt all over. His lungs ached when the air entered them.

The figure came into focus. The Atlantean—standing over him, watching him, waiting... for what?

Dorian tried to speak, but he couldn't fill his lungs enough. He emitted a scratchy sound and closed his eyes. There was a little more air. He opened his eyes. "What... do you want?"

"I want what you want, Dorian. I want you to save the human race from extinction."

Dorian squinted at him.

"We're not what you think we are, Dorian. We would never harm you, the same way a parent would never harm their child." He nodded. "It's true. We created you."

"Bullshit," Dorian spat at him.

The Atlantean shook his head. "The human genome is far more complex than you currently know. We had a lot of trouble with your language function. Clearly we still have some work to do."

Dorian was starting to breathe normally now, and he sat up. What did the Atlantean want? Why the charade? He clearly controlled the ship. *Why does he need me?*

The Atlantean answered him as if Dorian had spoken his thoughts aloud. "Don't worry about what I want." On the other side of the room, the heavy doors slid open. "Follow me."

Dorian got to his feet and thought for a moment. *What choice do I have? He can kill me anytime he wants. I'll play this charade out, wait for an opening.*

The Atlantean spoke as he led Dorian down another dimly lit, gray-metal corridor. "You amaze me, Dorian. You're intelligent, yet your hate and fear control you. Think about it logically: we came here on a spaceship that employs concepts in physics your race hasn't even discovered. You putt around this tiny planet in painted aluminum cans that burn the liquefied remains of ancient reptiles. Do you honestly think you could beat us in a fight?"

Dorian's mind went to the three hundred nuclear warheads aligned around the outside of the ship.

The Atlantean turned to him. "You think we don't know what a nuclear bomb is? We were splitting the atom before you were splitting firewood. This ship could withstand the force of every nuclear warhead on this planet. You would do nothing but melt the ice on this continent, flood the world, and end your civilization. Be rational, Dorian. If we wanted to kill you, you'd be dead. You would have been dead tens of thousands of years ago. But we saved you, and we've been guiding you ever since."

The Atlantean had to be lying. Was he trying to talk Dorian out of attacking?

The Atlantean smiled. "And still you don't believe. I guess I shouldn't be surprised. We programmed you this way—to survive, to attack any threat to your survival."

Dorian ignored him. He held his arm out, stepped closer, and ran his hand through the Atlantean. "You're not here."

"What you see is my avatar."

Dorian looked around. For the first time, he felt a glimmer of hope. "Where are you?"

"We'll get to that."

A door slid open, and the Atlantean walked inside.

Dorian surveyed the small room. Two environmental suits hung on the wall and a shiny, silver briefcase sat on the bench below them. His mind began working on an escape plan. *He's not here. He's a projection. Can I disable him?*

"I told you we could do this the easy way or the hard way, Dorian. I'm letting you go. Now put the suit on."

Dorian eyed the suit, then scanned the room, desperately searching for anything he could use. The door slammed shut, and Dorian felt the air draining. He reached for the suit and began putting it on. In his mind, a plan formed. He took the helmet under his right arm, and the Atlantean motioned to the silver case.

"Take the case."

Dorian glanced at it.

"What—"

"We're done talking, Dorian. Take the case, and don't open it. No matter what happens, do not open the case."

Dorian took the case and followed the Atlantean out of the room and down the corridors, back to the open space where the dead bodies lay. The sliding doors that had slammed shut were open now, and the vast tomb spread out before him. Dorian eyed the open tube David had exited. Both he and Dorian had... "resurrected" in the tubes after their deaths. Would David return again? If so, that could spell trouble. Dorian motioned to David's empty tube. "What about—"

"I've taken care of him. He won't be back."

Another thought occurred to Dorian: the time difference. His father had been down here eighty-seven years, but on the inside, only eighty-seven *days* had passed. The Bell at the perimeter formed a time dilation bubble. One day inside was a year outside. What year would it be out there? How long had he been in the tube? "What year—"

"I've disabled the device you call the Bell. Only a few months have passed. Now go. I won't tell you again."

Without another word, Dorian started down the corridor. There was a thin trail of blood—his father's. To Dorian's relief, the droplets of blood grew smaller with each step and eventually stopped. *We will be together again soon, and we will finish this.* His lifelong dream was once again within reach.

In the long decontamination chamber, he saw Kate's torn suit and the two smaller suits the children from her lab had worn.

Dorian walked to the portal door and secured his helmet. He waited with the case cupped under his right arm.

The three triangular pieces of the portal door twisted open, and Dorian stepped quickly toward them. Just before he crossed the threshold, he tossed the case aside.

An invisible force field as hard as a steel wall slammed into him, repelling him backward into the chamber.

"Don't forget your luggage, Dorian," the Atlantean's voice said inside his helmet.

Dorian picked up the shiny case. *What choice do I have? I'll leave the case outside the entrance. It won't matter.* He exited the ship and paused, taking in his surroundings. The scene was much as it had been when he'd walked through the portal initially: an ice chamber with a high ceiling, a mound of snow with a crumpled metal basket and a pile of steel cord, and an approximately ten-foot round ice shaft leading to the surface two miles above. There was something new, however. In the middle of the chamber, just below the ice shaft, three nuclear warheads sat on a steel platform, joined by a bundle of wires. One by one, tiny lights flashed on as the warheads armed.

10

Orchid District
Marbella, Spain

Kate followed Martin through the burning kitchen into the open dining room, what had been the main hospital wing. The devastation was more vast than she could have imagined. Half of the far wall had been blown away, and people were pouring out of the building, dodging falling debris and trampling the sick and the slow-moving.

Martin dashed into the throngs of people and elbowed his way forward. Kate fought to keep up. She was shocked at Martin's agility, especially given his head wound.

They cleared the building, and Kate got her first look at the camp—or what was left of it. Massive fires burned along the fence where the guard towers had stood. The fleet of trucks and jeeps spewed thick columns of white and black smoke, a toxic brew of burning rubber and plastic that made Kate choke and cover her nose and mouth with her shirt. The white hotel towers seemed untouched, but at the base of each, an endless flow of people poured out.

The resort grounds were covered. Hordes of people flowed in every direction, frantically searching for an exit, or for safety from the explosions that seemed to go off every few seconds. They almost looked like herds on the savanna, running from an unseen predator, each member simply reacting to the motion beside them.

Martin scanned the perimeter, looking for a way out.

Kate rushed past him and made a beeline for the lead-encased spa building. A small fire burned at one end, but it was otherwise untouched in the assault. Behind her, she heard the explosion from what had been Martin's office.

Kate reached the door to the spa building and raised her gun to shoot the lock, but Martin was beside her. "Save your bullets." He swiped his badge at the door, and the lock popped open. They raced down the corridors. Kate threw the door to Adi and Surya's room open, and relief washed over her when she saw the two boys sitting at their desks on opposite sides of the room, writing on their legal pads without a care in the world.

"Boys, we have to go."

Both ignored her.

She walked to Adi and picked him up. He was thin but still weighed probably forty-five pounds. Kate strained to hold him up, and he struggled in her arms, reaching desperately for his writing pad. She set him down, handed him the pad, and he settled down considerably. Across the room, she saw Martin following suit with Surya.

They practically dragged the boys out of the building, and this time Martin led Kate across the camp, into the swarming mass of people. Up ahead, a gun battle erupted, scattering the crowd. Through the fleeing people, Kate could see the Spanish troops fighting the group of survivors—a mix of the faces she had seen in the prison cell, and the new people who had been brought in. The light blue Orchid flag curled and blew in the wind as it burned above them.

Martin reached into the backpack and handed Kate a green egg with a handle. "Your arm is better than mine," he said. "If the Spanish lose, we won't get out." He pulled the pin, and when Kate realized what it was, she almost dropped it. Martin cupped her hand. "Throw it."

The stampede around her grew more intense as people slammed into her, tearing Adi's hand from hers and forcing the small boy to the ground. They would trample him. Kate launched the grenade toward the gate and the sound of the gunfire, then waded into the mob. She pulled Adi into her arms as the heat and sound of the explosion tore through the crowd.

As the smoke went up, the mass of people reversed course, flowing toward the gate. Kate, Martin and the boys fell in and managed to clear the gate just as the sound of gunfire resumed again—this time behind them.

The back of the resort opened onto a small road that joined the main highway. Kate stopped at the sight—it was amazing. Abandoned cars filled the freeway as far as she could see. On both lanes, the cars abruptly stopped near the entrance to the Orchid District. Doors stood open and the streets were strewn with garments, rotten food, and objects Kate couldn't make out. People had driven here for safety, for the life-saving drug. If Kate, Martin, and the boys could get in one of the first cars, they could get away quickly.

Martin seemed to read her mind. He shook his head. "They siphoned all the gas weeks ago. We need to get to the Old Town. It's our only chance."

They continued moving with the crowd, but with each step, the concentrated mass got thinner as families and loners broke off, taking their own course away from the coast and the death in the Orchid District. Martin continued to lead as he and Kate tugged the boys along by their hands.

Beyond the freeway, the streets were lined with the hallmarks of any Spanish resort town: beach shops, chain retailers, and hotels. All were empty, and most of the windows had been shattered. The sun had almost set now, and the gunfire in the distance still raged, but it had slowed.

As Kate walked, a new sensation gripped her: a smell, slightly sweet yet putrid. Dead bodies. How many would there be out here? Martin's earlier words echoed through her head: ninety percent die within seventy-two hours. How many had died before the Orchid District had been established? What would they find beyond its fence?

They walked a few more blocks in silence, and the streets changed. Asphalt gave way to cobblestones, and the buildings were different too. The shops were smaller and quaint. Art houses, cafes, and gift shops that had sold handmade trinkets dotted the streets. They had fared better than the stores along the main thoroughfare, but there were still signs of the mayhem here: burned-out buildings, abandoned cars, and trash.

Martin stopped to catch his breath at a white plaster wall that held an iron gate—presumably the gate to the Old Town. The rush of adrenaline that had propelled him in the camp seemed to have left him, and Kate thought he looked more haggard than ever—like a drunk the morning after a bender. He put his hands on his knees and drew long breaths.

Kate turned and surveyed the coastline behind them. Marbella's Old Town sat on a hill, and the vantage point was incredible. Without the columns of smoke, the view of the sun setting over the Mediterranean and the white sand coast would have been breathtaking. Through the smoke, a dozen black objects emerged: a fleet of helicopters.

She grabbed Adi's and Surya's hands and turned to run, but

Martin stopped her with an outstretched arm. He wrapped his fingers around her shoulder and corralled her and the boys behind him, putting his body between them and something. Kate peered over his shoulder and saw what it was.

At the cross street ahead, two wolves wandered into the intersection. The animals stood still for a moment, listening, then slowly turned their heads toward Kate, Martin, and the boys. A still, quiet moment seemed to stretch on forever. Then Kate heard the soft sound of paws padding across the stone street. Two more wolves joined the first two, then another joined them, and then three more, making eight in total, all standing in the street, staring.

The largest wolf broke from the pack and strode toward them, never taking his eyes off Martin. A second mangy animal followed close on his heels.

They stopped a few feet from Martin, studying him. Kate's hands started to shake. Moisture filled the space where her hands met the boys' hands.

Behind them, the thump-thump-thump of the helicopters grew louder.

11

Two Miles Below Immari Operations Base *Prism*
Antarctica

Dorian held his arms up, letting the case crash into the hard snow below. What did he expect his Immari comrades to do? He had just walked out wearing an Atlantean suit, holding a mysterious case. He would have already thrown the switch on the nukes.

The visor in the helmet was mirrored—they couldn't see Dorian's face. He needed some way to communicate with them, some method of sending a message. He scanned the ice room for something he could use. He couldn't scratch a message in the ice—it was frozen solid. With his hand, he began motioning in the air, writing the letters: D - O - R - I - A - N.

A second set of lights on the nukes came on.

He traced the letters again. It wasn't working. He cast a glance around the room, desperately trying to find anything that could—

A body, almost buried in ice, lay against the wall. Dorian

rushed to it and punched the ice around it, trying to dig it out. Maybe he could activate the suit's radio. He wiped the ice from the helmet and instantly reeled back in shock. His father. Rivers of frozen blood framed the face. The cold had preserved him perfectly. They had killed him—left him here to the Bell. Why? Who? Dorian sat there, staring at his father's dead body. He didn't care about the bombs anymore.

At the end of the corridor, the sound of steel slamming into ice echoed through the chamber. Dorian turned. A cage sat waiting for him. The lights on the bombs stayed active, but they didn't advance.

Dorian freed the rest of his father's body from the ice, hoisted him up in his arms, and walked to the basket. He set his father down gently and stood over him. The basket began rising to the surface.

12

Old Town District
Marbella, Spain

KATE COULD SEE IT NOW: the eight animals weren't wolves, they were dogs—emaciated, desperate...

Kate released her trembling hand from Adi's and reached for the gun in her pocket. As she drew it out, first the larger dog, then its feral companion, bared his teeth and growled. Both dogs' fur rose as they crouched to spring.

Martin's hand went to Kate's, and he slowly forced her to return the gun to her pocket, out of sight. He stared forward, but he didn't make eye contact with either dog.

Slowly, the air seemed to flow out of the dogs. Their fur collapsed back into matted mounds on their backs, their white foaming teeth disappeared, and they began blinking again. Then they turned and traipsed back to the pack, and swept out of the street without a sound.

Martin shook his head. "They're forming packs, but they're

just out here looking for food. And there's food here they can eat that we won't."

The sound of the helicopters was almost upon them now, and Kate saw a single spotlight carving into the sky above. What were they looking for?

Martin took Surya by the hand, and Kate and Adi chased after them. "There's a church a few blocks from here. It's close to our rendezvous point," he said. "If we can last 'til morning, we can meet the SAS team at the extraction point."

Kate pumped her legs faster, keeping pace with Martin. With every step, the last vestiges of daylight faded. Above, three lights now carved into the night.

Kate stopped in the street. The helicopters were dropping something. She and Martin practically dove into the nearest alley as the bombs descended. A large one exploded forty feet above them, raining down... sheets of paper all around them. Kate grabbed one. A flyer. The helicopters were dropping pamphlets. The page was in Spanish, but she turned it over and found an English translation.

To the People and Prisoners of Andalusia:

We have heard your call.
Freedom is at hand.
Immari International has come for you, to give you back the basic human right to liberty the Orchid Bloc has denied you.
Stand with us and reclaim your right to live and die as you choose.
Your dictators have revoked your right to select your own government.
Place bedsheets upon your roofs and show the world your choice.
We come in peace, but we will not turn away from war.

Kate scanned the horizon. White sheets drifted down from the helicopters, blanketing the city. The Immari were apparently rigging the "vote." What would they do? Take satellite photos and show the world, justifying their invasion?

Kate realized Martin was already back in the street, pushing as hard as he could toward the church. Kate stuffed the page in her pocket and rushed after him.

Behind her, the thump-thump-thump of another group of helicopters filled the air. They were dropping something different this time. Parachutes attached to... soldiers? Paratroopers?

Martin glanced back at the helicopters, and for a brief flash, Kate saw the fear in his eyes.

Their heart-pounding escape from the coast and their pace since then had no doubt sent his blood pressure through the roof —not exactly ideal for anyone with a head wound. Kate could see the blood seeping from the gash at the back of his head. She would need to close the wound and soon.

They charged on. Block after block of the Old Town district passed, almost in a blur.

Up ahead, a parachute drifted down, silently swaying back and forth.

Martin and Kate stopped, bringing the boys to a halt beside them. They had nowhere to go, but... the passenger at the end of the parachute's strings wasn't a person. It was a metal barrel.

The barrel clanged onto the cobblestone street, rolled around for a second, and then a plug at the end popped off, and it began spinning wildly as green gas spewed into the street.

Martin motioned for Kate to retreat. "They're gassing the city. Come on, we have to get inside."

They searched every building on the block for a store without broken windows, but every storefront was the same: chains around the door and plate-glass windows that had long since been broken out. Adi was slowing down, and Kate pulled at his arm. Both boys were tired. Kate stopped and picked Adi up. She saw Martin do the same with Surya. How far could they carry them? Ahead, a cloud of green gas flowed out of the intersection.

Kate needed to buy some time. She set Adi down and scrambled over to one of the sheets that lay in the street. She tore off four strips. She wrapped the boys' noses and mouths and handed Martin a piece of cloth.

In the alleys to their right and left, clouds of gas emerged. The scene was the same at the intersections ahead and behind. She lifted Adi and followed Martin into the gas.

13

Outside Operations Base *Prism*
Antarctica

Dorian waited calmly as the basket ascended in total darkness. The faint light of the ice chamber below had long since faded, and there was no sunlight or artificial light above, only complete darkness.

Dorian squatted over his father's body, thinking about what he would do when he reached the surface—and what they would do.

Sending the basket down for him was a shrewd move. They assumed Dorian was an enemy combatant. It was always better to fight on a battlefield of your choosing and near your own army. The Immari could only send a handful of troops down the shaft, and once they reached the bottom, they could find additional Atlantean troops there. Reinforcements couldn't be sent down quickly, so whatever force they sent could easily be lost—or worse: captured and worked for intel on Immari troop strength and defensive capabilities.

Dorian was certain of one thing: they would incapacitate him the second the basket reached the surface.

He lay down on his back in the basket, shoulder to shoulder with his dead father. He watched and waited. The floodlights of the platform above pierced the blackness, grew brighter, and finally took shape.

The basket snapped to a halt and wobbled slightly in the wind. Dorian listened to the crunch of snow as boots rushed toward him, and then he was surrounded by rows of men pointing automatic rifles at him.

There was no sound, and for a moment, nothing happened. They were waiting on him. Dorian didn't move. Finally a soldier stepped forward and bound his hands and feet, then two soldiers lifted him and his father and carried them toward the base. Bright lights bathed the area, revealing what had become of the base. The closest section was just as Dorian remembered it: a giant white caterpillar, stretching for over the length of a football field and curving around at the ends. But there were more of the caterpillars now—at least thirty—spread out as far as he could see. How many troops were camped here? He hoped there would be enough. He would find his father's killer and hold him accountable, but first he needed to deal with the threat below.

The soldiers entered a large decontamination room, and the sprinkler heads opened up, drenching Dorian and the contingent guarding him. When the liquid stopped, the men carried him out and threw him on a table.

The closest soldier popped the latch of Dorian's helmet and lifted it off. The man seemed to freeze.

"I escaped. Now untie me. They're awake. We need to attack."

14

Immari Training Camp *Camelot*
Cape Town, South Africa

Raymond Sanders watched the ridge as the first soldiers crossed. They ran at top speed—nearly thirty-five kilometers per hour—and carried twenty-seven kilogram packs. The sun was rising over the mountains of South Africa in the distance, but Sanders couldn't take his eyes off the growing army of super-soldiers training below.

"Time?" Sanders said to his assistant, Kosta, without turning.

"14:23." Kosta shook his head. "Incredible."

Sanders marveled at the time. The harder they pushed them, the stronger the soldiers got.

"We've got casualties though," Kosta said.

"How many?"

"Six. This cohort began with two hundred."

"Cause?"

Kosta flipped the pages. "Four dropped dead during yesterday's march. We're doing autopsies. Probably heart attack or stroke. Two more died in the night. Also pending autopsies."

"Three percent is a small price to pay for the gains. How about the other cohorts?"

"Improvement but nowhere near cohort five."

"End the other regimens. But let's keep testing," Sanders said.

"Same cohorts?"

"No. Let's start fresh. I don't want the previous training regimens to skew the results. The science team has a new protocol?"

Kosta nodded. "Tons of them."

"Good—"

"But I just have to say, sir. They're plateauing. We're well past the point of diminishing returns. These are people, not figures on a spreadsheet that can be adjusted. It feels like—"

"They're still getting better. Stronger, faster, smarter. The last cognitive tests were the best yet."

"True, but at some point we have to decide they're good enough. We can't keep moving the finish line. Procrast—"

"It almost sounded like you were going to say 'procrastinating,' Kosta. I can't recall exactly, but I believe I'm in charge, and you're the paper-toting helper." He shook his head theatrically. "There's one way to find out. If I tell them to put you in the next cohort, and it happens, then bam—we have our answer."

Kosta swallowed and motioned out the window, at the rows of tents and almost endless encampments. "I'm just trying to help, and... What I mean to say is... We have almost a million soldiers. We have a viable training regimen that makes them almost as strong as they're ever going to get. And we don't know how much time we have."

"We also know that we get one shot at this. The army we send into the tombs is the only one we'll ever send. They succeed or we face the uncertainty beyond that. I don't want to do that. Do you? You can follow my orders, or you can join them in the tents down there. Now tell me where we are on southern Spain."

Kosta picked up another folder. "We've taken the major cities in Andalusia—Seville, Cádiz, Granada, and Córdoba. We also have control of all the significant coastal towns, including Marbella, Málaga, and Almería. We're working on the news outlets, pressing them to release our story. Our agents say they're wavering. If they think we have a chance, they might start hedging their Orchid support. We'll know soon. Our landing troops are inbound to the coast."

"Any reaction from the Orchid Alliance?"

"Nothing yet. We don't expect much resistance. Clocktower says the Allies could be looking at a slowdown of Orchid production in France and northern Spain. Member nations are panicking."

The timing was perfect; Sanders couldn't have planned it better.

The door opened and an Immari general walked in. "Sir—"

"We're working here," Sanders snapped.

"The portal in Antarctica opened."

Sanders just stared.

"Dorian Sloane came out. He had a case with him. He says—"

"Where is he now?" Sanders said flatly.

"They brought him to the surface. He's in the primary conference room being briefed on the situation."

"You're shitting me."

The general looked confused. "He is the ranking Immari Council member."

"I want you to listen to me very carefully, general. *I* am the ranking Immari Council member. Dorian Sloane has been inside that structure for almost eleven weeks. We don't know what he's been doing down there, but I guarantee you it won't be good for us. We have to assume they have reprogrammed him, brain-washed him, and spit him out with a mission."

"What should—"

"Use the contingent of Clocktower agents on site. Have them tell Sloane there's something they need to show him. Lead him to one of the science labs. Gas him. Then take him to an interrogation room and strap him in real tight. Don't underestimate him. God knows what they've done to him. Post guards outside the door." Sanders thought for a moment. "You said there was a case. Where is it?"

"Sloane left it at the bottom of the shaft. He says he thinks it's dangerous. That we shouldn't open it."

Sanders thought for a moment. His first instinct was that the case was a bomb. Maybe Sloane really thought it was too. If they brought it up, it could destroy the entire camp or maybe something worse. There was the other alternative: that Sloane had left it down there because he or the Atlanteans needed it there. Did the Atlantean army need it outside so that they could exit the tombs? Did it serve another purpose there? Could it melt the ice and free the ship? He needed answers. He couldn't leave it there, and he couldn't move it until he knew what it was.

"What kind of science staff do we have on site?"

"Minimal. We evacuated almost everyone when we did the troop realignment for the attack."

"Send whoever we've got down the shaft. Find out what's in the case. But don't open it. Send someone without knowledge of our defensive capabilities. Call me directly when they know what it is."

The general nodded and waited.

"That's all, general." When the general left, Sanders turned back to Kosta. "Cancel the trials. This is happening now. We have to go to war with the army we have. And I have a feeling we're going to need more troops. Speed up the purge of Andalusia. Where are we on transport?"

"We're still trying to round up ships."

"Try harder. We need to move a million troops to Antarctica and soon."

15

YOU'RE LISTENING to the BBC, the voice of human triumph on this, the seventy-ninth day of the Atlantis Plague.

The BBC has confirmed multiple reports that the Immari have invaded continental Europe. The invasion began at dusk yesterday as helicopters and drones launched rockets at cities in southern Spain. Casualty figures are not known at this time.

Eyewitness reports from across the Spanish province of Andalusia say that the Orchid Districts were the primary targets of the Immari raid. Political experts have speculated for weeks that the Immari would begin assimilating vulnerable populations in Europe and Asia. It seems that they have begun their campaign in southern Spain.

Dr. Stephen Marcus, an expert at the think tank Western Century, had this to say earlier: "Nobody really knows the Immari endgame, but one fact is clear: they're building an army. You don't build an army unless you need it to protect yourself or you intend to use it to attack an enemy. It's hard to believe the Orchid Alliance could launch any sort of counterattack."

The weakness in the Orchid Alliance has prompted fears

around the world that the Immari incursion into Andalusia could be a prelude to a larger attack on mainland Europe—an attack the Orchid Alliance can't repel.

Janet Bauer, an expert on Orchid production, agrees with that assessment. "The Allies are doing well to sustain Orchid production as it is. They can't fight a war. Even if they wanted to, the practicality of getting Orchid to the front lines to keep soldiers alive makes it simply impossible. Forming an Allied army from survivors presents a completely new set of issues, namely loyalty. Most survivors who maintain healthy brain function are Immari sympathizers—they've been made to live in Orchid Districts, what many believe to be confinement, for nearly three months now."

Experts speculate that the Immari are simply nibbling at the fringes of Europe—that by taking a province the Allies can't defend, they're testing the Allied resolve and the will of the people. In essence, the Immari are taking the pulse of Europe.

Dr. Marcus elaborated on this point: "This is War Strategy 101: the aggressor takes a small step across the line, then waits for the result. Does he get appeasement or retribution? Our reaction determines his next move. If he senses weakness, he takes another step, and another."

That next step, many believe, could be Germany. Ms. Bauer agrees. "Germany is the real prize here. It's the key to the entire continent. Germany produces seventy percent of all the Orchid in Europe. If the Immari army gets to Germany, it's game over for Europe. As Germany goes, so goes the continent."

In fairness to the Immari, we've agreed to read their statement regarding the attacks:

"Immari International yesterday launched a vast rescue effort in southern Spain. For almost three months, the people of Andalusia have lived in concentration camps and been forced to take a drug against their will. Immari International was founded on the idea of creating one global society. Our origins were in trade, in linking the world. We carry on that tradition today, but the dire circumstances the Orchid nations have forced upon the world have made us pursue new avenues to global freedom. We are nonviolent, but we will protect the people of the world from oppression and any measures that violate their free will."

The BBC wishes its listeners to know that it does not take sides in armed conflicts. We report the news and will continue to report the news, no matter the victor or vanquished.

16

Immari One
Over the southern Atlantic Ocean—inbound to Antarctica

RAYMOND SANDERS TURNED AWAY from the plane's window and answered his satellite phone. "Sanders."

"We just got a report from the team examining the case. They say it's empty."

"Empty?" Sanders hadn't expected that. "How do they know?"

"They used a portable X-ray machine. They also say the weight indicates it couldn't hold anything but air."

Sanders leaned back in the seat.

"Sir?"

"I'm still here," Sanders said. "Is there anything else?"

"Yes. They think the case could be emitting some kind of radiation."

"What does that mean? It's—"

"The team doesn't know, sir."

"What's the working theory?" Sanders asked.

"They don't have one."

Sanders closed his eyes and rubbed his eyelids. Whoever was inside that structure wanted the case outside. "Sloane left the case right outside the portal. Is it possible the Atlanteans need it there to get out—that it serves some kind of purpose there?"

"Possible, I suppose. I'm not sure how we would test that theory. The science staff and equipment on site is very limited."

"Okay... Let's get the case out of there. Put it in some kind of lead box or whatever can shield the radiation, and take it to our primary research facility—somewhere we can get real answers."

"Who should we have look at it?"

Sanders thought for a moment. "Who was the cagey scientist, Chang?"

"He's on a plague barge in the Mediterranean—"

"No, not him. The nuclear guy."

"Chase?"

"Yes. Have him look at it. Tell him to report his findings directly to me."

17

Old Town District
Marbella, Spain

THE GREEN GAS was as thick as fog now, and Kate could only see a few meters in front of her. She followed Martin, hoping he knew where he was going and that they would find shelter soon. He had stopped inspecting the windows of the stores: he simply charged on as fast as he could now, carrying Surya. Adi's head rested on Kate's shoulder, and she kept her arms wrapped tightly around him. Every few seconds, he jerked slightly as he coughed.

The gas stung her eyes and left a bit of a metallic taste in her mouth. She wondered what it was, what it was doing to them.

Ahead, Martin abruptly turned to the right, into a small courtyard. A white plaster church stood at the end, and Martin raced to its heavy wooden door. As they approached it, Kate inspected the stained-glass windows. The desperate citizens of Marbella hadn't broken them.

Martin threw the door open, and Kate and the boys rushed

in. He closed it just as the first wisps of green gas drifted through.

Kate set Adi down and practically collapsed. She was completely drained, too sapped to even survey the cathedral. She used her last bit of strength to pull the cloth from Adi's and Surya's faces and give each of the boys a quick inspection. They were tired but otherwise okay.

She turned away, walked to the closest wooden pew and stretched out. A few minutes later, Martin was there, hovering over her with a protein bar and a bottle of water. She took both, ate a bit, drank a little, then closed her eyes slowly and drifted off to sleep.

Martin watched Kate sleep while he waited for the secure chat connection to activate.

The chat window expanded, and a line of text popped up.

Station 23.DC> Status?
Station 97.MB> Dire. Immari invasion of Marbella underway. Trapped. Have Kate as well as Beta-1 and Beta-2. Safe for now. Not much longer. Request immediate exfil. Cannot wait. Current loc: Church of Saint Mary.
Station 23.DC> Standby
Station 23.DC> Field team report from Present-2 hrs: outside Marbella. Town gassed, but dissipating. Will be at rendezvous loc at 0900 local time. /END REPORT/ NOTE: team consists of 5 heavily

`armed soldiers in Spanish military uniforms.`

Martin leaned back and exhaled. Maybe they had a chance. He glanced over at Kate. She twisted and grimaced. She was having a nightmare, and sleeping on the hard wooden pew probably didn't help, but it was the best Martin could do for her. He knew she would need the rest.

Kate was dreaming, but it felt so real to her. She was in Antarctica again, in the tombs of Atlantis. The shimmering gray walls and beady lights at the floor and ceiling sent a shiver through her. The place was quiet, and she was alone. Her footsteps echoed loudly, startling her. She looked down. She was wearing boots—and a uniform of some kind. Where was David? Her father? The boys?

"Hello?" she called out, but her words only echoed through the cold empty space.

To her left, a large set of double doors parted, sending light into the dim hallway. She stepped through the door and scanned the room. She knew this room. She had seen it before. The room held a dozen tubes, each standing on end, each holding a different human ancestor, a specimen from one of the human subspecies. But only half the tubes were full now. Where had the other bodies gone?

"We're getting more test results."

Kate turned quickly, but before she could see the face, the room disappeared.

18

`Immari Operations Base *Prism*`
`Antarctica`

DORIAN KNEW THE ROOM—IT was the same interrogation room where he had detained Kate Warner before she had escaped. Someone had added an interrogation chair—what could have been a dentist's chair with thick straps at the feet, wrists, and chest. The soldiers had strapped him in so tight he could barely breathe. The grogginess from the gas wouldn't seem to pass. Why had his people turned on him? Had the portal opened again? Had another Dorian Sloane walked out with another story? Or another case? Had the case Dorian carried out exploded?

Dorian didn't have to wait long for an answer. The door swung open and a smug man strolled in, two Immari special forces soldiers at his side. Dorian knew the man. What was his name? Sanford? Anders? Sanders. That was it. He was a middle manager, in Immari Capital. The look on Sanders' face told

Dorian what this was: a power struggle. The revelation sent relief through Dorian's body. He could handle a power struggle.

Dorian inhaled a shallow breath, but his adversary spoke first. "Dorian. Long time no see. How are you?"

"We don't have time for this—"

He nodded knowingly. "Right. Atlanteans. Waking up. Coming out. We're on it."

"There's something down there that controls the ship inside. We need to destroy it from the outside."

Sanders walked closer to Dorian, scrutinizing him, inspecting him. "What did they do to you? I mean, you look great. Almost like new. Smooth skin. You've really shaken off that used up, rode hard and put away wet look you wore so poorly."

This was Sanders' plan—to humiliate Dorian, to show whoever was watching through the glass that Sanders was in charge and that Dorian was no threat. Dorian strained against the chest strap, trying desperately to lean forward. He practically spat his words. "Listen to me very closely, Sanders. You're going to release me, and we'll forget all about this. If you don't, I swear to you, I will rip you open and drink your blood while I watch you die."

Sanders jerked his head back, raised his eyebrows, held the expression for a long moment, then laughed out loud. "My God, what did they do to you, Dorian? You're actually crazier than you were before. Who knew that was possible?" He paced away from Dorian and turned back, his expression serious again. "Now, I want you to listen to me very closely, because this is what's *actually* going to happen. You're going to stay strapped in that chair, where you'll wiggle and shout more crazy stuff. Then we're going to drug you, after which you'll tell us everything that happened down there, and when we're done with you, we're going to throw your limp body down that hole where you'll freeze to death, which is a better death than my predecessor gave your crazy daddy."

Shock spread across Dorian's face.

"Yes, that was us. What can I say, Dorian? Management change can be brutal sometimes. Here, I'll show you what I mean." Sanders turned to one of the guards. "Get the drugs, let's get started."

A cold rage ran through Dorian, a clear, calculating kind of hate that focused his mind. His eyes scanned the straps at his hands and chest. He couldn't break either. His arms would break first. He jerked his hand back on the left strap. It didn't give. He felt the pain radiate from his hand. He had almost broken his thumb. He pulled harder against the strap and felt his thumb pop out of its joint. The pain fought a war with the rage in Dorian's mind. The rage won.

Sanders gripped the door handle. "I guess this is goodbye, Dorian."

One of the guards cocked his head and stepped toward Dorian. Had he realized what Dorian was doing?

Dorian jerked his left arm with every ounce of strength he had. The knuckles of his index and pinky fingers buckled and popped below the middle fingers, allowing his arm to slide out of the strap. But the hand was badly damaged—he could only use the middle two fingers. Would it be enough? He reached over and grasped the strap that restrained his right arm. His middle fingers barely had enough strength to pin the strap to his palm. But he had it. The pain was overtaking him. He jerked back and the strap came free. The soldier lunged for him. Dorian ripped the chest strap off and rose, shoved the heel of his right hand into the guard's nose, and pivoted, lunging just in time to grab Sanders' legs.

The restraints at Dorian's feet held him to the chair, but he pulled Sanders down to the ground and then to him. Sanders cried out as Dorian bit into his neck. Blood sprayed all over Dorian's face and the floor, drenching the white surface in seconds. Dorian pushed off of Sanders just in time to see the other guard draw his sidearm. He fired two shots into Dorian's head.

19

The Church of St. Mary of Incarnation
Marbella, Spain

KATE AWOKE to the sound of someone typing feverishly. She brought a hand up to wipe the sleep from her eyes and instantly realized how sore she was. The frantic escape from the Orchid District and sleeping on the hard wooden pew had taken a toll on her. For the first time since Martin had brought her to Marbella, she missed the tiny bed in the spa building, and the quiet life of isolation she had lived there.

She sat up and looked around. The church was dark except for two candles burning in the center aisle, and the glow of a laptop screen illuminating Martin's face. Upon seeing her, he quickly closed the laptop, grabbed something out of the backpack, and edged over to her. "Are you hungry?" he asked.

Kate shook her head. She searched the dim cathedral for the boys. They were curled up beside each other on the next pew, wrapped in several layers of the white sheets the helicopters had dropped. They looked so peaceful. Martin must have gone back out to get the sheets after she had passed out. She focused on him. "I want to finish our conversation."

Dread filled Martin's face, and he turned away from Kate and drew two more items out of the backpack. "Fine but I need something first. Two things, actually." He held up a blood draw kit. "I need a blood sample from you."

"You think I'm connected to the plague somehow?"

Martin nodded. "If I'm right, you're a significant piece of the puzzle."

Kate wanted to ask how, but another question nagged at her. "What's the second thing?"

Martin extended a round plastic bottle filled with brown liquid. "I need you to dye your hair."

Kate stared at Martin's outstretched hands. "Fine," she said. "But I want to know who's looking for me." She took the blood draw kit, and Martin helped her with it.

"Everybody."

"Everybody?"

Martin glanced away from her. "Yes. The Orchid Alliance, the Immari, and all the dying governments in between."

"What? Why?"

"After the explosions at the facility in China, Immari International released a statement saying you carried out the attack and unleashed the plague, a weaponized flu strain—the product of your research. They had video footage, which was real of course. And it was consistent with the previous statement from the Indonesian government naming you for your involvement in the attacks in Jakarta and in performing unauthorized research on children with autism."

"It's a lie," Kate said flatly.

"Yes, it's a lie, but the media repeated it, and a lie repeated becomes perception, and perception is reality. Perception is also very hard to change. When the plague went global, everyone wanted someone to blame. You were the first story and for many reasons, the *best* story."

"The best story?"

"Think about it. A supposedly deranged woman, working alone, creating a virus to infect the world and accomplish her own delusional goals? It's a lot less scary than the alternatives: an organized conspiracy or the worst possibility—a natural occurrence, something that could happen anywhere, anytime. All the alternatives are ongoing threats. The world doesn't need an ongoing threat. They need a crazy lone gunman, presumed dead. Or better yet, captured and punished. The world is a desperate place; catching and killing a villain puts a win on the board and gives everyone a little more hope that we might get through this."

"What about the truth?" Kate said as she handed him the tube with her blood.

Martin dropped the tube into the top of the thermos. "You think anyone would believe it? That the Immari dug up an ancient structure, hundreds of thousands of years old, below Gibraltar, and that the device guarding it unleashed a global pandemic? It's the truth, but it's farfetched, even for fiction. Most people have a very limited imagination."

Kate rubbed the bridge of her nose. She had spent her adult life doing autism research, trying to make a difference. Now she was public enemy number one. Fantastic.

"I didn't tell you because I didn't want to worry you. There was nothing you could do about it. I've been negotiating for your safe passage and safekeeping. I just finalized a deal two days ago."

"A deal?"

"The British have agreed to take you," Martin said. "We'll meet up with their team in a few hours."

At that moment, Kate couldn't help but glance at the sleeping boys in the pew.

"The boys will go with you," Martin added quickly.

Hearing that Martin had a plan, that they would be safe soon, seemed to drain half the fear and tension from her. "Why Britain?"

"My top choice would be Australia, but we're too far away. The UK is closer and probably just as safe. Continental Europe will likely fall to the Immari. The British will hold out to the very end. They have before. You'll be safe there."

"What did you trade them?"

Martin stood and held the bottle of hair dye up. "Come on, time for your makeover."

"You've promised them a cure. That's what you traded for my safety."

"Somebody has to get the cure first, Kate. Now come on. We don't have a lot of time."

20

Immari Corporate Research Campus
Outside Nuremberg, Germany

Dr. Nigel Chase stared through the wide glass picture window into the clean room. The mysterious silver case sat upright on the table, glimmering, reflecting the room's bright lights. The team from Antarctica had delivered the strange case an hour ago, and Nigel had learned nothing about it so far.

It was time to run some experiments, time to start guessing. He carefully nudged the joystick. The robotic arm inside the clean room jerked wildly, almost knocking the case off the steel table. He would never get the hang of this. It was like that silly contraption at the grocery store where you fed it a quarter and tried to fish out a stuffed animal. That never worked either. He wiped the sweat from his brow and thought for a moment. Maybe he didn't need to turn the case. He would just use the arm to move the equipment.

"You want me to try?" Harvey, his lab assistant, asked.

Nigel loved his sister Fiona dearly, almost as much as he

regretted taking on her son Harvey as his lab assistant. But she wanted Harvey out of the house, and he needed a bloody job for that.

"No, Harvey. Thank you, though. Run get me a Coke Light, would you?"

Fifteen minutes later, Nigel had repositioned the equipment, and Harvey still hadn't returned with his Coke Light.

Nigel programmed the computer to begin a round of radiation bombardment, then sat back in the chair and stared through the window, waiting for the results.

"They were out of Coke Light. I checked every machine in the building." Harvey held out a can. "I got you a regular Coke."

For a second Nigel considered telling Harvey that another light drink would have been the logical course of action, but the boy had made a good effort, and that went a long way. "Thanks, Harvey."

"Any luck?"

"No," Nigel said as he cracked the can and sipped the caramel liquid.

The computer beeped, and a dialog filled the screen.

Incoming data.

Nigel quickly set the drink down and leaned in to study the screen. If the readings were correct, the box was emitting neutrinos—a subatomic particle that resulted from radioactive decay and nuclear reactions in the sun and nuclear reactors. How could they be here?

Then the readings flashed red and the neutrino readings slowly ticked down to zero.

"What happened?" Harvey asked.

Nigel was lost in thought. Was the case reacting to the radiation? Was it some kind of signal, like guiding lights flashing in the night? Or an SOS, a proverbial tap-tap-tap with subatomic particles?

Nigel was a nuclear engineer—he focused primarily on nuclear power systems, though he had worked with nuclear warheads a bit in the eighties and on the nuclear power systems on submarines in the nineties. Particle physics was way outside his wheelhouse. A part of him wanted to call in another expert, someone with a background in particle physics, but something made him hesitate.

"Harvey, let's alter the radiation regimen, see what the case does."

An hour later, Nigel finished his third Coke and began pacing the floor. The latest group of particles the box had emitted could be tachyons. Tachyons were theoretical, mostly because they could move faster than light: not possible according to Einstein's theory of special relativity. The particles could also conceivably make time travel possible.

"Harvey, let's try a new regimen."

Nigel began programming the computer while Harvey manipulated the joystick and the robotic arm. The young man was good. *Maybe video games and youth in general, are good for something*, Nigel thought.

Nigel finished programming the radiation protocol and watched as the device spun up inside the clean room. Nigel had a theory: Perhaps the case manipulated Chameleon particles—a postulated scalar particle candidate that had a mass that depended on its environment. Chameleon particles would have a small mass in space and large mass in terrestrial environments, making them detectable. If it was true, Nigel could be on the verge of discovering the basis of dark energy and dark matter and even the force behind cosmic inflation.

But Chameleon particles were only half his theory. The other half was that the case was a communications device—that it was simply guiding them, telling them what types of particles it needed to do whatever it was going to do. The case was asking for specific subatomic particles. But why did it need them? Were they "ingredients" to build something, or a combination to unlock it? Nigel believed they had found the key, the radiation regimen the case needed. Maybe it was a sort of Atlantean IQ test, a challenge. It made sense. Math was the language of the universe and subatomic particles were the proverbial writing stone, a kind of cosmic papyrus. What was the box trying to say?

The computer screen lit up. Massive output—neutrinos, quarks, gravitons, and particles that didn't even register.

Nigel looked through the window. The case was changing. The shiny silver exterior turned dull, then tiny pits popped up. It was as if the polished surface was turning to sand. Then the grains of sand shook in place briefly before sliding to the center, where a vortex formed.

The dark vortex was eating the case from the inside out. Then the case collapsed completely and the room filled with light.

The building exploded in a flash of white light that instantly consumed the six office towers around it before spreading out for miles around, pushing down trees and scorching the earth. Then the light instantly receded, collapsing back to the point where it began.

The night was dark and still for a moment, then a tiny thread of light floated up from the ground, like a phosphorescent string, swaying in the wind as it rose. Tendrils sprouted from the thread of light and linked with other threads until they became a mesh, and the mesh weaved so tightly it became a solid wall of light, arched at the top and about twice as tall as a normal door. The gateway of light shimmered silently, waiting.

21

The Church of St. Mary of Incarnation
Marbella, Spain

KATE PERCHED on the edge of the cast-iron tub in the bathroom, waiting for the hair dye to soak in.

Martin had insisted on overseeing the operation, as if Kate might try to skip out on the dye job. Knowing the whole world was after her was a strange, yet compelling, motivation to alter her appearance. However... the logical, ultra-rational part of her mind screamed out: *If the whole world is looking for you, dyeing your hair won't save you.* Then again, it wasn't like she had anything else to do, and it couldn't hurt her either. She twisted a strand of her now-brown hair between her fingers, wondering if the transformation was complete yet.

Martin sat across from her on the tile floor, legs straight out, his back against the solid wood door of the bathroom. He typed away on the computer, occasionally pausing to contemplate something. Kate wondered what he was doing, but she let that go for the time being.

Other questions circled in her mind. She wasn't sure where to start, but one thing Martin had said still bothered her: the plague had infected over a billion within twenty-four hours. That was hard for her to believe—especially given that Martin and his collaborators had been secretly preparing for the outbreak for decades.

She cleared her throat. "A billion infected within twenty-four hours?"

"Mm-hm," Martin murmured without looking up from the laptop.

"That's impossible. No pathogen moves that fast."

He glanced up at her. "It's true. But I haven't lied to you, Kate. No known pathogen moves that fast. This plague is something different. Listen, I'll tell you everything, but I want to wait until you're safe."

"My safety isn't my biggest concern. I want to know what's really going on, and I want to do something. Tell me what you're hiding. I'll find out eventually. Let me at least hear it from you."

Martin paused for a long moment, then closed the laptop and exhaled. "All right. The first thing you should know is that the Atlantis Plague is more complicated than we thought. We're just now understanding the mechanism of action. The biggest mystery has been the Bell."

The mention of the Bell sent a shiver of fear through Kate. The Immari had discovered the Bell in Gibraltar in 1918. The mysterious device was attached to the Atlantis structure Kate's father had helped the Immari excavate. The moment the Bell was uncovered, it had unleashed the Spanish flu on the world—the most deadly pandemic in modern history. The Immari had eventually dug around the Bell and removed it so that they could study it. Dorian Sloane, the head of Immari Security, had used bodies of recent Bell victims to seed the world with the Atlantis Plague, recreating the outbreak in an attempt to identify anyone with genetic resistance to the Bell. His end goal was to create an army to attack the Atlanteans who had created the Bell.

"I thought you knew how the Bell worked, the genes it affected," Kate said.

"We thought so too. We made two critical mistakes. The first was that our sample size was too small. The second was that we were studying bodies with direct contact with the Bell, never re-transmission. The Bell itself doesn't emit an infectious agent: there's no virus or bacteria. It emits radiation. Our working theory has been that the Bell radiation causes a mutation in an endogenous retrovirus, essentially reactivating an ancient virus that then transforms the host by manipulating a set of genes and epigenetic tags. We believe this ancient virus is the key to everything."

Kate held her hand up. She needed to process. Martin's theory, if true, was incredible. It indicated a completely new kind of pathogen and even a new pathogenesis—radioactive, then viral. Was it possible?

Retroviruses are simply viruses that can insert DNA into a host's genome, changing the host at a genetic level. They're a sort of "computer software update." When a person contracts a retrovirus, they are essentially receiving a DNA injection that changes the genome in some of their cells. Depending on the nature of the DNA inserted, getting a virus could be good, bad, or benign, and since every person's genome is different, the result is almost always uncertain.

Retroviruses exist for one purpose: to produce more of their own DNA. And they are good at it. In fact, viruses make up the majority of all the genetic material on the planet. If one added together all the DNA from humans, all other animals, and every single plant—every non-viral life form on the planet—that sum total of DNA would still be less than all the viral DNA on Earth.

Viruses didn't evolve to harm their hosts—in fact they *depend* on a living host to replicate, and that's exactly what they do: find a suitable host and live there, replicating benignly, until the host dies of natural causes. These reservoir hosts, as scientists refer to them, essentially carry a virus without any symptoms. For example, ticks carry Rocky Mountain spotted fever; field mice, hantavirus; mosquitoes, West Nile virus, Yellow fever and Dengue fever; pigs and chickens, flu.

Humans are actually reservoir hosts for countless bacteria and viruses that haven't even been classified yet. About twenty percent of the genetic information in the nose doesn't match any known or cataloged organism. In the gut, forty to fifty percent of all the DNA is from bacteria and viruses that have never been classified.

Even in the blood, up to two percent is a sort of "biological dark matter." In many ways, this biological dark matter, this sea of unknown viruses and bacteria, is the ultimate frontier.

Almost all viruses are harmless until they jump to another host—a life form different from their natural hosts. The virus then combines with a completely new genome and causes a new and unexpected reaction—an illness.

That was the ultimate danger with viruses, but Martin wasn't talking about these infectious viruses that entered a human body from the outside. He was describing the activation of a past infection, a dormant set of viral DNA that originated inside the human body, buried inside the genome. It was like contracting an infectious virus from oneself—a sort of DNA Trojan horse that activated and began to wreak havoc on the body.

These human endogenous retroviruses (HERVs), as they are known, are essentially "viral fossils"—the remnants of past infections that changed the host genome, were integrated with the DNA of the host's sperm, and were transmitted to future generations. Scientists had recently discovered that up to eight percent of the entire human genome was composed of endogenous retroviruses. These fossil records of past viral infections also appear in our closest genetic relatives, living and dead: chimpanzees, Neanderthals, and Denisovans. They had been infected with many of the same viruses we had.

Kate turned the idea over in her mind. Endogenous retroviruses had been considered inert and essentially part of a large group of "junk DNA" in everyone's genome. These retroviruses were not infectious, but they did influence gene expression. Scientists had recently begun to consider the possibility that endogenous retroviruses could play a role in autoimmune diseases such as lupus, multiple sclerosis, Sjögren's syndrome, even cancer. If the virus behind the Atlantis Plague was an endogenous retrovirus, it would mean...

"You're saying the entire human race is already infected. That we were infected the day we were born—that the virus behind the Atlantis Plague is already part of our DNA." She paused. "The Bell and the bodies from it only activated a dormant virus."

"Exactly. We believe the viral components of the Atlantis Plague were added to the human genome tens of thousands of years ago."

"You think this is intentional—that someone or something planted the endogenous virus—the Atlantis Plague—knowing it would be activated some day?" Kate asked.

"Yes. I believe the Atlantis Plague has been planned for a very long time. I think the Bell is simply an activation mechanism for a final transformation of the human race. The Atlanteans are either trying to cause another Great Leap Forward—a *final* leap forward—or a great leap backward, a regression to a point before the introduction of the Atlantis Gene."

"Have you isolated the virus behind the plague?"

"No and that's exactly what's holding us up. We actually think there could be two endogenous retroviruses at work, like a viral war going on in the body. These two viruses are fighting to control the Atlantis Gene, possibly to change it permanently. In ninety percent of the infected, this viral war overwhelms the immune system and causes death."

"Like the Spanish flu."

"Precisely. And that's what we had anticipated—a traditional biological outbreak, transmitted in common ways: bodily fluids, airborne, et cetera. That's what we prepared for."

"Prepared how?"

"There's a group of us—government employees and scientists mostly. Over the past twenty years, we've worked on a cure, in secret. Orchid was our ultimate weapon against the plague—a cutting edge therapy modeled on the cure for HIV."

"The cure for HIV?"

"In 2007, a man named Timothy Ray Brown, known later as the Berlin patient, was cured of HIV. Brown was diagnosed with acute myeloid leukemia. His HIV-positive status complicated his treatment. During chemotherapy, he battled sepsis, and his physicians had to explore less traditional approaches. His hematologist, Dr. Gero Hutter, decided on a stem cell therapy: a full bone marrow transplant. Hutter actually passed over the matched bone marrow donor for a donor with a specific genetic mutation: CCR5-Delta 32. CCR5-Delta 32 makes cells immune to HIV."

"Incredible."

"Yes. At first, we thought the Delta 32 mutation must have arisen during the Black Death in Europe—about four to sixteen percent of Europeans have at least one copy. But we've traced it back further. We thought perhaps smallpox, but we've found Bronze Age DNA samples that carry it. The mutation's origins are a mystery, but one thing is certain: the bone marrow transplant with CCR5-Delta 32 cured both Brown's leukemia and HIV. After the transplant, he stopped taking his antiretrovirals and has never again tested positive for HIV."

"And it helped with Orchid research?" Kate asked.

"It was a huge breakthrough, opening up all sorts of research avenues. CCR5-Delta 32 actually protects carriers not only from HIV but smallpox and even *Y. Pestis*—the bacteria that causes plague. We focused on it. Of course, we didn't fully appreciate the complexity of the Atlantis Plague at the time, but we developed Orchid to a point where it stopped the symptoms. It was nowhere near ready for release when the outbreak occurred. It doesn't fully cure the disease, but we had no choice. There was some element of the plague we couldn't isolate. Another factor. But... we thought we could use Orchid. Containment became our goal. If we could contain the infected and suppress the symptoms, we could stop it, buy ourselves some time until we could isolate the endogenous retroviruses that caused the plague and manipulated the Atlantis Gene—the true source. That's why... your work was so... intriguing."

"I still don't understand the transmission rate—radiation?"

"We didn't either at first. In the first hours of the outbreak, something unexpected happened. The plague blew through every quarantine and containment protocol we threw at it. Kate, it was like wildfire, like nothing we had ever seen. Infected individuals, even in containment, could infect others over three hundred yards away from them."

"Impossible."

"We initially believed that we had problems with our quarantine procedures, but it was happening worldwide."

"How?"

"A mutation. Someone somewhere had an endogenous retrovirus, another ancient virus, buried in their genome. When it was activated, the whole world fell in hours. A billion people were infected inside twenty-four hours. As I said, our sample size was too small to find it; there was no way to know about this other endogenous retrovirus. In fact, we're still looking for it."

"I don't understand how it could affect the transmission rate."

"It took us weeks to figure that out. All our containment protocols—around the world—decades of planning, it all broke down in those first days. The Atlantis Plague couldn't be stopped. Every time it entered a nation, it exploded across the population. What we discovered we never would have imagined. The infected were actually putting out new radiation, not simply carrying radiation from the Bell in their tissues. We believe that the second endogenous retrovirus actually turns on genes that cause the body to change the radiation it emits."

Kate tried to process what she was hearing. Every human body emitted radiation, but it was like noise, static, the subatomic equivalent of sweating.

Martin continued. "Every activated person becomes a radiation beacon, activating, infecting everyone around them—even if they're in bio-containment tents. A person standing a mile from you with no person-to-person contact could infect you. There are no protocols for anything like it. That's why governments around the world accepted universal infection—they couldn't stop it. The focus became controlling the population so that the Immari and the survivors didn't take over the world. They began building Orchid Districts and herding the surviving population inside them."

Kate thought about the lead-encased building where she had done the experiments. "That's why you used lead sheeting on the building—to stop the radiation."

Martin nodded. "We were worried about another mutation. Frankly, we're out of our element here. We're talking about quantum biology: subatomic particles manipulating the human genome. The intersection of biology and physics. It's way beyond our current understanding of either physics or biology. We're just scratching the surface of what's known. We're way behind the game, but we've learned a lot in the past three months. We knew you and the boys were immune to the plague because you survived in China. We're trying to isolate the retrovirus that causes the radiation. The ultimate fear was that radiation from the trial participants—from a new mutation—could leak into the camp and compromise the effectiveness of Orchid. If that happened, there would be nothing standing in the way of the plague. Orchid's efficacy is slipping, but we need it; we need a little more time. I think we're close to a cure. There's one last piece. I thought it was here in southern Spain, but I was wrong... about a few things."

Kate nodded. Outside she thought she heard rumbling, like thunder rolling in the distance. Something was still bothering her. As a scientist, she knew that the simplest explanation was usually the correct one. "How did you figure it out so quickly—that there was another endogenous retrovirus? What makes you so sure there are two retroviruses at work? Why not one? One virus could cause different outcomes—the evolving and devolving result, the radiation trigger."

"True..." Martin paused, as if considering what to say. Kate opened her mouth to speak, but Martin held his hand up and continued. "It's the ships. They're different."

"The ships?"

"The Atlantean ships—in Gibraltar and Antarctica. When we found the structure in Antarctica, we had expected it to be roughly the same age and make-up as the structure in Gibraltar."

"It's not?"

"Not even close. We now believe that the ship in Gibraltar

is, or rather was, a lander, a sort of planetary rover. The ship in Antarctica is a space vessel, a massive one."

Kate tried to understand what that had to do with the plague. "You think the rover came from the Antarctica vessel?"

"That was our assumption, but the carbon dating makes that impossible. The ship in Gibraltar is older than the one in Antarctica, and more importantly, it's been on Earth a lot longer, maybe a hundred thousand years longer."

"I don't understand," Kate said.

"From what we can tell, the technology in the two ships matches; both have a Bell, but they come from different time periods. I believe the ships belong to different factions of the Atlanteans and that they are at war. I believe that these two factions have been trying to manipulate the human genome for some purpose."

"The plague is their tool to bioform us."

Martin nodded. "That's the theory. It's crazy, but it's the only thing that makes sense."

Outside, the rumbling grew louder.

"What is that?" Kate asked.

Martin listened for a moment, then stood quickly and stepped out of the room.

Kate walked to the sink and looked at herself in the mirror. Her face was more gaunt than usual, and the dark, obviously dyed hair made her look almost gothic. She turned the water on and began rinsing the brown residue off her fingers. Over the water, she didn't hear Martin return. He steadied himself against the doorframe, trying to catch his breath. "Wash that mess out of your hair. We have to go."

22

Church of St. Mary of Incarnation
Marbella, Spain

KATE WOKE the boys quickly and corralled them out of the church. In the courtyard, Martin was waiting impatiently. The heavy backpack hung from his shoulders and a worried expression clouded his face. Beyond the courtyard, Kate saw why. An endless crowd of people coursed through the street, running madly, blindly, their feet pounding the cobblestones. The scene reminded her of the running of the bulls in Pamplona.

In the corner of the courtyard, two dogs lay dead against a whitewashed wall of the church. The boys struggled to cover their ears.

Martin closed the distance to her and took Adi's hand. "We'll carry them."

"What's going on?" Kate managed as she hoisted Surya up.

"The gas was for the dogs, apparently. The Immari are rounding up everyone. We need to move quickly."

Kate followed Martin into the flow of people. Without gas

clouding her view, Kate noticed that the narrow streets were crowded with debris from the fall of Marbella: burned-out cars, looted merchandise like TVs, and overturned tables and chairs from the long-abandoned cafes that lined the streets and alleyways.

The sun was rising over the buildings that lined the street, and she squinted her eyes, trying to shield them from the intermittent blasts of light. Little by little, she acclimated, and the constant thunder of feet became background noise for an early morning run.

Someone slammed into the back of Kate, almost throwing her to the ground. Martin caught her by the arm and steadied her as they pressed on. Behind them, a new group of runners was pushing through the crowd at even higher speeds, pushing past the joggers. Kate saw that some were sick—a day without Orchid was already letting the symptoms of the Atlantis Plague reemerge. They looked panicked, wild.

Martin pointed to an alleyway ten meters ahead. He mouthed some words Kate couldn't hear, but she followed his lead, edging closer to the buildings that flanked the thoroughfare. They ducked into the alley as more bodies filled the tiny hole they left in the crowd.

Martin pressed on, and Kate tried to keep up. "Where are they going?" she asked.

Martin stopped, put his hands on his knees, and panted. At sixty, he was far less fit than Kate, and she knew he wouldn't be able to maintain this sort of pace for long. "North. To the mountains. Fools," he said. "They're being herded. We're close to the rendezvous point. Come on." He lifted Adi again and resumed walking down the narrow alley.

The rumble from the flowing mass of people behind them faded as they moved east, to a deserted part of the city. Here and there, Kate heard stirring in the seemingly empty buildings.

Martin nodded to the buildings. "They can either run or hide."

"Which is smarter?"

"Hiding. Probably. After the Immari clear the city, they'll evacuate their forces to the next town. At least, that's what they've done in other countries."

"If hiding is safer, why are *we* running?"

Martin eyed her. "We can't risk it. And the SAS will get you out."

Kate stopped. "Get *me* out."

"I can't come with you, Kate."

"What do you mean—"

"They're looking for me, too. If the Immari have pushed north, there will be checkpoints. If they capture me, they'll be on the lookout for you. I can't risk giving you away. And there's something... I need to find."

Before Kate could protest, the roar of diesel engines rang out from the cross street ahead. Martin raced to the opening of the alleyway and knelt at the corner of the building. He drew a small mirror from his pack and held it out, angling it so that he could see into the street. Kate steadied herself beside him. A large truck with green canvas covering its cargo section, similar to the one Kate had seen bringing the survivors into the camp, was slowly creeping down the street. Soldiers with gas masks fanned out beside it. They were going door to door, sweeping the houses. In the street behind them, a cloud of gas rose up.

Kate began to speak, but Martin rose quickly and motioned to the narrow passageway between the buildings, near the middle of the alleyway. They resumed their frantic pace as they rushed through the cramped space.

Several minutes into their run, the narrow corridor opened onto a larger alley, which flowed into an open-air promenade with a large stone fountain.

"Martin, you have to come with us—"

"Stay quiet," Martin snapped. "This isn't a discussion, Kate." He stopped just shy of the promenade. He got the small mirror out of the pack again and held it up to catch the sunlight. Across the square, flashes of light mirrored his gesture.

Martin turned to her just as explosions rocked the square and dust filled the air. Kate's ears rang, and she could barely see through the dust. She felt Martin grab her arm, and she in turn grabbed Adi and Surya as they waded out into the chaos erupting in the courtyard.

Through the settling dust, Kate saw Immari troops pouring in from the side streets and alleyways. Soldiers wearing Spanish military uniforms—no doubt the SAS extraction team Martin had signaled—took cover behind the massive stone fountain and opened fire on the Immari. Within seconds, the sounds of grenades and automatic gunfire became deafening. Two of the SAS soldiers fell. The remaining men were outnumbered and surrounded.

Martin tugged at Kate, pulling her toward a street to the north. Just as they reached the opening, a wave of people rolled in from the cross street and flowed toward Kate, Martin and the boys.

Kate looked back at the square. The last pops of gunfire faded, leaving only the sound of thunder—the rumble from the wall of people bearing down on them. The SAS soldiers lay dead, two in the now-red water of the fountain, two others face-down on the cobblestone street.

23

Old Town District
Marbella, Spain

KATE COULDN'T TAKE her eyes off the Immari soldiers behind them. She had expected them to rush through the promenade and capture her, Martin, and the two boys, but they hadn't. They simply loitered at the streets and alleyways that fed into the square, pacing in front of the massive trucks, some smoking, others talking on radios, all holding automatic rifles, waiting for what, Kate didn't know.

She turned to Martin. "What are they—"

"It's a loading zone. They're just waiting for the people to come to them. Come on." He charged into the narrow street, running straight for the oncoming mob of people.

Kate hesitated, then fell in behind him. The crowd was a hundred meters away and closing fast.

Martin tried the closest door—that of a ground floor shop—but it was locked.

Kate ran across the street and tried the door to a cafe. It

wouldn't budge. She pulled the boys closer to her. The crowd was fifty meters away. She tried the door of the townhome next to the shop. Also locked. The crowd would be upon Kate and the boys in seconds, trampling them. Maybe she could put the boys in front of her, press them into the doorway, shield them. She moved them in front of her and waited.

She heard Martin run up behind her. He was positioning himself to protect her, in the same way she was covering the boys.

The crowd was thirty yards away. Several runners had separated from the pack. They charged on with determined, cold eyes. They didn't glance at Kate, Martin, and the boys as the first of them passed.

In a second-story window, someone pulled a thin white curtain back. A face filled the window, a woman about Kate's age, with dark hair and olive skin. She looked down, and her eyes met Kate's. A moment passed, and the woman's expression changed from alarm to... concern? Kate opened her mouth to call to her, but the woman was gone.

Kate pressed the boys into the doorway. "Be still, boys. It's important."

Martin glanced back at the oncoming crowd.

Then the door before them clicked and swung open, sending Kate, Martin, and the boys spilling onto the floor. A man pulled them up as the woman from the second-story window slammed the door. The low rumble of the crowd seeped in through the door and windows.

The man and woman led them deeper inside, out of the anteroom and into a living room with a large fireplace and no windows. Candles lit the eerie space, and Kate struggled to acclimate.

Martin began conversing rapidly in Spanish. Kate inspected the boys, but they twisted and resisted her prodding. They had

had about all they could take. Both boys were agitated, tired, and confused. What was she going to do? They couldn't take much more. *Can we hide here?* Those were Martin's words: run or hide.

She unzipped the pack on Martin's back and took the two notebooks and some pencils out, then handed them to Adi and Surya, who grabbed them and scurried off to the corner. They needed a little piece of normalcy, something they knew, if only for a moment, to calm them.

Martin was motioning with his hands, making it almost impossible for Kate to zip the backpack. He kept repeating one word: túnel. The couple looked at each other, hesitated, then nodded and gave Martin the answer he seemed to want. He glanced back at Kate. "We need to leave the boys."

"Absolutely not—"

He pulled her aside, toward the fireplace, and spoke in a low tone. "They lost their sons to the plague. They will take the boys. If the Immari follow their previous purge protocol, families with young children will be spared—if they take the pledge. Only teens and childless adults are conscripted."

Kate looked around, her mind searching for a rebuttal. On the mantel above the fireplace, she noticed a photo of the man and woman standing on a beach, their hands on the shoulders of two smiling boys who were about the same ages as Adi and Surya. The hair color and skin tones were roughly the same as well.

She glanced between the couple and the boys, who were hunched over their notebooks, quietly working in the corner by a stack of candles. She squinted and tried to think. "They don't speak Spanish..."

"Kate, they barely speak at all. These people will care for them as best they can. This is our only play. Think about it: we are saving *four* lives here." He motioned to the two adults. "If they catch the boys with you or me, they will instantly know who they are. We put them at further risk. We have to do this. We will come back for them. And besides, we can't take them where we're going. It would be... more stressful."

"Where are we—"

But Martin didn't let her finish. He spoke quickly to the couple, who started out of the living room.

Kate didn't follow them. She walked to the boys in the corner and pulled them into a hug. They fought at her, grabbing for the notebooks, but after a moment, they settled down. She kissed each of them on the top of the head and released them.

Outside the living room, the couple led Martin and Kate down a narrow hallway to a cramped study with a large oak desk and floor-to-ceiling bookcases. The man marched to a bookcase along the back wall and began throwing the heavy volumes onto the floor. The woman joined him, and soon the shelves were empty. The man planted his feet and pulled the bookcase away from the wall. He pressed a button in the adjoining bookcase, and the wall snapped and receded slightly. He pushed, and the section of wall swung open, revealing a dark, grimy stone tunnel.

24

Old Town District
Marbella, Spain

Kate hated the tunnels. The stone walls were moist and seemed to ooze a blackish slush that brushed onto her at every turn, and there had been too many turns to count. Some time ago, she had whispered to Martin, asking him if he knew where he was going, but he had quickly shushed her, which she took to mean no. But where else could they go? Martin led the way with a bright LED bar that illuminated just enough of the tunnel to keep them from running headfirst into a grimy stone wall.

Up ahead, the cramped tunnel opened onto a circular intersection that branched in three directions. Martin stopped and held the light bar to his face. "Are you hungry?"

Kate nodded. Martin unslung the pack and dug out a protein bar and a bottle of water.

Kate chewed the bar, chugged the water, and when her mouth was clear, said in a low tone, "You have no idea where you're going, do you?"

"Not really. In fact, I'm not sure the tunnels go anywhere at all."

Kate looked at him curiously.

Martin set the light bar on the ground between them and sipped his water. "Like most old cities on the Mediterranean, humans have been fighting over Marbella for thousands of years. The Greeks, Phoenicians, Carthaginians, Romans, Muslims. The list goes on. Marbella has been sacked a hundred times. I knew the old merchant houses in the old town would have escape tunnels. The wealthy used the tunnels to avoid all the nasty things that happen when a city gets sacked. Some tunnels are just shelters for hiding. Some might lead out of the city, but I doubt it. Best case, they link up with the newer city's sewer system. But I think we're safe down here. For now."

"The Immari won't search the tunnels?"

"I doubt it. They'll do a house-by-house sweep, but it's cursory. They're mostly looking for troublemakers and anyone they didn't catch with the wider sweep. I imagine the worst we'll face down here will be rats and snakes."

Kate cringed at the thought of an unseen snake crawling across her in the darkness. The thought of sleeping down here, with snakes and rats... She held her hands out in a pleading gesture. "You might hold back on some of the details."

"Oh, right. Sorry." He grabbed for the pack. "More food?"

"No. Thanks, though. What now? How long do we wait?"

Martin considered it for a moment. "Based on the size of Marbella, I would say two days."

"What's happening out there?"

"They'll round everyone up and do a preliminary sort."

"Sort?"

"First they separate the dying and devolving from the survivors. Every survivor faces a choice. Take the Immari pledge or refuse."

"If they refuse?"

"They'll put them with the dying and devolving."

"What happens..."

"The Immari will evacuate the entire population. They'll load those that pledge and the rest on a plague barge bound for one of their operations bases. Only those that pledge will arrive." He grabbed the light bar and held it up so he could see Kate's face. "This is important, Kate. If we're caught along the way and you face the choice, you have to pledge. Promise me you will."

Kate nodded.

"They're only words. Survival is what matters now."

"And you'll take the pledge as well?"

Martin let the light bar drop to the ground, and darkness again filled the space between them. "It's different for me, Kate. They'll know who I am. If we're caught, we must separate."

"But you'll pledge."

"It won't be an issue for me." Martin let out a ragged cough, like that of a lifetime smoker. Kate wondered what sort of particles they were breathing down in the tunnels. He shook his head. "I joined once. It was the biggest mistake of my life. It's different for me."

"They're just words," Kate chided him.

"Touché," Martin murmured. "It's hard to explain..."

"Try." Kate took another sip of the water. "We've got a little time to kill."

Martin coughed again.

"We need to get you some fresh air," Kate said.

"It's not the air." Martin reached inside the pack and brought out a small white case.

Through the dim light, Kate saw him slip a white pill into his mouth. The pills were shaped like a flower, with three large, heart-shaped petals and a ring of red in the middle. An orchid.

Shock spread over Kate, and she couldn't find her voice. "You're—"

"Not immune, no. I didn't want to tell you. I knew you would worry. If we're caught, I'll be in the camp with the dying. If that happens, you'll have to finish my research. Here." He handed her something from the pack—a small notebook.

Kate set it aside with disinterest. "How many pills do you have left?" she asked.

"Enough," Martin said flatly. "Don't worry about me. Now get some rest. I'll take first watch."

25

Old Town District
Marbella, Spain

"Kate! Wake up."

Kate opened her eyes. Martin stood over her. Through the dim glow of the LED bar, Kate saw the alarm on his face.

"Come on," he said as he dragged her to her feet. He grabbed the pack and handed it to Kate. He took something out. A handgun. "Put the pack on. Stay behind me," he said as he turned to the far opening in the circular room.

Kate saw nothing, but there was... a faint sound. Footsteps. Martin pointed the gun at the opening. With his other hand, he reached down and silently clicked the light off, plunging them into total darkness.

Seconds dragged by as the footsteps grew louder. There were two sets of footsteps. A glow emerged from the opening. Slowly it grew brighter, coalescing, forming a lantern. It crossed the threshold a half second before its bearer: a bearded, obese man who almost hid a younger woman trailing close behind him.

At the sight of Martin and the outstretched gun, the man dropped the lantern and scrambled backward, throwing the woman to the ground.

Martin closed the distance. The man threw his hands up and spoke in rapid Spanish. Martin looked from the man to the woman, then conversed with the man in Spanish. When they finished speaking, Martin paused for a moment, appraising them, seeming to consider the story he had heard. He turned to Kate. "Take the lantern. They say there are dogs in the tunnels and that soldiers are coming."

Kate grabbed the lantern, and Martin motioned with the gun for the man and woman to get up and exit through the other corridor—the way Kate and Martin had come. The couple complied like prisoners on a perp walk, and the four of them set out at a brisk pace, moving in silence.

The corridor opened onto another round room, where they found six more people. They conversed hurriedly, and the new group joined Kate and Martin's band, and they set off again.

Kate wondered how they would deal with the dogs and soldiers. Her gun was in the pack and almost against her will, she considered reaching back for it. But before she could make a move, the tunnel ended in a large cavernous room, this one square with a high ceiling. There was no exit.

Two dozen people stood inside. Every head turned as Kate and Martin's group entered.

Behind her, Kate heard the fat man shouting something. She turned. He was speaking into a handheld radio. *What—*

The far wall exploded, sending dirt, debris, and an invisible wave of force into the room. Kate felt herself hit the floor of the tunnel. Light flooded the room as the dust settled. She could see Immari soldiers pouring in through the breach. They dragged people out of the shattered stone room. The fat man and the woman and a half dozen others were helping them.

The bright light and ringing in Kate's ears were disorienting. Her head swam, and she thought she would throw up.

Kate saw one of the soldiers pocket Martin's gun from the ground, then hoist him up and carry him out. Then a soldier grabbed her. She struggled, but it was no use. They had her. They had them all.

26

DORIAN OPENED his eyes and gazed through the wide pane of glass. He wasn't in a tube—not the kind he had awoken in before. *Where am I? Am I dead, really dead this time?* He had to be. The guard had shot him in the head. He looked down. He wore a uniform—the same uniform the Atlantean had worn. The scene came into focus. The large window looked out into space. A blue and green planet filled the lower half of the window. Massive machines crawled across the surface, turning dirt and sending plumes of red dust into the atmosphere. No, it was more than dirt—the machines were moving mountains.

"The geological survey is in, General Ares. The tectonic plates in the northern hemisphere won't be a problem for four thousand years. Should we leave them?"

Dorian turned to look at the man. He stood next to Dorian on what must have been the observation deck of a space ship. Dorian heard himself speak. "No. They may not be able to fix them in four thousand years. Make accommodations now." He turned back to the window. In the reflection of the glass, he saw himself, but the man who stared back wasn't Dorian; it was the

Atlantean—a younger version. He had a full head of white-golden hair, pulled back flat against his head.

The glass disappeared, and the air and gravity changed. A bomb exploded in the distance, and Dorian realized he was in a large city. It wasn't any city on Earth, he knew that instantly. Every building seemed to have a unique shape. They sparkled as if they had been created yesterday from some material he had never seen. They were connected by catwalks that crisscrossed the city like a spider web joining the sparkling crystals of a geode. Then one of the buildings collapsed, and the skybridges connecting it to neighboring buildings tore free, like arms releasing, following a falling body. Another blast went off and another building fell.

The soldier beside Dorian cleared his throat and spoke quietly. "Should we begin, sir?"

"No. Let it go for a while. Let's show the world the type of people we're fighting."

Another blast went off, and the horizon faded to black as the clarity of space again came into focus. Now Dorian stood on a different observation deck—on a planet. No, a moon. He could see the planet on his right, but the view of space was far more impressive. A fleet of ships reached to the burning white star beyond. There were hundreds of them, maybe thousands. The sight of the full fleet took his breath away. He felt the hair on his arms stand on end. A single thought dominated his mind: *I have won.*

Dorian tried to focus his vision, but the image slipped away. He was somewhere else, on a planet, walking down a long concrete path towards a giant monolithic structure. He walked alone, but crowds lined the path on each side, many elbowing and jostling to get a look at him. A woman and two men waited at the base of the stone monument just outside the dark opening. Dorian couldn't quite read the inscription engraved above the entrance, but somehow he already knew what it said: "Here lies our last soldier."

The woman stepped forward and spoke. "We have decided. You will walk the long road of eternity."

Dorian knew the woman was playing for the camera, uttering the words for the historical record. She had betrayed him. "Every man deserves the right to die," he said.

"Legends never die."

Dorian turned, and for a split second, considered running. This is how they would remember him, his final act. He walked into the tomb, past the stone façade, into the vessel. The shimmering gray walls reflected the beady lights that shone from the floor and ceiling. The last rays of sunlight receded from the tunnel behind him, and the lights inside the vast chamber adjusted. Rows of tubes stretched out into the distance as far as he could see. They were all empty. The first tube in the row slowly hissed open, and Dorian marched to it. So be it.

As quickly as the tube closed, it was opening again, and Dorian was running out of the shrine. The sky was dark except for flashes all around him. He blinked, and then he stood in a deserted street of another spiderwebbed city. The blasts were far larger than the ones before. The entire city seemed to be coming down, and he saw ships descending from the sky.

Then he was in the vast chamber with the tubes again. They were all full now. He ran down the long corridor. He watched in horror as the Atlanteans, his people, awoke, screamed, stumbled out of the tubes, and died. The flow of people was endless. As soon as one died, a replacement body took shape in the tube, and the endless cycle of agony began again. Dorian raced to a control station and worked his fingers as the wisps of white and green light washed over his hand. He had to stop the resurrection sequence, had to end their purgatory. They could never wake up. But he could make them safe. He was a soldier. It was his job... his duty.

He stepped away from the control station, and he was on the observation deck of a ship again. Below, a blue, green, and white globe floated into view. Earth. The skies were clear, and the land below was untouched. No cities, no civilization. *A blank canvas. A chance to start over.*

He turned, and he was in the tombs again, but he wasn't in the chamber that held the tubes. He stood in a smaller room with twelve tubes, all empty. He blinked, and a body appeared in the center tube—a prehistoric man. He blinked again, and another human ancestor appeared.

The room faded, and he was outside, at the top of a mountain. The view was distorted by the curve of glass—a helmet's visor. He was wearing an environmental suit similar to the one the Atlantean had given him, and he stood atop a metal chariot that floated just above the tree line.

The sun was high in the sky, and the forest below was green and dense, interrupted only by the rocky ledges that descended like steps to the valley below.

Along the ridges, cavemen clashed with wooden and stone tools. There were two species, Dorian could see that now. One species was smaller, but they had better tools. They descended in waves on their larger adversaries. They threw spears and communicated in rough guttural sounds, coordinating their raids.

The sun advanced, and the valley filled with combatants. The war raged, and the carnage was near total. Blood flowed across the ground and stained the white and gray rocks. Dorian floated there on the chariot, watching, waiting.

Then the sun was setting over the valley, and just as quickly, it rose, and the valley was quiet. At the bottom, bodies were stacked so deep Dorian couldn't see the ground. Flies swarmed the mass grave. Buzzards circled overhead. On the rocky ridges, the victorious humans stood holding spears and stone axes. They stared down silently, their bodies painted red and black with the remnants of the battle. A large human—the chief, Dorian thought—stepped forward and lit a torch. He spoke some words, or rough sounds, and tossed the torch into the valley below. Around the ridge, others followed suit, until the rain of fire into the valley ignited the underbrush, then the trees and the bodies.

Dorian smiled and activated the helmet's recorder. "Subspecies 8472 shows a remarkable aptitude for organized warfare. They are the logical choice. Terminating other genetic lines." For the first time, he felt hope, looking at the primitive, warlike species.

Smoke filled the valley, then slowly drifted upward, engulfing the forest and finally the ridge. The band of triumphant humans disappeared into the smoke as the black and white plumes rose, surrounding Dorian. The columns of smoke engulfed him, and when they cleared, Dorian once again looked out of the tube at the chamber in Antarctica—the same vessel that had existed on the Atlantean home world. His thoughts were again his own, as was his body.

A new body. Another one.

The Atlantean stood there, watching him placidly. Dorian studied him, his face, the white shock of hair on his head. It had been him on the ship, in the dream. Or was it a dream?

The tube opened, and Dorian stepped out.

27

Two Miles Below Immari Operations Base *Prism*
Antarctica

Dorian eyed the Atlantean for a long moment. Then he looked around and said, "All right. You have my attention."

"You don't disappoint, Dorian. I show you the fall of my world and the origins of your species, and that simply earns your attention?"

"I want to know what I saw."

"Memories," the Atlantean said.

"Whose?"

"Ours. Yours and mine. Memories from my past, memories from your future." The Atlantean paced away from him, toward the opening to the chamber where Dorian's and David's dead bodies lay.

Dorian followed him, pondering what he had said. Somehow, Dorian knew it was true. The events were real—his memories. How?

The Atlantean spoke as he led Dorian down the gray-metal

corridors. "You're something different, Dorian. You've always known you were special, that you had a destiny."

"I'm—"

"You're me, Dorian. My name is Ares. I am a soldier, the last soldier my people ever had. Through a strange twist of fate, you inherited my memories. They've lain dormant in your mind all this time. I was only aware of them when you entered this vessel."

Dorian squinted at the Atlantean—Ares, not sure what to say.

"Deep down, you know it's true. In 1918, they placed a dying seven-year-old boy in a tube in Gibraltar. When you awoke in 1978, you weren't the same. It wasn't the time that changed you. You were possessed with hate, driven to seek revenge, to build an army to defeat the enemy of humanity and find your father. You had a sense of your destiny—to fight for the future of your race. That's what you came here to do. You even knew what you had to do: change the human race at the genetic level. *You* knew all this because *I* knew it. It was my desire. You have my memories. You have my strength. You have my hatred and my dreams. Dorian, there is an enemy in this universe more powerful than you can imagine. My people were the most advanced race in the known universe, and this enemy defeated us in a day and a night. They will come for you. It's only a matter of time. But you can defeat them—if you're willing to do what must be done."

"Which is?"

Ares turned on Dorian and looked him in the eyes. "You must ensure that the genetic transformation of your species is completed."

"Why?"

"You know why."

A thought ran through Dorian's mind: *to build our army.*

"Precisely," Ares said. "We're fighting a war. In war, only the strongest survive. I've guided your evolution for this single purpose: survival. Without the final genetic changes, the humans here won't survive. None of us will."

In the recesses of Dorian's mind, he knew it was true, had always known it was true. It all made sense now: his ambition, his blind, unreasoning desire to transform the human race, to defeat an unseen enemy. For the first time in his life, everything made sense. He was at peace. He had found *the* answer. He focused on the task at hand. "How do we build our army?"

"The case you carried out. It emits a new radiation signature that will complete the process. Not even Orchid can stop the mutated virus it will unleash. As we speak, a new wave of infection is emanating from the blast site in central Germany. Soon it will spread around the world. The final cataclysm will happen in the coming days."

"If that's true, what's left to do? You clearly have the situation well in hand."

"You must make sure no one finds a cure. We have enemies out there. Then you must free me. Together we can take control of the survivors. We can win the battle for this planet. They are our people. They are the army we will launch against our ancient enemy. We will finally win this war."

Dorian nodded. "Free you. How?"

"The case serves two purposes. It emits radiation that renders Orchid ineffective, and it has created a portal to my location—an artificial wormhole, a bridge across space and time." The Atlantean stopped, and Dorian realized they were in front of the door to the room that had held the case and the two suits. The door slid open, revealing an empty room, except for the last suit.

Dorian walked into the room without a word and began putting the suit on.

"There's something else you have to do, Dorian. You must bring the woman who was here. You must find her and take her through the portal with you."

Dorian pulled the last boot on and looked up. "Woman?"

"Kate Warner."

"What does she have to do with this?"

The Atlantean led him out of the room and down the corridor. "Everything, Dorian. She's the key to everything. At some point very soon, she will acquire a piece of information—a code. That code is the key to freeing me. You must capture her *after* she has the code and bring her to me."

Dorian nodded, but his mind raced. How did the Atlantean know?

"I know because I read her thoughts the same way I can read your thoughts."

"Impossible."

"It's only impossible with *your* scientific understanding. What you call the Atlantis Gene is actually a very sophisticated piece of biology and quantum technology. It utilizes principles in physics you have yet to discover. It has been the guiding hand in your evolution. It has many functions, but one of them is to turn on several processes in your body that control radiation."

"Radiation?"

"Every human body emits radiation. The Atlantis Gene turns that stream of static into an organized data feed—a continuous upload of your memories and physical changes, right down to the cellular level. It's like an incremental backup, transmitting data to a central server every millisecond."

They stood in the opening to the chamber that held the seemingly endless rows of tubes. "When this vessel receives a death signal and confirms there will be no further transmissions, it assembles a new body, an exact replica down to the last cell and very last memory."

"This place is—"

"A resurrection ship."

Dorian tried to wrap his head around it. "So they're all dead?"

"They died a very long time ago. And I can't wake them up; won't wake them up. You saw it. They died badly, in a world that hadn't known a violent death in too long to remember. But you and I can save them. They are the last of our people. They are counting on you, Dorian."

Dorian took in the expanse of tubes with a new appreciation. *My people.* Were there others? "What about the ship in Gibraltar? It's another resurrection ship?"

"No. It's something else. A science vessel. A local explorer, incapable of deep space travel. It's a lander—the alpha lander from the science expedition here. It has eight resurrection pods. Expeditions are dangerous work, and the scientists sometimes have unfortunate accidents. As you know, the resurrection chambers also have the power to heal. Resurrection only works for Atlanteans. And it has a limited range. The nuclear blasts in Gibraltar likely destroyed the pods there. These tubes are the only ones that can resurrect you. But if you venture past a hundred kilometers from here, you won't resurrect. The system won't make a copy if it doesn't have updated data—the Prometea rule. If you go out into the world, you will be mortal again. If you die, you die forever, Dorian."

Dorian looked over at David's body. "Why didn't he—"

"I disabled the resurrection for him. You won't have to worry about him."

Dorian glanced at the corridor that led to the outside. "They captured me before. They didn't trust me."

"They've seen you die, Dorian. When you walk out of here again, risen from the dead with memories of what happened to you, no one will oppose you."

Dorian hesitated for a second. There was one last question, but he didn't want to ask it.

"What?" Ares asked.

"My memories... our memories..."

"They will come, in time."

Dorian nodded. "Then I'll see you shortly."

28

David Vale opened his eyes. He stood in another tube but in a different place—not the seemingly endless chamber below Antarctica. This room was small, no more than twenty feet by twenty feet.

His eyes adjusted, and the room came into focus. There were three other tubes—all empty. A large screen dominated the far wall, just above a high-top bar, like the control panels he had seen in the Atlantean structure in Gibraltar and Antarctica. Below it, a crumpled-up suit lay on the floor. A closed door stood at each end of the room.

What is this? What happened to me? To David, the room seemed different from those in Antarctica; it was more like the science lab in the Gibraltar structure that Kate's father had described in his journal. Was this a science lab? *If so, why am I here? For some kind of experiment?* And beyond that, he wondered why he kept waking up in these tubes every time Dorian Sloane killed him. That he had now been shot to death multiple times was also hard to wrap his head around, but he had to focus on the more pressing issue: how to get out of the tube. As if on cue, the tube hissed open, and the thin clouds of gray and white fog wafted into the room and dissipated.

David paused, assessing his surroundings, waiting for his unseen captor to make the next move. When nothing happened, he stepped out into the room, struggling on barely responsive legs. He steadied himself at the control station. Below him lay the environmental suit. The helmet sat against the wall, behind the control station. David could now see that the suit was damaged. He bent and rolled it over. It was the same type of suit he had seen in the holo movies in Gibraltar. The Atlanteans had worn them when they had run out of the ship and saved a Neanderthal from a ritual sacrifice near the Rock of Gibraltar.

He examined the suit more closely. A large gash spread across the torso. The result of weapons fire? The material seemed to be severed but not singed. What did it mean? In the videos he had seen, the ship in Gibraltar had exploded after a massive tsunami washed it ashore, then pulled it back out to sea. The Immari had assumed that a series of methane pockets on the sea floor had exploded, ripping the ship into several pieces.

The explosion had incapacitated one of the Atlanteans in the suits, and the other had carried him or her through a door—presumably to Antarctica.

Was this suit from one of the two Atlanteans in Gibraltar? David stood and searched the room for any other clues. On a small bench behind the control station, he could see a garment of some kind, neatly folded.

He hobbled to the bench. His legs were getting better, but they weren't one hundred percent yet. He unraveled the bundle. It was a black military uniform. He held it up to the dim LED-like lights that shined from floor and ceiling. The suit glistened and seemed to reflect the light. It almost looked like a projection of a starry night. He moved it around, and the suit changed again, matching the light and walls behind it. It was some kind of active camouflage. The entire reflective top—the tunic of the uniform—was smooth and without markings except for the collar. Its right side had a square emblem: [II].

I.I. Immari International. This was an Immari Army uniform.

On the left side of the collar, a silver oak leaf spread out—the insignia of a lieutenant colonel's rank.

David tossed the uniform back on the bench. He was naked, and he'd rather stay that way than put the uniform on.

He walked over to the control station and waved his hand over it. Kate's father had learned to work these Atlantean control stations. For him, a blue and green light would emanate and interact with his hand, but this control station was dark and dead. David pressed his fingers to it, but it gave no reaction.

He glanced back and forth between the doors. There was nothing like being a rat in a cage. He walked to the closest door and stood for a moment, but it didn't slide open. He ran his hand over the panel beside it. Dead. He flattened his hands on the gray metal and pushed, but it didn't move. It was sealed shut, like the bulkhead door in a submarine.

He tried the same routine on the opposite door but got the same result. He was trapped. How much air did he have? How long could he last before he starved to death?

He sat on the bench in silence, alone with only his thoughts. No matter how hard he tried, they always drifted to Kate. David wondered where she was at that very moment. He prayed she was safe.

He thought about their one night together in Gibraltar, how different he felt in that moment. Then he had awoken to find her gone. He forgave her for that; she had been trying to save him. But he had made another mistake: letting her out of his sight again in Antarctica when he had stayed behind to hold off Dorian and his men.

David decided he wouldn't let that happen again. If he ever got out of this room, he would find Kate, wherever she was in whatever was left of the world, and he would never let her out of his sight again.

29

Marbella, Spain

Kate had awoken in the dark confines of a semi trailer filled to the brim with people, packed in like a fresh catch on the way to a fish market at the pier. Or at least, that was what it smelled like: sweat and fish. People coughed and elbowed as the trailer bounced incessantly. The truck pulling it must have been doing top speed through Marbella's bumpy streets.

Kate wanted to find Martin, but she could barely see a few feet in front of her. She settled for sitting quietly against the wall in a less-crowded section of the trailer, near the front, far away from the double doors at the end.

The truck slowed, stopped for a few seconds, and continued on, barely creeping this time. Then it came to an abrupt halt, and its air brakes squeaked loudly. The rumbling engine died a few seconds later.

A wave of panic seemed to sweep the trailer's inhabitants. They were all on their feet and rushing the door a split second before it opened.

The light from the setting sun revealed the scene beyond. Kate stood there, taking it in, letting the people flow around her.

The two blue Orchid flags that had hung on the fence were simply charred remains. The Immari had left the remnants hanging, perhaps as a symbol, a sign of their triumph. They had placed their own black flag on each side of the camp's entrance. Immari soldiers in black uniforms paced in the guard tower above—the one that hadn't been completely destroyed.

The trailer was emptying quickly now. Kate's mind grasped for a plan. She slipped the backpack off her shoulders and unzipped it. The pack had some kind of heavy lining. Fire and waterproof? Kate surveyed the contents: a handgun, the laptop, a sat phone, Martin's notebook, and the thermos-like device he had placed the sample in. She took the gun out. She couldn't shoot her way out of here; in fact, she wasn't sure she could shoot the gun at all. She needed a better plan, and if she was caught with the gun... She slid it into the darkened corner. She needed to keep the other equipment—Martin had saved it; it must be essential to finding the cure.

Martin had also told her what would happen next: the Immari would sort everyone. The dying would be left to die. The survivors could either pledge or perish.

She had a choice to make.

30

Centers for Disease Control and Prevention (CDC)
Atlanta, Georgia

Dr. Paul Brenner paced in front of the screens that covered the wall. The world map they displayed was covered with red dots: one for each Orchid district. A number floated above every point: the Orchid failure rate for that district. Since the outbreak, Orchid had been ineffective for roughly 0.3% of those infected. Now the numbers were climbing. In one district in Germany, almost one percent of the inhabitants were now dying from the plague. Was Orchid finally failing?

They had seen temporary, localized Orchid failures, but that had been due to formulation issues—manufacturing. This was global. If it was another... Paul resisted even thinking the word mutation but if it was...

"Roll it back," Paul said. "Show Orchid failure rates one hour ago, two hours ago. Keep stepping back an hour until they stabilize."

Paul watched the numbers gradually decrease, then level out. "Stop right there." He glanced at the time.

He walked to his station in the large conference room and rifled through a stack of papers. *What had happened then?* Had the Immari released a mutated virus—one Orchid couldn't stop? That was their plan, or at least that was the working theory. He focused on the memos regarding Immari activity. One caught his eye. He checked the time. It was close. He scanned it.

EYES ONLY

Suspected Nuclear Explosion at Immari Corporate Research Campus outside Nuremberg, Germany

Cause (best theory): industrial accident; detonation of an experimental weapon, part of Immari Research Advanced Weapons Program

Alternative Explanations:
(1) Immari believed to have removed object from location in Antarctica for study in Germany; possibly connected.
(2) Immari could have purposefully destroyed facility to prevent Allied seizure following their invasion of southern Spain.

Paul took a deep breath. He was sure of two things: one, that Orchid was failing around the world, and two, that it had begun with an Immari act. How much time did they have? One, possibly two days? Was there anything they could do in that amount of time?

"Get the group on the line," Paul said. It was time to throw a Hail Mary pass.

31

David Vale had tried the doors and control panel more times than he could count. He had even gone and stood in the tube, hoping it might activate an escape route. The room hadn't changed since he had awoken. He could feel himself getting weaker. He had a few hours left, maybe.

He needed to make a move. He walked to the damaged Atlantean suit that lay crumpled on the floor. Maybe if he put it on... He held it to his chest and let the legs hang down. They barely cleared his calves. David was six-foot-three and broad-shouldered. The owner had been under six feet and rather small in stature, a woman perhaps. He dropped the suit and looked over at the other suit—the Immari colonel's uniform, crisp and new.

He sat on the bench next to it for a long while. It was the only thing he hadn't tried. *What choice do I have?* He grudgingly slid the pants on, then the boots. He stood and held the tunic for a moment. The four oval glass tubes in the room each reflected a warped view of his figure. Gone were the fresh gunshot wounds in his chest and shoulder. Across his chest, older scars had also been erased: burns from a falling building that had trapped him in the 9/11 explosions, a stab wound just below his ribcage that he had received during an operation outside Jakarta, and a smattering of shrapnel impacts from Pakistan. He was a new man. But his eyes were the same—intense but not hard.

He ran a hand through his short blond hair, exhaled, and stared for a long second at the tunic, the last piece of the ensemble. He pulled the tunic on, and it glistened as it adjusted to the light.

David wondered if he would wake up in a tube again if he died. As if reading his mind, a small crack sprinted up the length of the first tube. Spider-like smaller cracks erupted at every angle, multiplying and expanding like cells dividing in a petri dish. The other tubes followed suit until the four clear glass tubes were so clouded with cracks they looked white. A series of soft pops rolled across the tubes, and the tiny pieces of cracked glass began falling inward.

Where the four tubes had stood, a series of cone-shaped piles of glass now lay, twinkling in the sharp light like stacks of diamonds.

Guess that answers that question, David thought. Whatever happened beyond this room, there would be no resurrection here.

The door to his right hissed as it slowly broke free from the wall and slid open. David walked to the threshold and peered out. A narrow, tight corridor spread out as far as he could see. Beady lights on the floor and ceiling barely illuminated the space.

He began down the long hallway, and the door to the tube room closed behind him. There were no doors on either side of the corridor, and it was smaller than the passages he had seen before. Was it an escape conduit or a maintenance tube? After a few minutes, the hallway ended at a large, oval door. It opened as he approached, revealing a round room that must have been an elevator. David stepped inside and waited. It didn't feel like he was moving, but he did have the sensation that the platform was rotating.

A minute passed, and the door opened with a shudder. The rush of air threw David against the back wall, but the force quickly dissipated.

The air was damp, definitely subterranean. The space beyond the door was dark as night. David crossed the threshold. The walls were rock, but they were smooth—a machine had bored this hole. *Where am I?* It was cool but not freezing. This wasn't Antarctica. Gibraltar?

The pathway was on an incline, maybe twenty degrees. Did it lead to the surface? There was no light at the end of the tunnel. Maybe it turned up ahead.

David spread his arms out and set off, dragging his fingers across the sides of the shaft, hoping to detect any change. None came, but the air grew warmer and dryer with every step. Still the end was dark. Then an electric wave swept over him, like a field of static electricity crackling and pricking across his skin.

The cool, dark tunnel was gone, and David stood outside in a mountainous place. It was night, and the stars above shone bright —brighter than he had ever seen them, even in Southeast Asia. If this was Europe or northern Africa, then all the light pollution was gone. And if so... In the distance, over the closest rock ridge, the sounds of gunfire and explosions echoed into the night. David rushed forward, stumbling over the uneven rock, and steadied himself at the top of the ridge.

To his left, the mountains dived into a coastline that stretched into the distance. David struggled to understand what he was seeing—it looked almost as though two worlds from different times had been thrown together.

Some kind of post-apocalyptic "fortress," or maybe an army

base from the future, lay on a peninsula with a long harbor. The peninsula jutted at least five kilometers into the sea and narrowed to perhaps only a hundred meters where it met the landmass—the perfect chokepoint to defend the base from ground attacks. A large wall rose there, towering above a burned-out wasteland beyond it. Waves of soldiers on horseback charged toward the wall, shooting and shouting. It looked almost like a medieval raid on a castle—a castle from far in the future. David stepped closer to the edge, marveling, trying to get a better view. The lead riders unleashed something.

A massive explosion erupted and a mushroom of fire rose from the wall, sending David staggering back and illuminating the area around the fortress. On the other side of the narrow sea, David caught a glimpse of a massive rock cliff jutting high above the water. The Rock of Gibraltar. He was in Northern Morocco, across the Straits of Gibraltar. The peninsula was home to Ceuta, an autonomous Spanish city. Or had been, before someone turned it into a fortress. There were still traces of the city, but—

Behind him, David heard trucks cranking. He turned just in time to see a spotlight snap on, blinding him. The light from the explosion had revealed him to someone in the mountains.

A man's voice called down to him from above. "Don't move!"

He jumped off the ridge as bullets raked the cliff. He stumbled back to the rock face where he had emerged and felt around desperately for the entrance. It wasn't there. Whatever he had passed through was a one-way door, some kind of force field that looked and felt like rock out here.

He heard boots pounding behind him. He turned just as Immari soldiers poured onto the ledge and surrounded him.

32

Immari Training Camp *Camelot*
Cape Town, South Africa

Dorian stood at the tall window. The Immari troops that spread out below were breaking down their camps and making their way to the harbor and the ships waiting there for them.

A woman was directing a group of soldiers. She had... poise, Dorian thought, and something else; he couldn't quite put his finger on it. "Kosta," he said to his new assistant, who was working at the desk behind him.

The short, fat man scurried over to join Dorian at the window. "Sir?"

"Who's that woman?"

Kosta peered down. "Which..."

Dorian pointed. "There, with the blond hair, and... striking features."

Kosta hesitated. "I... I don't know, sir. Is she underperforming? I can have her reassigned—"

"No, no. Just find out who she is."

"Yes, sir." Kosta lingered. "The rest of the ships are almost here. We're still trying to round up more cold weather gear—"

"We won't need it."

"Sir?"

"We're not going to Antarctica. We're sailing north. Our fight is in Europe."

PART II

TRUTH, LIES & TRAITORS

33

Immari Fleet
Off the coast of Angola

DORIAN RAN his finger down the length of Johanna's bare back, across her behind, and down her leg. Beautiful. Sublime.

When he lifted his finger from her, she rustled, then lifted her head and brushed her golden hair out of her eyes. "Was I snoring?" she asked sheepishly.

Dorian loved her accent. Dutch, he thought. Had her parents been first-generation South African settlers? Asking her would show personal interest. Weakness. He had tried to tell himself that she was dull and shallow, that she didn't warrant his interest, that she was one of any number of girls on this ship or another in his fleet. But... there was something about her. It wasn't the conversation. She had spent most of her time in his cabin lying there naked, flipping through old gossip magazines, sleeping, or pleasuring him.

He rolled away from her. "You wouldn't be here if you had snored."

Her tone changed. "You want to..."

"When I want sex, you'll know it."

As if on cue, a soft knock echoed from the steel door to his cabin.

"Enter," Dorian called loudly.

The door cracked open, and Kosta stepped in. Upon seeing Dorian and the woman on the bed, he spun and made for the door.

"For God's sake, Kosta, haven't you ever seen two naked humans? Stop. What the hell do you want?"

"They'll be ready for the broadcast to the Spanish captives in an hour, sir," Kosta said, still facing away from Dorian. "The communications teams would like to review some talking points."

Dorian stood and pulled his pants on. The girl hopped up and found his sweater. She smiled and handed it to him. Dorian didn't make eye contact with her. He threw the sweater over the chair in front of the desk.

"I write my own talking points, Kosta. Come get me when it's time."

Dorian could hear Johanna rolling around in the bed, trying to get his attention. He ignored her. He had to focus, had to find the right message. This address was important—it would set the tone for the subsequent push into Europe, for everything that came after.

He needed to make their cause about more than survival, more than self-interest. He needed to sell the choice to join the Immari as something more—the choice to join a movement. A declaration of independence, a new beginning. Freedom from Orchid... and what? What is the Spanish Zeitgeist? The issues?

What was their "plague" before the Atlantis Plague? What would the world respond to?

He scribbled on the page:

Plague = Global Capitalism: a Darwinian force that cannot be stopped; it seeps into every nation, discarding the weak, selecting the strong.

Orchid = Central Bank stimulus: easy money, a false cure that never solves the root causes, only suppresses symptoms, prolonging the agony.

Current outbreak = Like another Global Financial Crisis: uncontainable, incurable, irreversible. Inevitable.

It could work. He decided he would tone it down a bit though.

Ares is right, Dorian thought. The plague was the ultimate opportunity to remake humanity. A single human society with no classes, no friction. An army, working as one toward a common goal: safety.

Johanna threw the sheet off, exposing her spectacular body to him. "I've changed my mind."

Changed your mind? Dorian thought. He was surprised that she had made it up about something in the first place. And now she had reconsidered this "thought." He imagined what was next. Perhaps another comment about a potential breakup of "stars" Dorian had never heard of, or "do you think this dress would look good on me?" As if that dress were on sale down in the ship's commissary.

"Fascinating..." Dorian mumbled as he turned back to his work.

"I've realized that I liked you better when all you did was sleep, drink, and screw me."

Dorian exhaled and set the pen down. His speech could wait.

34

Immari Sorting Camp
Marbella, Spain

KATE STOOD IN THE LINE, surveying the camp, thinking, trying to figure a way out. The Orchid District lay in ruin, a burned-out wreck that barely resembled the five-star seaside resort it had been before the plague, or even the shelter Martin had shown her yesterday. Fires at the guard towers and motor pool still smoldered, sending thin columns of black smoke into the sky, like a snake crawling up the white hotel towers. The setting sun burned red and orange above the Mediterranean. Kate's line marched silently toward the sea like sheep to the slaughter.

The Immari soldiers were doing what Martin had predicted: sorting everyone. The sick were routed to the closest tower, where guards with guns and cattle prods herded them through the doors. Kate wondered what they would do with them. Leave them there to die? Without Orchid, those people would be dead within three days. Martin was in the group somewhere. Kate hadn't seen him since they were captured. She searched the crowd for him.

"Step forward!" a soldier called.

Maybe they had already taken Martin inside the tower, or perhaps he was behind her. She couldn't take her eyes off the tower that held the sick. What would they do in a few days, when it was filled with the dead? What about when they evacuated Marbella? In her mind's eye, Kate saw explosions rocking the bottom of the building and it collapsing to the ground. She had to get Martin out somehow. She—

"Move forward!"

Someone grabbed her arm and dragged her forward. Another man grabbed her neck, feeling her lymph nodes. He tossed her to the left and another man—not a soldier, a doctor, perhaps—ran a long swab inside her mouth, along the inside of her cheek. He placed the swab inside a plastic tube with a barcode. The tube was one of many lined up that went into a larger machine. DNA samples. They were sequencing the survivors' genomes. Kate's dyed hair and generally grimy appearance from the tunnels had given her some reassurance that the soldiers wouldn't recognize her—she looked nothing like she had twenty-four hours ago. But if they had a DNA sample from her and could match it, they would know exactly who she was.

At that moment, a guard on the other side of her grabbed her wrist and slammed it into a small round opening in another machine. A sharp pain erupted at her wrist, but before she could cry out, it was over. The guard shoved her hard in the back, and she was face to face with another guard who ran a wand over her body.

"Negative," he said, pushing Kate into the crowd on the other side of the technicians and machines.

Kate stood there for a moment, wondering what to do. The group parted slightly, and she saw two familiar faces: the man and woman who had herded them in the tunnels—the Immari loyalists who had helped capture her and Martin.

Another person, a pudgy middle-aged white man without even a hint of a tan stepped closer to her. "It's okay. It's over!" he said, his tone somewhere between nervousness and excitement. "You're a survivor. We're saved."

Kate looked back at the technicians, then at her wrist and the burning red welt that surrounded the black bar code.

"How did you know—"

"That you're a survivor? You didn't have an Orchid ID—an implant."

Implant? Martin had said nothing about an implant.

The nervous man seemed to read Kate's confusion. "You don't know about the implants?"

"I've been... out of the loop."

"Oh my God. Let me guess, you were here on vacation and went into hiding after the plague? Me too!"

Kate nodded slowly. "Yeah, something like that."

"Holy smokes! Where to start? Well, you didn't have an implant, so you were never captured, never made to endure the forced treatment. You're not going to believe it. After the outbreak, the Spanish government declared martial law. They took over everything and herded everyone—everyone left alive—into massive concentration camps. They made everyone take a drug, Orchid, that delayed the plague but didn't cure it. They gave everyone an implant, some kind of biotech device that could synthesize a cure from the body's own amino acids or something. Or that's what they said. Who knows what it does. But you didn't have one, you're definitely a survivor. We're going to be okay now. The Immari have liberated Marbella. There are rumors this is happening all over southern Spain. They're going to clean this place up and get the world back to normal."

Kate surveyed the crowd again. There were two divisions,

she saw it now. Her group was much smaller—the known survivors. The other group was larger. They must have been Orchid district residents who showed no signs of infection. The DNA samples, the barcodes... comprehension dawned on Kate. The Immari were cataloging everyone, conducting their own trials, out in the open, trying to isolate the endogenous retroviruses that controlled the Atlantis Gene. That was their goal—increasing their sample size. Liberation was a side effect. A cover. Or was there another outcome?

Martin's words echoed in her mind: *Promise me you will pledge.* Kate wouldn't. Not after what they had done. Were doing. What could she do if she did pledge? They would find her sooner or later. She couldn't delay it. And she couldn't see how she could save Martin. Given the choice, she'd rather die knowing she'd never taken a false pledge, never bowed to her enemy.

Behind Kate, a massive screen lit up. The soldiers had hung a series of white sheets together, making an outdoor screen like a drive-in movie theater. The scene that lit the screen was a rough wooden desk in front of a steel bulkhead. The captain's desk of a ship? A man walked past the camera, turned, and sat at the desk, his back rigid, his face hard and emotionless.

Kate felt herself tense up. Her mouth went dry.

"My name is Dorian Sloane."

Slowly, the words faded away, and Kate was alone with a single thought: *if Dorian is alive, David is dead.* The proof was there on the screen, ten feet tall, twenty feet wide, staring down lifelessly at the frightened crowd. *If Dorian is alive, David is dead.* Knowing for certain revealed just how much hope she had held out. Tears welled in her eyes, but Kate blinked them away. She inhaled and fought the urge to wipe her eyes. Around her, others were wiping away tears but for a wholly different reason. Throughout the crowd, people were clapping, embracing each other, and cheering. Some faces were hard, like Kate's, and many simply looked down or away from the screen. Through the cheers and somber stares, Dorian droned on, completely unaware.

"I come to you not as a liberator, not as a savior, not as your leader. I am a human being, a man trying to survive, a person trying to save as many lives as he can. I'm simply in a unique position. As the chairman of Immari International, I control the resources to make a difference. Immari has a security division, a private intelligence service, natural resources, communications companies, transport organizations, and perhaps most importantly, one of the most advanced global scientific research and development groups in the world. In short, we are in a position to do something to help in these difficult times. But our resources are limited. In a sense, we can only fight the battles we can win. But we won't turn away from that fight or our responsibilities as humans. We will save the lives we can. Look at your lot. Look at what the governments of the world have given you.

"We face an unprecedented threat in the course of human evolution. A turning point. A flood. We stand waist deep in the blood of those who cannot survive in this new world. Governments have chained you to these people who can't swim in this flood. They've left you to drown. We offer a way forward, an outstretched hand from a life raft. We offer a choice. Immari International has the courage to do what must be done, to save the lives we can and offer peace and closure to those we can't. That's what I come to offer you today: life, a new world built by survivors. We ask nothing in return, save for your loyalty and your help in creating this new world. We will need all the help, all the able-bodied individuals we can find. The true challenge lies ahead. We seek only the opportunity to play our role in the coming cataclysm, and I ask you now: join us or abstain. If you abstain, we will not harm you. We will deliver you to those who disagree with us so that you may seek your own solutions. We have no desire for bloodshed; the world has enough blood on its hands.

"Our adversaries call us an empire. They spread lies in a desperate attempt to cling to their own power. Consider what they've done with that power—built a world with two classes of nations: the third world and the first world. And they've let capitalism trample the citizens of every nation—first and third world—segregating us according to our economic value. A person's place in society determined by how much the world is willing to pay for whatever they can produce each day. This plague is simply the biological equivalent of the same programs they've used to divide us for centuries.

"Immari International's solution is simple: one world, with one people, all working together. If you prefer the old world, if you prefer Orchid, sitting in a concentration camp, waiting for a cure that will never come, waiting to live or die, you can. Or you can choose life, a fair world, a chance to build something new. Choose now. If you do not wish to be part of the Immari Solution, stand where you are. If you want to assist us, to help save the lives we can, step forward, toward the men holding the Immari International signs. The men at the desk will interview you, find out what skills you can offer, how you can help your fellow humans."

The crowd around Kate began dispersing. Maybe one in ten stood their ground. Possibly less.

Kate hated to admit it, but Dorian had given a convincing speech for anyone who didn't know what he was truly like. He was a smooth talker; she knew that all too well. As she stood there watching the people flock to the Immari soldiers, a procession of images flowed through her mind. Her father: died trying to prevent an Immari massacre. Her mother: dead at the hands of the plague they unleashed. David: dead at Dorian's hands. Now

Martin, her adoptive father, would soon be their latest victim. He had made so many hard choices and sacrifices—many of which had been all for her benefit, to keep her safe. He had tried to protect her for so long.

She couldn't leave him. Wouldn't, no matter what. And she would complete his research.

She felt the pack that hung on her back. Did it hold the keys to finding a cure?

She took a step forward. Then another. She would play the game—as long as she had to. That's what her father had done. But he had turned his back on them, and they had buried him in a mine under Gibraltar. She wouldn't relent.

She blended into the growing throngs of people swarming the tables, talking quickly. "There you are."

Kate turned. It was the middle-aged man who had spoken to her before. "Hi," Kate said. "Sorry if I wasn't very talkative earlier. I... wasn't sure what side you were on. It turns out I am a survivor."

35

Outside Ceuta
Northern Morocco

Through the dark of night and the glowing perimeter lights, David could see only glimpses of the massive military base ahead.

The area around it was another mystery. The convoy of three jeeps sped across what David would have sworn was a dormant lava field. Here and there, wafts of smoke floated up from the lumpy, charred ground. The smell confirmed David's worst fears. The Immari had dug a trench around this part of the city, then burned it, and flattened the remains—leaving an open area their enemies would have to cross in order to attack. Clever. Drastic, brutal, but clever.

The scene reminded him of something, a lecture. For a moment, he was back at Columbia, before the world had changed, had come crashing down on him, literally. His professor's voice had boomed in the auditorium.

"The Roman Emperor Justinian ordered the bodies to be

burned. This was mid-sixth century, people. The Western Roman Empire had fallen to the Goths, who had sacked Rome and assumed control of its administration. The Eastern Empire, centered around Constantinople, now Istanbul, was very much a force in the civilized world. At the time, it was the largest metropolitan center on Earth. It held sway over Persia, the Mediterranean, and every land its army could sail to. The plague that came in 541 changed everything, forever. It was a pestilence the likes of which the world had never seen before—or since. The city's streets ran red with the blood of bodies.

"There were so many bodies that Justinian ordered the dead to be dumped in the sea. But still there were too many. Just beyond the city walls, the Romans dug giant mass graves, each capable of accommodating seventy thousand individuals. The fires burned for days."

History repeats itself, David mused. If this had happened in Ceuta, what was the rest of the world like? The plague unleashed by Toba Protocol—the eventuality he had spent the last ten years trying to prevent—had come to pass. He had failed. How many were dead? Almost against his will, his mind focused on one: Kate. Had she gotten out in Gibraltar? If so, where was she? Southern Spain? Here in Morocco? She was a needle in a haystack, but assuming he survived the looming behemoth ahead, he would burn it down to find her. He would have to wait for his opening, a chance to escape. From the back of the jeep, he watched the last of the burned stretch of the city pass by.

The convoy slowed at the steel gate at the center of the giant wall. Two black flags hung on each side. As the gate parted to let the jeeps pass, a gust of wind caught the flags and they unfurled: [II]. Immari International. The high white wall reached at least thirty feet into the air, and here and there, it was charred with long stains of black, no doubt the scars from where the enemy on horseback had laid siege. The black-striped wall and gate looked almost like a zebra, opening its mouth to swallow the convoy. The flags waved like ears, flinching at the wind. *Into the belly of the beast,* David thought as they passed under the wall, and the gate closed quickly behind them.

The eight soldiers who had apprehended him in the mountains had bound his hands and tied them to his belt. He had ridden silently in the back seat of the jeep, enduring the bumpy, sometimes brutal journey from the mountains. He had gone through several escape scenarios, but each had ended with him leaping from the jeep, breaking a high number of bones and winding up in no shape to fight.

Now he squirmed in the seat and turned left and right, surveying the interior of the base, searching for an escape opening. Inside the high walls, Immari soldiers were rushing to resupply the towers that dotted the walls. The scale took David aback. How many troops were there? Thousands at least, working along the wall that faced inland. Others no doubt manned the other walls that faced the sea. Beyond the wall, past the towers and wide supply roads, rows of houses spread out along the street. They looked mostly unoccupied, but occasionally a soldier would step into or out of one.

Three rows of tilled soil ran along each side of the road. Every twenty feet or so, a wooden pole, like a shortened telephone pole, rose out of the ground. Each held two lumpy sacks, spaced several feet apart. At first, David thought they were giant wasps' nests.

Ahead, another high whitewashed wall loomed, almost exactly like the outer wall, and that told David what this was: a kill zone. If the Immari enemy ever breached the outer wall, they would shred them in this area in between. The tilled soil along the dirt road no doubt hid mines, and David assumed the sacks hanging from the poles were filled with spent shell casings, scrap metal, nails, and other debris that, when exploded, would rip apart anyone caught between the walls.

The ancient fortress had other modern upgrades. Each of the guard towers held massive guns. David didn't recognize the model. Something new? The tops of many houses were gone, and David figured they hid anti-aircraft batteries inside, sitting atop hydraulic lifts, ready to rise up and shoot down any incoming enemy aircraft. He doubted the horse raiders had any though.

Again the soldiers worked the radio, and the gate at the inner wall parted. This wall was less charred than the outer, but several zebra stripes still reached from its top and bottom. As he passed under the inner gate, David felt his chances of escape grow smaller. "Hit the closest guard and run" wouldn't cut it here. He had to focus.

Inside the inner gate, houses and shops lined another street, this one untouched by mines and improvised explosives. It looked more like a quaint ancient village. There were people in plain clothes here as well as more soldiers. This was clearly the main residential section of the base.

Beyond the second row of homes and shops, another wall rose, this one stone and much older. Another gate parted. The city was almost like one of those Russian matryoshka dolls with other dolls nested inside it.

Ceuta had probably been built like other villages along the Mediterranean. Thousands of years ago, the inhabitants of this place had no doubt built a small settlement on the shore. That settlement had prospered as a trading post. Prosperity had brought settlers and the less scrupulous opportunists: pirates and thieves. The ensuing commerce and crime had seen the first city walls built, and over the centuries the city had expanded, each time erecting a new outer city wall to protect its new citizens.

The buildings were much older here, and there was no one

in plain clothes, only soldiers and seemingly endless stacks of artillery, munitions, and other equipment. The Immari were preparing for war, and this was clearly a major launching center. This was also the city's citadel. He would be judged here.

David turned to the soldier sitting in the jeep beside him. "Corporal, I know you're following orders, but you need to release me. You're making a very big mistake. Take me past the city gate and release me. No one will be the wiser, and you might avoid a court-martial for interfering with a covert operation."

The young man eyed David, hesitated, then looked away quickly. "No can do, Colonel. Standing orders are to capture or kill anyone beyond the wall."

"Corporal—"

"They've already called it in, sir. You'll have to speak with the major." The young soldier turned away as the jeep crossed the threshold of a courtyard that housed the fleet of jeeps. The convoy stopped and the soldiers dragged David out and marched him inside the building, down several corridors, and parked him inside a cell with heavy iron bars and a small, high window.

David stood in the cell and waited, his hands still bound and fastened to his belt. After a time, loud footsteps echoed against the stone floor, and a soldier appeared. His black uniform was unruffled, and a single silver bar sat on his shoulder. A lieutenant. He squared with David but kept his distance beyond the bars. Unlike the corporal in the jeep, there was no hesitation in his voice. "Identify yourself."

David stepped toward him. "Don't you mean: Identify yourself, *Colonel*?"

Hesitation crossed the man's face, and he spoke slowly. "Identify yourself, Colonel."

"Have you been briefed on covert operations here in Morocco, Lieutenant?"

The lieutenant's eyes darted left and right. Doubt. "No... I've haven't been notified—"

"Do you know why?" David held up his bound hands. "Don't answer. It's rhetorical. You haven't been notified because, that's right, the operations are *covert. Classified.* You log my presence here, my operation will be blown. And so will your chances of promotion or ever doing anything besides peeling potatoes. Understand?"

David let the words linger in the young man's mind a moment. When David continued, his tone was less harsh. "Right now, I don't know your name, and you don't know mine. That's a good thing. Right now, this is just a mix-up, a stupid mistake by a low-ranking perimeter patrol. If you release me and provide me with a jeep, it will be forgotten."

The lieutenant paused for a moment, and David thought he was about to reach for something in his pocket, possibly the keys, when a set of boots began clacking against the stone floor and another soldier emerged in the hallway, a major. The higher-ranking officer glanced from the lieutenant to David as if he had caught them in the middle of something. His expression was mild, almost blank, somewhere near amusement, David thought.

The lieutenant straightened at the sight of the major and said, "Sir, they found him in the hills below Jebel Musa. He refuses to identify himself, and I don't have any transfer orders."

David studied the major. Yes, he recognized the man. His hair was longer, and his face was leaner, but the eyes were the same as those David had seen several years ago in a photograph paper-clipped to a printout of an after-action report. The operative had handwritten the report in neat block letters, as if every letter and word had been considered at length. The major had been a Clocktower operative—a member of the covert operations group David had worked for. David had recently learned that Clocktower had actually been under Immari control. The major might know who David was. But if not... Either way, David was finished if he didn't make a play.

He stepped to the iron bars. The lieutenant moved back and placed his hand on his sidearm. The major stood his ground. He slowly turned his head.

"You're right, lieutenant," David said. "I'm not a colonel. Just like the man standing next to you isn't a major." David continued before the lieutenant could speak. "I'll tell you something else you don't know about the 'major.' Two years ago, he assassinated a high-value terrorist target named Omar al-Quso. He shot him at dusk at a range of almost two kilometers." David nodded to the major. "I remember it because when I read the after-action report, I thought to myself, now, that's a hell of a shot."

The major cocked his head, then shrugged and broke his gaze for the first time. "Truth be told, it was a rather lucky shot. I had already chambered the second round when I realized that al-Quso wasn't getting up."

"I don't... understand," the lieutenant said.

"Clearly. Our mysterious guest has just described a classified Clocktower operation, which means he's either a station chief or a chief analyst. I don't think analysts get to the gym nearly as much as our colonel here. Release him."

The lieutenant opened the cell and unbound David's wrists, then turned back to the major. "Should I—"

"You should make yourself scarce, Lieutenant." He turned and began down the hall. "Follow me, *Colonel*."

As David walked down the stone hallway, he wondered whether he was now deeper in the trap or on his way out.

36

Immari Operations Base at Ceuta
Northern Morocco

THE MAJOR LED David out of the building that housed the holding cells, and across a wide courtyard that was crowded with pens. David could hear rustling inside. Were they keeping their livestock here? Sounds he couldn't make out drifted into the night.

The major seemed to notice David's interest. He glanced at the pens. "Barbarians waiting for the boatman."

David wondered what he meant. In Greek mythology, "the boatman" carried souls of the newly deceased across the rivers Styx and Acheron into the underworld. He decided to let it go. He had more pressing mysteries to unravel.

They walked in silence the rest of the way to a large building at the center of the inner city.

David quickly took in the major's office. He didn't want to seem too interested, but several things struck him. It was too large. This was clearly the base commander's office. And it was sparse. The walls had been stripped to the white drywall and there was very little else: a black Immari flag in the corner, a simple wooden desk with a swiveling metal chair behind it, and two foldout chairs across from the desk.

The major plopped down behind the desk, drew a pack of cigarettes from the top drawer, and quickly lit one with a match. He held the match and looked up at David. "Smoke?"

"I quit after the outbreak. Figured there wouldn't be any left in a few weeks."

The major shook the match out and tossed it in the ashtray. "Glad I'm not that smart."

David didn't sit at the desk. He wanted some distance between them. He walked to the window and stared out, thinking, hoping the major would tip his hand somehow, give David an opening.

The major blew a cloud of smoke between them and spoke carefully, as if measuring every word before he spoke it. "I'm Alexander Rukin. *Colonel...*"

He's good, David thought. Right to the point. No opening. *What do I have to work with?* The room. A major—commanding a base this large? It was unlikely. But David sensed that there was no superior officer on site. "I was told the base commander would be notified of my presence, should we come into contact."

"He may have been." Rukin took another pull on the cigarette. David sensed something changing. *Is he changing his approach?*

"He's in southern Spain, leading the invasion. He deployed almost everyone. We're running a skeleton crew. Our station chief, Colonel Garrott, got picked off two days ago. Stupid son of a bitch was making the rounds, visiting every guard tower, shaking hands like he'd been elected mayor of hell. Berber sniper got him with one shot. We assume the shooter was in the hills, that's why we added the patrols. And the boomerangs on the perimeter. Now I need to know why you're here."

Yes, Rukin was giving him useless details, hoping David would reciprocate, tell his story, make a mistake. "I'm here for a job."

"What—"

"It's classified," David said, turning to face Rukin. *How long do I have? Maybe an hour before he finds out I'm a fake? At best, I can buy some time.* "Call it in. If you have the clearance, they'll tell you."

"You know I can't."

"Why not?"

"The explosion." Rukin read David's face. "You don't know?"

"Apparently not."

"Someone exploded a sub-nuclear device at Immari HQ in Germany. Nobody's calling anything in right now, especially covert ops verifications."

David failed to hide his surprise. But it was the opening he needed. "I've... been in transit, with no comms."

"From?"

Now the test. "Recife," David said.

Rukin leaned forward. "There's no Clocktower station in Recife—"

"We were in startup when the analyst purge began. Then the plague hit. I barely got out. I've been on special assignment since."

"Interesting. That's a really interesting *story*, Colonel. Here's the reality: if you don't tell me who you are and why you're here *right now*, I'll have to hold you in a cell until I can verify your identity. It's my ass if I don't."

David stared at him. "You're right. It's... operational secrecy. Old habit. Maybe I was a Clocktower operative for too long."

Then David gave the story he had been working on since he crossed the first gate. "I'm here to help secure this base. You know how important Ceuta is to the cause. My name is Alex Wells. If HQ is destroyed, there's bound to be someone from special ops directorate that can verify me."

Rukin scribbled some notes on a pad. "I'll have to confine you to quarters under guard until then. You understand, Colonel."

"I understand," David said. *I've bought some time.* Would it be enough to get out of here? One goal dominated David's mind: finding Kate. He needed information to do that. "I do have one... request. As I said, I've been in transit. I'd like to hear any updates you have. Anything unclassified, of course."

Rukin sat back in the metal chair, seeming to relax for the first time. "The rumor is that Dorian Sloane has returned. Naturally he was arrested outside the Antarctica structure. But they say he carried a case. The morons in charge took that case back to HQ, and it blew up the building. Darwinism at work, if you ask me."

"What happened to Sloane?"

"That's the strangest part. The story is that in interrogation, he killed a guard and ripped open Chairman Sanders' throat. Then, get this, they kill him—double tap to the head, close range. An hour later, he walks out of the structure. A completely new body—with all his memories. Not a scratch on him."

"Impossible..."

"And then some. The Immari are desperate to create this mythical story around him. It's working. The rank and file worship him now. The end of days, Messiah, rapture rhetoric... here in Ceuta and every other place that flies the Immari flag. It's nauseating."

"You're not a believer?"

"I believe the whole world is circling the drain, and Immari International is the only piece of shit that floats."

"Then… let's hope it continues to float. Major, I'm a bit exhausted from my trip."

"Sure."

Rukin called two soldiers in and instructed them to escort David to quarters and arrange for round-the-clock guard.

Alexander Rukin stubbed out the cigarette and stared at the words on the page.

The door opened, and Captain Kamau, his second-in-command, entered.

The tall African spoke slowly in a deep voice. "You buy his story, sir?"

"Sure. It's about as real as the Easter Bunny." Rukin lit another cigarette and peered into the pack. Three left.

"Who is he?"

"No idea. He's somebody though. A pro. Maybe one of ours, probably one of theirs."

"You want me to call it in?"

"Please." Rukin handed him the strip of paper. "And put him under heavy guard. Make sure he sees nothing more than what the Allies can already see from the air."

"Yes, sir." Kamau studied the slip of paper. "Lieutenant Colonel Alex Wells?"

Rukin nodded. "I'm not certain it's a fake name, but it's strangely similar to Arthur Wellesley."

"Wellesley?"

"The Duke of Wellington. Defeated Napoleon at the Battle of Waterloo. Never mind."

"If he's a fake, why don't we take him now? Interrogate him?"

"You're a good soldier, Kamau, but you're lousy at intelligence work. We need to know what we're dealing with here. He could lead us to a bigger fish or reveal a larger operation at work. Sometimes you use the small fish as bait."

The major stubbed out the cigarette. He was good at waiting. "Bring him a girl. See if he's more talkative with her." He glanced at the cigarette pack again. "And get me some more smokes."

"The commissary ran out yesterday, sir." Kamau paused. "But I heard Lieutenant Shaw won some in a card game last night."

"Really? It's too bad they got stolen. Some men are sore losers."

"I'll see to it, sir."

David rubbed his eyelids. He was certain of two things: that Major Rukin hadn't bought his story, and that he couldn't shoot his way out of here. David decided he would rest, then try to take the guards at the door. After that, he wasn't sure.

A soft knock interrupted his internal debate.

David stood. "Come in."

A thin woman with flowing black hair and light caramel skin stepped in, quickly closing the door behind her. "Compliments of Major Rukin," she said softly, not looking at him.

The girl was beautiful, truly. The more of this world David saw, the less he liked it.

"You can go."

"Please—"

"Go," David insisted.

"Please, Mister. There will be trouble for me if you turn me away."

In his mind's eye, David saw the girl climbing on top of him after he'd fallen asleep and running a knife blade across his throat. He wouldn't put it past Rukin. He couldn't take the risk. "There could be trouble for me if you stay. Go. I won't tell you again."

She exited without another word.

Another knock, more urgent this time.

"I said no—"

The door opened, revealing a tall African man. He nodded to the two guards and walked in, closing the door firmly.

A single phrase ran through David's mind. *Game Over.* "Kamau," he whispered.

"Hello, David."

37

Immari Operations Base at Ceuta
Northern Morocco

For a long moment, neither David nor Kamau said a word. They simply stood there, staring at each other.

David broke the silence. "Have you come to take me to the major?"

"No."

"Have you told him who I am?"

"No. Nor will I."

A single question ran through David's mind: What side is he on? He needed a way to test Kamau's allegiances without revealing his own. "Why haven't you told him?"

"Because you have not told him. I believe you have not done so for a reason, though I do not know what it is. Three years ago, you saved my life in the Gulf of Aden."

David remembered the operation: a combined Clocktower strike force from several stations had worked to dismantle a pirate ring. Kamau had been an operative from the Nairobi station. He was a skilled soldier who had simply been unlucky that day. His team had boarded the second of three pirate ships and they had quickly been overrun—it had been impossible to estimate the number of combatants inside each ship. David's team had secured their boat, then moved to reinforce Kamau's team. It had been too late for many of the members.

Kamau continued. "I had never seen anyone fight the way you did. I have not since. If keeping your identity a secret, can help repay my debt to you, I will keep it. And I will help you, if you want it, if you are here to do what I believe you will do."

Was it bait, David wondered, to draw him out? In his mind, he inched toward trusting Kamau. He needed more information. "How'd you end up here?"

"I took a piece of shrapnel in the leg three months ago. Clocktower gave me medical leave, and I wanted to get out of Nairobi. I had family in Tangier. I recuperated there until the plague hit. It wiped the city out in a few days. I made my way here. They gave all the Clocktower operatives commissions in the Immari Army. I was assigned the rank of captain. Station chiefs were made lieutenant colonels, which is partly why Major Rukin believes your story. Northern Africa is dangerous for anyone alone, even a soldier. I took refuge here; I had no other choice."

"What is this place?"

Kamau looked confused. "You do not know?"

David focused on him. The next answer would reveal where Kamau came out, what he really believed. "I want to hear it from you."

Kamau straightened. "This is a wretched place. Hell's doorstep. It is a processing center. A place where they bring the survivors from Africa and the islands of the Mediterranean. And soon, those from southern Spain."

"Survivors..." David said. Then it occurred to him. "Of the plague."

Kamau looked at him with even more confusion.

"I've been... out of the loop for a while. I need you to bring me up to speed."

Kamau told him about the global outbreak and the fall of nations around the world. The rise of the Orchid Districts and the Immari master plan. David took it in. It was truly a nightmare scenario.

"They bring the survivors here," David said. "What do they do with them?"

"They separate the strong from the weak."

"What do they do with the weak?"

"They send them back, on the plague barges. They feed them to the sea."

David sat down at the table, trying to grasp the horror. *Why?*

Kamau seemed to read David's mind. "The Immari are building an army. The largest in history. The rumor is that they found something in Antarctica. But there are so many rumors. They say Dorian Sloane has returned. That he cannot be killed. What Rukin told you is true: there was an explosion yesterday in Germany, at the Immari Headquarters. There is talk of all-out war, but the Allies have another problem. They say that their miracle drug, Orchid, no longer works, that the wave of death has restarted around the world. People believe this is the end."

David rubbed his temples. "You said you thought you knew why I was here."

Kamau nodded. "You are here to destroy this place, are you not?"

As the words were spoken, David made up his mind. Was this the measure of a soldier, to fight a just fight, even if it was lost? What else could he do? He desperately wanted to find

Kate, but he wouldn't run, not from this. He would die fighting. Actually, it was becoming a habit for him. He tried not to think about that, about awakening in the tubes, about what he was. Here and now—that was what mattered. "Yes. I'm here to destroy this place. You said you would help me?"

"I will."

David eyed Kamau, still trying to decide whether he trusted him. "Why haven't you tried before? You've been here for..."

"Two months." Kamau paced away from David. "I did not know the Immari plan before I arrived here. Nor did I know Clocktower was their covert ops branch. I was shocked and horrified when I learned the truth."

David knew the feeling. He let Kamau continue.

"I was trapped here in Ceuta. The world was desperate. I only knew that survivors came here and found refuge. I had no idea... that I would make a deal with the devil to survive. There was no way for me to take the base. I had no choice. Before yesterday, there were almost a hundred thousand Immari troops stationed here."

"And now?"

"About six thousand."

"How many would fight with us?"

"Not many. I would trust no more than a dozen with my life. And we will be asking for their lives."

A dozen to fight six thousand. Losing odds at best. David needed an angle, some fulcrum to change the dynamic.

"What do you need, David?"

"Right now, some rest. Can you hold Rukin off, keep him from figuring out who I am?"

"Yes, but not for long."

"Thank you. Come back at oh-six-hundred, Captain."

Kamau nodded and left.

David climbed into bed. For the first time since he had walked out of the tube, he felt confident, grounded. He knew why: he had an objective now, a mission to complete and an enemy to defeat. That felt good. Sleep came quickly.

38

Immari Sorting Camp
Marbella, Spain

THE IMMARI SOLDIERS had directed Kate and the other survivors who had pledged to one of the white resort towers, assigning two people to each room. The sun had set hours ago, but Kate peered out the sliding glass door, just as she had seen the Orchid residents gazing out yesterday.

There were no lights on the Mediterranean. She had never seen it so dark. There was only a faint glitter across the sea, from a city in northern Morocco.

"You taking that bed?" her roommate asked. She motioned to the bed closest to Kate, near the window.

"Sure."

Her roommate set her things on the other double bed and began ransacking the room—looking for what, Kate couldn't imagine.

Kate wanted to open the pack and search for anything she could use, but she was too drained, physically and mentally.

She placed the backpack under the covers, climbed in, and let sleep take her.

She wasn't in an Atlantean structure, Kate knew that instantly. It felt more like a villa in a Mediterranean city, perhaps from Marbella's Old Town district. The marble-floored corridor led to an arched wooden door. Kate had the impression that if she opened it, something important would happen, some revelation.

She took a step.

There were two doors to her right. She heard movement inside the closest.

"Hello?"

The movement stopped.

She walked to the door and slowly pushed it open.

David.

He sat on the end of a king-sized bed with disheveled sheets. He was shirtless, bent over, unlacing his tall black boots. "There you are."

"You're... alive."

"Apparently I'm hard to kill these days." He looked up. "Wait. You thought you'd never see me again. You'd given up on me."

Kate closed the door. "I never give up on anyone I love."

Kate awoke with an eerie sensation: she could remember every second of the dream, as if she had been there. David. Was he alive? Or was her mind giving her hope? She needed to focus. Martin. Escape. Those were the priorities now.

The first rays of sunlight were creeping into the room, and her roommate was already up.

Kate opened the backpack and began searching it. She opened the small notebook and turned to the first page.

Martin had scribbled a message to her.

My Dearest Kate,

If you're reading this, they've caught us. For the past 40 days, this has been my greatest fear. I tried 4 times to get you out. But it was too late. Of the 30 patients who died in the trial, I hoped each one would lead us to a cure. But we ran out of time. Since your father disappeared 29-5-87, I spent every waking hour trying to make you safe. My failure is complete.

Grant my last wish: save yourself. Leave me. It's all I ask.

I am proud of the woman you've become.

Martin

Kate closed the notebook, reopened it, and read the message again. Martin's message to her was clear. And touching. But she sensed there was something else. She took a pencil from the pack and circled all the numbers. Together, they read:

4043029587

A phone number. Kate sat up in the bed.

"What is that?" her roommate asked.

Kate was so lost in thought she almost didn't hear her. "Um... a... crossword puzzle."

Her roommate set her book down and rolled over, suddenly interested. "Can I have it when you're done?"

Kate shrugged. "Sorry, I wrote on it."

Her roommate scowled, got up from the bed, and padded on heavy feet to the bathroom without another word. The lock clicked.

Kate fished the satellite phone out of the pack and dialed the number.

The sat phone beeped once, then clicked, and a voice began immediately, in a manner that told Kate that it was a recording. The voice was female, an American.

"Continuity. Status follows. Recording time: 22:15 Atlanta Local, Plague Day seventy-nine. Trial 498: result negative."

Trial 498. What was the last trial she had done—where Marie Romero had died? The tube Martin had begged her for, the result he uploaded into the thermos-like cylinder? 493? There had been five trials since then, obviously at other sites.

"Network status: down. Dial zero for operator." The speaker paused and then the voice changed. "Continuity. Unsere Situation ist..."

The message was repeating in German. Kate hit zero on the keypad. She heard rustling in the bathroom.

If her roommate saw the sat phone, she would report it immediately, and Kate would be interrogated. The soldiers had set forth the "honor code" of the survivors' tower: all "members" had to turn in any weapons or electronics. They weren't searched—part of the Immari brainwashing was apparently to pretend they were voluntary members, not prisoners, and forced searches would have shattered the charade. Still, the Immari had set out severe consequences for any signs of dissent. Anyone caught with anything suspicious, anything shiny and sharp or with an on-off switch, was immediately transferred to the other tower—with those who didn't pledge.

Kate held the phone behind the pillow, where her roommate wouldn't see it if she emerged from the bathroom. Kate lowered her head to the phone, halfway behind the pillow and listened.

A woman answered, speaking quickly. "Access code?"

It took Kate a second to process what she had said.

"I..."

"Access code."

"I don't know it," Kate whispered as she eyed the door.

"Identify yourself," the woman said, with a hint of concern or possibly suspicion.

"I... I work with Martin Grey."

"Put him on the line."

Kate thought for a moment. In the back of her mind, she wanted to hold back, to extract more information, but how? She was out of time—and options. What choice did she have but to tell her story and ask for help?

The bathroom door clicked.

Kate dropped the phone behind the pillow. Then remembered to hit the end button.

She looked up to see her roommate eyeing her.

Kate tried to focus on the notebook she held in her other hand. "What?" she said innocently.

"Were you talking to somebody?"

"Myself." Kate held up the notebook. "Helps me with spelling. I'm a terrible speller." *And liar*, she thought.

The suspicion lingered on her roommate's face, but she returned to her bunk and resumed reading.

The next three hours passed in silence. Kate lay on her bunk, thinking, wondering how she could get Martin out. Her roommate read, occasionally laughing.

The breakfast call came, and her roommate was up and at the door in seconds. She paused. "You coming?"

"Gonna let the line die down," Kate said.

The instant the door closed, Kate dialed the number again.

"Access code?"

"It's me again. I work with Martin Grey."

"Put Dr. Grey—"

"I can't. We're separated. We've been captured by the Immari."

"What's your access code?"

"Look, I don't know it. We need help. He kept me in the dark. I don't know anything, but Martin is going to die in a few hours if we don't get some help."

"Identify yourself."

Kate exhaled. "Kate Warner."

The line was silent, and Kate thought it had been disconnected. She glanced at the phone readout. The seconds were still counting up. "Hello?" She waited. "Hello?"

"Hold the line."

Two beeps came, then a man's voice, young, crisp, focused. "Dr. Warner?"

"Yes."

"This is Paul Brenner. I've been working with Martin for some time. I've actually been... I've seen all of your reports, Dr. Warner. Where are you now?"

"Marbella. The Orchid District. The Immari have taken it over and the city."

"We know."

"We need help."

"The operator said that you and Dr. Grey are separated."

"Yes."

"Do you have access to Dr. Grey's research notes?"

Kate eyed the bag. The question made her nervous. "I... can get access to it. Why?"

"We believe he has some research we desperately need."

"Well we *desperately* need to get the hell out of here, so let's make a deal."

"We can't help—"

"Why not? What about NATO? Can't you send some commandos in here to get us or something?"

"NATO no longer exists. Look, things are more complicated—"

"Tell me about it."

"Orchid no longer works on the plague. People are dying—everywhere. The president died a few hours ago, and the vice president followed shortly thereafter."

"Who's running the government—"

"The speaker of the house assumed the presidency, but he was then assassinated. He was a suspected Immari sympathizer. The rumor is that the Joint Chiefs have stepped in, and that the chairman is styling himself the emergency president. He's considering a plan to... Dr. Warner, we need that research."

"Why is Orchid failing?"

"Another mutation. Listen, we think Martin was working on something, but we don't know what it was. I need to speak with him."

Kate flipped the notebook open and began reading the pages. She didn't understand what she saw.

"Dr. Warner?"

"I'm here. Can you get us out?"

A long pause. "We can't get anyone into the Orchid District, but if you can get out... I'll see what I can do to arrange transport. But—our sources say the Immari plan is to evacuate southern Spain late tonight, the survivors at least."

Kate glanced out the glass door. The sun had almost risen now. It was going to be a long day.

"I'll call you back. Be ready."

39

Immari Operations Base at Ceuta
Northern Morocco

DAVID AWOKE to the second-loudest alarm he'd ever heard in his life. The loudest alarm had been in Langley, Virginia, in 2003: an air horn held at his head, prompting him to jump out of bed, half-naked. His CIA training handlers had hauled him out of the barracks, still half-naked, and dumped him in the woods of northern Virginia.

"There are six snipers in these woods. You have 'til dusk to reach the barracks. Their bullets carry paint, and if any is on you, we don't want you."

They had thrown him out, the van still rolling, and he had seen them again as the sun set behind the one-story barracks building.

Since that evening, he had never slept in his underwear again, save for that single time, a slight oversight, a moment of weakness, when he let his guard down in Gibraltar, with Kate.

Now a flood of footsteps echoed through the door. He took

up position in the opposite corner of the room, diagonal from the door, ready to assault anyone who entered. Had Rukin found out? Bugged the room? He would have heard everything.

The door clicked open, but it didn't swing. Two black hands peeked out from the door, extended straight out, showing that they were empty. The owner called through the rush of footfalls behind him. "Kamau."

"Step inside. Then close the door," David said from his crouching position, then quickly, silently, on bare feet, stepped to the other corner of the room, in the door's blind spot.

Kamau entered the room and pushed the door closed behind him. He instantly focused on the corner David's voice had come from, then spun to the other corner, facing David.

"We're under attack," he said.

"Who?"

"We don't know. The major has asked for you."

David followed Kamau into the hall, which was awash with men, all rushing to their positions, paying no mind to David and Kamau.

Outside the residential wing, the inner courtyard of the citadel buzzed with activity. David wanted to stop, to make a tactical assessment, but Kamau pressed on, jogging toward a high tower.

They raced up the rickety steel staircase, and Kamau grabbed David's arm just before the last landing. "They don't know what's going on either. He's testing you."

David nodded and followed Kamau into the command center. It exceeded David's wildest expectations. It had eight sides; every other wall was filled with a floor-to-ceiling window that allowed a clear view of each direction of the camp. The other four walls held computer screens that showed maps, charts, and readouts David couldn't begin to understand.

At the center, two technicians hunched over tables and

computer screens. A single chair was set off from them, and the major occupied it. "Deploy batteries four and five. Fire at will." He spun around to David.

"You knew about this."

"I don't even know what *this* is."

A technician spoke up. "The planes have dropped their payload."

The major eyed David.

Out the side window, guns along the north wall rotated quickly and fired into the night.

The shots seemed to instantly connect, exploding in a cascade of midair explosions. The remains of the attack planes rained down into the water below.

"Seven targets, seven kills," another technician said.

David marveled at the air defenses. He wasn't well versed on surface-to-air defense systems, but what he had just seen was more advanced than anything he was aware of.

This base wouldn't be taken from the air.

The tech who had fired the barrage of missiles punched his keyboard a few times and shook his head. "Radar's clear. It was just one group."

The major stood up and walked to the window. "I saw only seven explosions. Why didn't anything hit us? Did the missiles miss?"

"They fell short, sir."

Out the western window, a plume of water and light rose up.

"What the hell was that?" Rukin demanded.

The techs worked their computers. Another man stood up and pointed to one of the screens. "I don't think we were the target, sir. I think they deployed mines in the straits. A piece of one of the planes hit one of the mines as it sank, I assume."

The major stood there for a moment, staring at the water, at the point where the plane debris had exploded. "Get me the chairman's fleet. He needs to alter course," the major said as he waved David and Kamau out of the room.

Outside the command center, David got an aerial view of the pens he had heard on his way in. They were filled with people, huddled together, packed in. There must have been two or three thousand of them. *Barbarians waiting for the boatman*, Rukin had said. *Who could do this?*

On the way back to the residential wing, Kamau and David walked in silence. At David's room, he motioned for Kamau to stay. "What was that?"

"An RAF squadron. We haven't seen one in months. They tried to take the base shortly after the outbreak, before the Immari burned the city and got their air defenses in place. We thought the British were out of jet fuel."

"Why did they drop the mines?"

"Dorian Sloane is on his way here. He's leading the main Immari fleet north. They're going to invade Europe. I assume the British have mined the straits to cut him off from the Mediterranean."

"How far out is Sloane?"

"The main fleet is days away. I just read a memo that said Sloane flew up the coast and is leading a smaller, advance fleet. He's after something. He could be here as soon as tonight."

David nodded. Sloane. Here. Taking Ceuta before he arrived could save even more lives than David imagined—if he could kill or capture Sloane. And he had just seen the key to doing it. "What are those guns?"

"Rail guns," Kamau said.

"Impossible."

"They were a classified Immari Research weapons program."

David knew the US military had experimented with rail gun technology, but rail guns weren't in active use. The principle problem was power. Rail guns used massive amounts of electricity to propel a projectile at hypersonic speeds—over sixty-two hundred kilometers per hour. "How do they get the power?"

"They have a special solar array, several mirror complexes near the harbor."

"Range?"

"I'm not sure. I know that during the invasion of southern Spain they fired on targets in Marbella and even Málaga—over a hundred kilometers away."

Incredible. The guns at Ceuta could likely destroy any fleet that approached, possibly even the entire Immari army in southern Spain. Could they use them to—

Kamau seemed to read his mind. "Even if we took the control tower, the guns cannot be pointed inside the base."

David nodded. "Who are the horse raiders?"

"Plague survivors. Berbers. With the collapse of civilization, they have gone back to their cultural roots. Other than that, our intel is limited."

"How many are there?"

"Unknown."

David tried to assemble a plan. "Rukin. What's he like?"

"Cruel. Competent."

"Vices?"

"Only smoking and... women."

David pulled off the tunic of his Immari uniform. The mention of women reminded David of the girl who had come to his room. Instantly his mind replaced her with a mental image of Kate. He tried to push it away, but he had to know... It was a risk, but David asked the question he had wanted to since the second he had arrived in Ceuta. "Have you seen any reports about someone named Kate Warner?"

"About a thousand. She is the most wanted person in the world."

A current of fear went through David. He hadn't expected that. "Wanted by whom?"

"Everyone. The Immari, the Orchid Alliance."

"Suspected whereabouts?"

"The Immari doesn't know. Or at least, we haven't been briefed."

David nodded. She might still be alive. He hoped she was in hiding somewhere far away, out of reach of the Immari. Even if he went looking for her, he would likely never find her. And he had a job to do here. "Okay, I want you to get me some civilian clothes. And the best horse you can find."

40

Plague Barge *Destiny*
Mediterranean Sea

THE CAPTAIN TURNED to the two men. "We're clear. You can begin. And see if Dr. Chang and Dr. Janus have any bodies to dispose of."

The older of the two men nodded and they left the ship's bridge.

Below deck, they began strapping on the suits they wore each time.

"You ever think about what we're doing?" the younger man asked.

"I try not to."

"You think it's wrong?"

The older man glanced up at him.

"They're people, they're just sick."

"Are they? Are you a scientist? I'm not. Janitors don't get paid to think."

"Yes, but—"

"Don't do that. Don't *overthink* this thing. You've got my back out there. My life is in your hands. You overthink what we're doing, and you could get us both killed. And most importantly, you could get *me* killed. If the freaks on the deck don't get us, the lunatics in the control room will. We've got one chance here: we do our job. So shut up and suit up."

The younger man looked away, then resumed attaching tape to his suit, occasionally glancing at the older man.

"What did you do before the plague?"

"I didn't do anything," the older man said.

"Unemployed? Me too. Pretty much like everybody else my age in Spain. But I had just gotten some work as a substitute teacher—"

"I was in prison."

The young man paused, then asked, "What for?"

"I was in the type of prison where you don't ask what you're in for. And you don't make friends. It's a lot like this place. Look kid, I'm going to make it really simple for you: the world is over. The only mystery that matters is who's gonna survive. There are two groups left. The people with the flamethrowers and the people catching the flames. You're holding a flamethrower right now. So shut up and be happy. And don't make friends. You never know who you're gonna have to burn in this world."

At that moment, the door opened, and the scientist whom the crew called Dr. Doolittle—whose actual name was Dr. Janus—stepped into the small room. His face was blank and he made no eye contact with either man. Two lab assistants pushed carts with body bags in and left just as quickly.

"That all of 'em?" the older man asked.

"For now," the doctor said mildly to no one in particular. He turned to leave, but the younger man spoke up just as the scientist reached the door's threshold.

"Any progress?"

Dr. Janus paused a moment, then said, "That depends... on your definition of progress." He stepped out.

The younger man turned to the older man. "You think—"

"I swear, you say the word 'think' again, and I'll torch you myself. Now come on."

They donned their helmets, marched up the stairs, and opened the doors to the stalls that held the devolving and the survivors who refused to pledge. A few seconds later, the first people began falling into the sea.

41

Immari Sorting Camp
Marbella, Spain

KATE STARED out the sixth-floor window at the resort grounds below. She and the other survivors were housed in the tower closest to the sea. The soldiers had taken the middle tower for themselves, and the far tower, farthest inland and close to the gate, was filled to the breaking point with the dead and dying. Martin was in there. Kate wondered which group he was in: dead or dying? Kate stared at the tower, at the four guards who loitered at the entrance, smoking, talking, laughing, and reading magazines.

Waiting was excruciating but she had to. She had to bide her time until the moment came. She would get one shot at getting him out.

She turned back and sat on her bed. Across the room, her roommate lay in bed, reading an old book. "What are you reading?" Kate asked.

"She."

"She?"

The woman rolled over and rotated the cover toward Kate. "*She: A History of Adventure*. You want to read it when I'm done?"

"No, thanks," Kate said. "I'm getting all the adventure I can handle right now," she added, under her breath.

"What?"

"Nothing."

The rumble of heavy trucks at the edge of the gate rolled through the camp, and Kate sprang up and peered out the glass. She waited, hoping, and yes—they were bringing in a new shipment. The Immari had been continuously unloading people, perhaps from the rural areas beyond Marbella. This former Orchid District seemed to be their main staging area for the region. Every few hours, a new convoy brought more people, both sick and well, and troops with them. Confusion. An hour of chaos. An opening. Kate raced to the door.

"Where are you going? We've got room count in twenty minutes—" her roommate called, but Kate didn't stop. She bounded down the stairs. At the ground floor, she found the front desk and searched for a floor plan. Would this building have what she needed? What would she say if a guard stopped her or even found her out of her room? They counted twice a day, and she didn't know what they would do if the numbers didn't add up—it had never happened before.

At the front desk, she found the first item she needed: a name badge. Xavier Medina, Vargas Resorts. It wouldn't matter. She just needed a badge. If they checked it, she was caught already.

She moved past the gift store, and to her relief, a restaurant dominated the corner of the building beyond. She waded into the darkened dining room, through the stainless steel double doors, and into the kitchen. The stench was almost unbearable.

She pinched her nose and moved deeper into the room. It was dark, too dark. She propped the double doors open with a stool and resumed her search.

In the corner, she found what she needed: a chef's jacket. She unfolded it. It was soiled: green and red streaks coated the front. She knew she would need to cut it to make it work. She took a butcher knife off the center table and withdrew her hand from her nose long enough to reshape the garment. She turned it inside out and slipped into it. She clipped Xavier's badge to her newly carved lapel and surveyed her reflection in the stainless steel refrigerator: white coat, dangling name badge, brunette hair pulled back into a ponytail, gaunt cheeks, and a pale complexion. A single thought ran through her mind: *No freaking way this is gonna work.* She exhaled deeply and ran a hand through her ponytail. *What the hell am I doing?*

But what else could she do? She walked quickly out of the kitchen and back to the front desk. Sunlight bathed the lobby through the glass revolving door. Two guards waited beyond. *I should take this thing off and go back to my room.* She shook her head. What would they do if they caught her? But she couldn't turn back. She had to do something. She couldn't sit up there knowing Martin was dying, that the whole world was. She would take this risk. It was her only shot.

She walked to the revolving door and pushed through. The guards stopped talking and focused on her. She walked quickly past them, and they called to her. She looked back and waved. She walked a little faster. Not too fast, not fast enough to be suspicious. Were they following her? Another look back could give her away.

Out of the corner of her eye, Kate caught a glimpse of something that startled her: lights, on the water. Her hotel room had no view of the coast. She paused just long enough to take it in. The monstrous white ship glittering off the coast moved slowly, but there was no mistaking its destination: Marbella. It looked almost like... yes, a cruise ship, with large guns mounted at the ends. Was it a plague barge? Would the survivors—her included—be rounded up and loaded onto it? She had to get to Martin before it reached the harbor.

Up ahead, a thick line of people formed where the trucks were unloading. The people marched to the tables and processing attendants, just as Kate had done yesterday. Would they replay Dorian's speech? Like the outdoor movie at dusk every night? The thought of him made her angry, steeled her a bit.

She fell in behind a man and a woman, both coughing, hobbling toward the building for the sick.

The four guards were talking amongst themselves, ignoring the endless flow of sick into the building. As Kate reached the revolving door, a guard looked over at her, wrinkled his brow, and stepped toward her. "Hey, what are you—"

Kate pinched Xavier's badge and held it forward, not letting it unclip from the makeshift lapel. "O-Official business," she stammered.

She quickly ducked into the revolving door. *Official business?* God, she was going to get caught. The revolving door spilled her into the lobby, and as her eyes adjusted, Kate took in the scene. Nothing could have prepared her for it.

She almost staggered back, but people were rushing in behind her, pouring into the building.

Bodies were everywhere. Dead, dying, crying, coughing, and everything in between. This was a world without Orchid. And it was happening all across southern Spain—and if Paul Brenner was right, around the world. How many had died already, in the first day? Millions? Another billion? She couldn't think about that now; she had to focus.

She had seen people flowing into the building, but she had

no concept of how many people were here. There were a hundred, at least, here in the lobby, in this confined space. How many in the building? Several thousand, maybe? There were thirty floors. She would never find Martin.

Behind her, she saw the guard enter the revolving door. He knew. He was coming after her.

Kate took off, darting through the lobby and into the stairwell. If they were going to demolish the building, when would it happen?

She pushed those thoughts out of her mind as she bounded up the stairwell, which was relatively empty. What floor should she try? Below, the stairwell door flew open.

"Stop!" the guard yelled from the bottom floor.

Against her better judgment, Kate peeked over the rail and her eyes met his. He raced up the stairs.

Kate opened the door to the fourth floor, and—

The hallways were filled with people, some lying, others sitting, many already dead. At the sight of her, a woman grabbed her white coat. "You've come to help us."

Kate shook her head and tried to break the woman's grip, but others crowded around her, all talking at the same time.

Behind her, the door opened again, and the guard filled the doorway, his gun drawn. "Okay, turn around. Back away from her."

The people around her scattered.

"What are you doing here?" he asked Kate.

"I'm... taking samples."

The guard looked confused. He took a step forward and glanced at her badge. Her fake badge. Confusion turned to shock. "Turn around. Put your hands behind your back."

"She's with me," interjected another soldier as he casually exited the stairs. He was taller and more muscular than the guard who had chased Kate, and she thought he had a slight British accent.

"Who the hell are you?"

"Adam Shaw. I came in with the shipment from Fuengirola."

The smaller guard shook his head as if trying to clear it. "She's wearing a fake badge."

"Of course she is. You want these people to know her identity? You think they know what an actual Immari Research ID card looks like?"

"I..." The guard eyed Kate. "I have to call this in."

"You do that," the soldier said as he stepped behind the man, quickly gripped his head and neck and ripped hard, sending a loud crack into the hallway. The guard fell to the floor, and the people in the hallway, those left alive anyway, scattered, leaving Kate alone with the mysterious soldier.

He focused on her. "Coming here was a very stupid thing to do, Dr. Warner."

42

Immari Operations Base at Ceuta
Northern Morocco

MAJOR ALEXANDER RUKIN adjusted the sniper rifle. Through the riflescope, he could see the mysterious colonel approaching the Berber encampment on horseback. The man had ridden out wearing plainclothes, as if that could help his cause.

The colonel had been evasive about his purpose for leaving, and Rukin had only protested enough to seem believable. In truth, this was the opportunity Rukin had been waiting for. He had placed a tracker and a bug on the colonel's clothes; they would know exactly where he went and hear everything he said. A team was also shadowing the colonel, just in case he made a break for it. That would expose him as well. One way or another, Rukin would soon know what this "Alex Wells" was after.

The colonel brought the horse to a stop, then dismounted, his hands in the air.

Three Berbers ran out of the tent. They carried automatic rifles and shouted, but the colonel remained still. They surrounded him, hit him over the head, and dragged him into the tent.

Rukin shook his head. "Jesus. I assumed the fool had a better plan than that." He packed up the rifle and handed it to Kamau. "I'd say we've seen the last of our mysterious colonel."

Kamau nodded and gave a final look in the direction of the tent camp before following the major into the stairwell that led down from the roof.

"I've come here to help you," David insisted.

The Berber soldiers tore the last of his clothes off and carried them out of the tent.

The chief stepped forward. "Don't lie to us. You've come here to help yourself. You don't know us. You don't care about us."

"I'm—"

"Don't tell us who you are. I want to see it." The chief motioned to a man standing by the entrance to the tent. The man nodded once, left quickly, then returned with a small burlap sack. He closed the flap to the tent, plunging the room into almost total darkness, save for the dance of candlelight that played across the cloth walls. The chief took the sack from the man and tossed it into David's lap.

David reached for the sack.

"I wouldn't do that."

David looked up, then he felt it. Muscle, a finger sliding across his forearm. Then another rope gliding out over his thigh. Snakes. His eyes had almost adjusted to the dim light, and he knew instantly what they were: two Egyptian cobras. One bite would do him in. He would be dead within ten minutes.

David tried to control his breathing, but he was losing the

battle. He felt his muscles tense, and he thought the snakes reacted. The one on his forearm was creeping up his arm more quickly now, toward his shoulder, his neck, his face. He took another shallow breath. He wouldn't inhale fully—the contraction could alarm them. Slowly, he let the air escape his nose, and he focused his mind on the place where the breath touched the tip of his nose, observing the sensation, the absence of any other feeling. He stared straight ahead, at a dark spot on the floor. There was one last tingle, at his collarbone, but he kept his mind on his breath, taking in and breathing out, the sensation as the air met the tip of his nose. He couldn't feel the snakes.

Through his peripheral vision, he was vaguely aware of the chief pacing toward him.

"You are afraid, but you have control of your fear. No rational man walks the world without fear. Only those who control their fear live a life free of it. You are a man who has lived among snakes and learned to hide himself. You are a man who can tell lies, who can tell them as if you yourself believe them. That is very dangerous. At this moment, more for you than for me." The chief nodded to the snake handler, who crept carefully toward David and collected the snakes.

The chief sat across from David. "Now you can lie to me, or you can speak the truth. Choose wisely. I have seen many liars. And I have buried many liars."

David told the story he had come there to tell, and when he had finished, the chief looked away, seeming to contemplate.

In his mind, David began rifling through the chief's possible questions, mentally preparing responses. But no questions came. The chief stood and left.

Three men rushed into the tent, seized David, and dragged him out toward a communal fire that burned in the center of the makeshift village. The tribespeople gathered as he passed. Just before they reached the fire, David got his feet under him and threw the man on his right off, but the man holding his left arm held tight. David hit him hard in the face, and the man released his grip and fell listless into the sand. David turned, but three more soldiers were on him, dragging him to the ground, covering him, holding his arms. Then someone else loomed over him—the chief. Something rushed down, a sword, or a spear. It burned orange and smoke rolled off of it. The chief plunged the burning iron prod into David's chest, sending waves of searing pain throughout his body and the sickening smell of burning flesh and hair into his nose. David fought not to gag as his eyes rolled back into his head, and he lost consciousness.

43

Immari Sorting Camp
Marbella, Spain

KATE WAS SAFE, or so she thought. The tall British soldier, Adam Shaw, had killed the other guard and... he knew her name.

"Who are you?" Kate said.

"I'm the fifth man from the SAS team sent here to retrieve you."

"The fifth—"

"We had a bit of a disagreement over tactics. I submitted that we should alter our plans after the Immari invasion of Marbella. The other four didn't listen."

Kate eyed his uniform. "How did you—"

"There's a lot of confusion right now. A lot of new faces. We've been studying the Immari Army organization extensively. I knew enough to fake it. Getting the uniform was easy. Just had to kill one of them. Speaking of." He bent over the dead guard. "Help me get his uniform off."

Kate eyed the dead man. "Why?"

"Seriously? You want to walk out of here in that? Any idiot can see you sliced up a chef's jacket, and even if you can't see it, by God you can smell it a kilometer away. You're a walking compost heap."

Kate raised her shoulder and tried casually to sniff the white coat. Yeah, it was less than fresh. The overwhelming stench in the kitchen had apparently numbed her to the smell for a bit.

Shaw handed her the man's tunic, then stripped off the pants and held those up as well.

Kate hesitated. "Turn around."

He smiled. "Let me guess, Kate. Two well-shaped boobs, an unnaturally flat stomach, and toned legs. I've seen it before, Princess. I had the Internet before the plague."

"Well my body isn't on the Internet, so turn around."

He shook his head and turned his back to her.

Kate thought he mumbled something about "prudish Americans." She ignored him as she slipped into the uniform. It was slightly too large, but it would do. "What now?"

"Now I complete my mission—to take you to London. You'll complete the research, find a cure for this nightmare, and the world will live happily ever after. I'll get a picture with the Queen, et cetera, et cetera. Assuming you don't make any other stupid moves, we'll be okay."

Kate walked around the dead guard to face Shaw. "There's a man in here—Dr. Martin Grey. He's my adoptive father, and the man who made the deal with your government. We have to find him and take him with us."

Shaw led Kate out of the hallway and into the stairwell. "If he's in here, he's either dead or dying. We can't help him. You're my mission, not him."

"He is now. I'm not leaving here without him."

"Then you won't leave."

"And you won't accomplish your mission. No visit with the Queen."

He snorted. "I was being facetious. This is serious."

Kate nodded. "So is this. A man's life is a stake."

"No, Kate, billions of lives are at stake."

"Well none of them raised me."

Shaw exhaled deeply and motioned to the dead guard in the hall. "The other three are going to come looking for him soon. We need to get out of this building."

Kate considered Shaw's words for a moment. "That sounds like something you're going to have to handle." Kate thought for a moment. She could never search the entire building; she needed somewhere to start. Where would Martin go? He knew the layout of the buildings, and the Immari invasion protocol. Her mind flashed to the hotel safe. Could it withstand the fall of the building? No, that would simply trap him there, and his food wouldn't last—assuming anyone ever dug out the rubble, and that was a long shot. Food. Of course. "When you're done with the guards, meet me in the kitchen."

"The kitchen?"

"That's where Martin is." She started down the stairwell.

"Wait." Shaw picked up the guard's gun and belt and fastened both around Kate. "Wear this, but try not to use it."

"Why?"

"It draws attention, for one. And if you're shooting at someone around here who has a gun, they're probably a better shot than you are."

"How do you know I'm not some gun-shooting expert?"

"I read your file, Kate. Be careful." Without another word, he set off down the stairwell, practically leaping down the flights. He exited at the bottom before Kate could respond.

Kate followed at her own pace. At the lobby, the inhabitants scurried away from her, giving her a wide berth.

Through the glass revolving door, she saw Shaw talking with the three guards, waving his arms, the others laughing.

Kate made her way to the restaurant, which was similar to the other tower's restaurant, but she thought maybe it had had a different theme, though it was too disheveled to make out at this point. There were people here, but far less than she had expected. They crawled away from her as her footsteps echoed in the dining hall.

She pushed against the doors to the kitchen, but they wouldn't open. She pushed again, but they didn't give. She peered in through the oval glass window.

Martin sat there on the floor, slumped against the stainless steel cabinet below the counter. A pile of empty water bottles lay at his feet. Kate couldn't tell if he was alive or dead.

44

Immari Operations Base at Ceuta
Northern Morocco

THE GUARD ADJUSTED THE BINOCULARS, hoping to get a better look at the rider. The horse was one of theirs, the one the colonel had taken. The rider wore a bedouin headdress. The guard sounded the alarm.

Five minutes later, the guard stood with the other men of the perimeter detail as the rider stopped before the city gate and slowly raised his hands in the air. He reached for the red cloth wrapped around his head and unwound it.

The guard turned back to the men. "False alarm. It's the colonel." Then he looked back at the man. Something was different.

David walked into the officer's lounge and made a beeline for the major.

The major set down his cards, leaned back in his chair, and smiled. "The mighty horse warrior returns! We thought the savages might be having you for dinner."

David took a chair from an adjacent table without asking and inserted it between two men at the major's table, shoving them aside without a word. He opened his shirt, revealing the seared, inflamed flesh. "They tried. Too gamey for them." David glanced at the men around the table. "Give us a little privacy here?"

The major nodded and the men all grudgingly rose from their seats, taking one last look at their cards before muttering and tossing them back on the table, as if each knew he had the winning hand.

"I can solve your Berber problem."

"I'm listening," Rukin said.

"Return the chief's daughter. The raids stop."

The major turned his head slightly. "Who?"

"The girl you sent to my room."

"Bullshit."

"It's true."

"It's a ruse."

"That girl is all he wants. He'll relent, stop the attacks, hell, he'll even help us round up the other tribes. He's set a time and place for the attack. He'll serve them all up. But he wants his daughter and the other women first."

"Impossible. I can't turn them over."

"Why not?"

"First off..." Rukin seemed to be grasping, rationalizing. "Releasing the women will likely only empower them. The chief will parade the women as a sign of his own power and our weakness—our capitulation. It gives him the momentum. And that's just the half of it. I need those women for... *morale.* They're about the only joy I can give these men in this desolate hellhole. I'll have a mutiny on my hands the second they pass the city walls."

"Men can live without sex. They've done it before. And the chief will stop the attacks. Look, I had a mission—to secure Ceuta before Chairman Sloane arrived. I've given you the opportunity to do that. You can turn it down, but if horse raiders are taking pot shots at Sloane's helicopter convoy when he arrives, you'll have to answer for it."

The threat to Sloane and the possibility of failing at such a crucial moment seemed to weigh on Rukin. His tone changed. "You're certain the attacks will stop?"

"Certain."

"How? I mean, the idea that all these attacks, for months, have been to get her back?"

"Yes. Well, actually, those attacks were just to size you up. To test the city walls. You've only seen a tenth of their strength. There are other camps. They've just been figuring out the best way to take the base. They won't take prisoners."

"He'd risk them all for one girl?"

"Never underestimate what parents will do to save their child's life."

Rukin looked away, searching for something to say.

David preempted him. "We're going to give the girl back, and they're going to help us round up the other tribes. That will secure this base and give us the freedom to focus on the upcoming mission, our role in the larger Immari plan. If we're not ready, if we're fighting to hold our city walls... heads will roll, and it won't be mine. I've completed my mission. I've given you a means to secure Ceuta." David stood and began walking away. Throughout the officer's lounge, every table was quiet, every pair of eyes focused on him and the major.

The major spoke up. "If I release the women... the daughter. You honestly think that when the chief sees what we've done to his daughter, that he won't attack then and there."

"He won't—"

"He—"

"Made a promise to me, before his entire tribe. His honor hangs on it. He breaks his promise, even to an enemy, he loses the faith of his people. He can't afford it. And you're wrong. For months he prayed that he would see her again, that she wasn't dead. He'll be overjoyed to see her. Nothing else will matter." David turned and walked out. "Choice is yours, Major."

45

Immari Sorting Camp
Marbella, Spain

KATE RAMMED the butt of the gun into the glass again, and it finally broke, sending shards into the kitchen. The noise scared the remaining people out of the dining hall, leaving her alone.

She used the edge of the gun to clear away the sharp teeth of glass along the rim of the window and then tried to reach the metal bar that Martin had put through the door handles. She stretched, felt the last remaining shards of glass biting into her arm, and reeled back. She took the gun in her hand and reached again, and she had it. She pushed hard, and the bar fell to the ground with a loud clang.

She pushed through the doors and rushed to Martin. He was alive, but he was burning up. She held his head in her hands. Dark spots covered his cheeks. His skin was boiling.

Kate pulled his eyelids open. His eyes rolled around, revealing milky yellow where white should be. Jaundice. Liver failure. What other organs were affected?

"Martin?" Kate tried to shake him, and his breathing rate increased.

He cracked his eyes, and upon seeing Kate, drew back. He coughed violently.

Kate patted him down, searching for the case that held the Orchid pills. It was the only thing she could do, but the case wasn't on him. He coughed again, arching his back this time. He rolled off the cabinet to lie on the floor, and Kate saw the case—behind him, lying against the cabinet.

She opened it quickly. One pill. She glanced back at Martin, who was coughing quietly on the floor. He had rationed himself, hoping he might make it a little longer.

The double doors to the kitchen flew open, and Kate reeled around. Shaw stood there, a sack in his hands. He surveyed Kate and Martin. "Ah, bloody hell."

"Help me get him up," Kate said, as she struggled to right Martin against the cabinet.

"He's finished, Kate. We can't take him out of here like this."

Kate grabbed a bottle of water and forced Martin to take the last pill. "What was your plan?"

He threw the sack at her feet, and Kate saw that it held another Immari Army uniform.

Shaw shook his head. "I thought we could walk out of here. Maybe if he were in better shape. Immari soldiers don't look that sick, Kate. He'd paint a target all over us."

Martin turned his head and tried to say something, but the words came out in a jumble. The fever was consuming him. Kate used the uniform to wipe some of the sweat off of him. "If he was well, what would you do after we left this building? What's the plan?"

"We follow the crowd—the survivors. We get on the plague barge to Ceuta, the main Immari sorting center—"

"What? We need to *get away* from the Immari."

"We can't. There's no way out of here. They're burning a perimeter around the Orchid district walls—almost a half kilometer."

Kate's thoughts immediately went to the boys, to the couple in the old city. "Are they burning the Old Town district?"

Shaw seemed confused. "No. Just a defensive perimeter around the camp. They're turning it into a new processing center. Anyway, by nightfall, the fire will be at the walls, and the plague barge will be here. It's the only way out."

Kate made her decision. "Then we'll be on it."

Shaw opened his mouth, but Kate cut him off. "I'm not asking. There's a bag in my room. You know where that is?"

He nodded.

"Bring it to me. It has the research. Then find some..." She needed to try something to slow the disease progression. Normally, for any other virus, the key would be antivirals and patience. But if this disease behaved the same way it did in 1918, Martin was undergoing an immune system overload. His own body was attacking him. "Bring some steroids."

"Steroids?"

"Tablets." Kate tried to think of the European names. "Prednisolone, cortisone, methylprednisolone—"

"Okay, I get the picture."

"And we need some food. When the loading starts, we'll take him out. We'll say he's a drunk soldier."

Shaw let his head fall back. "This is a really bad idea." He focused on Kate, and seeing how serious she was, simply turned and walked out. He paused at the door and pointed at the metal bar that had blocked it. "Put that back in the door while I'm gone. And stay quiet."

46

Immari Advance Fleet Alpha
Near Cape Verde

DORIAN WALKED onto the ship's bridge and cringed as all the officers, including the ship's captain, stopped what they were doing and saluted him.

"For God's sake, stop saluting me. I'll demote the next sailor who salutes me to seaman zero class." He wasn't sure if that rank existed, but the looks on the faces around the room told him that his meaning was received. Dorian led the captain aside. "Any update from Operation Genesis?"

"No, sir."

In this case, no news was bad news. The lack of update from his operative told Dorian that his plan to capture Kate Warner was exactly nowhere. He debated changing course.

The Atlantean had been clear: *You must wait until she obtains the code.*

"Do you have new orders, sir?"

Dorian turned away from him. "No... Stay the course, Captain."

"There's something else, sir."

Dorian eyed him.

"An update from Ceuta. They say the British have mined the Straits of Gibraltar. We won't be able to pass them."

Dorian exhaled and closed his eyes. "You're sure?"

"Yes, sir. They've sent several ships in. They were hoping to find a way and guide us through, but the Brits sewed it up tight. But, we think there's some good news."

"Good news?"

"They wouldn't have mined the straits if they planned to face us off the coast of Spain."

The captain's logic made sense. Options formed in Dorian's mind, but he wanted to hear the captain's opinion first. "Options?"

"Two. We sail north, try to go around the British Isles and find a port in north Germany. We could fight our way south from there. But I advise against it. That's what the British want. They have to be low on jet fuel, maybe close to out. But their subs and half their destroyers are nuclear; assuming they have enough survivors to operate even some of them, they can field a small fleet. Off the coast of Britain, between their sea and air power, they could take us easily."

"And option number two?"

"We park off the coast of Morocco, fly you to Ceuta on a helicopter, and you sail across the Mediterranean on one of the ships they've collected."

"Risks?"

"You'll have a smaller fleet, with fewer battleships and fewer of our well-trained troops—just what we can fly with you in the five helicopters. You'll dock in northern Italy and make your way to Germany from there. Reports from the ground are that the

Orchid Districts are evacuating across Europe. It's complete pandemonium. Once you get to Italy, you'll have no problem."

"Why can't we just fly the whole way? Surely we can find a jet."

The captain shook his head. "There are still some air defenses in continental Europe, and they've got backup power to last for years. They're shooting down any unidentified aircraft—several each day."

"Ceuta it is, then."

When Dorian returned to his stateroom, Johanna was awake and naked, stretched out on the bed, reading an old gossip magazine, for reasons he would never understand.

He sat on the bed and pulled his boots off. "Haven't you read that thing two dozen times? Here's an update: all those idiots are dead and whatever they were doing didn't matter—even before the plague."

"It reminds me of the world before the plague. It's like revisiting the normal world."

"You think that world was normal? You're crazier than I thought."

She tossed the magazine aside and curled into him, gently kissing his exposed ribs where he had just pulled his shirt off. "Rough day at the office, Sir Broods-a-Lot?"

Dorian pushed her off of him. "You wouldn't talk to me that way if you knew me better."

She smiled innocently. It contrasted sharply with the cruelty on his face. "Then it's a good thing I don't know you better. But... I do know how to cheer you up."

47

Immari Operations Base at Ceuta
Northern Morocco

FROM THE WATCHTOWER, David adjusted the binoculars and waited for the battle to begin. The Immari divisions had been slowly chasing the Berber tribes for the better part of three hours. From his vantage point, David could see the trap they had set—a line of heavy artillery and fortified lines on the far side of a high ridge looking down on a small valley. The Berbers would cross the opposite ridge and descend into the valley soon, then the larger battle would begin. The Immari would win, capturing and killing every Berber in the valley.

"How are the tribes faring?"

David turned to see Kamau standing behind him on the platform.

"Not well. They're almost in the Immari trap. Where are we?"

"Eleven men."

David nodded.

"I can widen the net, but the risk grows."

"No. We'll have to make do with eleven."

Several hours later, the sound of heavy artillery echoed across the charred field that had been the city of Ceuta. David stood, walked to the edge of the watchtower, and held the binoculars up. The carnage in the valley was near total. On the farthest ridge, a group of riders on horseback charged up the hill toward the big guns camped there, but the Immari shot the horses out from under them, then raked them with automatic gunfire. Behind them, tribesmen fell in waves. David let the binoculars drop to his side, then returned to the bench and waited.

As the sun set, the Immari procession reached the outer gate. David watched from the guard tower. Major Rukin was the first to reach the gate, and as his jeep sped by, he and David shared a glance. The major's lips curled slightly, but David simply stared.

David sat in his room, waiting. He would take one last nap before the final battle began. The next few hours would determine his fate and that of millions more.

48

Immari Sorting Camp
Marbella, Spain

Kate forced Martin to eat a little more of the candy bar—part of the paltry "buffet" Shaw had rounded up. She held the bottle of water to Martin's lips, and he drank greedily. He couldn't seem to get enough water.

Shaw stood in the corner wearing an expression that said, *This is a waste of time and could get us killed.* Kate already knew him that well.

She jerked her head toward the silver double doors. Shaw rolled his eyes and wandered out.

"Martin, I need to ask you about your notes. I don't understand them."

His head rolled back and forth against the cabinet. "Answers are... dead. Dead and buried. Not among the living..."

Kate wiped a fresh layer of sweat from his forehead. "Dead and buried? Where? I don't understand."

"Find the turning points. When the genome changes. We searched... not alive. We failed. I failed."

Kate closed her eyes and rubbed her eyelids. She considered giving him more steroids. She needed answers. But there were risks. She grabbed the bottle of prednisolone.

The kitchen doors parted, and Shaw stuck his head in. "It's happening now. We need to move."

Kate nodded her assent, and she helped Shaw stand Martin up and escort him out of the building. Past the revolving door, the sight of the camp almost stopped her dead in her tracks. The tower of the survivors spilled people onto the grounds in an endless stream. The palm trees swayed above the unseen masses that flowed below them. Guards were waving flashlights, herding people. A massive cruise ship stood tall at the shore, towering over the coast. Two massive ramps loaded people onto it, as if it were Noah's Ark.

"The far ramp," Shaw said quietly and began tugging Martin.

Four guards were minding the far ramp, which Kate took to be the Immari loyalist loading point.

The ship came into focus. The once-white luxury liner now looked derelict, and Kate wondered if it would even float.

Shaw spoke quickly with the guards, something to the effect of "little too much cough syrup," and "be right as rain tomorrow."

To Kate's relief, they passed the checkpoint with ease and fell into the throngs of people climbing the ramp. At the top, they exited into a corridor that was closed on both sides but open to the moonlight above. It felt like a cattle stall at a state fair or a rodeo. They weaved endlessly, toward the center of the ship, Shaw leading the way. Twice they had to stop to let Martin catch his breath, standing against the wall as the flow of people snaked around them and filled the hallway beyond. There were doors that led to square compartments along the hallway, and people filled each room as they went.

"We need to get below, to a cabin. The topside compartments will be an inferno by morning." He motioned to Martin. "He won't fare well."

At the end of the hall, they descended the stairwell several flights, then worked their way through another set of corridors until they found an empty room. "Stay here, be quiet, and keep the door shut. I'll knock in three sets of three when I return," Shaw said.

"Where are you going?"

"To get supplies," he said and pulled the door shut before Kate could reply. She slid the latch, locking the door.

The compartment was completely dark. Kate felt around for a switch but found none. She took the light bar from the backpack and bathed the small space in light. Martin lay against the wall, panting. Kate helped him into the bottom of one of the bunks. This was clearly one of the crew quarters: two bunk beds and a small closet in the center of the room.

She took the satellite phone out and checked the display. *No Service.* She needed to go topside to finish her phone call. She needed answers. Her talk with Martin had been less than helpful. *The genetic turning points. The answers... dead and buried.*

Kate was utterly exhausted. She stretched out on the bunk opposite Martin. She would close her eyes and rest, just for a moment, just to help her think.

Periodically, she heard Martin cough. She didn't know how much time passed, but she thought she felt the massive ship move. Sleep took her sometime later.

Kate was barefoot, and her feet barely made a sound on the

marble floor. Ahead of her, the arched wooden door stood at the end of the long hall. On her right, the same two doors loomed. The first was open: the door where she had seen David. She peered in. Empty. She walked to the second door on the right and pushed it open. The circular room was bathed with light from windows that had been swung open and glass doors that opened onto a terrace. A blue sea spread out below, but there were no boats, just a peninsula of tree-covered mountains and water beyond, as far as she could see.

The room was sparse, save for a steel and oak-topped drafting table. David sat behind it, on an old iron stool.

"What are you drawing?" Kate asked.

"A plan," he answered without looking up.

"For what?"

"Taking a city. Saving lives." He held up an elaborate drawing of a horse made of wood.

"You can take over a city with a wooden horse?"

David set the drawing down and continued working on it. "Happened before..."

Kate smiled. "Yeah, right."

"Happened in Troy."

"Oh yeah. I thought Brad Pitt was great in that."

He shook his head. He erased a few lines on the drawing. "Like other epic tales, they thought it was just a story until they found scientific evidence of its existence." He made a few last strokes with his pencil, sat back, and scrutinized the drawing. "I'm mad at you, by the way."

"Me?"

"You left me. In Gibraltar. You didn't trust me. I could have saved you."

"I didn't have a choice. You were injured—"

"You should have trusted me. You underestimated me."

49

Immari Operations Base at Ceuta
Northern Morocco

Major Rukin poured himself a tall glass of whiskey, drank it down, and collapsed into a chair at the round table just beyond his bed. Slowly, he unbuttoned his tunic, and when it fell free, he poured himself another drink, just as high as the last. It had been a long day, but hopefully it would be his last dealing with those wretched barbarian tribesmen beyond the walls. Good riddance. Killing them all was ideal; killing a few and capturing the rest, just as good. The base was always woefully short of servant staff. And for that matter... where was she? It had been a very long, very stressful day.

He peeled his sweat-soaked tunic off and shimmied his arms out, letting the tunic fall back to wrap around the chair. He poured a third drink with less care this time, splashing brown liquid onto the table, drank it down, and bent to untie his boots. His feet throbbed, but the sensation had faded as the drinks had taken effect.

A loud knock echoed from the door.

"What?"

"It's Kamau."

"Come in."

Kamau swung the door open, but he didn't enter. Beside him stood a tall, slender woman Rukin hadn't seen before. Good. A new girl. Kamau had done well—the woman was older than Rukin's typical taste, but he was in the mood for something different. Variety was the spice of life. There was something else about her. Her posture. The eyes—strength, not quite defiance. Confidence. No fear. She will learn.

Rukin stood. "She'll do."

Kamau nodded slightly, pushed the girl at her lower back to usher her in, and closed the door with a click.

The woman stared at the major, not bothering to take in his enormous quarters.

"You speak English?"

She furled her brow and shook her head slightly.

"No, your lot never does, do they? No matter. We'll do this caveman style." He held a hand up, indicating for her to stay, then stepped behind her, pulled the garment off her shoulders, and untied it at her waist.

The garment dropped silently to the floor, and he spun her around to inspect—

She was nothing like he expected. She was muscular. Too muscular and her legs and lower torso were dotted with scars—knife wounds, some bullet wounds, others... arrows maybe? Unacceptable. He didn't want reminders of combat here. He shook his head and paced to the table, making for his radio. *Back to the stables with her*.

He felt a strong hand on his arm, and he looked back in shock. Her eyes met his. Feisty. Her confidence had turned to fire. Did she know he had rejected her? Rukin turned, reassessing her now.

As a smile spread across his face, her other arm flew to him, and her fist crashed into his gut, just below his diaphragm, knocking the wind out of him instantly. He fell to his knees and gasped. As he sucked desperately, she kicked his left side, just below his ribcage, rolling him over and sending waves of whiskey up his throat and out his nose and mouth. He gagged and gasped as the liquor burned with each desperate cough. He was drowning in fire. His abs burned and ached from the impacts and his violent heaving.

She stepped around him carefully, deliberately, never taking her eyes off him. A small smile played at the ends of her mouth, and her eyes narrowed.

She's enjoying this. She's going to watch me die, Rukin thought. He turned over and crawled to the door. If he could get his breath back, he could cry out. Maybe if he reached the door—

Her foot came down hard on his back, slamming him into the hard floor, breaking his nose. He almost lost consciousness.

He felt her hands wrap around his wrists and pull his arms back, her foot still planted in the center of his back. She was ripping him in half. He wanted to scream, but no sound came from his lungs, only an animalistic grunt. His right shoulder snapped, and the wave of pain hit him like a slap, almost taking him under. He would have passed out, but the liquor had numbed some of the pain, keeping him conscious. His left shoulder snapped, and the woman pulled both arms back unnaturally.

Rukin heard her pace away from him, and he hoped she was going for the gun. Death would be welcome. But he heard the rip of tape instead. She wrapped his wrists together behind him. Every touch sent a new shock of pain.

He almost had his breath back now and he pushed, trying to

call, but she brought the tape to his mouth and covered it, winding the roll around his head several times. She tied his legs from his ankles to his knees, then lifted him and practically threw him against the wall, face out. Pain, then hyperventilation came as he tried to breathe through his nose and endure the waves of pain that came from his shoulders pressing against the wall.

She stared at him for a moment, then casually strode to the table. Her naked, muscled body flexed only slightly with each leisurely step. She looked at the liquor bottle, then took the handgun from Rukin's belt.

Do it, he thought.

She ejected the magazine and pulled the slide back. No round ejected. Rukin never chambered his first round. She inserted the magazine again and chambered a round.

Do it.

She set the gun on the table, sat, crossed her legs, and gazed at him.

Rukin screamed through the tape at his mouth, but she ignored him.

She grabbed the radio, twisted the dial on top to change the channel, then held it close to her mouth. "Fire purges everything."

A few minutes passed. In the distance, Rukin heard a loud explosion, then another, and another, like rolling thunder. They were attacking the walls.

50

Plague Barge *Destiny*
Mediterranean Sea

KATE WAS TIRED of waiting for Shaw. She rolled off the bunk. She needed to get to the surface to make a call. She glanced at Martin. She couldn't leave him here. She pulled him up and helped him to the door. She opened it and looked out. The corridor was clear.

They made their way to the tiny doors for the elevator. Kate hit the up button, and the elevator dinged and opened a few seconds later, revealing a cramped compartment. What floor to hit? Kate pressed the button for level one and waited.

The doors parted. Two men in white coats, doctors she assumed, stood before her, holding clipboards, discussing something.

One was Chinese, the other was European. The Chinese doctor stepped forward, cocked his head, and said, "Dr. Grey?"

Kate froze. She was halfway off the elevator. She considered going back, but the Chinese doctor closed the distance quickly.

The European was close behind him. "You know this man?" he asked.

Martin was still listless, but he looked up. "Chang..." his voice was soft, barely audible.

Kate's heart raced.

"I..." Chang began. He turned to his colleague. "I used to work with this man. He's... a fellow Immari researcher." He looked at Kate for a moment. "Follow me."

Kate glanced down the corridor to her left and right. Guards loitered at each end.

She was trapped. Chang was walking down the narrow hallway directly ahead, and the European scientist was staring at her, his head cocked. Kate fell in behind Chang.

The hallway opened onto a large kitchen that had been converted to a research facility. The steel tables had been transformed into makeshift operating tables. It vaguely reminded Kate of the kitchen in the Orchid District, where Martin had told her the truth about the plague in the attached office.

"Help me get him onto the table," Chang said.

The European stepped closer to examine Martin.

Martin slowly turned his head to look at Kate. There was no expression, and he said nothing.

Chang stepped between the other scientist and Kate and Martin. "If you could... give us a moment. I need to talk with them."

When he had left, Chang turned to Kate. "You're Kate Warner, aren't you?"

Kate hesitated. The fact that he suspected it and hadn't turned her in... she thought she could trust him. "Yes." She nodded to Martin. "Can you help him?"

"I doubt it." Chang opened a steel cabinet and took out a syringe. "But I can try."

"What is that?"

"Something we've been working on. The Immari version of Orchid. It's still experimental, and it doesn't work for everyone." He focused on Kate. "It could kill him. Or it could give him a few more days. Do you want me to administer it?"

Kate glanced down at Martin, at his dying body. She nodded.

Chang stepped forward and injected him. He glanced at the door.

"What's wrong?" Kate asked.

"Nothing..." Chang murmured as he focused on Martin.

51

Immari Operations Base at Ceuta
Northern Morocco

DAVID STARED at the eleven men who stood around the armory room. "Gentlemen, our cause is lost. But it is just. This base is the gate to Hell, and the world the Immari seek to build. If we destroy it, we can give the people of Europe a fighting chance. However... we are outnumbered, outgunned, and sitting in the heart of enemy territory. We have three things: the element of surprise, the will to fight, and a righteous cause. If we see morning, we will win. Tonight will determine our fate and that of millions of others. Fight hard and don't fear death. There are far worse things in life—one being living a life you aren't proud of."

He nodded to Kamau, who stepped forward and began issuing orders to each man.

Shortly after the tall African finished, the radio in the corner crackled and pierced the silence. "Fire purges everything."

"It's time," David said.

David and Kamau ascended the catwalk with three of their men. The operations center for the base sat at the top of the tower, at the center of the citadel, far away from the walls, safe from any attackers but high enough to see exactly what was going on with a naked eye—or better yet, binoculars. It was smart. The base commanders didn't want to rely on cameras, surveillance, and field reports—they could all fail or be compromised. They wanted to see the fight with their own eyes.

David paused at the landing and clicked the flashlight into the night, sending the signal to the regiments of Berber soldiers waiting beyond the far wall.

When the last flash faded from the light, he resumed his climb to the top, his men following closely behind him. The room at the top of the tower was as he remembered it: a mix of an air traffic control center and the bridge of a battleship. Four operations officers sat at control stations, staring at banks of flat-screen monitors, occasionally typing. A pot of coffee brewed in the corner.

The closest tech saw David, spun around, stood, and saluted nervously as if not quite sure how to handle the unexpected visit. One by one, the other three followed suit.

"As you were, gentlemen," David said. "It's been a long day, and as you may have heard, Major Rukin won a great victory in the hills. He's downstairs celebrating, getting what he deserves." David smiled, a truly genuine smile. "Take a break. Join him in the mess. There's food, drink... and the spoils of war. New arrivals." David motioned to his men. "We'll take this shift."

The techs mumbled their thanks and hopped up from their stations. A colonel's orders were the best opening they would get to skip out on a shift.

When the men had left, David's soldiers took their places at the consoles. David looked at the screens suspiciously. "You sure you know how to work these things?"

"Yes, sir. I worked the day shift for a few months when I was first transferred."

Kamau circled the room, handing each of the soldiers a cup of coffee. He joined David, and the two of them stood for a moment, staring into the night. David thought it spoke well of him that he said nothing. After a few minutes, Kamau simply held up his watch: twenty-two hundred hours. David activated his radio. "All stations report." One by one, the men checked in, their voices crackling in David's earpiece. He waited for the last piece of the puzzle to click. The men had taken names from the Trojan War; they had all decided that David's call sign would be Achilles.

"Achilles, Ajax. The Trojans are in the banquet hall. We've begun the feast."

Begun the feast was code for locked them in and deployed the gas.

"Copy, Ajax," David said. He walked out of the command tower and down to the first landing. Again he held the flashlight up and clicked it. By the time he returned to the command center, the explosions along the perimeter had begun. Fire and plumes of smoke rose above the outer wall. The three men at the command station worked the radios and computers.

The screens revealed the scene. Waves of horseback riders besieged the wall. The automatic guns at the towers mowed rows of the riders down, but still they came, charging relentlessly.

A tech turned to David. "Tower Two wants authorization to use the rail gun."

Kamau glanced over at David.

The rail guns would decimate the Berber forces. Authorizing their use, however, would be very convincing to the troops, would prove the base was at risk.

David pointed to the sniper rifle at Kamau's side. "Take them after the first shot."

David walked to the command chair and activated the microphone. "Tower Two, this is Colonel Wells. The major has turned over command to me. Go weapons hot on rail gun delta and fire at will." He deactivated the radio and waited. The rail gun sent a streak of fire into the night, and a geyser of earth and blood exploded into the air, leaving a black cloud where horses and soldiers had been a second before. Everything seemed silent for a moment after that. David hoped the Berbers would keep coming. He needed them to.

On the landing below, David heard three shots ring out in rapid succession. The rail gun fell silent.

David clicked the microphone on the control panel again. "Battalions one, two, and three, move into zone one. I repeat, Battalions one, two, and three, this is Ceuta Command, outer wall is at risk, move into zone one and take up position."

Almost immediately, David saw motion in the citadel and the ring beyond. Troops pounded the ground, the inner gate opened, and trucks rushed through it. The Berbers pressed the attack, and the battle grew more intense.

"Command, Tower One. Tower Two is down, repeat Tower Two is down."

"Copy, Tower One," one of David's men said. "We're aware. Reinforcements are inbound."

Almost a minute after David's order, the area below the wall was filled with Immari soldiers, almost four thousand of them. This was the moment David had planned, their one opportunity to take the base. His hands shook slightly, and in that moment, he wondered if he could do it. What if he couldn't? There was no turning back now.

The technicians looked back at him, each knowing what

came next. Finally, one man quietly said, "Awaiting your order, sir."

Mass murder. The death of four thousand men—soldiers. Enemy soldiers. *Monsters*, David told himself. But they couldn't all be monsters. Just people on the other side of this fight, people who had been unlucky enough, whose circumstance had made them his enemy.

All David had to do was say the words. The tech would push the buttons, the mines below the wall would arm, the improvised explosives would detonate, and hell would break loose. Thousands of soldiers—people—would die.

"There will be no order," David said.

Shock spread across the men's faces, except for Kamau. His face was a mask that betrayed no emotion.

David stepped forward, to the primary technician's station. "Show me the buttons to press." This was his burden to bear; he alone should and would shoulder the responsibility. The man showed him the sequence of commands, and David memorized them. He entered the codes, and the ring below the wall exploded into a sea of carnage. Blood seemed to pool like a moat. The radio erupted in calls, and one of the techs instantly turned it down.

David activated his radio. "Ajax, Achilles. Outer wall is breached. Crack open the horse."

"Copy, Achilles," the soldier answered.

The screens flashed to the confinement wings. Three of David's soldiers raced through, opening the cells, freeing the captured Berbers, arming them. The fight for the citadel and for Ceuta began now.

"Open the gate," David said. "And make the call."

He slumped into the "captain's chair" and waited. The tech called over his shoulder. "You're on."

"Immari Fleet Alpha, this is Ceuta Command. We are under

attack. Repeat, we are under attack. Our outer wall has been breached. Request immediate air support."

"Copy, Ceuta Command. Stand by."

David waited for the words. Sloane was in that fleet, and David knew him—he would command the air assault himself. For all his faults, Sloane led from the front.

"Ceuta Command, Fleet Alpha. Be advised: we're scrambling air support now. ETA fifteen minutes."

"Copy, Fleet Alpha. ETA fifteen minutes. Ceuta Command out."

When he was sure the channel was closed, he issued his final orders to the techs. "I want you to wait until they're deep in our firing range. Don't take any chances."

"Even if they fire—"

"Even if they fire everything they've got. Wait. And don't position the rail guns until you're ready to fire. Someone on the ground could warn them. You take those helicopters down, and we could change the course of history." He walked over to join Kamau at the door. "It's been an honor, gentlemen. Now we're going to buy you some time."

David reached for the door, but a tech called out. "Sir, we've got incoming—"

"Air?"

"A plague barge. It's a little over a mile out. Inbound from Marbella. They just sent us their docking request and manifest."

David spun to face Kamau. "How could we not know about this?"

He shook his head. "The ships come and go as they please, there's no schedule. They can wait in the harbor to dock for days, so it doesn't matter." He crossed the room and punched the keyboard. The manifest scrolled across the large screen.

David looked around the room. "What's onboard? Weapons

capabilities? And for that matter, what the hell is a plague barge?"

Kamau spoke as he worked the computer. "This one's an old cruise ship. Weapons are minimal: two fifty-four-caliber guns on each end. But... they're carrying all the excess troops from the invasion of several cities in southern Spain." He stood. "Almost ten thousand troops—plus new recruits, those that took the Immari pledge. Who knows how many. There could be twenty thousand enemy combatants on board. There would have been devolving on board, but this close to Ceuta... they've already been offloaded."

David rubbed his forehead. "How long 'til it gets here?"

"Five, ten minutes."

There was no choice. Twenty thousand troops, pouring in from the harbor, reinforcing the citadel from the rear. "Hit it," David said. "Whatever it takes. Sink her." He grabbed his gun and raced out the door, and Kamau followed close behind him.

When the shots were fired from the rail guns along the harbor—at an Immari ship—the remaining Immari troops in the citadel would know they had been betrayed. The final battle for Ceuta would start in seconds.

As David and Kamau reached the bottom of the landing, they saw shots launch from the batteries along the harbor. The towering cruise ship exploded, then buckled and burned, floating listlessly like a funeral pyre.

Kosta burst into the room, but this time, he didn't retreat at the sight of Dorian and the woman laying there naked. "Sir, Ceuta is under attack. They've requested air support."

Dorian was up, dressed, and out of the room before the woman even woke up.

52

Immari Advance Fleet Alpha
Near Tangier, Morocco

Dorian marched down the cramped corridor. The hatch stood open, revealing the darkened deck. Four helicopters purred on the launch pad. Soldiers stood beside them, waiting for him, ready to fly into battle.

For the first time since he had awoken in that tube in Antarctica, he felt normal. He felt like himself. A soldier going to war. He felt at home.

Sailors poked their heads out of the intersecting passageways, hoping to get a glimpse of him—the chairman of the last empire humanity would ever see, the man who had died and arisen, someone more than mortal—a God or the Devil.

The pitter-patter of bare feet on the metal floor caught his attention, and he turned just in time to see Johanna, running full on for him. She jumped, and he caught her.

She wrapped her arms around him and kissed him. He stood

there, still as stone at first, but slowly he wrapped one, then another arm around her, held her tight, and kissed her back.

Whistles and hollers erupted down the corridor.

Dorian felt himself smile as he set her down. He quickly let it fade as he turned and walked through the hatchway toward the waiting soldiers and helicopters.

Martin opened his eyes. His head was clear. He could think again. Kate was there. He was in a lab or a hospital. A man leaned over him. Martin knew him. A memory came to him; he had spoken with the man over a videoconference. The doctor was the researcher in China, who had conducted the trials on the Bell. Dr... "Chang," Martin said, his voice raspy.

"How are you feeling?"

"Awful."

He heard Kate laughing, and she stepped closer to him. "At least you know how you're feeling. That's an improvement."

He smiled at Kate. He wondered what she had done to save him. Had she risked her life? He hoped not. It would be a waste. He had so much to tell her, so much she needed to know. "Kate—"

The ship shuddered, and Martin was thrown across the room. He slammed into a steel refrigerator, and dark spots crowded his vision.

53

Outside Ceuta
Northern Morocco

Dorian watched the wooded expanse fly by below him. Ahead, through the helicopter's windshield, he saw flashes in the distance, like fireflies in the night. Soon they would join the battle, and victory would follow soon after.

He pulled his helmet on. "Comm check, Strike Team Delta, this is General Sloane."

The four helicopters answered his call.

Sloane relaxed against the seat cushion. He watched the flashes a while longer and wondered what Johanna was doing, what she was wearing, what she was reading.

What was happening to him? Attachment. Sloppiness. Weakness. He would have to get rid of her when he returned.

The first bullets sprayed the metal scaffolding as David and Kamau reached the bottom.

They formed up, standing back to back, pressing into each other just enough to know where the other was, and opened fire. The empty shells fell to the ground as they jerked left and right.

Immari infantry poured out of the barracks surrounding the command tower, and David and Kamau cut down wave after wave of soldiers. But they kept coming. A group of Immari soldiers took up position across the yard and began focusing their fire on David and Kamau.

David began sidestepping to the building opposite the control tower, hoping to get to cover. Kamau matched his movements.

David's earpiece came to life. "Achilles, Ajax. I have the Myrmidons. We're closing on your position."

"Copy, Ajax," David said. "The sooner the better." He fired another blast until his automatic rifle clicked. He quickly reloaded and opened fire again.

Three massive explosions lit the night sky, then rose into a fire that burned over the water. Dorian could see the outline of Ceuta base now.

"What the hell was that?" Dorian asked.

"Probably another rail gun barrage from the wall," the pilot said.

"Probably not, you idiot. It's burning over the water. Who fired those shots?"

"The attacking tribesmen?" the pilot half-said, half-asked.

Dorian's mind raced. These barbarians—on horseback. Would they attack an incoming plague barge? Unlikely. Something was wrong.

"Strike Force Delta, hold your position, repeat, halt your assault on Ceuta."

The helicopters flew on into the night, barreling toward the burning base and the mysterious fire in the water.

He grabbed the pilot's shoulder. "Take us down. Take us down." The pilot complied, and the helicopter nose-dived into the trees below.

"Strike team—"

The lead helicopter exploded, and the two beside it instantly burst into flames. Shrapnel sprayed Dorian's helicopter. The rotors sputtered, and it began to spin. Smoke filled the cabin, and Dorian felt flames and heat from the top of the helicopter. The trees rushed up, and he felt branches reaching in, and then he was flying, falling, outside the helicopter.

David fired the last round from his rifle and drew his sidearm. They were coming too fast for him to keep up. Kamau spun around and fought side by side with him, cutting down a row of soldiers rushing out of the barracks. They were never-ending.

David's sidearm clicked. He didn't have another magazine. Kamau stepped in front of him and continued firing.

David activated his radio. "Ajax, Achilles. The Trojans are about to overrun our position."

Kamau slammed back into him, throwing David to the ground. He could hear Ajax responding in his earpiece, but all the words were lost. He grabbed Kamau's rifle and began firing from the ground, then got to one knee. How many rounds did he have left?

He glanced back at Kamau. He was writhing on the ground. David tried to turn him over, hoping to see where he had been hit.

Kate struggled to get up from the floor. The ship was shaking too much. The wail of bending steel was almost deafening. She felt for the pack at her back, making sure she still had it. She crawled over to Martin and pulled him into her lap.

Another shudder rocked the ship, and she was thrown across the room. The scientist, Chang, caught her, breaking her fall. "Are you okay?" he shouted.

The sprinkler system came on, and the ship's alarms rang out.

The door swung open, and Shaw ran in. "Come on. We need to get to the lifeboats."

The European scientist followed close behind him. He surveyed the room in horror. "Our research!" he shouted to Chang.

"Leave it!" Chang yelled.

Chang and Shaw took Martin, and Kate followed them.

Bullets whizzed by David from behind and he spun, ready to fire, but it was Ajax and the Berber forces. They rushed past him, consuming the Immari soldiers.

David pulled Kamau to the building wall and rolled him over. There was no blood. Kamau looked up, shaking his head. "Got my vest, David. Just knocked the wind out of me."

Ajax and the Berber commander converged on their position. "What's our status?" David asked.

"We've almost got control of the citadel," Ajax said. "They're starting to surrender, but a few units are fighting to the last."

"Come with me," David said. He helped Kamau to his feet, and they entered the barracks.

Outside, the gunfire was dying down. The occasional grenade explosion punctuated the din. They stopped at a large door, and David knocked gently. "It's Achilles."

The door opened, revealing the Berber chief. She wore a blue dress and held a pistol in her hand. She motioned them in.

Major Rukin was gagged and hogtied on the floor. A wry smile spread across David's face. The major struggled at his bindings and screamed into the gag.

David turned to the chief. "You intend to honor your word?"

"I will, just as you have honored yours. No harm will come to those who surrender." The chief glanced at the spot on David's chest where she had branded him. "A true chief never betrays a promise to her people."

David walked to the major and pulled the gag out.

"You're a fool—"

"Shut up," David said. "We have control of Ceuta. The only remaining question is how many Immari soldiers will die tonight. If you go up to the command center with the chief here —" David paused to enjoy the shock on the major's face. "Yes, that's right, she's the chief. It was her daughter, by the way. The Berbers have a long history of female tribal leaders. History and cultural understanding come in handy sometimes. Even in war. If you go with her and order your remaining troops to surrender, you could save lives. If you don't, that will please her and her people very much, I assure you."

"Who are you?" Rukin demanded.

"It doesn't matter," David said.

Rukin smiled contemptuously. "Men like you don't win wars like this. This isn't a world for *nice guys*."

"We'll see about that."

54

Plague Barge *Destiny*
Mediterranean Sea

KATE WATCHED Shaw open another door. He was about to step through it when flames filled the corridor ahead.

"Back!" he yelled as he slammed the door.

Kate glanced behind them. Smoke drifted in at the end of the corridor. She couldn't even see the end of it anymore. Fire was consuming the ship, bearing down on them, suffocating them.

They were trapped.

Above her, Kate heard debris falling onto the floor. She felt the heat from the ceiling. They would be crushed, or burned to death, or suffocate. There was no escape—they were too deep inside the ship.

Shaw grabbed her arm, opened a door, and led her deeper into the ship.

"We can't go—"

"Shut up," he said as he jerked a cabin door open and practically threw Kate inside. Chang helped Martin in behind them and the other scientist followed.

"We can't stay here—" Kate began, but Shaw was out the door, which he slammed behind him.

Kate jerked the door handle, but it was jammed. Shaw had locked them in.

The courtyard inside the base's citadel was almost quiet. Here and there, gun battles still raged where Immari soldiers and Berber fighters clashed. David walked behind the chief and three of her men, one of whom was pulling Major Rukin by the arm—inflicting pain with every step.

To David's right, the massive plague barge burned on the water. Occasionally an explosion went up.

Casualties of war, David told himself. Kamau had said that they were all enemy combatants—Immari soldiers or new recruits who had pledged: loyalists. There had been no alternative.

Kate heard a series of three explosions. The room was pitch black, and inside, the only sounds were the occasional grunt or cough from Martin, Chang, and the European scientist.

Kate heard clanging at the door, and it opened just as she reached it. Shaw grabbed her arm and pulled her behind him.

She looked back, hoping Martin was behind her, but she couldn't see anything. The smoke was too thick. It burned her eyes and filled her lungs.

She coughed and hacked as Shaw dragged her. He was going to rip her arm off.

The darkness and smoke ebbed at the intersection of the next corridor. Kate heard and felt the massive fire burning before she saw it.

The fire burned up one side of the hallway, licking the ceiling and reaching for the other side. Past the flames she could see the open air. The ship had been blown to pieces. Shaw had used grenades to clear a path. It was as though some giant creature had taken a bite out of the side of the ship, leaving a jagged hole.

Shaw pulled her toward the flames.

David leaned against the doorframe of the operations center at the top of the control tower.

One of the Berbers ripped the tape off Rukin's mouth and shoved him toward the microphone.

Rukin eyed the chief, then David, and finally began speaking into the microphone. "Attention all Immari forces. This is Major Alexander Rukin. I am ordering you to surrender immediately. Lay down your weapons. Ceuta has fallen..."

David tuned Rukin's words out as he surveyed the carnage the screens depicted: around the base, beyond the wall, and on the water.

What have I done? he wondered. *What you had to,* he told himself. Across the room, Kamau's eyes met his. He gave him one slight nod.

Kate closed her eyes as Shaw pulled her past the fire, then she was at the edge of the hall, and the walls on each side of her were gone, and they were falling—

She landed hard on her feet, her knees buckled and she rolled across the deck. Shaw was already getting to his feet. The guy was like a super-soldier. Above her, Kate saw Martin, Chang, and the other man fly out of the flaming opening, falling toward the deck below. They crashed down around her a second after she rolled out of the way. The three men were alive, but Kate suspected there were broken bones. She threw her backpack off and began crawling over to them, but an explosion overhead sprayed pieces of the ship into the air. The debris fell in piles, raining down on them. Kate curled into a ball, trying to protect herself.

Shaw pulled her up. "We have to jump!" He pointed at the water below.

Kate's eyes went wide. It was twenty feet or more. A massive fire burned over the water, ringing the ship. "No. Freaking. Way."

He grabbed her backpack and threw it over, then grabbed her arm and dragged her toward the edge. Kate closed her eyes and inhaled.

David took the Styrofoam cup of coffee from the soldier and thanked him.

He sipped it as he watched the screens around the room. The disarmed Immari soldiers were filing into the citadel. They would be the new inhabitants of the pens.

Two technicians were zooming in on the burning plague barge, assessing the damage and rate of disintegration, trying to decide whether they needed to hit it again.

On the screen, explosions blew out one side of the ship. An Immari soldier dragged a woman through the flames and threw her onto the deck below. She curled into a ball, then the soldier stood her up again.

David froze. Her hair was dark... but he knew her face. It was impossible. Yet, there Kate was. Or had David finally cracked? The pressure of the battle, of his choice, finally shattering reality. Was he seeing what he wanted to see?

He watched Kate fight with the Immari soldier, then he threw her into the water below, likely to her death.

David raced to the tech's station. "Rewind that feed."

The frames zoomed back.

"Stop."

David leaned closer. He was sure of it now. It was Kate. And a soon-to-be-dead Immari soldier who had tossed her about like a rag doll and thrown her from the ship.

He spun around and said to the chief, "You're in command until I return. Do not fire on that plague barge. No matter what."

He was out of the control station and down the first flight of stairs in seconds.

Kamau called down to him. "David! You want some help?"

55

Former Immari Operations Base at Ceuta
Northern Morocco

AT THE HARBOR, David surveyed the boats. There were a slew of fishing boats but only a few motor yachts. David tried to think. What was the priority? Range or speed? He needed both, but how much of each? There was a Sunseeker 80 yacht. He tried to remember the specs. He had looked at buying one two years ago. It was twenty-four and a half meters long, cruised at twenty-four knots and could do thirty, he thought. The range was maybe three hundred fifty nautical miles. But there was a monstrosity on the end, a forty-meter Sunseeker. With luck, it would have a submersible on the back dock. He nodded to it. "We'll take the larger motor yacht," he said to Kamau.

A few minutes later, the forty-meter yacht was cruising out into the Mediterranean, toward the cruise ship burning in the night.

Kate's arms and legs were tiring. She could barely keep her head above the water. The ship continued to spew smoke into the air and spit splintered pieces of wreckage into the water, almost taking her under every few seconds.

But they had nowhere to go: a wide wall of fire burned over the water, a ring that trapped them in a small area of water close to the ship.

Her body ached all over, and her lungs hurt just to breathe.

Shaw was swimming for something—a piece of wreckage. He towed it back to her and the three men. "Grab on. We'll have to wait the fire out, then try to swim to shore."

David surveyed the listless cruise ship. It burned like a wildfire on the water. The ship was collapsing in on itself, and periodically, explosions erupted from random places. The gas tanks that fueled the turbine engines had ruptured at some point, and the gas burned over the water in a stunning half-ring of fire around the ship. People jumped from all decks, some no doubt to their deaths. They disappeared into the water beyond the wall of fire. David didn't see how they could get out. They certainly couldn't swim through the fire, and the field of flames was too wide to dive under.

His only hope was that Kate had survived the fall and was waiting there for him.

David went belowdecks and checked the submersible. He opened it and checked the controls. Out of oxygen. What did that leave? Waiting for the flames to die? What if she was injured?

"David, what do you need?"

"Oxygen."

Kate caught a glimpse of something beneath the water a split second before it grabbed Shaw and pulled him under.

At first, Kate thought it was a shark or some other sea creature, but Shaw surfaced, flailing his arms desperately. He reached back, felt the end of the floating wreckage, and clawed his way up onto it. The thing rose out of the water, pummeling Shaw's body, slamming him into the wreckage. It was a man, Kate saw that now, and he was unbelievably powerful. His muscles were huge. He wore scuba gear and several tanks on his back. Shaw fought bravely, swinging with his last bit of strength, but the monster was too powerful. One of his blows connected with Shaw's face, forcing his head into the hard surface below. Shaw fell limp against the wreckage, and the man grabbed him and began receding into the water.

Kate made for them, throwing herself into the fray. She pushed against the scuba diver's face mask. She gripped Shaw with her other hand, trying to free him.

The monster ripped his face mask off. "What the hell are you doing?"

David.

Kate froze. A flood of emotions overwhelmed her. She felt her limbs go numb, and she gulped a mouthful of seawater.

David released Shaw and reached for her. He looked into her eyes for a moment, then opened his mouth to say something. Shaw's fist connected square with David's face, sending him below the water. Shaw dived after him, but Kate regained her composure and fought her way between them.

"Boys, boys!" She pushed at each of them, putting herself between them.

"You're protecting him?" David spat.

"He saved my life," Kate said.

"He threw you off the ship."

"It's uh, it's... *complicated.*"

David stared at her. "Whatever. We're getting out of here." He unslung one of the tanks from his back and pushed it toward Kate. "Take this."

Kate motioned to Martin, Chang, and the other scientist. "What about them?"

"What about 'em?"

"They're coming with us," Kate insisted.

David shook his head. He started putting the tank straps around Kate's shoulders.

She pulled away from him and swam to the men. "I'm not leaving Martin and the others behind."

"All right, the three of you," he glanced back at Shaw coldly, "four of you can share a tank."

"Kate, I need to speak with you. It's urgent," Martin said. He could barely keep his head above water.

The European scientist spoke up. "I will not need to share the oxygen. I can cross alone."

All heads turned to him.

"I am an extremely strong swimmer," he said, explaining.

David tossed the other tank to Shaw. "Right, well you all have a committee meeting to sort it out. We're going." He took Kate by the arm.

"Wait," she said. "Martin has been injured. He's sick. You take him, David."

"No." He swam to her. "I'm not letting you out of my sight. Not again."

She heard Shaw groan in the background, but time seemed to stand still. She felt herself nod.

"For God's sake," Shaw said. "I'll take Martin. You all take the scientist; he won't take much oxygen anyway." He motioned to the European scientist. "And you... can swim strongly I suppose."

The European ducked under the water. Martin protested, but Shaw had him, and they were under. David put the face mask on Kate, and they dove, but she fought to get to the surface.

"What?" David asked.

"Chang."

David looked over.

Dr. Chang was treading water. "I thought you were going to leave me."

He saved Martin's life, Kate thought. "We're not going to leave you." She motioned to David. "Take his hand."

"You overestimate my comfort zone."

"Oh please!" She grabbed Chang's hand, tightened her grip on David's, and the three of them dove.

Kate took the first turn with the oxygen, then Chang. David seemed to need less than the two of them.

Kate couldn't see Shaw and Martin or the other man. The space below the fire seemed to stretch on forever. Through the mask, she looked up. The fire above the water was beautiful, like nothing she had ever seen. A flower of orange and red, blooming at the top of the water, expanding, receding, like a time-lapse photo.

Chang paddled beside her. His eyes were closed. There must have been gas in the water.

David led them on. He wore fins on his feet, and his powerful legs propelled them through the water.

Finally, the field of fire ended, and Kate saw the black night above the water. David guided them upward, and he and Chang gasped for air as they broke the surface.

Kate held an arm up to block the bright lights that blinded her. Another ship floated just past the fire. A white yacht with black windows. It was three stories tall. She knew there was probably some nautical term for "three stories," but that's what it looked like to her: a three-story white condo building with telescoping decks at the front and back.

David pulled her and Chang toward it. A towering black man stood at the back of the boat. He reached into the water, grabbed both of Kate's arms, and pulled her effortlessly into the boat.

Kate peeled the backpack off as the African lifted Chang up by one arm and deposited him beside her.

David began climbing up the ladder. "Are we the first?"

The African nodded.

David stopped, grabbed the face mask from Kate, and was halfway back down the ladder when a head popped out of the water.

The European scientist.

"Did you see the other two?" David called to him.

"No." He wiped the water from his face. "My eyes were closed. There is gas in the water."

Kate thought he was barely winded. She desperately wanted to talk to David, but he was gone, back into the black water.

Seconds passed that felt like hours.

"I'm Kamau."

Kate turned to him. "Kate Warner."

His eyebrows rose quickly.

"Yeah, I get that a lot." She turned back to the water.

Another head surfaced. Shaw. Martin wasn't with him. Kate walked to the rail. "Where's Martin?"

"He's not here?" Shaw spun himself in the water. "He freaked out, thought he was drowning. I thought he swam ahead of me. I couldn't see a bloody thing." He dove back below the surface.

Kate stared at the wall of flames. If Martin had come up in the middle...

She waited. She felt a blanket being wrapped around her shoulders. She murmured her thanks without turning to see who had placed it.

Two heads broke the water, and one man pulled the other to the boat: David—leading Martin.

Martin's head was badly burned, and he was almost unconscious.

David carried Martin aboard and laid him on a white leather couch in the saloon. Chang raced over to Martin and began assessing his wounds. Kamau set a first-aid kit down, and Kate began rifling through it.

The water parted again. "Do you have him?" Shaw called.

"Yes!" Kate shouted.

The second Shaw reached the ladder, David shouted to Kamau, "Get us out of here."

Kate and Chang continued to work on Martin until his head was properly bandaged, and his breathing stabilized.

"He's going to be fine," Chang said. "I can take it from here, Kate."

David took Kate by the arm, leading her belowdecks. His hand was tight around her bicep. She was soaked and utterly exhausted, but seeing him, knowing he was alive, somehow exhilarated her, gave her an indescribable rush.

He closed the door and latched it.

"We need to *talk*," David said, still facing the door.

56

Northern Morocco

Dorian awoke to a searing pain in his side.

He rolled over and screamed in agony. The motion only intensified the pain. Whatever had hit him was still in him, digging, moving around his insides like a hot knife.

He ripped his helmet off, then bent over to see what had him.

The tree limb had speared him all the way through just above his pelvis, where his upper body armor ended. He gently unstrapped his body armor. The motion sent a second wave of pain through him, and he had to pause. He tossed the armor aside and pulled his undershirt back.

The limb was just a few inches from his side. Had it been farther in, it might have gotten his liver.

He gritted his teeth and methodically drew the wooden shard out.

He inspected the wound. He was bleeding, but he would be all right. Right now he had bigger problems to deal with.

Even in the night sky, he could see three columns of smoke rising above the trees, the remains of the helicopter fleet burning.

Ceuta had no air support—it had all been deployed to southern Spain, but whoever had taken the base obviously had plenty of ground troops. Would they send them?

He got to his feet.

Screams—from the crash site. His instincts took over. He grabbed his helmet and body armor and ran toward the burning wreckage.

The helicopter had set fire to the forest, and it burned violently, a wall of flame Dorian couldn't see through. The screams grew louder, but Dorian couldn't make out the words.

He donned the body armor, then the helmet, and ran around the perimeter of the fire, looking for a way through. On the other side, the fire wasn't as thick, but he still had no clear line of sight to the helicopter. He thought he could make it through.

He drew his sidearm and tossed it on the ground, along with the spare magazines. He also placed his satellite phone on the ground. He tucked his hands in the armor and stepped to the edge of the blaze. The boots, suit, and helmet were fire-resistant, but there were limits to how much heat they could take, and then there were the parts of his body that the armor didn't cover.

He drew a deep breath and raced into the fire. His feet pounded the ground. The burn was overwhelming. He held his breath, and... broke through the fire, into a small clearing. Dorian saw it now: three of the helicopters had gone down close to each other and their fires had joined, creating the ring. Each of the helicopters was in full blaze. Dorian wouldn't get anything from them, and the screams hadn't come from anyone inside.

Another wave of screams erupted. Dorian spun and found their source. The pilot's black Immari armor made him almost impossible to see against the dark earth and pitch-black night, even through the light of the fires.

Dorian ran to him. The man's leg lay at an unnatural angle, and there was a deep cut up the side. The man had already tied it off at his thigh, and that had saved his life, but Dorian wasn't sure that was good news. The man had been able to crawl from the burning helicopter, but he couldn't run or so much as stand.

"Help!" he screamed.

"Shut up," Dorian said mechanically from behind his dark helmet. What to do? The man had lost too much blood already, and there were no medical supplies. Dorian automatically reached for his sidearm, then remembered he had left it beyond the fire. *Put him out of his misery and move on. The enemy will be here soon, searching the area. He'll get you killed.* But Dorian couldn't do it, couldn't bring himself to leave the man, to leave one of his own soldiers to the fire. He bent and took the man's arm.

"Thank you, sir," the pilot said, panting.

Dorian paused for a moment, then stood from the man, walked over to his helmet and returned with it. "Keep this on. We're going through the fire."

Dorian braced himself for the pain as he hoisted the man onto his shoulder. The wound in his side raged, cutting him, jabbing him. It felt like he was ripping apart.

He ran to the edge of the flames, drew a breath, then moved into them. He charged on more slowly this time but with every ounce of energy he had.

When he cleared the fire, he threw the man to the ground and collapsed himself. The blaze was moving the other way, with the wind. They were safe for now.

Dorian was breathless, and he wanted to puke from the pain. The agony was total. He couldn't even identify where it hurt. Out of the corner of his eye, he saw the gun, magazines, and phone lying there. He could end this man's misery if he could reach it... Dorian tried to push up, but the pain and exhaustion met him, holding him against the ground, forcing him to lie still.

The pilot crawled over to Dorian and began doing something. Dorian tried to shove him off, but the pilot fought him back. Another jolt of pain surged up his legs. The man was torturing him. Dorian tried to kick his legs, but the man threw his body across them. The pain swelled, moving up Dorian like a wave. It would drown him, was drowning him. The woods faded.

When Dorian awoke, it was still dark, but there was no fire at the helicopter crash site, only smoke. And pain. But he could move again. Beside him, the pilot lay asleep.

Dorian sat up, grimacing with every move. His feet. They were a burned, mottled mess. The unlaced, melted boots lay close by. The bottoms were smooth where the rubber had turned to liquid, flowing onto and over his feet. The pilot had removed them, likely saving Dorian's feet. How long would it have taken the melting rubber to cool? If the boots had stayed on, Dorian may have never walked again.

An untouched pair of boots lay just beyond Dorian's charred set.

Dorian glanced over at the snoring pilot again. He was barefooted. Dorian held the boots up to his feet. A little small, but they would do, depending on how far he had to go. And he needed to find that out.

He crawled over to his sidearm and sat phone. He glanced again at the pilot and considered his next move. The area around the gash in the pilot's leg already showed signs of infection.

Dorian punched the phone.

"Fleet Ops."

"It's Sloane—"

"Sir, we've—"

"Shut up. Put Captain Williams on."

"General—"

"Captain, why the hell am I stranded in the woods inside enemy lines?"

"Sir, we've sent two rescue missions. They've shot them both down. You're deep in their firing range."

"I do not want to hear how many times you've *failed*, Captain. Send a topographic map to my phone with an overlay of their firing radius."

"Yes, sir. We think Ceuta may be sending ground troops to your location—"

Dorian held the phone out and studied the map, ignoring the captain. From his location, Dorian thought he could reach the nearest rendezvous point outside Ceuta's firing range in about three hours. He glanced at his burned feet. Four hours was more realistic. It wouldn't be an easy trek, but he could make it.

The pilot let out a snore that caught Dorian's attention. He looked over, annoyed. What to do? The gun and magazines loomed just beside him, silently presenting the solution.

His eyes drifted away as his mind explored alternatives. Every other option he considered was met with a single thought, cold and final: *Don't be a fool. You know what must be done.* For the first time in Dorian's life, he had a face to put with that voice: Ares. He knew it now. For the first time, he could feel his own thoughts, his true thoughts, the person he was before the first outbreak, when his father placed him in the tube. This moment was a microcosm of every difficult decision he had ever made: a struggle between what his emotional, his *human* self wanted to do, and that cruel, cold voice. Ares. Ares was the drive that had lingered in the background, unseen, prodding Dorian, shaping his thoughts. Dorian had never been fully aware of the struggle within him until this moment. Ares cried out again: *Don't be weak. You are special. You must survive. Your species is depending on you. He is another soldier lost to our cause. Don't let his sacrifice cloud your judgment.*

Dorian raised the phone to his face. "Captain, I just sent you some coordinates."

He looked at the pilot, then at his burned feet—feet he could still walk on.

"Sir?"

Dorian's mind rocked back and forth like a tiny ship on rough seas. The voice was firm now. *This world wasn't built for the weak. Dorian, you are playing the greatest chess game in history. Don't risk a king to save a pawn.*

"I'm here," Dorian said. "I will be at the extraction point in..."

Don't—

"...eight hours. Be advised, I have another survivor. If we're not at those coordinates, the rescue team's orders are to move into the woods and search for us on a heading bearing four-seven degrees."

And like that, the voice was gone, silenced. Dorian's thoughts were his own. He was free. He was... different, or was he the person he was always meant to be? The voice in his ear interrupted his reflection.

"Copy, General. Godspeed."

"Captain."

"Sir?"

"The girl in my quarters," Dorian said.

"Yes, sir. She's here—"

"Tell her... that I'm all right."

"Yes, sir, I'll see to it—"

Dorian ended the call.

Dorian fell back to the ground. He was hungry. He needed to eat, needed his strength, especially with the extra weight he had to carry. He would have to hunt.

In the distance, he heard a low rolling rumble. Thunder? No. It was the beat of horses charging through the forest.

57

Somewhere off the coast of Ceuta
Mediterranean Sea

For the better part of the last hour, Kate and David hadn't done any talking, and that made her very happy. They lay there, both naked, in the sheets of the king bed centered in the wood-paneled master stateroom.

It felt almost surreal to her, like they were lying in a luxury hotel room, as if the world outside had only been a bad dream. She felt safe and free, for the first time since... since she could remember.

Kate's face rested on his chest. She loved listening to his heart, watching his body rise and fall with every breath. She traced her finger around the red burn marks on his chest. It looked like he had been branded. "This one is new," she said softly.

"Cost of a wooden horse in this screwed-up world." His voice was serious.

Was it a joke? She pushed up and looked him in the eyes, hoping for an answer, but he didn't look at her.

He was different somehow. Harder. More distant. She sensed it when they made love. He was not as gentle as he had been in Gibraltar.

She returned her head to his chest, half-hiding. "I had a dream about a wooden horse. You were drawing—"

David pushed her off of him. "I was at a drafting table—"

The shock gripped her. She nodded, hesitating. "Yes... a veranda looked out on a blue bay and a forested peninsula—"

"Impossible..." David whispered. "How?"

Martin's words echoed in her mind, *We believe the Atlantis Gene is connected to a quantum biological process. Subatomic particles transmitted faster than the speed of light...*

Kate had given David a blood transfusion, but that couldn't have changed his genome, couldn't have given him the Atlantis Gene, yet there was some connection between them. "I think it has something to do with the Atlantis Gene—it activates some sort of quantum biological link—"

"Okay, stop right there. No more scientific mumbo jumbo. You and I have to talk."

Kate drew back. "So talk. You don't need a formal invitation."

"You left me."

"What?"

"Gibraltar. I trusted you—"

"Can I just remind you that you had been shot—*three times*? Keegan was going to kill you."

"He didn't."

"I made a deal with him—"

"No, you didn't. He needed me. He wanted me to kill Sloane. He was playing us both. You should have come to me—"

"Are you serious? David, you could barely walk. Keegan told

me the house was crawling with his men—Immari agents. And they *were* his men, weren't they?"

"They were—"

"And what would you have done? You were surrounded—"

"I wouldn't have lied to you. I wouldn't have slept with you and left in the night."

Rage coursed through Kate. She fought to regain her composure. "I never lied to you—"

"You didn't trust me. You didn't talk to me—"

"I saved your life." Kate stood and shook her head. "I did what I did. It's done."

"Would you do it again?"

Kate resisted the urge to answer.

"Answer me!"

She stared at him, and he glared back at her. He was so different. Yet, it was still the man she had...

"Yes, David. I'd do it again. You're here. I'm here. We're both alive." There was something else she wanted to say, but she couldn't do it, not while he was looking at her like that, with those cold dead eyes.

"I won't have anyone under my command who doesn't trust me."

Kate exploded. "Under your *command*?"

"That's right."

"Well, that's convenient, because I'm not looking to join the army or whatever the hell you're running around here."

There was a knock on the door, and to Kate, it felt like water to a dying man. She opened her mouth, but David cut her off.

"It's a bad time—"

"It's Kamau. It's urgent, David."

David and Kate each replaced the sheets that they had held with clothes. They dressed with their backs to each other. David glanced at her coldly, courteously, and when she nodded, he opened the door.

"David—" Kamau began.

"What—"

"The old man."

"What about him?"

"He's dead."

David glanced back at Kate, his face changed, the hardness instantly gone. She saw sympathy, and the man she had fallen in love with. The exhilaration fought against the hurt she felt at hearing Kamau's news. Then there was the shock: Martin's face was burned, but he wasn't that badly injured. Had Chang's plague treatment failed suddenly? What would Kate do without him? She had never thanked him. What were her last words to him?

"Thank you for... telling us," David said.

"You need to come now, David. Arm yourself."

"What?"

Kamau glanced around, making sure they were alone. "I believe someone murdered him."

Martin lay peacefully on the white leather couch in the enclosed living space of the upper deck.

Everyone was there: Kate, David, Kamau, Shaw, and the two scientists: Chang and the European scientist, who had finally introduced himself as Dr. Arthur Janus. Kate stared at Martin for a moment before crossing the room to kneel at his side. She tried to keep her emotions in check. He was the closest thing she'd had to a father. He hadn't been up to the job, but he had certainly tried. And for some reason, that made it even harder for Kate. She tried to clear her head. She had to focus.

Kamau's words echoed in her mind: *I believe he was murdered.*

She didn't see any signs of a struggle. Kate checked his fingernails. No skin, no blood. There were a few bruises, but nothing Kate thought was more recent than the injuries from their escape from the plague barge. Martin looked the same as when Kamau had pulled him from the water. She looked up at the African, her eyes asking, are you sure?

He tilted his head slightly.

Kate felt Martin's neck. Yes... She moved his head a little, testing its range of motion. Someone had broken his neck... Kate felt her airway constrict. Whoever had done it was in this room, staring at her right now.

"Kate, I'm very sorry about Martin," Shaw began. "I truly am, but we have to get off this boat and be on our way. You're not safe here."

Had Shaw seen it too? Did he know?

"She's not going anywhere," David said.

"She is," Shaw insisted. "Now tell me where you're taking us, and I'll make arrangements for someone to retrieve us."

David ignored him. He took a step toward Kate.

Shaw grabbed his arm. "Hey, I'm talking to you."

David spun and pushed him, almost forcing Shaw to the floor. "Touch me again, and I'll throw you off the back of the boat."

"Why wait? You can give it a go right now."

Kamau stepped behind David, letting Shaw know it would be two to one.

Kate rushed between the three men. "Okay, that's enough of the testosterone show."

She grabbed David's arm and dragged him away.

58

Northern Morocco

"Thank you, sir, for saving me," the pilot said.

Dorian tore off a piece of the overcooked meat with his knife and scarfed it down. "Don't mention it. I'm serious. To anyone."

The pilot hesitated. "Yes, sir."

They ate in silence for a bit, until the best of the meat was gone.

"This reminds me of camping with my dad when I was a kid."

Dorian wished the sappy jerk would shut up or pass out. He looked at the man's wound again, at the signs of infection. He would definitely lose the leg... if he made it to morning. Something about that thought made Dorian respond. "My father wasn't into... camping, per se."

The helicopter pilot began to speak, but Dorian continued.

"He was in the military. He took a great deal of pride in that. And his interests in Immari International, of course, though when I was young it was more like a club he was in, a social commitment. It didn't become a preoccupation until later. About the only thing we ever did together was attend military parades. At the first one, I knew what I wanted to be. Seeing the Kaiser's men all lined up in rows, marching in rhythm, the beat of the music in my chest."

"Amazing, sir. You knew even then that you wanted to be a soldier?"

Dorian had told his father that night. *I want to march at the front, Papa. Please buy me a trumpet. I will be the best trumpet player in all the Kaiser's army.* Dorian's rebirth in the tubes had removed the scars from his legs and lower back, but he could still remember the beating his father had given him. *This is what the world does to trumpet players, Dieter.*

"Yes. I knew it even then. A soldier..."

But when had he known it, become what he was? That day in 1986 when he had emerged from the tube. He was different. He was Ares. It was true. It was so clear now. But— "Wait. Sir, did you say the *Kaiser's* army?"

"I did. It's... a long story. Now button up and get some rest. That's an order."

Dorian had stayed up half the night and only slept a few hours, but he felt incredibly refreshed when he awoke. The first rays of sunlight were emerging in the east, and here and there, the forest was coming to life.

Dorian had also awoken with an idea. Why hadn't he thought of it before? He needed to act fast for it to have any chance at success.

He crept over to the pilot. His breathing was shallow. The

wound continued to seep blood onto the forest floor, spreading a black and crimson pool around him. He twitched periodically.

Dorian paced away from him and sat on a rock for a long while, listening, trying to get a direction. When he was sure, he checked his gun and set off.

From the bushes, Dorian could see two of the Berber tribesmen. One slept on the ground; the other, likely an officer, in a tent. He was pretty sure there were only two; only two horses were tied to a tree nearby.

At the smoldering fire, lay a large machete. Dorian would use it. Gunfire would draw attention, and there was no need for it. Two sleeping Berber tribesmen would be no problem.

Dorian kicked the horse again. It glided through the forest. At the camp, he would make the call first, moving up the extraction time. How fast could he and the pilot get there on the horses? A better question: how long did the man have? Dorian wished he knew. That would be the deadline. The horses would save the pilot's life. He kicked the horse again, and it responded. He pulled the other behind him by the reins, and it matched their pace. Amazing animals.

At the camp, Dorian slowed and dismounted before the horses stopped.

"Hey! Get up."

Dorian made for the satellite phone.

There was no answer from the pilot.

Dorian stopped. *No.* He turned. He knew what he saw, yet he ran to his comrade. He held two fingers to his neck. Dorian felt the cold skin long before he knew there was no pulse, but he held his fingers there for a second, staring at the closed eyes.

Rage pulsed through him. He almost kicked the man's body. He wanted to fall to his knees and punch him in the face—for dying, for stringing him along, for... everything. He stood, and the horses erupted, backing away from him. One neighed and jumped. Stupid, smelly beasts. He turned to strike one of them, but they were out of reach. It didn't matter. He would ride one to death, then mount the other and follow suit.

He raced to the sat phone.

"Fleet Ops."

"Give me Captain Williams."

"Identify yourself."

"Who the hell do you think this is?! How many wrong number calls do you get these days? Put Williams on, or I will split you down the middle when I get out of this hellhole!"

"St-stand by, s-sir."

Two seconds passed.

"Williams—"

"Change of schedule. I will be at the LZ in less than an hour."

"We can be there—"

"In less than an hour! One hour or less. They can develop photos that fast, you sure as hell better get your ass down here. If I have to make my own way back to the fleet, your lifespan plummets, Captain."

Dorian heard the captain screaming to scramble helicopters.

"We'll... be there, sir."

"The girl—"

"We're taking good care of her—"

"Get rid of her."

"You want—"

"I don't care where she goes, she just better be gone when I get back."

Dorian disconnected the line.

He mounted the closest horse and kicked it as hard as he could.

59

Somewhere off the coast of Ceuta
Mediterranean Sea

"SHAW KILLED HIM," David said flatly.

Kate cringed and glanced at the closed door of their stateroom. "Keep your voice down."

"Why? He knows he did it. He knows I know it."

Kate looked him in the eyes. He was so angry. She could see it in his body, hear it in his voice, but she could also feel it—on a more basic level, as if some part of her was in him and vice versa. The anger seemed to rise off of him and seep into her, like heat off an asphalt highway. She felt it infecting her, felt herself digging in against him, subconsciously readying for another fight. Everything was spinning out of control. She had to stop it, had to start somewhere. Kate made a decision: she would start with David. She needed him, wanted him, couldn't do this without him... *wouldn't* do this without him.

David was pacing the room, thinking—dark thoughts, Kate felt it. She held her hand out and waited for him to walk into it.

Without a word, she guided him to the bed and sat him down. She knelt in front of him.

"I want you to talk to me. Will you?" She took his face in her hands.

David still looked down, avoiding her. "I'll zip-tie them all, Kamau too, just for good measure. We'll set them out somewhere. It doesn't matter where. Be more food for the two of us. Then I need to get in touch with the British and Americans." He shook his head. "Sloane's fleet is off the coast of Morocco. Why haven't they hit it yet? Why wait? We could end the war quickly. Are they out of fuel? Jet maybe but they have nuclear subs—tons of them. We take 'em out, then we start rounding up the Immari camps, do war trials on site. Do it quick."

"David—"

He was still looking away from her. "It sounds harsh, I know, but it's the only way. Maybe this is what it's all about: the plague. It's the ultimate test. The Rapture, the day of reckoning where people are exposed for what they truly are. You should have seen what they were doing, Kate. Yes, it's a test, an opportunity—to purge the world of anyone with no morals, no values, no compassion for their fellow man."

"People are desperate, they're not themselves—"

"No, I think the plague reveals what they *really are*, whether they help the less fortunate or whether they turn and desert their own kind, leave them to die. And now we know who they are. We round up every Immari and Immari sympathizer and wipe them out. The world after will be a better place. A peaceful place, a world where people care about each other. No war, no hunger, no—"

"David. David. This isn't you."

He looked at her for the first time. "Well, maybe this is the *new* me. That's sort of an inside joke."

Kate gritted her teeth. She wanted to smack him. "You

sound like someone else I know. He wants to reduce the world's population, eliminate people that don't fit his view of the ideal human."

"Well... maybe Sloane had the right idea, just the wrong execution. Pun intended."

Kate was ready to explode. She closed her eyes. She had to turn the argument, redirect, draw him out so she could figure out what had happened to him, why he had changed. Focus on the facts. She heard David mumbling in the background.

"I mean if there was a problem with the subs, they could just launch some cruise missiles if they—"

"I know why they aren't attacking the Immari fleet."

"Wait, what?"

"I'll tell you, but you have to tell me what happened to you."

"Me? Nothing. Just another day at the office."

"I'm serious."

"Well, let's see... where to start... Sloane killed me—twice, actually." He held his shirt up. "See, no more scars."

The skin was smooth, like a newborn. Kate hadn't noticed it before, when they were... With every bit of willpower she had, she fought the urge to draw away from him. What *was* he? "I... don't understand."

"Join the club. Heard enough?"

"Tell me *everything*."

"Okay, after the second death of David Vale, I of course woke up in a mysterious Atlantean structure, which, you know, makes total sense. There was only one way out, like a rat in a maze. Said maze dumped me out in the hills above Ceuta." He stared, as if remembering it. "It was horrifying. It was a burned-out wasteland. The sum of all my fears, everything I had fought to stop: the Immari, Toba Protocol, right there in front of me, in all its horror. My total failure. Seeing it was surreal. The Immari patrols captured me, took me inside the base. Then I saw what it was, what they were doing there."

Kate nodded. "And you decided to fight them."

"No. Not at first, and I'm ashamed of that. Very ashamed of that. My first impulse was to escape the camp and find you." He looked at her, and in that fraction of a second, she saw the man she had fallen in love with. He was strong and vulnerable, and... David.

He glanced away from her. "But I had no idea where you were, no clue where to start. That's when I decided to fight, to take the base."

"David, it's changed you somehow."

"Before today, I had killed hundreds of people—hell, I don't even know how many. Most were bad guys trying to kill me or my team at the time—well, except the ones I shot with a sniper rifle but same general principle. Ceuta was different. Different than following orders. *I* drew up the plan, sold some men on my plan, and when the hour came, I pushed the button that killed thousands of soldiers and plunged that place into war. It was my carnage, and I thought it was just, that they deserved it. And I want to finish the fight. I feel the impulse burning inside me like a fire. I want more. I want to wipe them all out, now, while we can."

Kate understood. Her leaving him in Gibraltar, his decision to fight in Ceuta. His wounds wouldn't heal overnight, and his rage wouldn't fade anytime soon. But there was an opening, a window she could slip through to get to him. David fidgeted on the bed. He was vulnerable now, and she sensed that her next words would determine what happened to "them" and perhaps the fate of many others. She spoke quietly. "I need your help, David."

He turned his head but said nothing.

"In the next forty-eight hours, ninety percent of the world's population is going to die."

"What?"

"The plague, it has mutated. There was an explosion in Germany—"

"Sloane. He carried a case out of the structure in Antarctica."

"Whatever was in that case emitted a radiation signature that swept the globe. The radiation changed the plague. There's no defense against it now. Orchid has failed. Every nation on earth is facing widespread infection and death. They're collapsing. But I think I can find a cure. Martin was working with an underground consortium, Continuity. It includes the people at the CDC. I think he was close to finding a cure. I have his notes, but I need your help."

"You think—"

"There's something else. Something I have to say. I'm in love with you, David, and I'm sorry I hurt you by leaving in Gibraltar. I'm sorry I didn't tell you about Keegan. I'm sorry I didn't trust you. It won't happen again. No matter what happens, from here on out, you and I will finish this together. And for the record, I don't care how many times you've died or what scars you do or don't have."

He kissed her on the mouth, and it was like the kiss in Gibraltar. She seemed to feel the rage draining out of him, as if the kiss were releasing some pressure valve that had been about to blow.

When they separated, he stared at her, the softness back in his eyes.

"And one more thing: I will follow your orders."

"Actually... I think maybe you should give the orders for a while. I'm just kind of... zooming out here, getting a little perspective, remembering some of the things I just said." David shook his head. "Not the sanest stuff that's ever come out of my mouth or entirely rational for that matter. And you seem to know what's going on. You do the thinking, I'll do the shooting."

"I can do that."

David stood and glanced around the stateroom. "Murder mystery cruise and a countdown to a global apocalypse. Hell of a second date."

"You're certainly not boring."

"Just trying to keep you interested. Now where do you want to start: with the plague or Martin's murderer?"

"I think—"

The boat suddenly lost speed. Kate felt as though it was coming to a stop in the water. "What's going on?"

"I don't know." David put his arm around her and guided her across the room. He pointed at the hallway that led to a short flight of stairs and at the bottom, an elaborate master bathroom. He handed her a gun. "Stay in there. Lock the door. I—"

She kissed him again. "Be careful. That's your first order."

60

Immari Advance Fleet Alpha
Near Tangier, Morocco

DORIAN STRODE onto the ship's bridge. The men turned quickly and stood rigidly. "Attention on deck!"

"You have a message for me," Dorian said to the captain.

The captain held out a slip of paper, and Dorian unfolded it.

I have Warner.

She has code.

Request exfil.

She is well guarded.

On yacht near Ceuta.

Destination unknown.

Be ready.

Dorian considered his options. If those damn British hadn't mined the straits, his fleet could reach them. The Berber control of Ceuta and northern Morocco also further limited his options.

"We've sent ships from Fuengirola after them," the captain said.

"Estimated intercept time?" Dorian asked.

"Unknown."

"What do you mean, *unknown*?"

"They're moving at almost thirty knots. We don't have a ship fast enough to catch them."

Dorian shook his head.

"But if they slow down or stop, we'll be on them. Or—if they enter port somewhere, we can corner them."

"Notify our source. And get me a map of Ceuta's firing radius. I need to know how to fly around their guns."

61

Somewhere off the coast of Ceuta
Mediterranean Sea

DAVID WAITED at the door to his and Kate's stateroom, listening, hoping for any sound, any clues as to what was happening on the ship. The engines had completely stopped, and the one-hundred-thirty-foot yacht was cruising almost silently now. David glanced out the floor-to-ceiling glass windows that led out to their balcony.

He backed away from the door. If whoever had killed Martin was taking the boat, they would be set up outside the master stateroom, waiting for him.

He exited onto the balcony. There were no other boats in sight. Even the lights from Ceuta had faded, leaving only the moon to light the boat.

David inched forward on the balcony and peered into the saloon—the living space beyond the bedroom. Empty.

Tiny recessed lights twinkled, illuminating the lavish living and dining accommodations.

The main deck was devoted entirely to the master stateroom and living and dining spaces. The lower deck below them housed the crew quarters and guest rooms.

Assuming he lived through the next few minutes, he would have to move Kate belowdecks, to a room with no balcony and fewer windows. It would be easier to defend her there. However, he could also fold the balcony off the master into the ship, closing off the side entrance to the master stateroom. Which would add better protection? He'd have to sort it out later.

At that moment, he heard a footstep on the deck above: the upper deck. It housed the ship's cockpit, a spacious guest stateroom, as well as indoor and outdoor lounging space.

David exited the stateroom quickly and rushed up the stairs, his gun leading the way.

The upper saloon was empty.

He heard voices in the cockpit. David stepped quietly toward it.

Dr. Janus stood there, the same impassive look on his face, no hint of concern at the sight of David and his gun. David panned around the room. Kamau and Shaw stood on the port side, arguing. They turned toward him and stared.

"David—" Kamau began.

David's mind raced. Chang. "Where's Chang?"

"We haven't seen him—"

David darted out of the cockpit, back through the upper saloon. He was about to round the stairs when the door to the saloon's bathroom opened. Chang glided out, seemingly talking to himself.

David wheeled around, still holding his sidearm straight out, and closed the distance between them.

Chang almost collapsed back into the bathroom. He held his hands up, shaking. "I... I'm sorry, I didn't know whether to flush... then I felt the boat stop... I..."

Kamau, Shaw, and Janus walked into the saloon. The African spoke first. "We're out of gas."

David let his gun fall to his side, but he still gripped it tightly. "That's impossible. We had over half a tank when we left the harbor in Ceuta."

"True," Kamau said. "But there's a hole in the fuel line. We've been leaking."

David stared at the four men. One of them had killed Martin, and now he had cut the fuel line. He wanted the boat stranded. For what? An extraction?

Shaw spoke up. "There could be other damage. There are bullet holes in the engine room."

Kamau nodded slightly, confirming that the damage was there.

Bullet holes, David thought. Could the boat have taken fire from soldiers on the plague barge or during the firefight at Ceuta? It was possible...

A plan formed in David's mind. He would need to fix the fuel leak before they could go on, but the size of the leak—whether it had been cut or simply severed by a bullet—might reveal the killer. "Where were each of you just now?"

"I was in the galley, preparing a meal," Janus said.

"I was in the cockpit," Kamau said. "I hadn't thought to check the fuel, but when I saw our status, I killed the engines."

"I was..." Chang began. "...using the restroom."

Shaw cleared his throat and straightened his back. "I was actually about to knock on your door and demand you release Dr. Warner to me. A demand I now press, especially in light of our circumstances—"

David had hoped one of the scientists had seen Kamau, had hoped he had an alibi. David desperately wanted to rule him out. His primary suspects were Shaw and Chang—in that order.

"I want your guns."

"I... don't have a gun—"

"I'm not talking to you, Dr. Chang." David stared at Kamau and Shaw. Neither made a move.

"David, there are pirates on the Mediterranean," Kamau said. "We need to be armed—"

"It's an order."

Kamau nodded, glanced at Shaw, then extended his pistol, butt outward.

"Well, you can't order me, and I won't relinquish my—"

"Hand me your gun, or I'll shoot you right here, Shaw. Try me." David took another step closer to him, lifting his pistol to chest height.

Shaw cursed and muttered but handed over his gun. He made to leave the saloon.

"You stay here, all of you." He nodded to Kamau. "Bring me my sniper rifle and our automatic rifles."

David knew that neither Kamau nor Shaw needed a gun to kill him or Kate, but ensuring they had to do it hand-to-hand gave David a bit more comfort. If it came down to fighting hand-to-hand with either man, he liked his chances.

Kate strained to hear what was going on up above. She heard footsteps occasionally, but no gunfire. That was a good sign. She considered leaving the bathroom long enough to retrieve the sat phone and call Continuity. She wanted to find out how much time she had, what the status was. She heard the outer door—the door to the stateroom—click open.

She started to call out for David, but she hesitated. Someone was running around the room, ransacking it.

A knock came from the bathroom door.

"Who—"

"It's David."

She opened it. Relief washed over her. "What's happened?"

"We're losing gas."

"Losing—"

"Either someone sabotaged the ship or one of the bullets nicked the fuel line. I'm thinking sabotage." He led her into the room. He had turned it upside down.

"What were you looking for?"

"A safe." He pointed to a wall safe with a combination. It was closed, but a smaller, portable safe—what might have held a large necklace—stood open. Several handguns and magazines from rifles lay inside. David closed it and handed Kate the key. "You and I have guns now. Only us. We need to decide what to do from here. Stay focused. One of them is not who he claims to be. Their next actions could reveal who."

62

Somewhere off the coast of Ceuta
Mediterranean Sea

David led Kate up the stairs to the upper deck where the four men were waiting. Kamau and Shaw stood and paced impatiently; Chang and Janus sat, staring out the boat's windows like nothing was amiss.

David focused on Kamau. "How much fuel do we have left?"

"Less than a quarter of total capacity."

"Range?"

"Depends on our speed—"

"Can we make it to the coast?"

Kamau wavered. That made David nervous. "Assuming we fix the leak, I think so, but there is no guarantee that we will find fuel there."

"We're sitting ducks out here," Shaw said. "This luxury liner is the juiciest bait on the Mediterranean. Pirates will be on us within hours, certainly by sunrise."

David wanted to rebut the argument, but... it was true. In the post-plague world, for those who had survived the initial outbreak and avoided the Immari or the Orchid Districts, the seas were safer than the shore. A lot of people were waiting the plague out on boats scattered across the Mediterranean. Survivors could fish and catch rainwater—a lot of it on a boat this big. The one-hundred-thirty-foot-long motor yacht was irresistible bait, and it would draw pirates.

When David didn't respond, Shaw continued. "Kate, I need to use your sat phone. I'll have my government airlift us out of here within hours. You know we're racing the clock here. We'll be in London soon. You can continue your research there and hopefully save some lives."

Chang and Janus both stood. "We'd like to join you—"

"Nobody's going anywhere," David said.

"We've been doing our own research," Chang said.

"What sort of research?" Kate asked.

"Research on a cure," Janus said. "We were close to a permanent cure, or at the very least, an Orchid alternative. We have worked in secret, withholding our findings from the Immari."

"The treatment you gave Martin," Kate said.

"Yes," Chang said. "That was our latest prototype. It's not one-hundred-percent effective, but it was worth a shot."

Kate whispered in David's ear. "Can I speak with you?"

Below deck, Kate turned to David and said flatly, "You know Shaw is right."

David stared out the window. Shaw's option was their best. David couldn't take Kate back to Ceuta. Everyone would know who she was. The brunette look wouldn't fool anyone. If word got out that she was in Ceuta, the entire world would storm the base.

He wondered what he would do in London. He was likely a wanted fugitive, but he could probably sort that out.

But if Shaw had killed Martin, if he had cut the fuel line to set this up, David would be delivering Kate to him.

"Let me think about it," David said, still not looking at Kate.

"David, what's there to think about? Come with us."

"Just... give me a few hours, Kate. Let us fix the boat."

David thought Kate was going to press him, but she eyed him for a moment, then nodded. "While you do that, I want to work with Chang and Janus. I want to show them Martin's notes. They're written in a code I haven't been able to break."

David had to smile. In Jakarta, Martin had sent him a coded message that had set the entire chain of events of the past few months in motion. The old man had been trying to warn David, but he and his team hadn't unraveled the message fast enough. "Martin did love his codes." David considered the implications. It certainly helped his cause: Kate could be making progress on a cure while he stewed on what to do.

"Just make sure they don't make any phone calls," he said.

Kate had spent the last hour discussing Martin's notes with Doctors Chang and Janus. Both men had listened intently, occasionally raising their hands and asking a question.

When Kate finished, they presented their own research, beginning with a bit of their personal backgrounds. Both men stood when they presented to the group.

Kate thought that Dr. Chang's story was very much like Martin's. Shen Chang was sixty-one and had joined Immari Research right out of medical school. He had been enamored with the research, with the possibilities, but had soon learned the truth about the Immari. He had spent his career trying to prevent the Immari's worst atrocities, but ultimately, like Martin, he was trapped and had failed.

"There's something I need to tell you, Dr. Warner. And I will completely understand if you no longer wish to work with me. I was the chief scientist at the Qino Immari facility. I was on site the day they put you in the Bell room."

A long silence passed and finally Kate said, "We're working on the same side now. Let's focus on the work at hand, on finding the cure."

"I'd like that very much. There is one other thing. You look... very familiar to me. I wonder if we've met."

Kate studied his face. "I... don't think so."

"Ah, well, my memory isn't what it used to be, Dr. Warner."

"Call me Kate. Both of you."

When Chang finished, Janus shared his story. Dr. Arthur Janus was an evolutionary biologist and virologist with an interest in viral evolution—the study of how viruses mutate and adapt.

"I was on assignment for the World Health Organization in Algiers when the plague hit," Janus said. "I barely got out. I made my way to Ceuta. The Immari sorted me there, and I was placed on the plague barge, assigned to be Dr. Chang's assistant."

Dr. Chang laughed. "But I'm the one who has done the assisting since then. Dr. Janus is the genius on our team. He's responsible for the breakthroughs."

Each man tried to deflect the credit.

After that, they described their research and their approach. Kate was blown away. The men had tackled the plague from another angle—looking for similarities to past outbreaks and trying to find someone with natural disease resistance who might have a genetic anomaly that provided immunity to the plague.

Janus made some tea and handed it out, and now they sat, sipping their tea and talking in turn. After each person spoke, they paused to consider the others' assertions.

Disagreements were never direct. It was so nice, Kate thought. The relaxed environment and collegiality made it so much easier to focus on the work, the theories.

All their civility aside, the group was making no progress on Martin's notes.

Their work now focused on one particular page that contained some sort of code:

PIE = Immaru?

535...1257 = Second Toba? New Delivery System?

Adam => Flood/A$ Falls => Toba 2 => KBW

Alpha => Missed Delta? => Delta => Omega

70K YA => 12.5K YA => 535...1257 => 1918...1978

Missing Alpha Leads to Treasure of Atlantis?

Theories had been thrown around and collectively shot down. Kate had begun to fear they were out of ideas.

Periodically, she heard banging from the engine room below, which was inevitably followed by a bout of cursing, always Shaw and David at each other. It only ended when Kamau spoke up in his deep baritone voice, always the same refrain interrupting the chorus of cursing and clanging: "Gentlemen, please!"

Kate wondered if there would be anything left of the engine when they were done.

Overall, it sounded like a bar brawl belowdecks and a book club up above.

After yet another bout of intense banging and a final "Gentlemen, please!" from Kamau, David emerged from below, covered in grease.

"We're almost there," he said. "But that's all the good news. We don't have enough fuel to make it to the coast."

Kate nodded. She considered bringing up Shaw's plan to call his government, but she decided now wasn't the time. David still seemed wound up. What would they do if these pirates showed up? Race down to their room, pass out guns and hope they could repel them? And that whoever killed Martin didn't take a shot at her or David in the crossfire?

David headed toward the galley, probably to wash himself up.

Janus set his teacup down. "The part that puzzles me most is PIE = Immaru? It seems almost a comedic reference. Perhaps it is meant to throw off any nefarious readers? A sort of camouflage. We should consider omitting it—"

"What did you say?" David was out of the galley.

"I—"

David picked up the page with Martin's code with his greasy hand.

Kate tried to snatch it from him. "David, you're smudging it..."

"You know what this means?" David asked Kate.

"No. Do you?"

"Yeah."

"Which part?"

"All of it. I know what the whole thing means. These aren't scientific notations. They're historical references."

63

Somewhere off the coast of Ceuta
Mediterranean Sea

David glanced at Kate and the two scientists, then read Martin's code again.

PIE = Immaru?

535…1257 = Second Toba? New Delivery System?

Adam => Flood/A$ Falls => Toba 2 => KBW

Alpha => Missed Delta? => Delta => Omega

70K YA => 12.5K YA => 535…1257 => 1918…1978

Missing Alpha Leads to Treasure of Atlantis?

Was he right? Yes, he was certain of it. But he wouldn't start with the first part—it was too out there, too… fantastic, even for him to believe.

"Will you please wash your hands?" Kate pleaded.

David lowered the page. "It's not the Magna Carta—"

"It is to me. And it could be the key to finding a cure for the plague." In that moment, David thought she couldn't be any cuter. She sat on a white leather club chair in the lavish upper-deck saloon, the other two scientists sitting side by side on the adjacent couch. Three white porcelain cups, all half-full of a brown tea, sat on the coffee table before them. The whole scene seemed bizarre, like the aftermath of a brunch in a penthouse apartment in Dubai.

David handed her the page and walked back into the galley. He scrubbed his hands and thought again about the code. Yes, he was right. Below, he heard banging sporadically in the engine room. Shaw and Kamau were almost finished. Then what? David had to figure out their next move. His decision was crucial, and he felt the weight of it. If he guessed wrong, played into the hand of whoever had killed Martin and disabled the boat...

He walked back out. "You guys seriously don't know what this is? You're not messing with me?"

"No."

The looks from the three scientists were skeptical at best, and David had to smile. "You mean you've got every scientist in the world on this, and you need little ol' me, a lowly grad-school dropout with a half-finished PhD to unravel this thing?"

"I didn't know you... Really, a PhD—"

"In European History at Columbia—"

"Why'd you drop out?" Kate asked, some of her skepticism waning.

"For... health reasons. In September of 2001." Being buried under a building after a terrorist attack and a year of physical rehab wasn't the typical "health reason," but David wasn't sure how else to describe it. That day had changed his life, his career.

He had abandoned his academic life instantly, but he had never given up his love of history.

"Oh, right..." Kate said quietly.

"I told you before I liked history." He wondered if she would remember the reference, his words in Jakarta.

"Yes, you did," Kate said, still somber.

He took a second to collect his thoughts. His theory was that the code was a broad outline of human history, specifically of the major historical turning points. But... he would start with what he was most certain about. "First thing's first: PIE is not pie or any other pastry. It's a group of people."

Blank stares greeted him.

"PIE stands for Proto-Indo-Europeans. They're arguably one of the most important ancient groups in world history."

"Proto..." Kate began. "I've never heard of them."

"Nor have I," Dr. Chang said.

"I too am unfamiliar," Dr. Janus said.

"They aren't well known. The irony is that they are the precursor civilization for almost everyone living in Europe, the Middle East, and India today. In fact, half the world's population is *directly descended* from Proto-Indo-European groups."

Janus sat forward. "How do you know? The gene pool—"

David held up his hand. "We historians have another tool, just as important as the gene pool. It's passed down from generation to generation. We can mark changes in it across time, and we can trace its dispersal across the world—it changes in different places."

None of the three scientists offered a guess or comment.

"Language," David said. "We know that almost everyone in Europe, the Middle East, and India speaks a language that is descended from a common root language: the Proto-Indo-European language, which was spoken by a single group, the Proto-Indo-Europeans, about eight thousand years ago. We believe these people lived in either Anatolia or the Eurasian Steppes—present day Turkey or southwestern Russia."

"Fascinating..." Janus mumbled as he glanced out the window.

"David, it's interesting, but I'm just not sure how this would connect with the plague," Kate said gently.

Janus glanced at David, then Kate. "I agree, but I for one would very much like to hear more about this."

David gave Kate a look that said, *At least someone around here appreciates me.*

Janus continued, "I have two questions. First: how do you know what you're saying is true?"

"Well we didn't even know about the PIE until 1783 when a British judge named William Jones was assigned to India. Jones was a brilliant scholar and linguist. He knew Greek and Latin and began studying Sanskrit—mostly to familiarize himself with native Indian laws, many of which were written in Sanskrit. Jones made a remarkable discovery: Sanskrit and the ancient classical Western languages were eerily similar. This was completely unexpected. As he further compared Sanskrit, Greek, and Latin, he realized that they all had a common ancestral language. Here we have three languages, separated by thousands of miles and thousands of years of development, yet they had all evolved from a common root language: what we now call the Proto-Indo-European language. Jones was a true scholar, and he dug deeper into the mystery. The revelations were shocking. Other languages were also Proto-Indo-European, and not just obscure ones: every major root language from India to Great Britain. Latin, ancient Greek, Norse, Runic, Gothic—they're all derived from the Proto-Indo-European language. The list of modern-day languages is extensive. All the Germanic languages, including Norwegian, Swedish, Danish, German, English—"

Janus held his hand up and spoke softly. "If you would

indulge us a moment, I would like to hear more about the PIE. You said there were other derivative languages?"

"Oh yeah, tons of them. All the Italic languages: Italian, French, Portuguese, Spanish... let's see... all the Slavic languages: Russian, Serbian, Polish. What else, Balkan languages. Of course Greek; the Greeks were PIE descendants. Sanskrit, as I mentioned; Hindi, Farsi, Pashto. There are also tons of extinct PIE languages. Hitite, Tocharian, Gothic. In fact, scholars have been able to work backwards to actually reconstruct the Proto-Indo-European language. And that's actually the basis of about everything we know about them. They had words for horse, wheel, farming, animal breeding, snow-capped mountains, and for a sky god."

David paused, not sure what to add next. "In general we know the PIE were extremely advanced for their time—their use of horses, the wheel, tools, and agriculture made them a force in the region, and their descendants went on to dominate the world from Europe to India. As I said, today roughly half the world speaks a Proto-European language. In many ways, they are the ultimate lost civilization." David stopped again, then glanced at Janus. "You said you had two questions?"

Janus was deep in thought. After a second, he realized the room was waiting for him. "Oh yes. I... would like to know... where they are now."

"That's the real mystery. We're not even sure where to look for them. What we know of them is based on language reconstruction and myths—specifically the mythology they passed down to their descendant groups along with their language. Those are the tools of history: language, stories, and artifacts. In this case, we don't have many artifacts, just their language and myths."

"Myths?" Janus said.

"Here again, we're reconstructing the past based on shared

myths across cultures—these are instances where the same story appears with slight changes. Obviously, the names are changed, but the shape of the narrative is the same. One common belief is that there were two progenitors of mankind: brothers, sometimes twins. For the Indic, it was Manu and Yemo; the Germanic have tales of Mannus and Ymir. These mythologies were eventually incorporated into histories. For the Romans, Remus and Romulus; the Hebrews, Cain and Abel. Another common myth is that of the Great Flood—it appears in some form in every PIE culture. But overwhelmingly, the most common myth is that of an epic battle ending with the slaying of a serpent, usually a dragon of some sort."

Chang picked up the page. "It seems Dr. Grey had some inkling of who the PIE were. What does it mean: PIE = Immaru? I am not familiar with Immaru."

David looked at Kate. *Do we tell them?*

Kate didn't hesitate. "The Immaru are, or more likely were, a group of monks in the mountains of Tibet. After the incident in China, where David was almost killed, they rescued us."

Chang winced, and David thought he was going to say something, maybe an apology, but Kate continued.

"I talked with several of the monks. A younger one, Milo, took care of us, and an older monk, Qian, showed me an ancient artifact: a tapestry. He believed it was a historical document that had been passed down for generations, thousands of years. It depicted four floods. The first was a flood of fire, which I believe to be the Toba Catastrophe—a volcanic eruption seventy thousand years ago that changed the human race. The tapestry showed a god saving a dying band of humans. The god gave them his blood. I believe that depiction was an allegory, a representation of a gene therapy an Atlantean gave those dying humans. That gene—the Atlantis Gene—helped that small band of humans survive in the volcanic winter that followed."

Dr. Chang nodded vigorously. "This matches the Immari assumption—that the Atlantis Gene was introduced seventy thousand years ago and that it caused the cataclysm: a change in brain wiring that set the human race apart from other hominins."

"Qian also told me that the Immari are actually a splinter group of the Immaru—a faction of monks who separated thousands of years ago. The Immari had grown tired of allegory and myth. They wished to pursue answers in science and archeology," Kate said.

"That may be, but I can't comment," Dr. Chang said. "I never advanced high enough to know the true Immari history. It was closely guarded and assigned its own mythological status. Dr. Grey would have known the history—he was a member of the Council—one of the three highest-ranking officers. Do you think that's why he included the note on the Immaru and PIE? Do they have something that relates to the plague?"

Kate considered that. "I know Martin was looking for something. His words to me were: 'I thought it was here in southern Spain, but I was wrong.' Maybe he was trying to trace the history of the Immaru and the Proto-Indo-Europeans to find the object... Maybe they have it." Another thought occurred to her. "The Immaru did have something, a box. The second flood depicted on the tapestry was the flood of water. In it, the god returns and tells the humans to repent and move inland, but many refused, ignoring the warnings. But the Immaru had faith. They heeded the warning and carried a large box into the highlands."

"What was in it?" David asked.

"I don't know—"

"You didn't ask?"

"Qian didn't know."

"Well... what did it look like?"

"A large plain box they were carrying on poles."

"What was the rest of the tapestry?" He hoped it would shed

more light on Martin's code. The first two depictions had confirmed David's theories. He was close to unraveling the message.

"The third was the flood of blood. A global apocalypse. The fourth was the flood of light. Our salvation. Qian said they were events yet to come."

"You think the plague is the flood of blood?" David asked.

"I believe so."

"You told Martin about the tapestry?"

"Yes."

David nodded. "The tapestry is a chronology. It chronicles the major turning points in human history. I believe this code is also a chronology: a timeline that Martin was creating to decode the tapestry and try to isolate specific events in the past—events that are key to finding a cure for the plague."

"Interesting," Kate murmured.

"Bravo," Janus said.

"I concur," said Chang.

David leaned back in the chair. That was the purpose of Martin's code—he was sure of it now. The mystery that remained was: who killed him and why? It was someone on this boat. Was it one of the scientists—because of Martin's research?

The sound of boots on the thin carpet interrupted his thoughts, and David turned to see Shaw charging into the room.

"We're ready. We need a decision—" He glanced around the room, taking the four of them in for the first time. "What the hell is this? A bloody tea party?"

"We're discussing Martin's notes," Kate said, pointing to the page on the coffee table.

Shaw snatched it up.

David lunged for him and grabbed the page out of his hand. "Don't. You're getting grease on it." He placed the page back on the coffee table. The look on Kate's face said, *It's tough dealing with barbarians, isn't it?* He knew her so well. In the background, he heard Shaw erupt.

"Are you kidding me? We're in the middle of—"

David slowly turned his head to Shaw, ready for battle, but a faint glimmer on the horizon caught his attention. He stared at it a moment, then stood and crossed to the window. Yes—lights in the night. A boat. Two. On what appeared to be a direct course for them.

64

From Tibet to Tel Aviv

MILO unslung the heavy pack and walked to the edge of the rock ledge. The untouched green plateau in western Tibet stretched to the horizon, where another mountain ridge met the setting sun. The serene, picturesque landscape reminded him of the monastery. His mind instantly flashed to his last moments in that place, the only home he'd ever known. He had stood at the top of another rock ledge, looking down, watching the wooden buildings burn, crumble, and tumble down the mountain, leaving only a burnt, blackened rock face.

Milo pushed the scene from his mind. He refused to think about it. Qian's words echoed to him: "A mind that dwells in the past builds a prison it cannot escape. Control your mind, or it will control you, and you will never break through the walls it builds."

Milo cleared his mind and turned back to the pack. He would make camp here, then leave at first light as he had done each day before. He took out the tent, then the animal traps and the map, which he consulted every night. He thought he had to be somewhere near the Kashmir region of northern India or Pakistan or possibly somewhere in eastern Afghanistan, but truth be told, he had no idea where he was, and he hadn't seen a single soul, no one to offer any clues. Qian had been right about that: "You will walk a long and lonely road. But you will have all that you need."

At each of Milo's questions, Qian had issued a quick retort. Food? "The beasts of the forests will be your only companions, and they will sustain you." Milo moved into the forest as he had each night before and began rigging the traps. Along the way, he ate nuts and berries. He usually consumed enough to maintain his energy levels until his protein-rich breakfast of animal meat the next morning.

When the traps were set, he erected his tent and laid out his mat. He sat and focused on his breathing, seeking the stillness within. Gradually, it came, and the memories and musings of his mind melted away. He was vaguely aware of the sun slipping behind the far ridge, pulling a curtain of darkness down the mountain.

In the distance, he heard the snap of one of the traps he had laid. There would be breakfast tomorrow, that much was certain.

Milo retired to the tent, where the last two items Qian had given him lay waiting in the corner. Both were books. The first was entitled *Anthems of the Dying*, but to Milo's surprise, there were no songs inside, only three simplistic stories.

The first story was about a father who sacrificed himself to save his daughter. The second was about a man and woman who traveled across a vast wasteland to find the treasure their ancestor had left them, which was their only hope to cure their dying people. The last part told the story of a humble man who slew a giant and became a king but renounced his power, giving it back to the people.

Qian had pointed to the book. "This book is a guide to our future."

Milo had hesitated. "How can the future be written?"

"It is written in our blood, Milo. The war is always the same, only the names and places change. There are demons upon this earth. They live in our hearts and minds. This is a history of our struggle, a chronicle of the past war that will be repeated. The past and our nature predict our future. Read it. Learn it well."

"Will there be a test?"

"Be serious, Milo. Life is a test we take every day. You must focus. You must be there for them when they need you."

"Who?"

"You will meet them soon enough. They will arrive here, and they will need our help, now and even more in the future. You must be prepared."

Milo considered this for a moment. Somehow, it excited him. He felt filled with purpose. "What must I do?"

"A great dragon pursues them. Their respite will be brief. The dragon will find them and breathe fire down upon us. You must build a chariot for the sky to carry them away. They must survive."

"Wait, there's a dragon? It's coming here?!"

Qian shook his head. "Milo, it is a metaphor. I don't know what will come, but we must be ready. And you must prepare for the journey after that."

Milo had spent the following weeks building a basket—for the chariot that would carry these people away from the dragon. He had thought it was all a diversion—something Qian had made up to keep him from pestering the older monks. But then they had come—Dr. Kate and Mr. David—just as Qian had said.

Mr. David was just as Milo had seen him before: at death's door. But Dr. Kate had healed him.

Qian's other prediction had come true as well. The dragon had come, flying through the air and breathing fire, and Dr. Kate and Mr. David had barely escaped. Milo was again at the top of the mountain, staring up at the basket he had built. It hung from a massive balloon, one of many floating toward the horizon, away from the burning monastery below him. They had known—the older monks. They had taken only one younger monk. Milo. They had not run from their fate. "It is written," Qian had said. But who wrote it?

Milo opened the second book, *The First Tribes of Humanity: A History*. He understood this book even less. It was written in an ancient language Qian had made him learn. Milo had been thrilled to learn English, but this language was different—far more difficult. And the text... what did it mean?

"When you know the answer, only then will your journey begin," Qian had said.

"If you know the answer, why not just tell me?" Milo asked, smiling. "We can save some time, and I can take off in the balloon and be there soon—"

"Milo!" Qian steadied himself against the table. "The journey is the destination. Finding the answers for yourself, achieving understanding, is part of your journey. There are no shortcuts along the path."

"Oh. Right."

By the time Milo reached what was left of Tel Aviv, he thought he understood the books. And he had changed, because of what he had seen, and the things he had done to survive.

He found a fishing vessel he thought would take him.

"What do you want, kid?"

"Passage," Milo answered.

"Where you headed?"

"West."

"Got anything to trade?"

"Only my willingness to work hard. And... the greatest story you ever heard."

The fisherman eyed him suspiciously. "All right, get on the boat."

65

Somewhere off the coast of Ceuta
Mediterranean Sea

David stared at the two sets of lights on the water for another second. "Kamau!" he shouted.

Within seconds, the tall African appeared in the saloon, covered in sweat and grease.

"Get us underway," David said.

"To where?" Shaw cried.

David turned to him. "Kill all the lights on the boat." To Kamau he said, "Make our heading away from those lights." David pointed out the window. "Best speed."

"Jesus," Shaw said. He ran out of the saloon. The lights throughout the boat went out.

David retrieved the binoculars from the cockpit and focused on the lights on the water. Just as the boats came into focus, they cut their lights. Through the moonlight, David couldn't make out any markings on the boats or even what type, but one thing was certain: they had cut their lights the second Shaw had killed theirs.

David felt the yacht lurch forward, and they were underway.

Shaw returned to the saloon. "They cut their lights—"

"I saw it."

"They're following us."

David ignored him. He said to Kamau, who was standing in the doorway, "Bring the map. Mark our position."

"Let me make the call, David. My government can airlift us out of here. It's our only way out. You know it," Shaw said.

Kamau returned with the map and spread it out on the coffee table, covering Martin's notes. He pointed at a dot in the water between Spain and Morocco. "We're here."

David's mind raced.

"Fine," Shaw said flatly. "I'll say it. Someone killed Martin."

Every set of eyes in the room went to Shaw. "We all know it. There are three doctors and three soldiers in this room; we all know enough to know that he was murdered. One of us killed him. It wasn't me, and it wasn't Kate. So I propose the following: Kate locks herself in the master stateroom with all the guns. We five gentlemen remain here in the upper deck until the SAS soldiers get here. That ensures Kate's safety." He focused on David. "Which is our priority, I believe."

David read Kate's body language, which was subtle but said: *not a bad idea*. And it *was* a good idea: if Shaw could be trusted. But if he had killed Martin, it would be the perfect trap. Disarm everyone, call in whomever he's working with and easily capture Kate.

David pointed to a small dot on the map. "What is this?"

"Isla de Alborán," Kamau said.

"You said in Ceuta that the Immari had taken control of the islands in the Mediterranean."

"Yes. They have Alborán as well. It is a very small outpost."

"How small?"

"Tiny. The entire island is less than a tenth of a square kilometer. That would be... maybe fifteen or twenty acres. There is a lighthouse and a building with maybe six guards. A helipad with two large helicopters. No significant defenses..." He seemed to read David's mind. "But... it would be difficult to take with only two people." His eyes cut to Shaw, almost involuntarily.

"Defenses?" David asked.

"Yes, some. A few fixed artillery batteries. We'd have to figure that out. The outpost mainly serves as air support to Immari ships that run into trouble—rescue, fending off pirates."

"The helicopters are long range?"

"Yes, definitely. There was discussion of having them support the invasion of southern Spain, but they were held back."

David nodded. If they could take the outpost at Alborán, they could fly anywhere.

Shaw finally broke. "You can't be serious. You have the option of being airlifted out of here, and your choice is to assault an Immari outpost? It's ludicrous."

David folded up the map. "It's what we're doing. This isn't a discussion." He handed the map to Kamau. "Set our course."

Shaw simply stood there.

"David," Kate began. The *I need to speak with you* look was the only cue David needed. He followed her downstairs to their stateroom.

She closed the door gently behind him. "I'm sorry, but I think we have to—"

"I want you to trust me, Kate. Let me do this." He waited for her.

Slowly, she nodded. "Okay."

"We'll reach Alborán inside five hours—assuming whoever is

chasing us doesn't catch us first. We need to figure out who killed Martin before we get there."

"I agree. But first, I want us to decipher the rest of Martin's code, then I want to call Continuity and relay our findings. If... something bad happens at Alborán, at least they will have our research. Hopefully they can find a cure."

This was her deal: David would help her work on a cure, and she would go along with his plan—and trust him. Tradeoffs, compromises, trust. This was turning into a real relationship. *I'm good with that. I like that.* He nodded. "Yeah, okay."

Dorian rolled over in bed. "Enter."

The door to his room opened, and a shy sailor inched in. He held out a closed envelope.

Dorian snatched it and ripped it open.

Where the hell are you?

Warner close to deciphering code.

Our destination is Isla de Alborán.

ETA 5 hours.

Be there.

Be ready.

66

Mediterranean Sea

When David and Kate returned to the saloon, the two scientists were there waiting for them, sitting side by side on the white leather couches, placid expressions on their faces, as if the world weren't dying from a global pandemic, and they hadn't just been accused of murder. David had to marvel at them. He wasn't sure if he felt envy or sheer surprise at their composure.

"We are ready to resume. If you are, of course," Janus said.

Kate and David sat in club chairs adjacent to the couch.

The wood-paneled, glass-accented room was lit only by three candles on the coffee table now, and the feeling had changed from a science conference to a late-night sleepover.

David turned the paper with Martin's code around on the coffee table, positioning it to face the others as if it were a Ouija board.

Everyone took a moment to reread the note.

PIE = Immaru?

535...1257 = Second Toba? New Delivery System?

Adam => Flood/A$ Falls => Toba 2 => KBW

Alpha => Missed Delta? => Delta => Omega

70K YA => 12.5K YA => 535...1257 => 1918...1978

Missing Alpha Leads to Treasure of Atlantis?

"Several items still confuse me," David said. "I believe the first two lines are simply notes—one about PIE. As we discussed, I'm quite certain Martin believed the Immaru were the PIE, Proto-Indo-Europeans, or at least a descendant group. The other note refers to an event in 535 and again in 1257. I know what it is, and I'll explain that in a moment. Then the three lines are a chronology—a time line that overlaps and corresponds to the Tibetan tapestry Kate saw at the Immaru monastery. But I believe Martin's chronology may be incomplete. Let's take it step by step."

David pointed at the word Adam. "Adam, Alpha, 70K YA."

"In research," Kate said, "the alpha signifies the first person in a clinical trial—the first to receive a test therapy."

"Yes," David said. "I think *Adam* is the first human who received the Atlantis Gene. That's the event in the flood of fire in the tapestry, and the first major event in Martin's chronology. The next is the *Flood, A$ Falls*, 12,500 years ago. I believe A$ is shorthand for Atlantis. So *Flood, Atlantis Falls.* When I was in the Atlantis structure in Gibraltar, there was a chamber with a series of... holomovies. I believe they showed this event—the fall of Atlantis at the foot of the Rock of Gibraltar. In the movie, the Atlantean ship hovered just above the water, then set down on the coast, just outside a prehistoric megalithic settlement. Two Atlanteans in suits exited the craft and interrupted a prehistoric tribal ritual, saving a Neanderthal. As soon as they returned to the ship, it was hit by a tidal wave that drove it inland, destroying the ancient city. As the water pulled the ship back out to sea, explosions rocked it, destroying the ship."

"Where it lay buried for almost thirteen thousand years, until 1918, when my father helped the Immari find it," Kate said.

"Exactly. The puzzling part is the notation: Missing Delta?"

"Delta signifies change," Kate said. "'Missing Delta'... So a change didn't happen?"

"If we piece together Martin's code, the tapestry, and what I saw that night in Gibraltar... In the first two floods on the tapestry, the Atlanteans interact directly with humans. Saving them or warning them. This implies a direct relationship."

Kate sat back in her chair. "What if the Atlanteans were somehow guiding human evolution? Like an experiment with periodic intervention—and that intervention failed to happen 12,500 years ago because of the ship's explosion: the fall of Atlantis."

"I believe that's what Martin thought." A thought struck David; did he have the other piece of the puzzle?

In Antarctica, when David was in the tube, the Atlantean had released Dorian first—given him a head start. The Atlantean had watched David and Dorian fight to the death, as if he knew the outcome, as if the Atlantean were simply waiting for his champion to triumph—Dorian.

David had died a second time in Antarctica. But unlike his first death, he hadn't resurrected in Antarctica. He had awoken in the Atlantis structure in Gibraltar—a section at the base of Jebel Musa in Morocco. Someone had made David resurrect there. Another Atlantean? David had noticed another damaged suit on the floor of the resurrection room. He tried to think back to the holomovie. Neither of the suits had been damaged during the events, he was sure of it.

Yet, the fact was undeniable: another Atlantean had brought him back—after Dorian and the Atlantean in Antarctica had killed him.

Another faction? One clearly wanted him dead. The other had saved him.

David was now sure of two things. One, that the Atlanteans were waging some sort of civil war. And two, that there was no way he was telling Kate or the two scientists what had happened to him.

"I have a theory," David said. "I believe what I witnessed—the Atlantis disaster—wasn't a natural phenomenon. I think it was an attack."

"By whom?" Chang asked.

"I don't know," David said. "But what if there were two factions of Atlanteans or a traitor, someone who sabotaged the ship, preventing some intervention? I mean look at the broad arc of human history. All the major stuff happened in the last thirteen thousand years—agriculture, cities, writing, you name it. The population chart explodes around this time. It coincides with the end of the glacial maximum and warmer weather, but..."

Janus leaned forward. "I find your 'missing intervention' theory intriguing. I see one hole, however. The next step in the chronology: '535...1257, Toba 2, Delta'—that implies a change did happen then—recently. And from the videos, you say the ship was destroyed."

David nodded. "I think those two Atlanteans must have died in Gibraltar. It's the only explanation. I think whoever killed them facilitated the change in 535."

Janus nodded. "Which leads me to my conclusion: if an Atlantean intervened in 535—another delta, as you say—where are they? If they have the power to control human evolution, where are they hiding?"

David pondered the question. He didn't have an answer, and it was, in truth, a very good question. The fact that he had advanced so many ideas made him feel a little defensive, as if he had to keep throwing out more possibilities to corroborate his theory. He felt himself tensing a bit, readying for battle.

Dr. Chang set his teacup down. "I too find it a valid question. However, I would like to hear more about the actual event —Toba 2, in 535 or is it 1257? Was Dr. Grey uncertain on the actual date?"

The question brought David back, made him focus. "No. I don't think so. I believe the dates are the beginning and end of a period, marked by two specific events."

"What period?" Janus asked.

"The dark ages in Europe."

"And two... events?"

"Volcanos and then plagues," David said. "One that ushered in the dark ages, another that led Europe out. There's strong evidence that the first outbreak—in 535—was linked to a massive volcano near mount Toba in Indonesia." He thought for a second. "You could think of it as a sort of *Second Toba Catastrophe*."

"I would have heard about a Second Toba Catastrophe," Kate said.

David smiled. Him, telling her about a volcano that changed the fate of humanity. "It's not well known," he said, echoing her words to him in Jakarta when she had first told him about the Toba Catastrophe Theory.

"Touché," Kate said.

"What we know is this: in 535, temperatures around the world dropped rapidly. We're talking about an eighteen-month-long winter—a harsh, bitter winter with very little sunlight. This is what was described in historical records. It's actually the most severe climate event in recorded history. In China, snow fell in August. Throughout Europe, crops were lost and famine ensued."

"A volcanic winter."

"Yes. The historical accounts across Asia and Europe attest to it. Ice core samples confirm it, and tree-ring evidence from Scandinavia and western Europe also reveals a huge reduction in tree growth in the years 536 to 542, not recovering fully until the 550s. But it wasn't the years-long winter that plunged humanity into darkness, it was the plague that followed—the worst pandemic in known history."

"The Plague of Justinian," Kate whispered. "In terms of casualty rates, it was the worst catastrophe in recorded history. But I don't see how it could be connected to a volcanic eruption. And wait, tell me again how you know all this?"

"It might be hard for you to believe, but I was *this close* to a PhD. My thesis was on the origins and impact of the Dark Ages in Europe." He stared at her for a moment, then shrugged theatrically. "I'm more than a pretty face and a skinny waist, you know."

Kate shook her head, her face somewhere between embarrassment and disbelief. "I stand corrected. Please continue."

"Here's what we know: up to a third of the eastern Mediterranean's population died in the outbreak. The Eastern Roman Empire was devastated. The capital, Constantinople, went from a city of half a million to less than a hundred thousand after the plague. They named the plague after the Roman Emperor Justinian. It's hard to exaggerate the carnage of this plague. It was like nothing the world had ever seen. Some victims would take days to die. Others became ill and died within minutes. On the streets, bodies were simply stacked up. The smell of death was everywhere. In Constantinople, the emperor ordered the dead be buried at sea." David's mind flashed to Ceuta. He focused. "But there were too many of them. Dead bodies were dangerous in ancient cities. So the emperor ordered that mass graves be dug outside the city. Bodies of the dead were burned there. The historical record says that they stopped counting after three hundred thousand."

None of the scientists said a word. David took a sip of water and continued.

"As a historian, this plague is remarkable not because of its mortality, but for how it reshaped the entire world. In many ways, the world we inhabit grew directly out of the events of the sixth century."

"What do you mean?" Kate asked.

"In the wake of the plague, we see the end of the supercities of the ancient world. Ancient Persia, once a super-nation, crumbles. The Eastern Roman Empire had been close to retaking its western half—the 'Rome' everyone talks about. But in the wake of this pandemic, it's besieged and almost falls. It eventually becomes the Byzantine Empire. We see these falls across the world—mighty empires recede and barbarian tribes actually gain ground. The major lesson from the Plague of Justinian is that the most connected civilizations, the most advanced, those with established international trade routes and supercities: they suffered the most. It was the isolated, simple societies that fared the best. Take sixth-century Britain—it's a great example. Britain at the time of the plague was dominated by the Romano-British. Based on artifacts, we know they traded with nations as far away as Egypt—that's where the plague first appeared, by the way, or that was the first account."

"I don't understand," Dr. Chang said.

"The trade routes brought the plague. The British had been at war with several Germanic tribes that had settled their western coast. At the time of the outbreak in the mid-sixth century, these tribes were mostly contained and regarded as barbarians. No one traded with them, and the British refused to intermarry with them for the most part. In the wake of the outbreak, these tribes seized the initiative, spreading throughout Britain and eventually taking control. The primary tribes were the Angles and the Saxons. In fact, some believe the legend of King Arthur is a composite of British knights who fought these Angle and Saxon invaders. The fact that people in Britain and around the world speak English—a Germanic language—is because of the plague... and the Angle and Saxon triumph after. It wasn't just Britain, this happened around the world: advanced civilizations, with cities and population density and established trade routes, fell. The barbarians beyond their gates rose, invaded, and most of the time, just moved on. In cases where the barbarian invaders set up their own government, they were usually sacked a century later by the next roving band of raiders. This was the real end of an era, a time of great cities and civilizations. The Dark Ages came after and they lasted for a very long time—almost a thousand years. It was the greatest reversal of progress in history. In fact, the Dark Ages only really ended after the next major outbreak—"

"Hold on," Kate said. "I have to confess my ignorance here. I'm a geneticist. I just don't see how a volcano and a volcanic winter are connected to the Plague of Justinian."

"Part of history is tracing artifacts and looking at patterns. One pattern that emerged from the outbreak is that it began in northern Africa, moved into Egypt, and from there, exploded into the eastern Mediterranean. Once it hit Constantinople, the rest of the modern world fell like dominos as trade ships carried the plague around the world. There's still some debate, but many historians believe that the plague came to Europe on grain barges from northern Africa, and that it was the rats on the barges that initially carried the disease."

"What David says is true," Dr. Janus said. "It is a great irony: the real danger from rapid climate change has nothing to do with the weather. The danger is destabilizing ecosystems, causing organisms that normally have no interaction with each other to come into contact. We know that most outbreaks are caused when wild-animal reservoir hosts that benignly harbor a deadly pathogen are forced out of their natural habitats. In the wake of this second 'Toba volcano,' ecosystems around the world were destabilized. If Dr. Grey's theory is correct, it is incredibly intriguing. The ancient world would have been a very difficult place to manage a global genetic change. A plague is the perfect vehicle, but there remains one very big problem."

"Distribution," Kate said.

"Precisely," Janus said. "The world was very disconnected. Visiting all the cultures and spreading a disease would have been impossible. A volcano that blanketed the world with ash, a global delivery system, would be perfect. The volcano brings a winter, in some places drought, then excessive rainfall. Vegetation growth plummets, then rebounds. In places like northern Africa, rodent populations would fare quite well. A breeding explosion occurs. The larger population seeks new territory as their existing ecosystem can't support their larger numbers. Some of these rats carry plague, and they push into areas of human population. While the rats are immune to plague—they are reservoir hosts—the fleas on their backs are not. So fleas die of plague, and the mechanism of their demise causes them to spread the disease. Fleas infected with plague literally starve. The plague bacteria multiply in their gut, blocking the ability to ingest nutrients. They go mad, jumping off the rodents onto any host they can find, spreading the disease to humans. Of course rodents, and the fleas hitching a ride on their backs, have spread plague for thousands of years. The *genius*, if you will permit the term here, of this outbreak was a genetic modification to the plague bacteria, which I believe was carried by the volcano. The ash that rained down changed the bacteria residing in the rats—it didn't unleash a pandemic on humans. A human pandemic would have simply burned out and been over with. Dr. Grey's notation—'Second Toba? New Delivery System?'—I believe refers to his own uncertainty on the subject. Based on our research, the work Dr. Chang and I have done, we can confirm that it was a new delivery system, an extremely ingenious one. By modifying an existing bacterial line in rats, whoever did this ensured there would be multiple waves of outbreak, a sustained genetic transformation. It lay dormant, in the reservoir hosts—rats in this case—waiting for the correct moment in time."

"That matches the historical record," David said. "The first wave of outbreak was around 535, but others followed, some even more violent. We can't imagine the toll. The bouts of plague lasted for two hundred years. Up to half of all Europeans died. Then after about 750, the outbreaks stop until around 1257—which is the next part of Martin's note. In 1257, another volcano erupted, again from Indonesia. These are recent discoveries, but we are pretty sure that the Samalas volcano, on Lombok Island in Indonesia, erupted with an incredible force. The impact was greater than that of the Tambora event in 1815, which caused what's known as the Year Without a Summer. From the tree-ring samples, we see the same thing in 1257: a volcanic winter that lasted for over a year. The plague rats return, and plague returns to Europe. By this time, nearly seven hundred years later, the historical records are more clear. This outbreak is almost exactly like the last, but it gets more press and mention in the historical record. They call it 'the Black Death' in Europe. But it was the same plague—"

"Bubonic plague," Kate said.

"Exactly," David confirmed. "The same plague, separated by almost a millennium, returning to wreak the same havoc—"

"Stop," Kate held up her hand. "The Black Death began in Europe around 1348—almost a hundred years after this volcano—"

"True," David said, holding up his hands. "Look, here's the history: in 1257 a massive volcano, strangely similar in location and effect to the one in the sixth century, caused a volcanic winter and widespread famine in Europe. I can only assume the plague returned, but there was a difference this time—some sort of immunity—"

"CCR5 Delta 32," Kate said, lost in thought.

"What?"

"Martin mentioned it to me. It's present in up to sixteen percent of Europeans. It's a mutation that makes them immune to HIV, smallpox, and other viruses. Possibly the bacteria that causes plague."

"Interesting," David said. "One of the great mysteries of history has been the origins of the Black Death. We're pretty sure the outbreak in the sixth century, the Plague of Justinian, moved up through Africa into the eastern Mediterranean. But the Black Death was different. Same scenario—volcano, same plague—but this time, we believe the Black Death originated in central Asia. The peace provided by the Pax Mongolica enabled the Mongol armies based in central Asia to carry the disease east along the Silk Road. During the Mongol siege of Caffa in the Crimea, the invading Mongols actually catapulted infected bodies over the city walls."

"Seriously?" Kate asked.

"Hey, it was pretty ingenious for the times. Call it medieval biological warfare. After Caffa, the plague quickly spread across Europe. Historians have assumed that migration from Asia is the reason for the one-hundred-year time difference, but it could have been—"

"The mutation," Kate said.

"Possibly." David wanted to get back to what he knew, away from speculation. "In the following years, thirty to sixty percent of the entire population of Europe died from the Black Death. One third of everyone in China died. In fact, it took a hundred and fifty years for the global population to recover to the level it was before the Black Death. But I'm afraid that's where my knowledge ends. In general, I don't know what the chronology is leading up to. I just knew what the references were, and I knew the dates."

"I can shed light there," Dr. Chang said. "As Dr. Janus mentioned before, our working theory has been that the current plague is simply activating past outbreaks, trying to complete some genetic transformation that was half-finished. We've been trying to isolate those past outbreaks to better understand how the human genome changed." He motioned toward David. "Mr. Vale, you had it right about the link between the plagues. A few years ago, a group of researchers discovered that the Plague of Justinian was caused by *Yersinia pestis* or *Y. pestis*—the bacteria that causes bubonic plague. The discovery was very intriguing: the two worst pandemics in recorded history—the Plague of Justinian and the Black Death—were both instances of bubonic plague. We believe in both cases there was a genetic mutation of the Y. pestis bacteria. We've been using the Immari to gather evidence. They procured samples from plague victims from both outbreaks. We sequenced those genomes, as well as samples of *Y. pestis*, from both eras. We also have samples from the Spanish flu of 1918. We found some common genetic sequences. We think they are connected to the Atlantis Plague. Based on Dr. Grey's notes and our discussion here, I believe our data is a key piece of the puzzle, the key to finding a cure. Unfortunately, it was lost when the plague barge went down."

Janus sat up on the couch. "Dr. Chang, I owe you an apology."

Chang's face glanced over, confused.

"I never fully trusted you," Janus said. "I was assigned to you. You went along with our research, but until now, I thought that you might have been an Immari loyalist, someone working to obtain my research. I withheld much of what I learned from you." He took out a memory stick. "But I saved it on this device. Along with the research we did together. It's all here, and I believe it will reveal the genome changes Dr. Grey was searching for—this Delta-2—the root genetic structure of the Atlantis Plague."

Chang glanced at the memory stick. "What matters is that you have the data. In your place, I think... perhaps I would have done the same thing. However, there seems to be one final piece—the Omega. To me, that signifies the endpoint—the eventuality of this genetic change. The notation '1918...1978' seems to indicate that Dr. Grey believed it could have happened in one of those years. The 'KBW' in the first line is unfamiliar. Mr. Vale, is this another historical reference?"

David had been turning "KBW" over in his mind since he had first seen the code. He didn't even have a guess. "No. I'm not sure what it means."

"I know what it means," Kate said. "'KBW' are my initials. Katherine Barton Warner. I think I'm the Omega."

67

Somewhere off the coast of Ceuta
Mediterranean Sea

Through the window of the helicopter, Dorian watched the water fly by below. The sun glistened on the black expanse like a beacon leading him to his destiny.

He thought about the white door of light in Germany. Where would it lead? To another world? Another time?

He activated the microphone in his helmet. "What's our ETA?"

"Three, maybe three and a half hours."

Would they beat Kate and her entourage there? It would be close.

"Get the outpost on the line."

A minute later Dorian was speaking with Isla de Alborán's commanding officer.

The Immari lieutenant at Isla de Alborán ended the call and looked back at the four other soldiers playing cards and smoking. "Put some coffee on. We need to sober up. We're going to have company."

David tried to process what Kate had said: "*I'm the Omega.*"

Shaw glided into the room. "I'm putting coffee on—" He looked around. "What's all this? You lot look like you've seen a ghost."

"We're working," David snapped.

Kate broke the tension. "I'd love some coffee. Thank you, Adam."

"Sure," Shaw said. "Dr. Chang? Dr. Janus?"

David noticed that he hadn't made the coffee roll call. He was fine with that.

"Oh yes, much appreciated," Dr. Chang murmured, still deep in thought.

Dr. Janus stared out the window, an unreadable expression on his face. When he realized everyone was waiting on him, he quickly said, "No. Thank you though."

Shaw returned with the two cups of coffee, then lingered by the window, diagonally behind David. David couldn't see him, but he knew he was there. He was less than fine with that.

Janus was the first to speak. "I do not doubt what you've said, Kate. I want that clear at the outset. I would, however, like to review our key assumptions and explore several... possibilities."

David thought Kate tensed a little, but she simply sipped her coffee and nodded.

Janus continued. "The first assumption: that this Tibetan tapestry was a document depicting Atlantean interaction with humans, specifically their intervention to save humans seventy thousand years ago—the introduction of the Atlantis Gene which changed human brain wiring and the fate of humanity—and then, their warning to humans before the Great Flood. The balance of the tapestry we assume to be events yet to come. I have a question about that, but I will hold it for now.

"Our second assumption is that Martin's note is a chronology—an attempt to decode the past, to identify the genetic turning points of humanity—to lead us to a cure for the plague."

"Our third and final assumption is that this chronology identifies a missing delta: a point at which Atlantean intervention in human evolution failed—sometime around the Great Flood and the fall of Atlantis. Mr. Vale's theory is that a battle between the Atlantean factions led to that event. Having said all that, I would have postulated that the Omega—the eventuality of all the Atlantean intervention in human evolution—would have been the survivors of the Atlantis Plague. Specifically, the rapidly evolving. Are they not the outcome the Atlanteans have been pursuing? They are the most obvious choice. As a scientist, I always evaluate the simplest explanation first before exploring more... exotic possibilities."

To David, Janus's argument was convincing. He started to speak, but Kate beat him to it. "Then why did Martin put my name in the chronology, above Omega?"

"To me, that is the question," Janus said. "I believe examining Martin's motives reveals that. We know that everything he did, all his research, his deals, his compromises, were for one purpose: to protect you. I believe that is his motive here. If his notes were found, he wanted the reader to find you, to ensure your safety so that you could be on hand to decode them, to be close to anyone pursuing a cure."

David nodded involuntarily. It was convincing.

"The pattern makes sense," Chang said. "As I see it, there's a problem with the timeline though. 70K YA: Adam, the introduction of the Atlantis Gene. 12.5K YA: the fall of Atlantis, the missing delta. 535 and 1257: Second Toba, the two volcanoes and subsequent outbreaks of bubonic plague, the beginning of the Dark Ages, then its end, followed by the Renaissance. Then 1918: the Bell, an Atlantean artifact that unleashed the Spanish flu. And this year, the second outbreak from the Bell. The Atlantis Plague. Martin has the dates wrong: 1918...1978. 1978 should be this year—the current outbreak creates the Omega."

"That would be logical," Janus said.

"When were you born?" David asked. "Uh, I'm inquiring for purely scientific purposes here."

"Cute," Kate said. "I was born in 1978. However... I was conceived in 1918."

"What?" Janus and Chang said, almost in unison.

David heard Shaw move from behind him and stand before the group, his first sign of interest in the conversation.

"It's true," Kate said. "Martin was my adoptive father. My biological father was a miner and an officer in the US Army during World War I. He was hired by the Immari to excavate the Atlantis structure under Gibraltar. He did it in return for my mother's hand in marriage. What he unearthed, the Bell, unleashed the Spanish flu epidemic. In a twist of fate, the outbreak claimed my mother's life. But the structure he uncovered contained a room with four tubes. He discovered that they were healing and hibernation pods. He put my mother—and me inside of her—in one, where we stayed until 1978: the year I was born."

Dr. Arthur Janus sat back on the couch. *This could change*

everything.

Kate's words shocked Dr. Shen Chang, even though he had already known about the Bell and the hibernation—that part was no surprise.

In 1978, Shen had been a researcher on a project funded by Immari International. He had gotten a call one morning from Howard Keegan, a man he had never met before. Keegan told him that he was the new head of the Immari organization and that he needed Shen's help, that Shen would be handsomely rewarded, would never have to worry about research funding again, and would do incredible work—work that could save the world but that he would never be able to tell anyone about.

Shen had agreed. Keegan led him into a room with four tubes. One held a young boy, the man he came to know as Dorian Sloane. The other held Patrick Pierce, the man who Keegan said had found the tubes. The last tube held a pregnant woman.

"We will release her last, and you will do everything you can to save her, but your first priority is the child."

Shen had never been so afraid in his entire life. What happened next was permanently burned into his memory. He remembered holding the child, her eyes... the same eyes Kate Warner now stared at him with. Incredible.

Adam Shaw marveled at Kate's story. *There's more to this than I thought; more to* her *than I thought. But I will deliver her safely, no matter what.*

Kate was tired of waiting. "Will someone please say something?"

"Yes," Janus began. "I would like to revise my earlier assertions. I now believe you *are* the Omega. And... it changes some things. My understanding of Martin's work, for one. I no longer think his note is just a chronology. That is only the half of it. Martin's code is much more than that. It is a roadmap to fix the human genome—to correct the problems with the Atlantis Gene, to create a viable Human-Atlantean hybrid, a new species, of which you are the first. Martin's sequence starts with the introduction of the Atlantis Gene—with Adam—then tracks the interferences, the missed correction at the time of the Flood, the Dark Ages that followed... and ends with you, Kate, someone with a stable, functioning Atlantis Gene, thanks to the tube that saved your life and your extraordinary birth. But... the real question, the practical matter becomes: what do we do now? We have our research, we understand Martin's notes. We need to find a lab—"

Kate interrupted. "There's one last thing I haven't told you all. Martin was one of the founders of a consortium called Continuity. It's a group of researchers from around the world. They've been running experiments for years, looking for a cure. In Marbella, Martin had a research site." A thought occurred to her. "I worked in a lead-encased building. I did a series of experiments, and Martin periodically took DNA samples from me."

"Do you think he was experimenting on you or on the subjects?" Dr. Chang asked.

Kate was sure of it now. "Both. Martin told me that he believed I was the key to everything. Seeing the code, Omega... yes, I know it. Continuity has all his results. I've been in contact with them."

Shock spread across David's face.

"What?" Kate asked him.

"Nothing." He shook his head.

She focused on Chang and Janus. "I think we should send Continuity our research and discuss our theories with them."

Dr. Janus took the memory stick out of his pocket. "I agree."

Chang nodded.

68

Somewhere near Isla de Alborán
Mediterranean Sea

THE CALL with Continuity had been intriguing.

Kate felt that she finally understood the experiments she had been a part of in Marbella.

For years, Continuity had developed an algorithm called the Genome Symphony. The principle was that whenever a gene therapy or retrovirus introduced a genetic change into a given genome, the Symphony algorithm could predict gene expression. Those predictions, when combined with knowledge about where the Atlantean endogenous retroviruses were buried in the genome, could predict a person's response to the Atlantis Plague and a given therapy.

Chang and Janus's research, which isolated the genome changes from the two plague outbreaks at the beginning and end of the Middle Ages, was the missing piece—or so Continuity hoped.

Kate watched Dr. Janus manipulate the computer, loading

the research into Symphony. He was a genius. Kate had never seen anyone his age with that sort of computer aptitude.

Kate spoke into the sat phone, which was in speaker mode. "What happens now?"

"Now we wait," Dr. Brenner said. "The algorithms will run and come up with possible therapies. Then we test them and hope to get lucky. If we find an effective therapy, we can deploy it quickly. Did Martin describe our gene implants?"

"I am not familiar," Dr. Janus said.

"Essentially we implant a biotech device subdermally that allows us to deliver a customized therapy to each person. The implants are connected wirelessly to a server inside each Orchid District."

The revelation shocked Kate. "I thought the implants were for tracking. And doesn't Orchid deliver the therapy?"

Brenner spoke quickly. "Well, yes and no. The implants do provide an inventory control—I mean, tracking apparatus, which is vitally important. Since the human genome is so diverse, we found that each therapy needs to be customized a bit, tweaked."

Kate nodded her head. It was extremely cutting-edge—an implanted biotech device delivering a genomically tailored therapy to every person. It was decades ahead of anything in use. It was a shame that it had taken the Immari threat and the plague to reach such a breakthrough.

"If the implant delivers the true therapy, then why still give everyone Orchid?" Dr. Janus asked.

"Three reasons. In some early trials, we found that the implants couldn't build a viable therapy for everyone. The implants build antivirals from the enzymes and proteins in the host's body—it essentially does a complicated bit of snipping to create the therapy it needs. But the process with an implant alone only worked for about eighty percent of hosts. So we give the implants a sort of viral stock—a proverbial block of viral clay it can carve a therapy out of. That's what's in the Orchid pills—viral stock."

"Very interesting..." Janus seemed lost in thought.

"The other reasons?" Kate asked.

"Oh, yes," Brenner said. "I get lost in the science. The second reason was speed. We knew we would need to deploy a new therapy quickly: manufacturing a new drug was out of the question, and of course this is a variable solution. We knew we could be looking at a base therapy with possibly thousands of small tweaks by the implants to make it work worldwide."

"And the last reason?"

"Hope. People taking Orchid everyday... we felt we needed to give them something they could see and hold, something tangible, something they knew: a drug for a disease. And now, I hope, you've given us the missing piece—the formula we need to pass to the implants. Symphony is processing your data now. Assuming it finds a corrective therapy, we can deploy it globally across the Orchid Alliance within hours."

Around the small saloon, the scientists nodded. David and Shaw eyed each other.

Dr. Brenner interrupted the tension. "There's something I haven't told you, Dr. Warner."

"What?" Kate asked through the speakerphone, not bothering to make the call private.

"The Orchid leadership has ordered us to execute Euthanasia Protocol."

"I don't—"

"We had standing orders," Brenner went on. "If either Orchid failed or the Immari ever became a viable threat, our orders were to issue cancellation commands to the implants—to let the dying die quickly. That would leave a world of Orchid survivors, a base to save the Alliance. So far, we have simply ignored those orders. We've focused on our research and hoped the leadership wouldn't actually go through with the plan. But we've heard rumors. If we don't execute Euthanasia Protocol, Allied troops may take control of Continuity and do it for us."

Kate sat back against the white couch.

No one said a word.

"Can you slow down Euthanasia Protocol?" Kate asked.

"We can try. But... let's hope your therapy works."

Downstairs, in their stateroom, David almost screamed at Kate, "You mean you had an open line to a global consortium this whole time?"

"Yes. What?"

"Call them back. Here's what you say..."

Kate called the Continuity number. *Dr. Brenner?—No, everything is fine. I need a favor. I need you to contact British Intelligence and ask them if they have an officer named Adam Shaw. Also, could you inquire with the World Health Organization about someone named Dr. Arthur Janus?—Yes, that would be very helpful.—Fine. Call me back as soon as you know. It's very important.*

Dr. Paul Brenner hung up the phone and glanced at the names. Shaw and Janus. What was happening on board that boat? Was Kate in danger?

He had actually grown quite attached to her. Seeing her in the videos for weeks, then talking with her in person. He hoped she would be all right. He picked up the phone and dialed his contacts at the WHO and British Intelligence. Each promised they would call back as soon as they had answers.

Paul had one more call to make—he hoped—but it would have to wait on Symphony, on the results.

He exited his office and walked down the hall of the CDC office building. The mood was dismal; everyone was overworked and burned out. Spirits were low, and for good reason: they had made no progress on a cure for the plague and had no prospects—not until the call from Kate nearly half an hour ago.

How long would it take Symphony? If there even was a cure to find in the research Kate and her team had sent...

The glass wall that held Orchid Ops parted, two glass pieces sliding to let him pass. Every head in the converted conference room turned to him. The scene was like the study hall of a college dorm, where students had crammed for sixty days straight: the conference tables were arranged haphazardly, littered with laptops, stacks of papers, maps, coffee-stained reports, and half-full Styrofoam cups.

The looks on their faces told Paul everything he needed to know.

The four large screens that dotted the walls confirmed it. The flashing text read: *One therapy identified.*

They had seen this text so many times before, and the celebration each time had been a little more muted than the previous. But the atmosphere felt different now. The team swarmed Paul, and everyone was talking excitedly about the new data and what to do next. Research sites were proposed and shot down.

"We test it here, on our own cohort," Paul said.

"Are you sure?"

"We've got some people who can't wait." He glanced at the Euthanasia Protocol countdown. Less than four hours left. There were a lot of people that couldn't wait.

But he wanted to be sure before they rolled it out worldwide. He had a phone call to make.

On his way back to his office, Paul stopped by the makeshift infirmary.

He stood at his sister's bedside. Her breathing was shallow, but he knew she recognized him. She reached out for his hand.

He stepped forward to take her hand. Her grip was weak.

"I think we've found it, Elaine. You're going to be just fine."

He felt her hand squeeze his, ever so slightly.

Paul picked up the phone. Several minutes later, he was connected to the Situation Room in the White House.

"Mr. President, we have a new therapy. We're extremely optimistic. I'm asking you to delay Euthanasia Protocol."

69

Somewhere near Isla de Alborán
Mediterranean Sea

"How LONG?" David demanded.

"Brenner said he would get back to me as soon as possible. Continuity has their hands full—"

"We'll be at Isla de Alborán within three hours. When we get there, I'll have to arm Shaw and Kamau and do something with the scientists. We need to figure out which one of them killed Martin and disabled the boat. "

Kate sat on the bed. She knew if they began debating the killer it would simply devolve into another fight. And she didn't want to fight, not with him, not at that moment. She slipped her shirt off and threw it on the chair.

David's eyes flashed. He took out his sidearm and covered it with a pillow. He pulled his shirt off, then his pants.

He stepped toward Kate, and she kissed his abdomen. He pushed her down onto the bed and crawled on top of her.

For a moment, the entire world outside faded away. She didn't think about the plague, or the Immari, or Martin's note, or the killer on board. David. He was all she wanted, the only thing in the world that mattered to her.

It was hot as blazes belowdecks, but David hadn't bothered to adjust the air.

He rolled over on the bed and lay there naked, beside Kate, both of their bodies soaked with sweat. His breathing slowed before hers, but neither said a word.

Time stood still. They both stared at the ceiling. David didn't know how long it had been, but Kate turned to him and kissed his neck just below his chin.

The sensation brought him out of the moment, and David asked the question he had avoided thinking about since the call with Dr. Brenner. "You think this is going to work? That Continuity can just take Janus and Chang's research and just... I don't know, '*snap it together*' like the Triforce and magically have the cure?"

"Triforce?"

"Seriously?"

"What?"

"From Zelda," David said. "You know, Link collects the Triforce to rescue Princess Zelda and save Hyrule."

"I never saw it."

"It's uh... a video game, not a movie." *How can she not know this?* That was more shocking to David than Martin's code. But... it was a discussion for another day. She probably also didn't know the difference between *Star Wars* and *Star Trek*. He likely had a lot of work to do, assuming they lived through the next few hours. "Look, forget Zelda, my question is whether this can work. Do you believe it?"

"I have to. We're doing all we can, and that's all we can do."

David lay back on the bed and stared at the ceiling again. What was the point he was trying to make? He didn't even know. All of a sudden, he felt scared. Apprehensive. It wasn't the battle that loomed on the horizon. It was something else, a feeling he couldn't put his finger on.

Kate sat up again. "How do you know so much about boats?" She was trying to change the subject.

"I used to own one in Jakarta."

"Didn't know secret agents had time for leisurely activities like boating," she said, somewhat playfully.

David smiled. "It wasn't a boat of leisure, I assure you. But it could have been. It was an element of an escape plan—if I ever needed it. And it came in handy, if you recall."

"I can't recall. I wish I could." She straightened the covers.

She was right; David remembered now. The Immari had drugged her during her interrogation. She remembered very little from his rescue of her and their escape.

"What did you do with it?" she asked.

"The boat? Gave it to a Jakartan fisherman." He smiled and looked away. "It was a good boat though." At that moment, he wondered where the boat was, if Harto had taken his family from the main island of Java to one of thousands of smaller uninhabited islands in the Java Sea. They would have a chance there. Harto could fish, and his family could gather. The plague couldn't touch them there, and the Immari wouldn't come after a few people on a deserted island. The way the world was going, they could end up being the last people on earth. Maybe the world would be better off that way, if simple people inherited the earth and lived as humans had for ninety-nine percent of its history.

"Where'd you learn boating? You just pick it up?"

"From my father. He used to take me sailing when I was a kid."

"You talk to him much?"

David shifted awkwardly on the bed. "No. He died when I was young."

Kate opened her mouth to speak, but David cut her off. "Don't worry about it. It was a long time ago. '83. Lebanon. I was seven."

"The bombing at the Marine barracks?"

David nodded. His eyes drifted over to the Immari uniform and to the silver oak leaf of a lieutenant colonel. "He was thirty-seven and already a lieutenant colonel. He might have made brigadier general or even higher. That was my dream as a kid. I had this image in my mind of standing in a Marine Corps uniform with a general's star on my shoulder. It's funny, I can still see the picture of myself that I held in my mind for so long. It's amazing how clear your dreams are when you're a kid and how complicated life gets after that. How a single ambition turns into a hundred desires and details—most of which are about what you want and who you want to be."

Kate took her eyes away from him, then turned in the bed and lay beside him, looking away.

Was it her way of giving him space? David didn't know, but he liked having her beside him, how her soft skin felt on his, her warm body heating the places where they touched.

"The day of the funeral, my mother came home and placed the folded-up flag over the mantel. It sat there for the next twenty years, in a triangle-shaped dark wood case with a few too many coats of varnish and a glass door. Beside it she placed two pictures: a headshot of him in his uniform and a picture of them together, somewhere tropical, somewhere they were happy. The house was filled with people that day. They kept saying the same things. I went into the kitchen, got out the biggest black trash bag I could find and filled it with my toys—anything that was a soldier, a tank, or even remotely connected to the military. Then I went in my room and played Nintendo for about the next three years."

Kate gently kissed his head where his forehead met his hairline. "Zelda?"

"I got the Triforce like two million times." He looked over at her and smiled. "Then, at some point, I got really interested in history. I read everything I could get my hands on. Military history in particular. Especially European and Middle Eastern history. I wanted to know how the world got to be the way it is. Or maybe I thought being a history teacher would be the safest job in the world, the farthest place on the planet from an actual battlefield. But when 9/11 happened, the only thing I wanted to do was be a soldier. It's like when my world was turned upside down, I wanted revenge, but I also wanted to do the one thing I thought I would be good at—what I was destined to do all along but afraid to do. Maybe a man can't escape his fate. No matter what you do, you can't change what you really are, what's deep down inside you, supposedly dead and buried but driving you all along."

Kate didn't say anything, and David appreciated that. She simply pressed her body next to his and buried her face in the space between his head and his shoulder.

Sometime later, David felt her breathing slow, and he knew she was asleep.

He kissed her forehead.

As his lips released, he realized just how exhausted he was. Mentally, from discussing Martin's notes; physically, from his time with Kate; and emotionally, from telling her the things he had never told anyone.

He moved the gun out from the pillow and laid it next to him, where he could get to it easily. He glanced at the door. He would hear it if it opened. He would have time if anyone came for them. He would just close his eyes for a second.

70

When David opened his eyes, he knew he was back in the Mediterranean villa. Kate stood beside him. An arched wooden door loomed at the end of the hall. On their right, two open doors flooded the narrow space with light.

David knew the doors and the rooms beyond—he had seen Kate there.

This is her dream. I'm in it, David thought.

Kate walked to the end of the hall and reached for the door.

"Don't," David said.

"I have to. The answers are behind it."

"Don't do it, Kate—"

"Why?"

David was scared, and here in the dream, he knew why. "I don't want anything to change. I don't want to lose you. Let's stay here, where we are."

"Come with me." She opened the door, and light consumed the corridor.

He raced after her, bounding through the door—

David sat up in bed, panting, fighting for air.

He had thrown Kate off of him, but it hadn't awoken her.

He rolled her head to face him. "Kate!"

Sweat poured off of her. But her pulse was faint. She was burning up. And she was unconscious.

What do I do? Get one of the doctors? I can't trust them. Terror—of a magnitude he'd never felt before—gripped him. He pulled her close to him.

To Kate's surprise, the door led her outside.

She turned to look at the door, but—a massive ship towered above her. She stood on a beach, and the ship spread out on the shore. Somehow Kate knew what it was—the *Alpha Lander*. What the primitive humans on this world would call Atlantis.

She looked down. She wore an environmental suit.

The sky above her was dark, ash-filled. At first she thought it was night, but she saw a dim sun directly overhead, struggling to break through the ash that blanketed the clouds.

Impossible, Kate thought. This is the Toba Catastrophe, seventy thousand years ago.

A voice echoed in her helmet. "Last recorded life signs are just beyond the ridge, bearing two-five degrees."

"Copy," she heard herself say as she set off at a brisk pace across the ash-covered beach.

Beyond the ridge, she saw them: black bodies stacked on the ground from the valley all the way to the mouth of a cave.

She crossed the distance and entered the cave.

The infrared sensors in her suit confirmed it: they were all dead.

She had almost given up hope when a single sliver of crimson lit up her display. A survivor. She moved closer.

Behind her, she heard footsteps. She turned to find a large

male, an incredible physical specimen. He barreled toward her with something in his hand.

She gripped her stun baton, but the male broke off his charge. He collapsed next to the female and handed her something: a rotting piece of flesh. She tore into it wildly.

Kate saw it now. The female carried another life sign. An infant. Two hundred forty-seven local days since inception.

The male collapsed back against the wall of the cave. Had he been the chief of his tribe? Perhaps. These two would die here, in this cave, and it would be the end of their species.

My species too, Kate thought. *They are my people, maybe the last of them. With one genetic change, I can save them. I can't watch them die. I won't.*

Before she knew what she was doing, she had hoisted both hominins onto her shoulders. The suit's exoskeleton and computerized weight distribution bore their bulk with ease. They were too weak to fight back.

On the ship, she rushed them to the lab.

Their species was too young for a full genetic modification. That would kill them. She made a decision: to give them the genetic precursor. That would save them. But it would cause problems. She would be here to help them, to guide them, to fix the issues. She had all the time in the world, in the universe. She would raise them. Full activation would come later, when they were ready.

"What are you doing?" a man's voice called from behind her.

It was her partner. Her mind raced. What should she tell him? "I'm..."

He stood there in the doorway, light spilling into the lab from behind him. Kate couldn't see his face. She had to find out who he was. She stood and walked toward him, but she still couldn't see his face.

Kate knew he was waiting for her answer. *I have to tell him something. I'll use the truth, but spin it.*

"I'm conducting an experiment," she said, just as she reached him. She grabbed his shoulder, but the light still hid his face.

David wiped another sheet of sweat off Kate's face. *That's it, I have to get a doctor. I won't let her die in my arms.*

He set her down on the bed, but she grabbed him and inhaled sharply. She gulped mouthfuls of air, and her eyes fluttered wide open.

David searched her face, trying to understand. "What the hell happened? I ran through the door, but—"

"I did it," she gasped.

"What?"

"Toba. Seventy thousand years ago. I saved the dying humans."

She's delirious, David thought. "I'm going to get the doctors."

She gripped his forearm tightly and shook her head. "I'm fine. I'm not crazy. These aren't just dreams. They're memories." She was finally getting her breath back. "*My* memories."

"I don't—"

"In 1978, I wasn't just *born* from the tube—I was *resurrected.* There's so much more going on here than we realized."

"You're—"

"I'm the scientist who gave us the Atlantis Gene. I'm one of the Atlanteans."

PART III

THE ATLANTIS EXPERIMENT

71

Somewhere near Isla de Alborán
Mediterranean Sea

David tried to process what Kate had said. "You're—"

"An Atlantean," Kate insisted.

"Look, I..."

"Just listen, okay?" Kate had regained her breath.

A knock came from the door.

David grabbed his gun. "Who is it?"

"Kamau. We're T minus one hour, David."

"Understood. Anything else?"

A pause.

"No, sir."

"I'll be out shortly," David called to the door. He turned to Kate.

"What the hell is going on?"

"I remember now, David. It's like a flood, like a dam has broken. Memories. Where to start—"

"How do you have these memories?"

"The tubes—the Immari thought they were healing pods. That's only half of what they are. They heal, but their main purpose is to resurrect Atlanteans."

"Resurrect?"

"If an Atlantean dies, they return in the tubes, with all their memories, just as they were before they died. The Atlantis Gene—it's more than what we think it is. It's a remarkable piece of biotechnology. It causes the body to emit radiation, a sort of subatomic download of data. Memories, cell structure, it's all collected and replicated."

David stood there, unsure of what to say.

"You don't believe me."

"No," he said. "Trust me, I believe you. I believe everything you just said is true." His thoughts drifted to his own resurrection, his rebirth, both in Antarctica and Gibraltar. He sensed that she needed him. She was going through something he couldn't begin to understand. "If anyone in the world believes you, it's me. You heard my story—my resurrection. But let's walk through it. First things first: how could you have an Atlantean's memories?"

Kate wiped the sweat from her face. "In Gibraltar, the ship was damaged, almost destroyed. The last thing I remember was going back into the ship. During the explosions, I was knocked out, and my partner... he grabbed me. I don't know what happened after. I must have died. But I didn't resurrect. The ship must have turned the resurrection off—either because it was damaged or there was no escape. Or maybe he turned it off—my partner." Kate shook her head. "I can almost see his face... He saved me. But somehow I didn't return in the tube. In 1919, my father put Helena Barton—my mother—in the tube. I was born in 1978. The tube is programmed to bring the Atlantean back to the moment it died. It grows a fetus, implants the memories, then matures the fetus to the standard age."

"Standard age?"

"About my age now—"

"The Atlanteans don't age?"

"They do, but you can disable aging with a few simple genetic changes. Aging is just programmed cell death. But it's taboo for the Atlanteans to disable aging."

"It's taboo not to age?"

"It's seen as... oh, it's hard to explain, but a sort of *greed for life*. Wait, that's not exactly right. It's that and it's a sign of insecurity—forgoing aging signifies clinging to an unfinished youth, as if you're not ready to move on. Forgoing death implies a life unfinished, a life one is not happy with. But certain groups are allowed to disable aging and maintain the standard age—deep-space explorers being one group."

"So the Atlanteans—" David hesitated. "You're... a space explorer?"

"Not exactly. I'm sorry, I keep using the wrong words." She held her head for a moment. "Will you see if there's some kind of headache medicine in the bathroom?"

David returned with a bottle of Advil, and Kate took four and dry-swallowed them before David could object to the dose. *She's the doctor. What do I know?*

"The two of us, we were a science team—"

"Why were you here?"

"I... can't remember." She rubbed her temples.

"Scientists. What kind? What's your specialty?"

"Anthropology. What would be the closest term? Evolutionary anthropologists. We were studying human evolution."

David shook his head. "How could that be dangerous?"

"Primitive world research is always dangerous work. In case we were killed in the field, we were programmed to resurrect so we could resume our work. But something went wrong with my resurrection. With me, it implanted the memories, but it couldn't advance me—my unborn body was trapped inside my mother. These memories have lingered in my subconscious for decades until now—until I reached the standard age." She slumped onto the bed. "Everything I've ever done has been driven by these subconscious memories. My decision to become a doctor, then a researcher. My choice to develop a gene therapy for autistic individuals, it's simply a manifestation of my desire to correct the Atlantis Gene."

"Correct it?"

"Yes. Seventy thousand years ago, when I introduced the Atlantis Gene, the human genome wasn't ready for it."

"I don't understand."

"The Atlantis Gene is extremely sophisticated. It's a sort of survival and communications gene."

"Communications... Our shared dreams?"

"Yes. That's how we were able to access it—to communicate subconsciously via subatomic particles, radiation, passed between our brains. It began when you were in northern Morocco, and I was in southern Spain. It's because we both have the Atlantis Gene, and we're linked. Humans won't be able to use 'the link' for thousands of years. I gave humans the Atlantis Gene so they could survive. The survival aspects were the only goal. But it spun out of control."

"What?"

"The humans, the experiment. We had to make periodic genetic modifications—changes to the Atlantis Gene." She nodded to herself. "We used gene therapy retroviruses to make the modifications—yes, that's it: the endogenous retroviruses in the human genome, that's what they are—fossils from past gene therapies we gave the humans, the incremental updates."

"I still don't understand, Kate."

"Martin had it right. It's incredible. He was a genius."

"I—"

"Martin's chronology of Atlantis Gene modifications—they don't stop at twelve thousand five hundred years ago."

"Right..."

"His 'missing delta' and 'Atlantis Falls' refers to the destruction of our ship and my science team's demise. The end of our changes in the human genome."

"So that means—"

"The changes went on. Someone else has been interfering with human evolution. Your theory was right. There are two factions."

Dorian closed his eyes. He could never sleep before battle. They were only hours from Isla de Alborán, from capturing Kate and taking her to Ares. When he freed the Atlantean, he would finally discover what he truly was, who he was. He felt nervous. What would he learn?

Dorian tried to picture Ares. Yes, he was there, staring back at him, a warped image reflecting off the curve of glass—an empty tube.

Dorian stepped back. A dozen tubes spread out in a semicircle. Four held primates or humans. It was hard to tell.

The doors behind him opened with a hiss.

"You should have never come here!"

Dorian knew the voice, but he could hardly believe it. He turned slowly.

Kate stood before him. She wore a suit that was similar to his but different. His was a uniform. Hers was more like the coveralls of someone working in a sterile research facility.

Kate's eyes grew wide when she saw the tubes. "You have no right to take them—"

"I'm protecting them."

"Don't lie to me."

"*You* put them at risk. You gave them part of our genome. You underestimate our enemy's hatred. They will hunt every last one of us."

"Which is why you should never have come—"

"You are the last of my people. And so are they."

"I only treated one subspecies," Kate said.

"Yes. I realized that when I took the samples. That species will never be safe now. You need my help."

72

Somewhere near Isla de Alborán
Mediterranean Sea

KATE WENT to the sink and washed her face, as if doing so could clear away the cobwebs in her mind and help her remember. She felt the answers, the whole truth was there in the recesses of her mind, just out of reach.

When she returned, David was waiting for her in the stateroom, his body armor on, that "ready for war" expression on his face that she knew by instinct now.

"How do you know there are two Atlantean factions?"

"I just know it. And the ships. Martin had it right. They're from two different groups."

"There are miles of tubes in Antarctica. What do they hold? More scientists? Soldiers? An army?"

Kate closed her eyes and rubbed her eyelids. It was all a jumble, yet the answers were there. "I... can't remember. I don't think they're explorers."

"Soldiers, then."

"No. Maybe. Just give me some time. It's like my whole brain is burning."

David sat on the bed and put his arm around her. They sat in silence for a few minutes. Finally he said, "We'll make landfall in less than an hour. We have to make a guess about the killer."

Kate nodded.

"My suspects are Shaw and Chang, in that order," he said.

"Let's work backwards here," Kate said. "Let's start with motive. Who would want to kill Martin—why would any of them want to kill him?"

"Martin was close to a cure—we know that from his notes."

"So anyone who wanted to prevent him from finding a cure should be our chief suspect," Kate said. "It's clear to me that Chang and Janus want to find a cure. That rules them out for me. We know preventing a cure is priority number one for the Immari. There's only one person on this boat who was a loyal Immari soldier when this all began. Kamau."

"It's not him," David shot back.

"How can you be so sure?"

"He saved my life in Ceuta."

"That may have been his mission—to save you and follow you to me."

David exhaled. "Let's move on. Chang was also an Immari loyalist when this began." Kate could see that he was angry now. "Hell, he's the biggest mass murderer on this boat. How many did he kill in China? Hundreds, thousands?"

"I don't think he could have broken Martin's neck," Kate said.

"Maybe not while he was alive, but what... what if Chang had already killed Martin? You said he gave him a therapy on the plague barge. What if that therapy killed him, and Chang broke his neck *after the fact* to hide it?"

"We can't test that theory. There's no way to do an autopsy here. Kamau is a better suspect. He's a trained killer."

"So am I. So is Shaw."

"You haven't mentioned Janus."

"I just... don't think it's him. I don't know why."

"Shaw saved my life in Marbella," Kate said.

"That could have been his mission—"

"That *is* his mission—"

"His *Immari* mission," David said. "There's another motive. Forget the cure. What if Martin knew who the SAS operatives were, and he knew that Shaw wasn't one of them?"

David's words silenced Kate.

"You said Shaw sure knew his way around that Immari camp."

"From the sounds of it, you got up to speed pretty quickly too."

David shook his head. "Touché."

There was something Kate wanted to say before the discussion, or argument, or whatever it had become, went any further. "Look, I don't know who killed Martin or what we should do. But I know this: whatever you decide, I will go along with it."

David kissed her burning forehead. "That's all I need."

Everyone was assembled on the yacht's upper deck. David handed Kamau an automatic rifle and a sidearm. A matching automatic rifle hung from David's shoulder.

Shaw looked from David to Kamau. "You're not arming me—"

"Shut up," David said. "We'll arrive at Isla de Alborán in twenty-five minutes. This is what we're going to do."

When David had finished relating his plan, Shaw shook his head. "You'll get us all killed. Kate—"

"This is what we're doing," she said flatly.

In the ship's cockpit, David nodded to Kamau, who then activated the radio. "To the outpost at Isla de Alborán, we are Immari officers, survivors from the battle of Ceuta. We request permission to dock."

The outpost responded, asking for Kamau's rank and Immari officer code. He called it out quickly and calmly, his back to David.

"They've cleared us to dock," Kamau said.

"Good. Let's proceed."

73

Isla de Alborán

DAVID ADJUSTED THE BINOCULARS. From the ship's cockpit, Isla de Alborán was coming into view. The rising sun illuminated the tiny rock platform that rose out of the Mediterranean. It was smaller than a city block. At the far end, stood a simple two-story stone and concrete building. It looked almost like a medieval jail. A lighthouse rose at the center, looming over the plain building.

On the other end of the island, the helipad held three helicopters that waited silently.

A dock spread out at the base of the twenty-foot-high cliff where the stone island met the sea. David adjusted the boat's course for the dock.

"Do they usually keep a complement of three Eurocopter X3s?"

Kamau shook his head. "No. Usually only one. They have received reinforcements. They could be from the primary Immari fleet or the invasion force in southern Spain."

David considered the development. Each helicopter could carry a dozen people. There could be over forty armed soldiers in the building, waiting to attack. Too many.

He made a mental adjustment to his plan.

Kamau tied the boat off at the dock and began climbing the staircase that led out of the cliff, up to the surface.

There had been no soldiers on the dock, and at the top of the stairs, he stopped, surveying the bare rock-and-sand landscape that spread out before him. There were no soldiers here either, just dust blowing in the wind. The lighthouse waited fifty yards ahead. The tower cut a dark shadow out of the rising sun, like a pathway of darkness leading into the unknown.

Kamau stepped out of the shadow. He wanted them to see that he was unarmed—that might save his life. He held his hands out at his sides.

Approaching an armed installation without a single weapon made him uneasy, but there were no alternatives.

A shot rang out and dust flew up from the ground three feet beside him.

Kamau stopped and raised his hands.

On the roof of the building, three snipers emerged.

Seven soldiers ran out of the building and surrounded Kamau.

"Identify yourself!" one of the soldiers barked.

Kamau kept his hands up and his voice calm. "I take it you received my message. You need to arm me, and we need to storm the boat now. They're onto me."

The soldier hesitated. "How many on the boat?"

"Two soldiers, well armed and well trained. They're on the upper deck, waiting for me to return. Three scientists belowdecks, each locked in a separate cabin. Unarmed. The female is the package. We need her unharmed."

The Immari soldier spoke into his radio, and three more soldiers exited the building and joined the seven standing around Kamau.

"You need to arm me—"

"Shut up. Stay here," the soldier said. "We'll sort you out after." He motioned for his men to follow him. He set off with seven of them, leaving two to guard Kamau. There were only two men on the roof now; one of the snipers must have joined the raiding party.

Kamau stood there, his hands still slightly raised, and watched as the troops reached the end of the rock platform, stormed the stairs, and descended toward the dock below.

He focused intently on the boat.

Five seconds, ten seconds, fifteen seconds, twenty—

A massive explosion erupted from the dock, sending a wave of fire up the rock cliff. The blow sent Kamau and the two soldiers beside him to the ground. He rolled and punched the closest one, knocking him out. The other was on his knees now, and Kamau lunged for him. The man tried to land a blow, but Kamau pulled him in close. He slammed the man's head into the ground and felt his body go limp.

Without looking up, he grabbed a grenade from the man's side and hurled it onto the top of the building, hoping to take out the snipers before they regained their positions. He took another and lobbed it onto the roof—in case he had missed. The two explosions rang out just as Kamau threw a third grenade through a plate glass window on the building's first floor.

He grabbed the soldier's automatic rifle and barreled toward the building. He had to make it to the building, get to cover beside the window. If the grenade exploded before then, it would spray shards of glass and debris, shredding him.

David pumped his legs faster. The fins propelled him through the water, and he couldn't help but take in the reefs surrounding Isla de Alborán. Under different circumstances, he could spend days diving here, taking it all in. But he had to hurry. He pushed on. He tried to form a map in his mind, tried to estimate how far he'd gone. If he came up too soon, near the outpost building, the snipers on the roof could easily pick him off.

Finally, he decided to emerge from the water. He quickly shed the tank and scuba gear. He was unarmed, save for his knife.

He walked to the face of the rock cliff and waited. He wanted to look over, to see how close he had gotten to the helicopters, but he didn't dare risk it.

He waited.

The booms of the explosions echoed. David instantly sprang into action. He pulled himself up onto the flat dusty platform and ran full-on for the helicopters. They were at least sixty yards away.

From the outpost, he heard two more explosions.

Kate adjusted her grip on the gun. She felt so awkward holding it. The tiny life raft bobbed wildly in the sea.

"For what it's worth, I'm really sorry about this, guys."

"I understand completely," Dr. Janus said.

"I concur," Dr. Chang agreed. "This was truly the only course."

Shaw muttered under his breath. Curse words were the only phrases Kate could discern, and she thought she was probably glad she didn't hear what he'd said.

In the distance, an explosion rocked the tiny island, and Kate watched pieces of the one-hundred-thirty foot yacht rain down onto the Mediterranean.

To her surprise, she felt a sense of loss as she watched the ship burst into flames. For all the stress and worry during the ship's voyage, she had treasured her time belowdecks with David. She wondered what the future held.

David had almost reached the three helicopters when he saw Kamau emerge on top of the building.

David stopped in his tracks, turned to the building, and waited.

Kamau shouldered a sniper rifle, pointed it at David and the helicopters, and swept left to right several times.

He relaxed his grip on the rifle and signaled to David: all clear.

David hadn't expected that. He assumed there would be at least one soldier guarding the helicopters. Sloane wouldn't have left the helicopters unguarded. He wasn't there—David was sure of that now.

The base commander had put all his resources into taking the boat. Or...

David reached the first helicopter, quickly looked inside, then darted between the others. All empty. Kamau was right: there was no one here.

Why? Had they booby-trapped the helicopters? David needed to find out which one had the most fuel. He approached the door of the closest helicopter and looked in. There was no trip wire. He gripped the handle and began to turn it.

Kamau raced through the building, searching for spare fuel tanks. He found them in a first-floor storage room. He grabbed two of them and exited the building. David was there waiting for him.

"Any sign of Sloane?"

Kamau shook his head.

"This must be an advance team—a test to see if the rail guns would shoot them down. Sloane would never risk his life. We should hurry; he can't be far behind." David considered something. "Did you see any explosives inside?"

"Yes."

"Bring them. Let's leave a surprise for Sloane."

Five minutes later, David sat in the helicopter, calmly watching the ground of Isla de Alborán float away. The view changed to open sea, and Kamau adjusted the helicopter's path. The life raft that held Kate and the three men had drifted a bit, but it was still easy to find.

They followed the protocol David had laid out on the yacht: Kate and the bag with the guns and computer equipment came up first, followed by Janus, Chang, and Shaw—in that order.

When everyone was aboard, Kamau spoke over the radio in David's helmet. "Where to?"

In truth, David had no idea. But... they couldn't go north toward Spain, or south toward Morocco, or west to the Atlantic. "East. Stay low."

74

Isla de Alborán

Dorian saw the two thick columns of smoke long before the tiny island of Isla de Alborán came into view.

The pilot stopped Dorian's lead helicopter to hover a half kilometer from the island, allowing everyone in the three-helicopter convoy to survey the outpost.

A massive yacht burned at the dock. A stone and concrete two-story building with an attached lighthouse also burned violently. Dorian hadn't missed them by much. Maybe an hour.

"Sir," the pilot said, "it looks like we missed the party."

The man was clearly suffering from "compulsive state-the-obvious syndrome"—a situation Dorian felt had grown to epidemic proportions among the men surrounding him.

"Very perceptive. You should have been an analyst," Dorian mumbled, pondering what to do.

"Bravo-leader, this is Bravo-three. Our fuel is down to forty percent. Request permission to put down and acquire fuel—"

"Negative, Bravo-three," Dorian barked into the helmet.

"Sir?" The pilot in his own helicopter turned to face him. "We're at less than fifty percent as well—"

"Bravo formation: maintain your distance from the outpost. Bravo-three, light up the closest helicopter."

The adjacent helicopter launched a missile that decimated one of the two remaining helicopters on the island's helipad. A split second after the impact, a second, more violent eruption spewed from the island.

"They booby-trapped the helicopters?" the pilot said.

"Yes. Hit the other one too," Dorian said. "What's our closest fuel source?"

"Marbella or Grenada. The invasion force reports both areas are secured—"

"They're going east."

"How do you—"

"Because they know we're behind them, and they have nowhere else to go." Dorian focused on Kosta, his assistant, who sat across from him. "Do we have a plague barge in the area—to the east?"

Kosta typed feverishly on his laptop. "Yes but it's almost to port in Cartagena."

"Turn it around. Tell them to head south on an intercept course with us."

"Yes, sir."

"Any word from him?" Dorian asked. The last message had said *Isla de Alborán. Hurry.* Was he in danger?

"No, sir." Kosta glanced out the window, down at the burning island. "He could be KIA—"

"Don't ever say that to me, Kosta."

Dr. Paul Brenner was sleeping on the couch in his office when the door burst open, slamming into the wall, practically scaring him to death.

Paul pushed up from the couch and fumbled for his glasses on the coffee table. He was groggy, disoriented. The hours of sleep were the best he had had in... quite some time.

"What—"

"You need to see this, sir." The lab tech's voice was shaky.

Excitement? Fear? By the time Paul got his glasses on, the man had fled the room.

Paul raced after him, down the hall of the CDC command center, to the infirmary. Rows of beds surrounded by plastic tents spread out before him. Paul could see only blurry glimpses of what lay inside. What he *didn't* see scared him most. No motion, no lights, no rhythmic "beep, beep, beep."

He walked deeper into the room. He pulled the plastic back at the closest bed. The cardiac monitor was silent, dead, turned off. The patient that lay below it was still. Blood flowed from her mouth, staining the white sheets.

Paul slowly walked over to his sister's bed. The same.

"Survival rate?" he asked the technician in a lifeless tone.

"Zero percent."

Paul trudged out of the wing, dreading every step, forcing himself to go on. He was hollow, truly hopeless, for the first time since the outbreak had begun, since Martin Grey had invited him to Geneva twenty years ago and told him that he needed his help with a project that could save humanity in its darkest hour.

At the Orchid Ops room, the glass doors parted again. The screens that had displayed the Symphony algorithm result a few hours earlier had been replaced with a map of the world. It bled red with the casualty statistics from around the globe.

The faces around the room reflected the quiet horror of the

image on the screen. Solemn stares greeted Paul as he stepped inside. There were fewer faces peering at him than there had been. Some members of the team were plague survivors, immune, just as Paul was. But for most, Orchid was their key to survival, and it had finally failed them. Those team members were in the infirmary. Or the morgue.

The remaining men and women, who usually hovered around the tables pacing and arguing, all sat silently now, dark black bags under their eyes. Full Styrofoam cups of coffee littered the tables.

The team leader stood and cleared his throat. He began speaking as Paul advanced into the room, but Paul didn't hear a word. He focused on the map, as if in a trance, as if it were drawing him in.

Boston Orchid District: 22% of total population confirmed dead.

Chicago Orchid District: 18% of total population confirmed dead.

He scanned the statistics.

In the Mediterranean, just south of Italy, a single island glowed green, like a single pixel that had burned out or malfunctioned.

Paul pressed the interactive screen, and the map zoomed.

Malta

Valletta Orchid District: 0% confirmed dead.

Victoria Orchid District: 0% confirmed dead.

"What is this?" Paul asked.

"A ruse," one of the analysts shouted.

"We don't know that!" another put in.

The standing team leader held his hands up. "We're getting mounting casualty reports around the world, sir."

"Malta hasn't reported?" Paul asked.

"No. They have. They report no casualties."

Another analyst spoke up. "The Knights of Malta have issued a statement saying they 'provide shelter, care, and solace in this dark time of crisis and war as they have before.'"

Paul glanced back at the map, unsure what to say.

"We think," the team leader began, "that they're simply trying to perpetuate the myth of the Knights Hospitaller, or worse, to attract any able-bodied individuals to help them hold the island."

"Interesting..." Paul mumbled.

"Everyone else is reporting anywhere from fifteen to thirty percent casualty rates at this point. We think the numbers in some places are a little off. The Vatican Orchid District is claiming twelve percent; Shanghai-Alpha District is thirty-four percent, while Shanghai-Beta is roughly half that..."

Paul wandered toward the door, his mind racing.

"Sir? Is there another therapy?"

Paul turned to the analyst. He wondered if the White House had put a man on the team, someone who could report back to his superiors with a firm up or down on the latest treatment, an informant that could tell Washington whether to proceed with the takeover of Continuity and then the Euthanasia Protocol.

"There is... something else," Paul said. "Something I'm

working on. It's related to Malta. I want you to contact the directors of Victoria and Valletta Districts. Find out whatever you can."

Paul's assistant ran into the room. "Sir, the president's on the line."

75

Over the Mediterranean Sea

It was quiet in the large helicopter, and David credited the slight vibration for helping Kate fall fast asleep shortly after boarding. He sat straight up against the seat, staring out the window. Kamau and Shaw were up front, in the cockpit, with Kamau flying; Janus and Chang sat across from him. Both wore exhausted, impassive looks on their faces.

Kate had slumped into him, her head resting on his shoulder. David didn't dare move. He held his sidearm under his right leg, ready to use it at a moment's notice.

With Kate sleeping on his shoulder, his gun in his hand, and all four suspects straight ahead, David felt better than he had since they'd found Martin dead. Knowing they had delivered a cure didn't hurt either.

Kate's breathing was even and calm, unlike the sweaty, torturous dreams she had endured on the yacht. David wondered where she was, what she was dreaming... or remembering.

Janus spoke softly, careful not to wake Kate. "I want to commend you, Mr. Vale. I am rarely so impressed with anyone as I was with your performance on the boat. Your grasp of history was... remarkable. I had taken you for a simple soldier."

"Don't worry about it. Happens all the time." David suspected Janus was working up to something, priming him like a suspect who had valuable information, but he couldn't imagine where the scientist was going with it.

"For me, one mystery remains."

David raised his eyebrows. Extraneous words ran the risk of waking Kate.

Janus held Martin's code out, letting David take it in once again.

PIE = Immaru?

535...1257 = Second Toba? New Delivery System?

Adam => Flood/A$ Falls => Toba 2 => KBW

Alpha => Missed Delta? => Delta => Omega

70K YA => 12.5K YA => 535...1257 => 1918...1978

Missing Alpha Leads to Treasure of Atlantis?

"The last line of Martin's code: 'Missing Alpha Leads to Treasure of Atlantis.' What do you think it means?" Janus folded the note back up. "I am also curious why Martin included the note about PIE at the top. It seems... unnecessary—if our theory is that the cure lies in the genome of Kate and the survivors of the two bubonic plague outbreaks in the past."

David had to admit: the man had a point. "Could be camouflage, or a false path to throw off anyone who found the notes."

"Yes, perhaps. But I have another theory. What if we have

missed a piece—another genetic turning point. Alpha. Adam. The introduction of the Atlantis Gene."

David considered the theory. "Maybe... but plague bodies from the sixth and thirteenth centuries aren't exactly easy to find, and there are millions of them buried throughout Europe. You're talking about a single body, buried somewhere in Africa, seventy thousand years ago... It would be beyond impossible to find."

"That is true," Janus said with a sigh. "I only mention it because you seemed to have most of the insight into the notes. Your history background appears to be more relevant than my science, strangely." He glanced out the helicopter's window. "I wonder if Martin found it. If he somehow located the remains of Adam, if he left a clue somewhere in this note."

David considered his words. Was there something else there?.

"Another consideration," Janus said, "is Martin's intention. He obviously knew Kate was part of the genetic puzzle, but his primary goal was to trade the cure for her safety. If he had identified all the pieces, perhaps he designed the final clue—the location of Adam—just for her."

"Except there's no clue, no dates, no locations. Just 'Missing Alpha Leads to Treasure of Atlantis.' We don't even know what the *treasure* is."

"Yes; however, I have a theory. If we consider the Tibetan tapestry, which we all agree is the key to Martin's code and chronology, there is a very clear piece of treasure in the depiction: the ark the primitives carry into the highlands at the time of the flood and the fall of Atlantis."

David nodded, almost involuntarily. Why hadn't he seen it before? And what did it mean? How could Adam lead to this treasure? And what was inside the box—the Ark? "Yes... that's interesting..." David mumbled.

"One last point, Mr. Vale. The first line in the code: 'PIE = Immaru?' Why do you think Martin put it in there?"

"To direct us to the tapestry?"

"Yes but clearly Kate already knew about that. Might it be a trail to something? It seems... extraneous. It could be taken away, and the chronology would be intact. It adds no further practical information, nor does the last line that references treasure. Unless, of course, they are actual clues, leading us to Adam and this treasure, somehow unlocking the secrets of this 'Atlantis Experiment.'"

Chang looked up, as if he had awoken from a dream. "You think—"

"I think," Janus said, "that there is still more to this. I wonder if we could wake Kate to get her opinion. It seems the entire mystery hinges upon her."

David involuntarily pulled Kate closer to him. "We're not waking her."

Janus swept his eyes over her quickly. "Is she not well?"

"She's fine," David said, in the loudest tone he'd managed since the conversation began. "She needs her rest. Let's all take a break."

"Very well," Janus said. "May I ask our destination?"

"I'll tell you when we get there."

76

Kate thought this dream was far more vivid than the others. Not a dream... a memory. She stepped into the ship's decompression chamber and waited. *Alpha Lander*, that was the ship's name.

The suit she wore moved slightly as the air swirled around it.

The massive doors parted, revealing the beach and rocky cliff she had seen before. The blanket of black ash that had covered the land before was gone.

The voice in her helmet was crisp, and Kate jumped slightly at the sound. "Recommend you take a chariot. It's a long walk."

"Copy," Kate said. Her voice sounded different, mechanical, emotionless.

She walked to the wall and held her hand to the panel. A cloud of blue light emerged, and she worked her fingers to manipulate it. The wall opened, and a hovering alloy chariot moved out into the room and waited for her.

Kate stepped onto it and worked the control panel. The chariot rotated and zoomed out of the room, but Kate barely felt any motion—the device created some sort of bubble that kept the inertia from swaying her.

The chariot moved over the beach, and Kate looked up. The sky was clear—no traces of ash. The sun burned brightly, and Kate saw green vegetation looming beyond the rock cliff that bordered the beach.

The world was healing. Life was returning.

How long had it been since she had administered the therapy—the genetic technology the humans would come to call the Atlantis Gene? Years? Decades?

The chariot rose to clear the rocky ridge.

Kate marveled at the green, untouched landscape. The jungle was returning, rising from the ashes like a new world that had been created from scratch—a vast garden built as a sanctuary for these early humans.

In the distance, a column of black smoke rose into the air. The chariot charged on, and the settlement emerged on the horizon. They had built it at the base of a high rock wall, to better protect them from predators in the night. The camp was arranged so that there would be only one way into it, and that entrance was heavily guarded. Shanties and lean-tos formed a circle, the largest structures built directly into the wall at the rear of the camp. The blazing communal fire at the center of the camp also helped ward off predators.

Kate knew the humans would learn to make fire later, but at this point in their development, they could only keep fires that had already been created by sources like lightning. And keeping the fire burning was imperative to the camp—for the protection it offered and for cooking the food that would help their brains develop.

Four males stood around the fire, feeding it, tending it, ensuring it never went out. The fire rose from a square stone pit. Large boulders ringed the towering blaze, forming a wall that kept the children from the inferno. And there were so many children, maybe even a hundred of them, scurrying about, playing, and motioning to one another.

"Their population is exploding," her partner said. "We must do something. We have to limit the tribe's size."

"No."

"Unchecked, they will—"

"We don't know what will happen," Kate insisted.

"We will make it worse for them—"

"I'm going to inspect the alphas," Kate said, changing the subject. The issue of their rapid population expansion was a concern, but it didn't have to be a problem. This world was small, but it was big enough for a much larger population—if they were peaceful. That would be her focus.

The chariot set down, and she stepped out. The kids around the camp stopped and stared. Many wandered toward her, but their parents rushed forward and shoved them to the ground. They fell down as well, placing their face to the ground and extending their arms.

Her partner's voice was even more solemn. "This is very bad. They take you for a god—"

Kate ignored him. "Proceeding into the camp."

Kate motioned for the humans to stand, but they remained face-down. She walked to the closest one, a woman, and stood her up. She helped the next person up, and then everyone was standing, rushing to her. They mobbed her as she waded past the crackling fire at the center of the camp.

She spotted the chief's hovel instantly. It was larger and adorned with ivory tusks. Two muscled men stood guard at the entrance. They stepped aside as she approached.

Inside, an elderly man and woman sat in a corner. The alphas. They looked so old, so withered. They had never fully recovered from their near-starvation in the cave. Three males sat around a square stone platform in the center of the hut, discussing what looked like a map or some sort of drawing. They all rose. The taller male stepped toward Kate, but the elderly man stood on shaky limbs and waved him back. He bowed to Kate, then turned and pointed at the wall. A series of primitive drawings were spread out in a line. The helmet translated them:

> Before the Sky God, there was only darkness. The Sky God remade man in his image and created a new world, lush and fertile for him. The Sky God brought back the sun and promised that it would shine so long as man lived in the image of God and protected his kingdom.

It was a creation myth. A surprisingly accurate one. Their minds had advanced in a great leap forward, achieving self-awareness and problem-solving abilities they had never before known. They had focused their newfound intellect on the greatest questions of all: *How did we get here? What are we? Who created us? What is our purpose?*

For the first time, they realized the mysteries surrounding their existence, and they groped for answers, as all emerging species do. In the absence of absolute answers, they had recorded their interpretations of what they believed had happened.

Her partner sounded nervous now. "This is extremely dangerous."

"Maybe not—"

"They are not ready for this," her partner declared with finality.

They were too young for mythology, but if their minds had already come this far, the religion that followed could be a powerful tool. "We can fix this. This... could save them."

Her partner didn't answer.

The silence weighed on Kate. It would be easier if he argued. The silence demanded she justify her claim.

"We have to end this experiment now, before we make it worse for them," her partner said, softly now.

Kate wavered. Developing religion this early was indeed dangerous. It could be corrupted. Selfish members of the tribe could use it for their own benefit, manipulating the others. It could be used as a justification, a basis for all sorts of evil. But if used correctly, it could be an incredibly civilizing force. A guide.

"We can help them," Kate insisted. "We can fix this."

"How?"

"We give them the human code. We'll embed the lessons, the ethics, in their stories."

"It cannot save them."

"It has worked before."

"It will only last so long. What happens when they stop believing? Stories won't satisfy their minds forever."

"We will address that problem when it arises," Kate said.

"We can't be here to hold their hand. We can't solve all their problems."

"Why can't we? We made them. Some of *us* is in them now. It's our responsibility. And helping them may be the most important thing we could possibly do. We certainly can't go home."

Kate's words brought only silence now. Her partner had relented. For now. She hated the disagreement, but she knew what she had to do.

She held her forearm out and tapped at the controls. The ship's computer quickly analyzed the primitives' symbolic language. It was crude, but the computer easily fashioned a dictionary. She held her palm out, and the light shone from it onto the stone wall. The symbols she projected lined up just below the lines the tribe had written.

The elderly alpha nodded. Two males rushed from the hovel and returned with two large green leaves filled with a thick burgundy liquid. Kate thought it was crushed berries at first, but then she realized what the leaves held: blood.

The males began painting the gray stone walls with it, copying the symbols she projected.

Kate opened her eyes. She was back in the helicopter with David. The door was open, and the sea glistened below. The breeze filled her lungs, and she realized how much they hurt. She wiped a sheet of sweat from her forehead. David's eyes were on her.

He pointed to the headset hanging in the middle of the space. Kate lunged for it and pulled it over her ears. He leaned forward and clicked the dial.

"We're on a private channel now," he said.

She involuntarily glanced at Chang and Janus sitting across from them.

"What's wrong?" David asked, focusing on her, ignoring the scientists who sat impassively.

"I don't know."

"Tell me."

"I don't know." Kate wiped another layer of sweat off her face. "The memories are coming; I can't stop them now. I'm reliving them... it's like they're... taking over... I think, I don't know. I'm scared that I'm losing... some of myself."

David's eyes raked over her, as if he were not sure what to say.

Kate tried to focus. "Maybe I'm at the age when the Atlantean therapy, whatever the tube does, the memory restoration, takes over and—"

"Nothing is taking over. You're going to stay exactly the way you are."

"There's something else. I think we're missing something."

David cut his eyes to the two scientists. "What?"

"I don't know."

Kate closed her eyes, but no memories came this time. Only sleep.

77

Over the Mediterranean Sea

KATE AWOKE to vibrations on her thigh. The first thing she saw was David's eyes.

She took the vibrating phone from her pocket and glanced at the number. It was a 404 area code. Atlanta, Georgia. The CDC. Continuity. Paul Brenner. Understanding washed over the stupor of her sleep as she answered the call. She listened. Paul Brenner was panicked now. He spoke quickly, the phrases hitting her like punches. *Trial failed. No alternative therapies. Euthanasia Protocol has been authorized. Can you help?*

"Hang on," she said into the phone.

She sat up. "It didn't work," she said to David, Chang, and Janus.

"There's more, Kate. Another piece of the genetic puzzle," Janus said. "We need more time."

"We have something," Kate said into the phone. She listened, then nodded. "Yes, okay. What? Okay, no, we're..."

She looked at David. "How close are we to Malta?"

"Malta?"

Kate nodded.

"Two hours, maybe a little less at top speed."

"The Orchid Districts in Malta report no casualties. Something is happening there."

David didn't say a word. He climbed past Chang and Janus in the seat across from her and began talking to Shaw and Kamau in the cockpit—setting a course for Malta, Kate assumed.

Kate rubbed her head. There was something different about the way she felt. She was more... detached, clinical, numb. Almost robotic. She had full command of her mind; she just experienced the scene as if it were happening to someone else. The danger was intense—the annihilation of ninety percent of the human race... yet she felt as though she were in the middle of a science experiment, where the outcome was uncertain but would have no impact on her. *What's happening to me?* Her feelings, her emotional core seemed to be slipping away.

When David returned, he slumped back onto the bench beside Kate. "We can be in Malta within two hours."

Kate held the phone to her ear and began conversing with Paul. *We're going to check it out—Can you hold them off—We don't know what's there—Do your best, Paul—This isn't over.*

She ended the call and focused on the group.

Janus spoke before she had a chance. "It was here the entire time, under our noses." He pointed to the page containing Martin's note. "Missing Alpha Leads to Treasure of Atlantis. *MALTA.*"

Kate watched as David scanned the code. His face changed. What was that: guilt?

She interrupted the pause. "Martin had been looking for it—whatever it is—for a long time. He thought it was in southern Spain, but he told me he had been wrong about the location. He must have added the last note regarding Malta, after the fact."

"Do you know what it is?" Janus asked. "The Treasure of Atlantis?"

Kate shook her head.

David pulled her close to him. "We'll know in a few hours." However, the look in his eyes said something different: *Do you remember?* Kate closed her eyes and tried to focus.

The rustle of the suit under the pressure of the decompression chamber was unmistakable.

The voice in Kate's helmet was crisp. "There are two settlements now."

"Copy."

"Sending coordinates of original settlement."

Kate's helmet displayed a map. Their ship, the *Alpha Lander*, was still off the coast of Africa, where she had originally administered the Atlantis Gene.

A floating chariot waited silently in the middle of the chamber. The doors opened slowly, revealing the scene beyond. Kate mounted the chariot and zoomed from the ship.

The world was even more green. How much time had passed?

At the camp, she realized exactly how much. There were at least five times as many huts as she had seen before. At least a generation had passed.

And the nature of the camp had changed. Muscled warriors, dressed in clothes and wearing war paint, patrolled the perimeter. They turned to her and raised their spears threateningly as she floated in.

She gripped the stun baton.

An elderly man hobbled out to the warriors and shouted to them. Kate listened in amazement. Their language progress was stunning: they had already developed a complex linguistic structure, though the words used at this moment were a bit more "informal."

The warriors lowered their spears and backed away from her.

She set the chariot down and ventured into the camp.

There was no bowing and groveling this time.

Up ahead, the chief's shanty had grown as well. The simple lean-to had morphed into a temple with stone walls, built directly into the rock cliff.

She marched toward it.

The villagers lined up on each side, keeping their distance, fighting to see her.

At the threshold of the temple, the guards stepped aside, and she entered.

In the altar at the end of the cavernous room, a body lay. A circle of the black humans knelt before it.

Kate paced to them. They turned.

From the corner of her eye, she saw an elderly male making his way toward her. The alpha. Kate was amazed that he had survived so long. The treatment had produced remarkable results.

Kate glanced back at the dead body, then read the symbols above the altar. *Here lies the second son of our chief. Cut down in the fields by his brother's tribe, for greed of the fruit of our lands.*

Kate quickly read the remainder of the text. It seemed that the chief's oldest son had formed his own clan—a group of nomads that roamed the countryside, foraging.

The chief's younger son had taken over the fields where this tribe hunted and gathered. The younger son was seen as his father's successor, the next chief. They had found him dead in the field, and the trees and shrubs picked clean. He was the first victim of the older brother's raids, and they feared there would be many more. They were preparing for war.

"We must stop this," her partner said into Kate's helmet.

"And we will."

"War will sharpen their minds, enhance their technology. It is a cataclysm—"

"We will prevent it."

"If we move one of the tribes," her partner said, "we can't manage the genome."

"There is a solution," Kate said.

She held her hand up and projected symbols onto the wall.

You will not take retribution on the unworthy. You will leave this place. Your Exodus begins now.

Kate opened her eyes to see David staring at her.

"What?"

"Nothing." She wiped sweat from her forehead. The memories were changing her more quickly now. Taking over. She was becoming more of what she'd been in the distant past and less of the woman she had become, the woman who had fallen in love with David. She pulled closer to him.

What can I do? I want to stop this. I opened the door, but can I close it? It felt as if someone was holding her down and pouring the memories down her throat.

Kate stood in another temple. She wore the suit, and the humans before her crowded around another altar.

Kate looked out of the opening of the temple. The landscape

was lush, but not as fertile as it had been in Africa. Where were they? The Levant, perhaps?

Kate walked closer.

The stone box on the altar; she had seen it before—in the Tibetan tapestry, in the depiction of the Great Flood, when the waters rose and consumed the coast, wiping out the cities of the ancient world. The Immaru had carried this box to the highlands, she was sure of it. Was this the treasure that waited in Malta?

The members of the tribe rose from the ground and turned to face her.

In the alcoves flanking the temple's main corridors, Kate now saw dozens of members of the tribe kneeling, meditating, seeking the stillness.

They would become the Immaru, the mountain monks who had carried the Ark into the highlands, who had kept the faith and tried to live a life of righteous observance.

Kate walked down the aisle.

"You know what must be done," her partner said.

"Yes."

At the altar, the crowd stepped aside, and she climbed the stairs and peered into the stone box.

The alpha, the tribe's founder and chief, lay there, still, cold, finally dead. His countenance was eerily similar to how it had been on the day when Kate had first seen him, in the cave, when he brought the rotting piece of flesh to his mate, when he collapsed against the wall and lay dying. She had hoisted him up then and saved him. She couldn't save him now.

She turned back to the masses gathered around the altar. She could save *them*.

"This is dangerous."

"There is no alternative," Kate said.

"We can end this experiment, here and now."

Kate involuntarily shook her head. "We can't. We can't turn back now."

When she had finished the modification, she stepped off the altar. The attendants swarmed around her, rushing past the box. They brought something out—a stone top—and placed it upon the box.

She watched as they engraved a series of symbols on the side of the Ark.

Her helmet translated them:

Here lies the first of our kind, who survived the darkness, who saw the light, and who followed the call of the righteous.

Kate opened her eyes.

"I know what's in Malta, what the Immaru were protecting."

David's eyes said, *Don't say it.*

"Is it part of the cure?" Janus asked.

Chang leaned in.

"Maybe," Kate said. She focused on David. "How long to Malta?"

"Not long."

Dorian pulled the sat phone out of his pocket and read the message.

```
Heading east. Destination Malta. Where
the hell are you?
```

He walked back across the plague barge's deck and climbed into the helicopter. "Let's go."

78

KATE STOOD in an immense command center. Holographic displays, the likes of which she'd never seen, covered the far wall. The maps tracked the human populations on every continent.

At the corner of the room, an alarm flashed to life.

Incoming vessel.

Her partner raced to a control panel and manipulated the blue cloud of light that emerged. "It's one of ours," he said.

"How?"

Fifty thousand local years ago, Kate and her partner had received a transmission: their world, the Atlantean home world, had fallen—violently, in a day and a night. How could there be survivors? Had the home world distress call been wrong? Kate and her partner had heeded the call, had hidden their science expedition, assuming they were the last of their kind, assuming they were now alone in the universe, marooned, two scientists who could never go home. Had they been wrong?

"The vessel is a life raft." Her partner turned to her. "A resurrection ship."

"They can't come here," Kate said.

"It's too late. They're already landing. They intend to bury the ship under the ice-capped continent at the southern pole." Her partner worked the control panel. He seemed to tense up. *Is he nervous?*

"Who's on the ship?" Kate asked.

"General Ares."

A current of fear ran through Kate.

The scene changed. Kate stood on another ship—not the lander. This vessel was massive. Glass tubes stretched out before her for miles.

Footsteps echoed in the space.

"We are the last," came a voice from the shadows.

"Why did you come here?" her partner called.

"For the protection of the Beacon. And I read your research reports. The survival gene you gave the primitives. I find it... very promising." The owner of the voice stepped into the light.

Dorian.

Kate almost reeled back. General Ares was Dorian. How? She focused. The man's face wasn't Dorian's, but the overwhelming sense Kate got was that Dorian was inside this man. Or was it the opposite? Was Ares inside Dorian and Kate was sensing that element—seeing it in its purest form now? When Kate looked at Ares, all she saw was Dorian.

"The inhabitants here are of no concern to you," her partner said.

"On the contrary. They are our future."

"We have no right—"

"You had no right to alter them, but what is done is done," Dorian said. "You endangered them the instant you gave them part of our genome. Our enemy will hunt them, as they will hunt us, to the far reaches of the universe, no matter where we go. I wish to save them, to make them safe. We will advance them, and they will be our army."

Kate shook her head.

Dorian focused on her. "You should have listened to me before."

The endless rows of glass tubes faded, and Kate was in a different room in the same structure. There were only a dozen glass tubes here, standing on end, spread out in a semicircle before her. It was a room she had seen before—in Antarctica—where she, David, and her father had met up.

Each tube held a different human subspecies.

The door opened behind her.

Dorian.

"You... are conducting your own experiments," Kate said.

"Yes. But I told you I cannot do this alone. I need your help."

"You delude yourself."

"They will die without you," Dorian said. "We all will. Their fate is our fate. The final war is inevitable. Either you give them the genetic equipment they need, or they perish. Our destiny is written. I am here for them."

"You're lying."

"Then leave them to die. Do nothing. See what happens." He waited. When Kate said nothing, he continued. "They need our help. Their transformation is only half complete. You must finish what you have started. There is no other way, no turning back. Help me. Help them."

Kate thought of her partner, his protests.

"The other member of your little expedition is a fool. Only fools fight fate."

Kate's silence was a signal—to her and to Dorian. He seemed to feed on her indecision.

"They are already splintering. I have collected the candidates, conducted my own experiments. But I don't have the expertise. I need you. I need your research. We can transform them."

Kate crumbled. She felt herself falling under his spell. It was the same as before—*her* before, in San Francisco. She tried to rationalize, tried to think of a deal, but her mind drifted to her experiences in Gibraltar and then in Antarctica when he had cornered her. It was history repeating itself. The same players, playing out a different game, with the same end, on a different stage. Except this was long before, in another life, in another era.

"If I help you," she said, "I want to know that no harm will come to my team."

"You have my word. I will join your expedition—as a security adviser. There are additional steps you all need to take to cloak our presence here. And you will program your resurrection tubes to my radiation signature—just in case something... unfortunate were to happen to me."

Dorian leaned his head against the helicopter's back rest and closed his eyes. It wasn't a dream. It wasn't a memory. He was there, in the past.

And Kate had been there, opposing him, then helping him. He had taken her research, used it, and betrayed her when he was done with her.

Across the ages, they were playing out the same scenario, fighting to transform the human race: her advocating for them, him trying to create an army to face a superior enemy.

Who was right?

He sensed something more: Kate was remembering these events at the same time he was, as if they were connected to the same network, each receiving signals, memories from the past, driving them on to some destination. She would receive the code this way. That's what Ares had planned. Had he programmed the case for this?

Seeing Kate had energized Dorian. Her fear, her vulnerability. It was the same as before. He'd had the power then, and he would have it again. She had the research and information he needed. And soon *he* would have it. She just had to remember.

But it wasn't only what had happened. It was some piece of information—a *code* that she would remember. Ares had known that. Dorian was close to Kate, and she was close to remembering the rest, remembering the code he needed. He had timed it perfectly. Soon, he would take her and take the last secret, the thing she held most dear, and her defeat would be complete.

79

Somewhere near Malta
Mediterranean Sea

ON THE HORIZON, David saw the two larger islands of Malta come into view.

In the last six hundred years, this tiny group of islands, which covered just one hundred twenty-two square miles of land, had been the most fought-over place on the entire planet.

During the Second World War, no place on Earth saw as much bombing per square foot as Malta. The German and Italian air forces had leveled it, but the British had held strong.

In some cities, like Rabat, the residents had retreated underground, living in stone rooms connected by miles of tunnels. The catacombs there were legendary. They had been used in Roman times to bury the dead, but they had kept countless Maltese residents alive during the carnage of the Second World War.

Almost four hundred years before the Luftwaffe had unleashed hell on Malta, a different devil had appeared on their doorstep: the armada of the Ottoman Empire. In 1563, Sultan

Suleiman the Magnificent had brought his fleet of almost two hundred ships, carrying nearly fifty thousand troops—the largest fighting force in the world at the time.

The months that followed became known as the Great Siege of Malta, and it had changed the history of the world. The siege was a clash of unimaginable brutality, one of the bloodiest battles ever fought. An estimated one hundred thirty thousand cannonballs were fired at or from the island. One in every three inhabitants of Malta was left dead. The Knights Hospitaller, along with a ragtag group of around two thousand soldiers drawn from Spain, Italy, Greece, and Sicily, held the island for four months, until the Ottoman fleet, counting its dead in the tens of thousands, turned and sailed home.

Had the Ottomans taken Malta in 1565, many historians agree that their forces could have easily taken mainland Europe, disrupting the Renaissance to come and forever changing the fate of the world.

The residents of Malta had fought to the death. Were they defending something besides their lives?

David glanced at the paper. *Missing Alpha Leads to Treasure of Atlantis.*

What was there on Malta? Some ancient treasure? What could it have to do with the plague ravaging the world?

David was a historian. He believed in facts: the truth culled from multiple sources, verified by eyewitnesses, ideally with differing backgrounds and motivations.

Treasure was the lure of fools. As were mythical objects. The Ark of the Covenant. The Holy Grail. He didn't believe in either of them. Military history was always more reliable. Generals counted their dead. Somewhere between the sums on each side lay the truth.

And the truth was that countless armies over the ages had fought for Malta, and rarely had it fallen.

The memories were clearer now, and Kate felt almost as though she could control them, as though she could move backward and forward in time.

She wore the Atlantean suit again, and the scene around her was of a one-room primitive hut. She looked out the door of the hovel. The climate seemed different. It was damp, rainy out, and the vegetation was almost tropical. Not Mediterranean. Perhaps they were in southern Asia.

Three women sat on the ground, working feverishly on something. Kate walked to them and peered down. The Tibetan tapestry. *They are creating the warning, in case we fail*, she thought.

The Atlanteans had given it to them—*she* had given it to them—as a backup plan.

She knew that now.

She walked out of the shack, into the open air of the camp. The settlement felt nomadic, as if it had been erected hastily and would be abandoned soon.

A makeshift temple loomed at the center. She walked to it. The guards at the entrance stepped aside, and she wandered in. The stone Ark was here. Monks circled it, sitting cross-legged, heads bowed.

At the sound of her steps, one man rose and hurried to her.

"The floodwaters will come soon," Kate said.

"We are prepared. We will leave tomorrow for the highlands."

"Have you warned the other settlements?"

"We have sent word." He continued to look down. "But they will not heed our warning. They say they have mastered this world. They do not fear the water."

The primitive temple disappeared, replaced by glass and steel walls, covered mostly by holographic displays.

Kate stood in *Alpha Lander*'s control center, beside her partner, staring at the global map.

The coastlines across southern Asia wavered. The floodwaters were advancing, changing the continent forever, sinking the settlements along the coast, some of which would be lost permanently.

The hologram switched to a satellite view of a group of humans hiking into the mountains, away from the floodwaters. They carried the stone box she had seen—the Ark.

Kate still couldn't see her partner, but out of the corner of her eye, she saw Dorian, standing rigidly, glancing at the display with only a hint of interest.

"This is not all bad," Dorian said. "A population reduction could allow us to consolidate the genome, perhaps eliminate some of the problems."

Kate didn't want to answer. Dorian was right, but she knew the solution, and she dreaded it. The "problems" he had left unspoken had been accelerating in the past ten thousand years—uncontrollable aggression, a tendency to war, to preemptively eliminate any perceived threats. This increasing trend was a fundamental dysfunction of the survival gene: the humans' logical minds knew that their environment had a finite amount of resources, that with their current technology their habitat could support only a limited number of people. They wanted to ensure that it was *their* people, *their* genetic line that survived. War—eliminating any competitors for the finite amount of resources—was their solution. But their race to genocide was happening too fast, as if there were someone else intervening, working against them.

At the back of Kate's mind, another possibility lingered: Dorian had done this. Had he betrayed her? Taken the research she had provided him and modified it? She had kept her collaboration with Dorian/Ares from her partner. She knew her partner would disagree, but she saw no alternative. The tribes of humanity would need every genetic advantage they could get—if Dorian's story, his assertions about their enemy, were true.

What else could I do? Kate asked herself. She had chosen the only logical course.

The holographic display began changing. Red spread out across the map: casualty readings.

Her partner spun back to the control station. "Population alarms."

"We must intervene," Dorian said.

"No. Not at these levels," her partner shot back. "We follow our own local precedent—only in the event of an extinction risk."

Kate nodded. Their "precedent" had been set seventy thousand years ago—when she had chosen to provide the Atlantis Gene to the humans in that cave, their subspecies teetering on the brink of extinction.

She opened her mouth to speak, but the holographic wall exploded in alarms.

`Population Alert: Subspecies 8471: 92% Extinction Risk.`

Kate traced the location. Siberia. The Denisovans. The floodwaters couldn't have touched them there. What was happening?

Another alarm emerged on the screen, in another location.

Population Alert: Subspecies 8473: 84% Extinction Risk.

This subspecies was confined to the islands of Indonesia. The Hobbits. The subspecies that would come to be known as homo floresiensis. What was driving their population collapse? The pressure of the flood, combined with the aggressive humans who had settled the islands relatively recently? Kate already knew the history. They would go extinct. What was the year? She glanced at the hologram, deciphering the Atlantean dating scheme.

The memory was from approximately thirteen thousand years ago. Another realization struck her at that moment: she would witness the fall of Atlantis. She would see what had happened. The missed delta.

A third population alarm went off.

Population Alert: Subspecies 8470: 99% Extinction Risk.

Neanderthals. Gibraltar.

Her partner raced to a control panel and began working it with his fingers. He turned to Dorian.

"You did this!"

"Did what? This is *your* science experiment. After all, I am merely a military adviser. Doctors, do not let me get in your way."

Her partner paused, waiting for Kate's input.

"Prioritize. Save the ones we can," she said.

He manipulated the panel, and Kate felt the ship lift up. The map traced its trajectory. It flew across Africa, barreling toward Gibraltar.

Dorian stood still as a statue, staring at her.

Her partner paced to the door, then stopped. "Are you coming?"

Kate was lost in thought. Three extinction alerts—at the same time. What did it mean?

Was Dorian eliminating all the other subspecies? Was he testing his weapon, ending the experiment? Did he have what he wanted? Had he betrayed her? Or was it something else?

Was this the work of their enemy?

Chance? Pure coincidence?

Either alternative was possible, yet remote.

Kate would know the truth soon.

Her partner's back was to her.

Another question dominated her mind. Who was he?

She needed to see his face, needed to find out who her ally was.

She needed answers.

She tried to focus. "Yes. I'm coming."

Dr. Paul Brenner stared at the patchwork of screens in the Orchid Ops room. Casualty rates were climbing.

Budapest Orchid District: 37% of total population confirmed dead.

Miami Orchid District: 34% of total population confirmed dead.

A countdown clock in the corner read:

1:45:08

Less than two hours to the near extinction of the human race. Or at the very least, the next stage in human evolution.

After the Euthanasia Protocol, there would be two groups of humans left: the evolving and the devolving. There would be two separate subspecies of humans for the first time in thousands of years. Paul knew that state would end soon, just as it had before: with a single subspecies. And it wouldn't be the less-evolved.

The survivors would have the world to themselves, the genetically inferior cleared away.

80

You're listening to the BBC, the voice of human triumph on this, the eighty-first day of the Atlantis Plague.

This is a special news bulletin.

A cure, ladies and gentlemen.

Leaders from across the Orchid Alliance, including America, the UK, Germany, Australia, and France, have announced that they have finally found a cure for the Atlantis Plague.

The announcements couldn't have come at a better time. The BBC has acquired classified reports and received eyewitness accounts from around the world that claim the death rate is now as high as forty percent in some Orchid Districts.

The announcements were issued in terse statements, and the heads of state have denied all requests for interviews, leaving experts and pundits to wonder about this mysterious cure—specifically, how it could seemingly be manufactured overnight.

Directors of several Orchid Districts, speaking on the condition of anonymity, have insisted that the existing Orchid production plants were already set up to manufacture the new drug, and that it will be handed out within hours.

This has been a BBC special news bulletin.

81

Kate was in the decompression chamber again, wearing the suit. She turned quickly, glancing at her partner. He was also suited up.

"The drones only identified one survivor."

One survivor. Incredible. Too... convenient. "Copy," Kate said.

She turned. Dorian was there. He wasn't wearing a suit. "You two go. I'll manage the ship."

Kate tried to read his expression. Her partner strapped the rest of his field gear on.

Dorian fled the room just as the last of the air was sucked out.

Two floating chariots issued from the walls, and she and her partner each mounted one and flew out of the lander.

The scene was breathtaking: a prehistoric settlement surrounded by stone monuments, like an outdoor amphitheater centered around a vast stone hearth that sent a blazing inferno toward the sky.

Several humans were leading the Neanderthal to the

communal fire, but they released him and backed away as the chariots approached.

Her partner grabbed the Neanderthal, injected him with a sedative, and threw him across his chariot. They turned and raced back to the ship.

"I don't trust him," her partner said on a private channel.

I don't either, Kate thought. But she held her tongue. If Dorian had betrayed them, set this up, it was partly her fault. She had done the research he needed.

Dorian watched the glistening water of the Mediterranean fly by below. He was half-awake, exhausted from lack of sleep.

The memories seemed to assault him now, like a movie he was forced to watch. Another scene came, and he couldn't turn away, couldn't escape. There was nowhere to run from his own mind. The helicopter and the Immari strike team sitting across from him dissolved, and a room rose up around him.

He knew the place well: the structure in Gibraltar.

He stood in the control center, watching Kate and her partner race to save the primitive.

Fools.

Bleeding hearts.

Why can't they accept the inevitable? Their science and their morals blind them to the truth, the unmistakable reality: that this world and the universe that surrounds it, has enough room for only one sentient race. Resources are finite. It must be *us*. We are at war for our lives. These scientists will be remembered as those who were seduced by morality. The code we gave to the primitives, to maintain peace, to perpetuate a lie: that coexistence is possible. In an environment with limited resources and unlimited population growth, one species must triumph over the other.

He manipulated the controls, programming the bombs.

He stepped out of the command center and raced down the corridor.

The turns went by in a flash, and he stood in a room with seven doors. He activated his helmet display and waited. Kate and her partner entered the ship.

Dorian detonated the first bomb—the one buried out at sea. The blast sent a tidal wave at the ship, sweeping it inland. As the receding water dragged it back out to sea, Dorian activated the other bombs. They would tear the ship, the *Alpha Lander*, apart.

He walked through one of the seven doors, and he knew he was in Antarctica, in his own ship. *Soon, I will free my people, and we will retake the universe.*

He walked past the control station and picked up a plasma rifle.

He returned to the middle of the seven-door room.

There was one escape route for them, only one way out of Gibraltar. He would be waiting.

Kate watched her partner dump the Neanderthal into a tube.

"Ares betrayed us. He is working against us."

Kate was silent.

"Where is he?"

"What should we—"

An alarm lit up her helmet.

Incoming tidal wave.

"He set off a bomb on the ocean floor—"

The shockwave hit the ship, throwing her against the bulkhead.

Pain coursed through her body. Something else was happening to her.

She was losing control. The memories were too real now.

She fought to focus, but everything went black.

David poked his head between Kamau and Shaw, into the cockpit of the helicopter, and surveyed Valletta, the capital of Malta, below. Valletta's narrow harbor was packed with boats. They covered almost every inch of the water, radiating out of the harbor and into the sea. A seemingly endless flow of people raced across the abandoned boats, using them like a series of floating platforms forming a path to the shore. From high above in the helicopter, they looked like ants marching out of the harbor. When they reached land, the four streams of people converged into one horde that coursed through the main thoroughfare of Valletta, making a beeline for the Orchid District. The rays of the rising sun peeked out from behind a tall building's domed top, and David held a hand up to shield his eyes.

Why are they fleeing here? What's here that could save them?

A shudder ran through the helicopter, throwing David into the back seat.

"They've got anti-aircraft missiles!"

"Take us out!" David shouted.

He grabbed Kate and held her. She was almost listless, her eyes absent.

Kate opened her eyes. Another shockwave hit her, but this was a different one—not a tidal wave. She was back in the helicopter, with David. He looked down at her.

What was happening to her? She felt different now. The things she had learned, the memories, they had changed her in some indescribable way. Humanity was... an experiment. Was he part of it?

"What?" he asked her.

She shook her head.

"Are you okay?" he demanded.

She closed her eyes and shook her head, not wanting to confront reality.

David strapped Kate into the helicopter's bench seat and held her as it banked and swerved, the bombs exploding around them. Malta was guarded, as it had been in the past, quite heavily.

They were accepting refugees by boat, but no one could reach it by air.

He picked up the satellite phone. "Dial Continuity," he said to Kate. "Tell them we're in an Immari helicopter, but we are friendlies. Instruct Malta to stop firing on us. We need to land."

He watched as Kate opened her eyes, eyed him briefly, then fought to dial the numbers. A second later, she began conversing quickly with Paul Brenner.

Paul Brenner hung up the phone. Kate and her team were in Malta.

"Get me the director of the Valletta Orchid District," he said to his assistant.

Dorian watched the explosions in the distance. Valletta was firing on any incoming aircraft.

He activated his helmet's mic.

"Find us a refugee boat."

"Sir?"

"Do it. We can't access the island by air."

Ten minutes later, they were hovering above a fishing trawler.

Dorian watched the rope lines descend. His men fell to the boat's deck and raised their weapons. The ship's crew and passengers retreated back into the boat's cabin.

Dorian landed on the deck and glided to the huddling group of people.

"No harm will come to you. We just need a lift to Malta."

David felt the helicopter touch down on the pad. He brushed Kate's hair out of her face. "Can you walk?"

He thought she was so warm, not burning up, but... too warm. *What's happening to her? I can't lose her. Not after all this.*

She nodded, and he helped her out of the helicopter, then wrapped his arm around her and ushered her away from the platform.

An enemy was behind them: Chang, Janus, or Shaw. David didn't know which. But he knew Kamau was behind him as well and that he would watch David's back. Kate was his concern now.

"Dr. Warner!" A man wearing designer glasses and a slept-in

suit greeted them. "Dr. Brenner has informed us about your research. We are here to help—"

"Take us to the hospital," David said. He didn't know what else to say. Kate needed help.

David couldn't believe his eyes. The hospital was state of the art, yet dying bodies were everywhere, and no one seemed to be interested in helping them.

"What's going on here? Why aren't you treating these people?" David asked the district director.

"There is no need. Refugees arrive here sick, and they rise from it in hours."

"Without treatment?"

"Their faith saves them."

David looked at Kate. She was getting better. The sweat had stopped pouring off her brow. He took her aside. "Do you believe this?"

"I believe what I see, but I don't know how it's happening. We need to find the source. Get me something to write on."

David took a legal pad from one of the bedside tables.

Kate sketched quickly.

David looked back at the Orchid District director, who seemed to be watching them like a hawk. In a corner of the hospital wing, Janus was setting up Kate's computer and the sample collector, the thermos-like device he had seen before. Kamau and Shaw stood beside them, eyeing each other as if they were waiting for the bell to ring and a fight to begin.

Kate handed her rough sketch to the director. "We're looking for this. It's a stone box—"

"I—"

"I know it's here. It's been here for a very long time. A group called the Immaru hid it here thousands of years ago. Take us to it."

The director looked away from them, swallowed, then led them away from the people, out of earshot. "I've never seen it. I don't know what it is—"

"We just need to find it," David said.

"Rabat. The rumor is that the Knights of Malta have retreated into the catacombs there."

Dorian flowed with the barbarian hordes of people coursing into the Maltese capital. God, they stank. They carried their sick, pushing and shoving, hoping to rush them to safety.

He held the scratchy blanket around his head, hiding his appearance, trying not to breathe in the putrid odor that assaulted him. Talk about suffering for your cause.

In the distance, beyond the hospital, he saw an Immari helicopter lift off the ground and move further inland.

Dorian turned to the Immari special ops soldier beside him. "They're moving on. Find us a helicopter. We need to get out of here."

82

Malta

From the helicopter's window, David could see the entire small city of Rabat below. It was nothing like he expected.

Rabat was deserted, utterly abandoned, as if every soul had fled the tiny town with only the clothes on their backs. When the plague hit, the people here would have flocked to one of Malta's two Orchid Districts, either Victoria or Valletta.

Across from him, he scanned Janus's and Chang's faces. Blank. Impassive. Through the split in the helicopter's seats, he could see the reflection of Shaw's and Kamau's faces in the glass. Blank. Hard. Focused. The six of them would be alone in Rabat, and Martin's killer would make his move—for Kate, or for the cure, or for whatever his endgame was.

David glanced out the window again, and his mind drifted to history, to safety, to what he knew best.

Rabat lay on the other side of Mdina, the old capital of Malta, a city historians believed had been settled before 4000 B.C.

Malta itself had first been settled by a mysterious group that had migrated down from Sicily around 5200 B.C.

In the twentieth century, archaeologists had found megalithic temples all over the two islands of Malta: eleven in total, seven of which had since been declared UNESCO World Heritage Sites. They were true wonders of the world. Some scientists believed them to be the oldest freestanding structures on the planet. Yet, no one knew who built them or why. They dated back to 3600 B.C. or possibly even earlier. The age of the structures—the history of Malta itself—was an anomaly, a fact that didn't fit into the current understanding of human history.

The dark ages of ancient Greece only reached back to 1200 B.C. The first civilizations, first cities, in places like Sumer, only dated back to 4500 B.C. Akkadia had been settled around 2400 B.C., and Babylon, supposedly, 1900 B.C. Even Stonehenge, the closest megalithic monuments, at least in character, was thought to have been created in 2400 B.C.—which was still over a thousand years *after* some mysterious group had built the towering temples on the isolated island of Malta. There was no explanation for Malta's megalithic structures; their history, and the history of the people who built them, had been lost to the ages.

Historians and archaeologists still debated the birthplace of civilization. Many argued that settlements had arisen in the Indus Valley of present-day India or the Yellow River Valley of present-day China, but the overwhelming consensus was that civilization, defined as functioning, permanent human settlements, had been founded around 4,500 years ago somewhere in the Levant or the wider region of the Fertile Crescent—thousands of miles from Malta.

Yet the remains of those primitive settlements in the Fertile Crescent were sparse and crumbling; a stark contrast to the undeniable, comparatively impressive, and technically advanced stone structures on Malta—which may have predated them. An isolated civilization had thrived here, had erected structures to some higher power, but had somehow vanished without a trace, leaving no history, save for the temples where they had worshiped.

The first settlers on Malta to leave a historical record were the Greeks, followed by the Phoenicians around 750 B.C. About three hundred years later, the Carthaginians succeeded the Phoenicians on Malta, but their reign was cut short with the arrival in 216 B.C. of the Romans, who conquered the islands in a few short years.

During the Roman rule of Malta, the governor had built his palace in Mdina. Almost a thousand years later, in 1091, the Normans had conquered Malta and altered the city of Mdina forever. The Nordic invaders had built defensive fortifications and a wide moat, separating Mdina from the nearest town —Rabat.

Perhaps the most enduring legend of Mdina, however, was that of St. Paul. In the year A.D. 60, the apostle Paul had lived there after having been shipwrecked on Malta.

Paul had been on his way to Rome—against his will. The man who would later be declared an apostle was to be tried as a political rebel. Paul's ship was caught in a violent storm and wrecked on the Maltese coast. All aboard swam safely to land, some two hundred seventy-five people in total.

Legend has it that the Maltese inhabitants took Paul and the other survivors in. According to St. Luke:

And later we learned that the island was called Malta.

And the people who lived there showed us great kindness,

and they made a fire and called us all to warm ourselves...

Luke's testament relates that as the fire was lit, Paul was bitten by a venomous snake but suffered no ill effects. The islanders took this as a sign that he was a special man.

According to tradition, the apostle took refuge in a cave in Rabat, opting to live a humble existence underground, refusing the comfortable surroundings offered to him.

During the winter, Publius, the Roman governor of Malta, invited Paul to his palace. While Paul was there, he cured Publius's father of a serious illness. Publius is then said to have converted to Christianity and was made the first Bishop of Malta. In fact, Malta had been one of the first Roman colonies to convert to Christianity.

"Where should we land?" Kamau called over the radio, interrupting David's reverie.

"In the square," David said.

"At the Church of St. Paul?"

"No. The catacombs are a little farther away. Put us down in the square. I'll lead the way."

He had to focus. Some mysterious group had settled Malta, and the world had fought over this tiny island for thousands of years since. Legends of miraculous healing, evidence of megalithic stone temples that predated civilizations around the world, and now, something on Malta was saving refugees from the plague. How did it all fit together?

He turned to Kate as the helicopter landed. "Can you walk?"

She nodded.

David thought she seemed... distant. Was she okay? He had the irresistible urge to put his arm around her, but she was already out of the helicopter, and the two scientists were shuffling out of their seats, following her.

Shaw and Kamau joined them.

"I assumed the catacombs would be under St. Paul's Church," Janus said.

"No," David half-shouted over the dying roar of the helicopter behind them. He glanced over at St. Paul's Church, the stone building that had been built in the seventeenth century atop the cave—now referred to as St. Paul's Grotto—where the apostle had lived so simply.

As the group cleared the helicopter's dying roar, David explained. "The catacombs are just ahead. For sanitary reasons, the Romans wouldn't allow their citizens to bury their dead inside the city walls of the capital of Mdina. They built an extensive subterranean network of catacombs—burial chambers—here in Rabat, just beyond the city walls." David wanted to add more —the historian in him could hardly resist. The catacombs in Rabat held the bodies of Christian, Pagan, and Jewish bodies, laid side by side, like members of the same denomination, an act of religious tolerance almost unheard of in Roman times, where many officials routinely persecuted religious leaders.

At the same time that the families of Pagans, Jews, and Christians were laying their loved ones to rest in adjacent subterranean burial chambers in the catacombs of Roman Malta, a man named Saul of Tarsus, a Jew and a Roman citizen, was zealously persecuting the early followers of Jesus. Saul had violently tried to destroy the upstart Christian church in its infancy but later converted to Christianity on his way to Damascus—after Jesus's death on the cross. Saul of Tarsus would become known as the apostle Paul, and the catacombs in Rabat had been renamed in his honor.

David focused on the task at hand.

They ducked down another alley, and he stopped at a stone building. The sign read:

MUSEUM DEPARTMENT
S. PAUL'S
CATACOMBS

Janus pushed the iron gate open, then the heavy wood door, and the group wandered into the museum's lobby.

The large marble-floored room was quiet, eerily still. The walls were adorned with placards, photos, and paintings. Glass cases were filled with stone items, and smaller artifacts David couldn't make out crowded several corridors off the main room. Yet all eyes focused on David.

"What now?" Chang asked.

"We set up camp here," David said.

As soon as the words were spoken, Kamau cleared off a table, set down his duffel bag, and began sorting their weapons: handguns, assault rifles, and body armor.

Janus rushed to Kate and held a hand out for the backpack. "May I?"

Kate handed him the backpack absently, and Janus began setting up a research station. He powered up the computer and connected it to the thermos-like device that Martin had given Kate to extract DNA samples.

Janus placed the sat phone on the table. "Should we call Continuity? Report our status?"

"No," David said. "We only call when we have something to report. No sense in... revealing our location."

He glanced at the phone. One member of the team had been doing just that—revealing their location. He grabbed the phone from the table and handed it to Kate. "Hang on to this."

Shaw stood a few feet from Kamau, watching him sort the weapons and armor. David locked eyes with him, and they each stared for a moment.

Shaw broke off first. He strolled nonchalantly to one of the small tables flanking the stairwell that descended into the catacombs. He picked up a folded brochure and began reading it.

"What now, David?" Shaw asked casually. "We wait for a medieval knight to come wandering out, and we ask him if he's seen an old stone box?"

Janus spoke up, trying to break the tension. "I want to point out the urgency of our situation—"

"We're going in," David said.

Kamau took the words as a cue. He attached his body armor and handed another set to David.

"It's a needle in a haystack," Shaw said. He held up the brochure. "The network is extensive. Only a few of the catacombs are normally open to the public, but this... *device* could be anywhere down there. We're talking miles of tunnels."

David tried to read Kate's expression. It was emotionless, almost cold. Was she having another flashback?

"I feel we should split up," Janus said. "We can cover more ground."

"Wouldn't that be... dangerous?" Chang said sheepishly.

"We could go in teams of two: one soldier, one scientist in each one," Janus said.

David considered the proposal. His other choices were leaving someone behind, here in the museum, where they could close the catacombs or acquire backup. He had no good options.

"Okay," David said. "Shaw and Chang, lead the way." David wanted to put his two suspects together, have them break off first, put distance between them and the rest of the group. "Kamau and Janus next. Kate and I will bring up the rear."

"We have no bloody clue what's down there," Shaw half-shouted. "I'm not going down there unarmed. You can shoot me if you like, David."

David walked to the table, picked up a tactical assault knife and threw it at Shaw, point first. Shaw caught it by the handle. His eyes flashed.

"You're armed. You're going first, or I *will* shoot you. Try me."

Shaw paused for a moment, then turned and led the way down the stairway, followed closely by Chang and then the other four.

83

St. Paul's Catacombs
Rabat, Malta

The catacombs were musty and dark. The museum lighting system wasn't functioning, but the glow of the LED lanterns revealed a scattering of display cases and write-ups where tours would pause and read about the chambers.

After about ten minutes, the tunnel split.

"We rendezvous in the lobby in one hour, no matter what. Turn back if you don't find anything," David said. "Try to make a map of where you've been."

"Sure thing, Mom. Back in an hour, and we'll bring our homework," Shaw snapped. He turned and led Chang down the darkened corridor.

Kate, David, Kamau, and Janus walked in silence after that. Five minutes later, the tunnel forked again. Kamau and Janus edged toward the new path.

"Good luck, David," Kamau said.

Janus nodded to both Kate and David.

"You too," David said.

He and Kate walked without a word for a bit. When David thought they were out of earshot of the others, he stopped. "Tell me you know what's going on here. What's saving the people in Malta from the plague?"

"I don't know. In the past, I saw the Ark, but I don't know what happened to it. I saw the Immaru carrying it into the highlands, but I don't know what happened after that."

"There are megalithic stone temples here that are almost six thousand years old—the oldest known ruins in the world. There are legends of miraculous healing dating back to the Roman period, when St. Paul landed on Malta. Could the Immaru have brought the Ark here for safekeeping?"

"It's possible," Kate said, seeming distracted.

"How can it be healing these people?"

"I don't know—"

"What's inside it?"

"The body of Adam, our alpha—the first person we gave the Atlantis Gene. At this point, just his bones."

"How could his bones be healing people?"

"I... I don't know. We did something to him in the past. I was there, but I couldn't see it. I couldn't even see my partner's face. The human genome was splintering—we were having trouble managing the experiment."

"The... experiment."

Kate nodded but didn't elaborate. "David, something is happening to me. It's hard to concentrate. There's something else. Dorian was there—"

"Here—"

"No. He was there in the past. I think he has the memories of another Atlantean, a soldier named Ares who came to Earth after the science expedition."

David stood there, stunned.

"How?"

"He was on the expedition, in Gibraltar. The tubes were reprogrammed to his radiation signature. When Dorian was put in there after the Spanish flu outbreak, he must have awakened with the memories, the same way I got the scientist's memories."

"Incredible," David whispered. A new kind of fear slowly surrounded him, setting in slowly. Dorian had knowledge of the past, possibly even more than Kate. That gave him a tactical advantage.

"What's your plan, David?"

David snapped back to the moment, to the dimly lit stone tunnel. "We find whatever is down here, see if we can use it to find a cure, then get the hell out of here."

"The others?"

"One of them is a killer and a traitor. We leave them down here. We have to put some distance between us. It's the only way to secure you."

Kate followed David through the tunnel.

The catacombs reminded her of the stone passages Martin had led her through below Marbella. In fact, the small town of Rabat itself reminded her a great deal of Marbella.

Kate felt as though a memory were just out of reach—the conclusion of her old life, the balance of the truth of what had happened in Gibraltar. Yet, she felt that if she allowed it to come in, the last of her would flow out. And she would lose David. To her, the memory uncovered was the greatest enemy down here, but she knew David was right: a killer lurked in one of the other tunnels.

84

CDC
Atlanta, Georgia

Dr. Paul Brenner slowly opened the door to his nephew's private hospital room.

The boy lay still. Panic ran through Paul.

A second passed, and Matthew's chest rose slightly.

A breath.

Paul gently pulled the door closed.

"Uncle Paul!" Matthew called as he rolled over and coughed.

"Hey, Matt. I was just checking on you."

"Where's Mom?"

"Your mother's... still helping me with something."

"When can I see her?"

Paul froze, not sure what to say. "Soon," he mumbled absently.

Matthew sat up and broke into another fit of coughing, spraying tiny specks of blood onto his hand.

Paul stared at the droplets of blood that slowly began to flow across the boy's hand, coalescing into small ravines of red.

Matthew eyed it, then wiped his hand on his shirt.

Paul grabbed his arm. "Don't wipe it—just... wait, I'm going to get a nurse." He rose and fled the room. He heard Matthew call to him, but Paul was already out of the room, walking quickly. He couldn't watch, couldn't stay in the room another second. *I'm finally breaking, losing it,* he thought.

He wanted to go to his office, lock the door, and wait until the whole thing, the whole world was over.

His assistant rose at the sight of him. "Dr. Brenner, you have a message—"

He waved his hand at her as he quickly paced past. "No messages, Clara."

"It's from the World Health Organization," she said. She held up two pieces of paper. "And another from British intelligence."

Paul snatched the pages out of her hand and read them quickly. Then he read them again. He turned and stumbled into his office, his eyes still on the pages. *What does it mean?*

He closed the door and quickly dialed Kate Warner. The sat phone didn't ring. Straight to voicemail. Was it off? Out of reception?

"Kate, it's Paul. Uh, Brenner." Of course she knew which "Paul." Somehow even leaving a message for Kate made him nervous. "Look, I heard from my contact at WHO. It seems there's no record of a Dr. Arthur Janus. And I also heard from British intelligence. They have no agents named Adam Shaw. They even checked the classified records." He paused, not sure what to add. "I hope you're okay, Kate."

Dorian slammed the helicopter door and watched the hordes of swarming people grow smaller as he and his special ops team rose above Valletta.

"What's our destination, sir?" the pilot called back to him.

Dorian pulled out his phone. No messages.

"They went west," he shouted. "We'll have to look for their helicopter. Try the cities first."

In the catacombs of St. Paul, below the city of Rabat, Kamau walked in front of Janus. The tall African led the way with an assault rifle. The beam from the flashlight he'd strapped to the gun barely illuminated the wide tunnel. The glow from the lantern Janus carried behind him didn't help much.

"Where are you from, Mr. Kamau?" Janus asked quietly.

Kamau hesitated, then said, "Africa."

"What part?"

Another pause, as if Kamau didn't want to answer. "Kenya, outside Nairobi. Now we should—"

"Near the birthplace of the modern human race. I think it's only fitting that we should have someone from east Africa on our expedition, hunting for the one African who changed history, who set humanity on its course."

Kamau turned back, shining the flashlight in Janus's face. "We should remain silent."

Janus held a hand up to shield his eyes. "Very well."

In another part of the catacombs, Dr. Chang walked just ahead of Shaw. The British soldier had made Chang walk first. "For safety," Shaw had said.

Chang stopped and swung the lantern back to face Shaw.

"Are you recording our path?" Chang asked.

"And leaving breadcrumbs, Doctor. Keep moving."

The lantern light only half-illuminated Shaw's face, and in that instant, Chang thought the man, who was likely in his early thirties, momentarily appeared much younger.

The face—that younger face—Chang knew it. Where had he seen it?

Years, decades ago. Right after he had delivered Kate from her mother's body, from the tubes.

In the memory, Howard Keegan, the Director of Clocktower and one of two members of the Immari council, sat behind a massive oak desk in his office. Chang fidgeted nervously in the chair across from him.

"I want you to do a thorough exam of the boy you extracted from the tube. His name is Dieter Kane, but we call him Dorian Sloane now. He's having some trouble getting... acclimated."

"Is he—"

Keegan pointed his finger at Chang. "You tell me what's wrong with him, Doctor. Don't overlook anything. Just give him a full workup and come back here, understand?"

When Chang had finished the examination, he returned to Keegan's office, taking the same seat in front of the gargantuan desk. He unfolded his pad and began making his report. *Physically, quite fit. Two centimeters taller than the average for his age. Several recent bruises. A few significant scars, also recent...* Chang looked up. "Do you suspect abuse?"

"No, for God's sake, Doctor! *He's* the abuser. What the *hell* is wrong with him?"

"I'm afraid I don't—"

"Listen to me. Sixty years ago, when he went into that tube, he was the sweetest kid in the world. When he came out, he was as mean as a damn snake. He's a borderline sociopath. That tube did something to him, Doctor, and I want to know what it is."

Chang just sat there, unsure what to say.

The side door to the study burst open, and Dorian ran in.

"Stay out, Dorian! We're working here."

Another boy ran in behind Dorian, bumping into him. He peeked out from behind Dorian's shoulder. The face.

The two boys retreated, pulling the heavy door closed behind them.

Keegan sat back in his chair, pinching the bridge of his nose.

Chang hated the silence. "The other boy..."

"What?" Keegan leaned forward. "Oh, he's my son, Adam. I'm raising Dorian as his brother, hoping it will help give him some stability, some sense of family. Dorian's own family is dead. But... I'm scared to death that Dorian's darkness, his sickness, will infect Adam, corrupt him. And this *is* a sickness, Doctor. Something is very, *very* wrong with him."

Chang was back in the stone corridor, the memory gone, the dim light returned. He stared at Adam Shaw, the half of his face he could see. Yes, it was him. Dorian's adoptive brother. Keegan's son.

"What?" Shaw demanded.

Chang took a step back. "Nothing."

Shaw closed the distance on him. "Did you hear something?"

"No... I..." Chang grasped for words, some excuse. *Think. Say something.*

Shaw smiled slowly. "You remember me, don't you, Chang?"

Chang froze. *Why can't I move?* It was like some invisible snake had bitten him, and a paralyzing venom was coursing through every inch of his body.

"I was wondering if you would. It's too bad. Martin remembered me too."

"Help!" Chang yelled out, a split second before Shaw drew the knife from his belt and slashed quickly across Chang's throat and windpipe, spraying blood on the stone wall and sending Chang to the ground, gurgling, clasping his opened throat, fighting for a breath that wouldn't come.

Shaw wiped the bloody knife on Chang's torso, then stepped over the dying man. Shaw placed an explosive on the floor of the tunnel, quickly armed it, and ran deeper into the tunnel.

Kamau stopped at the sound. It sounded like a cry for help. He turned to Janus. The man had something. A weapon?

Kamau raised his rifle.

A blinding light, brighter than anything Kamau had ever seen, assaulted him. A sound, not a vibration, some sort of tuning fork went off in his head. He fell to his knees. What was Janus doing to him? He felt as though his head were swelling, as if his brain were exploding from the inside out.

Janus stepped past him without a word.

The cry for help stopped David in his tracks. Who was it? The killer was making his move.

The sound was close. An adjacent tunnel? An intersecting tunnel?

Kate's voice was a whisper. "David—"

"Shhh. Keep moving." He led the way, racing through the tunnel now. Before, David had paused at every opening, sweeping his assault rifle left and right.

Now speed was the key, putting some distance between them and the sound, getting to a safe, defensible position.

Up ahead, the tunnel ended in a large burial room with a stone table that had been carved out of the rock.

David slowed his pace, his mind wondering what to do. Turn back?

He came to a stop, and an eerie feeling ran up his back. He moved to turn, but a voice called out, "Don't move."

85

St. Paul's Catacombs
Rabat, Malta

DAVID HELD HIS HANDS UP. He could feel Kate's eyes on him, watching his lead, wondering if he would turn and fire on the man behind him. David wanted to, but he didn't know who or how many were back there.

Another voice broke the silence, a voice David knew.

"Lower your weapons. They're the ones we've been waiting for."

David and Kate turned slowly, focusing on the young man who stepped from the shadows of the tunnel.

"Milo," Kate whispered.

"Hello, Dr. Kate." Milo nodded at David. "Mr. David."

"Come with me," Milo said. He turned and led the way through the tunnel, two heavily armed soldiers—Knights of Malta, David assumed—flanking him.

The tunnel opened onto a large square, stone room that was

much larger than the other burial chambers. A half dozen guards stood around the room, guns at the ready.

At the end of the chamber, a stone box lay on a slightly raised altar.

Kate rushed to it and unslung the backpack. She turned back to the soldiers. "Can you lift the top off?"

Milo nodded to them, and four guards released their guns and moved to the box.

"Milo, how did you get down here?" David asked.

"It is a long story, Mr. David, but let's just say... that I wouldn't want to do it again."

"Yeah, I know what you mean."

At the altar, Kate was leaning over into the stone ark, working on something. David walked up beside her and peered into the box. Through the faint light, he could just make out the bones of a single person.

Beside him, Kate manipulated a device David didn't recognize, something from the pack. He knew she was collecting a genetic sample, but he had no idea how.

He turned to the men spread out around the altar in the room. Milo stood silently in the center of them. David thought there was something distinctly different about this young man he had first met at the monastery in Tibet. A maturity, a poise.

David glanced back at Kate. "You have what you need?"

She nodded.

"Milo," David said, "we need to get back to the surface, to our computer, where we can process the sample." He paused. "We think there could be a killer down here."

"We will be fine here, Mr. David." Milo nodded toward the soldiers. "They have been guarding this place for a very long time. And they can see you safely out of the catacombs."

Several soldiers broke from the pack and stood at the

opening to the tunnel that led to the surface. David and Kate fell in behind them.

Out of the corner of his eye, Dorian caught a glimpse of a helicopter on the ground. An Immari helicopter.

He pointed at it. "There! They have to be close by."

As the first rays of sunlight broke across the tunnel, David realized that he no longer heard the guards' footsteps behind them. He glanced back, but the guards were gone. He shook his head. *Add it to the list of mysteries*, he thought.

At the surface, Kate raced to the computer, set down her backpack, and quickly began working.

David checked the magazine in the rifle, a nervous habit, and paced the room, never taking his eyes off the entrance.

"What happens now?" he called over his shoulder to Kate

"I need to upload the new dataset to Continuity and hope they find a therapy from it."

"How long?"

She rubbed her forehead and stared at the screen. "I don't know—"

"Why not?"

She glared up at him. "Well my brain is pretty much fried at this point, and Janus did the last round—he's much better at this than I am."

He took a second to tear his eyes away from the tunnel. "Okay, okay. I just think... that expediency is the order of the day."

A chirping sound broke the tension.

"What's that?"

Kate took the sat phone from her pocket. "There's a voicemail."

Kate set the phone on the table and resumed typing and scanning the computer screen. "You listen to it if you want. I hear *expediency* is the order of the day, and I have work to do."

David glanced at the phone, then swiveled back around to the tunnel and raised his weapon. He made a mental note not to pressure Kate when she was working, and not to use ridiculous phrases that might come back to haunt him.

Deep in the cave, beyond the light, he heard footsteps. They were faint, cautious, as if someone were approaching the entrance—someone who didn't want to be heard.

David got Kate's attention, raised his finger to his lips, and sidestepped away from the opening, taking a position outside the tunnel. He pointed his rifle at it, ready to fire. It would be Shaw—he was sure of it, and he would be ready.

Dorian leaned into the cockpit and eyed the Immari helicopter that sat in the square below.

"Put down beside them?" the pilot asked.

"Of course. May as well send a text message saying where we are. Or light a flare."

The pilot swallowed. "Sir?"

"Put down somewhere else. They could be waiting near the helicopter to ambush us. We'll survey the ground by foot."

Dorian checked his phone again. No messages. Why?

Was Adam dead?

He hoped not. That would be the final loss, the very last family he had, his only relationship. His brother. The only person in the world he trusted to capture Kate Warner. And he was somewhere in Rabat, Dorian could feel it. But why? What was here? Dorian was sure history could be his guide, reveal the exact significance of Rabat, but who gave a damn? History was so much work.

"Do any of you know the history of Rabat? Any significant cultural points?"

The soldiers turned to him, blank looks on their faces.

The pilot called over the intercom, "Mdina was the Roman capital in ancient times. The Phoenicians and the Greeks before them governed from there as well."

Who fills their head with this useless shit? Dorian thought. "Very interesting... But we're not in Mdina, are we? What's in Rabat?"

"They buried their dead here."

"What?"

"The Romans placed a premium on sanitation. And safety. They built walls around their cities and wouldn't let the dead be buried within the walls. Rabat was a suburb—"

"What the hell are you saying? Get on with it!"

"There are burial chambers here. Ancient ones. The catacombs of St. Paul."

Dorian considered this. Yes, it was exactly what David and Kate would be here for—dead bodies, ancient genetic clues to the cure. How many thousands of years were buried below this ancient city, in the stone chambers used over the ages? Had someone hidden an ancient body among these burial chambers, cloaking it, hiding it in plain sight? It didn't matter. All he needed was her, the code, the knowledge in her mind.

Slowly, the figure emerged from the darkness. David gripped the trigger. He depressed it slightly, ready to fire.

The man emerged from the tunnel, his hands raised.

Janus.

Kate stood from the table. "Thank God. I need your help."

Janus closed the distance to her. David instinctively followed the scientist with his gun.

"You found it?" Janus asked.

"Yes—"

"The Ark—from the Tibetan tapestry? It was here? All this time. The alpha. Adam?" Janus asked.

Kate nodded.

"Extraordinary..." Janus mumbled as he eyed the computer. "May I?"

"Of course, please." Kate stepped aside.

"Where's Kamau?" David called, over his shoulder.

"We got separated after the scream."

"He's alive?"

"I certainly hope so," Janus said, as he typed on the computer, his eyes scanning back and forth.

A minute passed with David focusing on the tunnel entrance and Kate and Janus staring at the computer.

Janus nodded. "This is it—the point of origin, the first human to receive the Atlantis Gene. If we combine the genome with those bodies from the bubonic plague and survivors of the Spanish flu outbreak, it all makes sense. I think they can isolate all the endogenous retroviruses from this dataset." He turned to her. "This is it, Kate."

Kate grabbed the sat phone and plugged it into the computer. She worked the computer. "It's uploading."

Janus paced away from the computer, toward the entrance to the tunnel.

"You can't go down there," David said.

"I am afraid I must," Janus answered. He turned to David. "For a scientist such as myself, this is the opportunity of the ages.

The first human of a wholly new tribe, the genetic cataclysm that began all that came after. The history, the science. Despite the risk, I have to see it with my own eyes."

"Stay here—"

Janus slipped into the tunnel before David could stop him.

Kate disconnected the sat phone from the computer and dialed quickly. David took up position between her and the tunnel's entrance.

Paul, I just sent a new data set—Yes—What—No, I didn't check the message.

Kate's eyes went wide. "No... I... thank you for letting me know. Call me back when you have the data." She ended the call. "Janus and Shaw. They're both fakes."

From the tunnel, David heard footsteps approaching the opening. He raised his gun, ready to fire, but the figure emerging from the darkness stopped.

86

St. Paul's Catacombs
Rabat, Malta

KATE FOCUSED on the tunnel entrance, trying to see who was coming. The figure stepped out, his arms in the air.

Kamau.

He stood in the entrance of the tunnel, fighting the light with his arms as if it were drowning him.

"Are you okay?" David asked.

"I... can't see."

David rushed forward and helped Kamau out of the tunnel and to a chair at the long table where Kate sat. She thought he looked disoriented, weakened somehow.

"What happened?" David asked.

"Janus. He blinded me with a light weapon. It disabled me for a while."

David focused on Kate. "He could have manipulated the data."

Kate opened her mouth but stopped when the sat phone began vibrating on the table. She snatched it up and answered quickly.

One result—no—I think you have to—I agree, Paul—Call me back when you know.

She ended the call. The one therapy was their only shot. But...

"They found one therapy," she said. "They're going forward with it. They don't have any alternatives." She stared at David. "We need to talk to Janus."

David walked closer to Kamau. "How bad is your sight?"

"Getting better. Still blurry."

He's putting up a front for his commanding officer, Kate thought.

David handed him an assault rifle from the table. "I want you to shoot anything that comes out of that tunnel."

He turned to Kate. "Chang is dead, I'd bet on it. It's just Shaw and Janus down there. We know where Janus is going. I'll bring him back." To Kamau, he said, "When I'm at the tunnel entrance, I'll call 'Achilles coming out' before I exit."

Kamau nodded.

Then David was gone, into the darkness of the tunnel.

Kate walked to the table and picked up a handgun. She ran her finger over the words engraved into the side. *SIG SAUER*.

"Do you know how to use that?" Kamau's deep voice echoed in the space.

"I'm a real quick learner."

Adam Shaw placed another pack of explosives into the stone cutout in the tunnel. Where to go next? He should have made a map back to the museum lobby; the tunnels were never-ending. Somewhere in the distance, he heard footsteps. He clicked his lantern off.

He receded deeper into the burial chamber that lay just off the tunnel. The rubber grip of the knife made a slight sound against his fingers as he drew it from the sheath.

The approaching figure was carrying a lantern. The light grew brighter with each passing second.

Shaw crouched and waited. The burial chamber was small, a roughly six-foot by ten-foot narrow chamber, one of many hollowed out appendages off the main tunnel.

He tried to pace the footsteps in his mind, knowing he would have only a split second to time his lunge and take his prey.

Closer.

Closer.

The figure came into view.

Janus.

Shaw let him pass. He exhaled. But there were more footsteps behind Janus. Kamau?

They had been together.

Shaw froze.

David.

Chasing Janus.

Then he was gone. And Shaw was glad. In the recesses of his mind, he could admit, barely, that Vale could take him hand-to-hand, even if Adam had the element of surprise. He had read David's file, his Clocktower personnel report, before he had begun this mission. He had been searching for a way to kill him since the second he first saw him, since David had risen out of the waters of the Mediterranean and slammed him against the floating wreckage of the plague barge—impressing upon Shaw, literally, how capable he was at hand-to-hand combat.

But Adam didn't have to worry about David now—he was zooming deeper into the tunnel, away from Kate, the thing David valued most, leaving Shaw open to capture her, complete his mission, and get his revenge upon David.

Adam stepped from the burial chamber and turned left, following the path David had revealed, to Kate.

Janus ran as quickly as he could. Up ahead, the soft glow of lanterns illuminated the stone room.

It would be guarded—if history was any indication.

Janus took the quantum cube from his pocket and slowed his pace. He could see it now, the Ark, lying at the end of the chamber. Amazing. It was just as it had been.

Two guards pivoted from behind the stone walls, blocking his path.

Janus activated the cube, flooding the area with blinding light. He adjusted it, turning it higher.

The men collapsed, and he heard more bodies hit the stone floor inside the room.

He stepped across the threshold and surveyed the scene. Six heavily armed European soldiers and someone else—an adolescent Asian wearing a ceremonial robe.

Janus stepped to the Ark and peered down.

There he was. The first. They had kept him. Told his story. After all these years. They were a remarkable species. They had exceeded all his expectations. It still didn't change what had to be done. He told himself that he had no choice.

He took hold of the alpha's femur bone, lifted it, and swung it violently against the wall of the stone box.

A small metallic chip fell out, then disappeared under the rain of gray dust that covered it.

Janus reached in, brushed the dust aside, and searched for the chip.

It had taken months to find it. It was the last piece. When it was gone...

He held it up to the light, glancing at the technology he and his partner had embedded almost seventy thousand years ago. The small radiation implant had enabled them to make changes to the human genome for tens of thousands of years. Each time they programmed a new radiation regimen, it altered the genome of humans within the implant's range, adjusting the course of humanity. The device was old now, and its power source was almost spent, reducing its range considerably. Janus had wondered if he could find it. But in the face of the current plague, it had performed as planned, running its emergency program, activating the Atlantis Gene, saving those who flocked to be near it. It was a shame so many had to die for Janus to find it. But without the device, nothing stood in the way of the final genetic transformation he had already unleashed.

At that moment, curiosity overcame Janus. He activated the implant's memory module and watched the telemetry scroll by. The implant's records began with the tribe they had altered. They had carried the ark out of the tropical locales, into the mountains, across the desert, and onto a ship. They sailed here, to Malta, where they remained, hoping the island's isolation would protect them until Janus and his partner returned. But they never had, and the island's protection had proved only temporary.

Barbarians made their way to the island and brought with them something the isolated tribe had almost forgotten: violence. The Immaru had fallen to the invaders, just as Janus' own people had to another violent race. History had repeated itself. Had he steered them wrong? In a world too civilized to fight, the last barbarians become kings.

The barbarians who inherited Malta began to explore the megalithic temples the Immaru had left. Deep inside one of these temples, where the ark and the body of the alpha lay hidden, a group of these humans were changed by the implant's radiation. First, it happened to the Phoenicians and then to the Greeks who ousted them from Malta. The Greek invaders took the genetic benefits back to their homeland, where the changes in brain wiring flourished for centuries.

The environment in Greece cultivated minds in ways that had never occurred before. A few enlightened individuals were able to access something: a shared memory buried deep within the subconscious. The shared memory emerged in the form of a myth —a story about an advanced city called Atlantis that sank off the coast of Gibraltar. Janus saw it now: the implant had added the shared memory, hoping a civilized society would find the ship and come to Janus and his partner's rescue. In some sense, the implant and the Atlantis myth it had conveyed had saved him as well. The Greeks were the first to realize the Atlantis story, to record it and spread the word, but the story of Atlantis would come to reside in the recesses of all human minds in the centuries after.

Janus watched as the Greeks met the same fate as the Phoenicians before them. The Greeks grew ever more civilized and in the process, became unable to fend off a vast army beyond their walls—the Romans.

In the years after the Romans absorbed Greece and arrived on Malta, their empire surged and civilization with it. The Romans built roads, established laws, and created a calendar still in use. Humanity was at its height. Rome's expansion seemed to have no end, but each time it extended its borders, those borders grew harder to defend. In time, Rome too declined and fell to the barbarian tribes who slipped past its poorly defended borders, settled in its lands, and eventually laid siege to its grand cities.

As Rome fell, fire and ash rose from a supervolcano near the equator in present-day Indonesia. The falling ash brought with it the greatest pandemic in recorded history, what would become known as the Plague of Justinian, and a new wave of genetic changes. Trade ground to a halt and with it, the flow of people across Malta. The implant's radiation couldn't reach enough survivors to turn the tide. The world receded back to a more primitive existence and waited for hope and deliverance.

Darkness followed. For almost a thousand years, there were no great civilizations. Malta and the entire human race around it grasped for direction. Against this backdrop, another volcano erupted, and the Black Death descended.

Refugees landed on Malta, and the implant unleashed a new wave of radiation and genetic changes. Those survivors sailed home from Malta, preventing Ares' final transformation of humanity and ushering in the Renaissance.

The implant had lain dormant after that—until the Atlantis Plague. The global failure of Orchid had finally reactivated it, revealing its location and allowing Janus to find it.

Janus could grasp it all now: the entire march of history after the fall of Atlantis. The tiny implant inside the ark and the humans it protected had waged a war against the darkness and the genetic changes that Ares rained down in the ash and plagues that came in the sixth and fourteenth centuries and then finally from the Atlantis Plague.

Across the millennia, the humans had clung to life. How they had fought. The resilience of species 8472 was remarkable. Now their history would come to an end. But they would be safe. He was sure of that.

He tossed the chip into the box and crushed it.

Behind him, he heard footsteps stop abruptly. Janus turned to find David standing in the opening of the chamber, holding one of the primitive weapons that shot hardened elemental projectiles.

Janus reached for the quantum cube.

"Don't, Janus. I swear I will shoot you."

"Now, Mr. Vale. That's no way to treat someone who saved your life."

87

CDC
Atlanta, Georgia

Paul Brenner walked to the Symphony control room. The feeling around the room was jubilation. Two flashing words on the center screen read:

ONE RESULT

They had a new gene therapy for the Atlantis Plague. A new hope.

"Do it," Paul said. "Deploy it across all the districts. Upload the data to all our affiliates."

He raced down the hall and burst into his nephew's hospital room.

The boy lay still. He didn't turn to face Paul. He was only semi-conscious.

But there was still time, Paul thought.

At the lobby that led to the Catacombs of St. Paul, Kate leaned back from the table, wondering what else she could do.

The figure that flew out of the tunnel was a blur. Kate spun, but it was too fast. It bowled Kamau out of the chair. The assault rifle clanged to the ground as the two figures rolled across the floor, into one of the museum's glass display cases. Kamau struck the figure, but Kate could see that he was disoriented, blind, bewildered. He would never make it.

Kate staggered forward and raised the handgun.

They writhed violently on the ground. Kate tried to get a lock on the other figure. Some part of her knew it was Shaw, but she didn't want it to be true. She'd suffered betrayal by someone she'd trusted once before; she'd sworn she wouldn't let that happen again. Shaw had saved her in Marbella. But...

The figure rose from Kamau, a knife in his hand. Blood flowed out onto the white marble floor. Kamau twitched a few times, then came to rest.

The figure turned to face Kate.

Shaw.

Kate wanted to squeeze the trigger, but she simply froze. She couldn't do it.

Shaw snatched the gun out of her hand.

"It's not in you, Kate. Be glad of that."

The door across from the lobby opened, and Dorian Sloane strolled in. The four men who followed him fanned out, taking up positions around the lobby, two flanking the entrance to the tunnel.

"Where the hell have you been?" Shaw demanded.

"Relax," Dorian said casually. "Car trouble." He scanned the room. "Vale?"

"In the tunnels," Shaw said.

Dorian nodded to the soldiers flanking the entrance.

"No," Shaw said. "There's only one way out." He took a small box from his pocket and clicked a button. Eruptions echoed from the tunnels, like rolling thunder growing closer. He looked up at Dorian. "Make that no way out."

Dorian smiled. "It's good to see you, little brother."

David heard the explosions before he felt them at his back. The ceiling was coming down.

He could see Milo in his peripheral vision, lying there, lifeless. He dove for the boy, covering his body with his own.

The stone fell on and around him, echoing in his ear. Milo's body felt so fragile under his. Would Milo survive?

Another stone slammed into David's body, and he winced. And another—into his leg. The pain was complete, but he didn't move. He remained, waiting for the end.

It came, but it was not what he expected. A dome of light, covering him, arching over, blocking the falling rock. But David still didn't move.

Kate glared at Dorian. "I won't help you. We already have a cure."

Dorian's smile grew, like someone who knew a secret. "Oh, Kate, you don't disappoint. I couldn't care less about a cure. I'm here for the code in your head."

"I don't have—"

"You will. You will remember, and then we'll have what we need."

One of Dorian's men grabbed her and dragged her out of the museum lobby.

88

St. Paul's Catacombs
Rabat, Malta

David felt a hand grip his shoulder and roll him over. The stone room was dark and quiet now. He still couldn't see a thing.

Slowly, a yellow glow expanded out into the room.

The figure seemed to be lighting the room from the palm of his hand. He cupped something—a tiny cube that sparkled.

David stared into the face. Janus. He had shielded David from the falling stone with the cube.

"Who the hell *are* you?" David said, his voice hoarse.

"Language, Mr. Vale."

"Seriously?"

Janus stood and spoke quietly. "I am one of two scientists who came here a very long time ago to study the hominins on this planet."

David coughed. "An Atlantean."

"What you call an Atlantean, yes."

David studied Janus's face. Yes, he knew it. He had seen

Janus before. In Antarctica, days ago, when David had been in the tube, he had seen that face staring at him at the end of the chamber. Then the face had disappeared. "It was you—in Antarctica."

"Yes, though not in person. What you saw in Antarctica was my avatar, a remotely controlled representation of me."

David sat up. "You saved me. Why?"

"I'm afraid I need to be going, Mr. Vale."

"Wait." David stood and glanced at the rifle, considering whether to pick it up. No. Janus had incapacitated the soldiers with the cube. He could do the same to David. And Janus had saved his life—twice now. "The cure you sent to Continuity. It's a fake, isn't it?"

"It is quite real—"

"Does it cure the plague?"

"It cures what ails humanity."

David didn't like the sound of that, or Janus's demeanor, which said: this conversation is over.

Janus focused on the cube in the palm of his hand. He stuck his other hand into the light that radiated outward from the cube and began wiggling his fingers. It was as if he was programming it.

David considered his situation. Someone had planted bombs and set them off down here; it wasn't a bomb from above. During World War II, the Germans and Italians had dropped countless bombs on these catacombs and had not brought them down. Shaw. He closed the catacombs. And he would have Kate. Had he already delivered her to Dorian?

"Shaw has Kate," David said.

"Yes, I imagine so." Janus said, not looking up.

"She has your partner's memories."

"What?" Shock spread across Janus's face—the first emotion David had seen him display.

"The memories started coming several days ago, first in her dreams, then when she was awake, she couldn't stop them."

"Impossible."

"She said there was a third person who joined your expedition—a soldier. She colluded with him to change the genome. She said his name was Ares."

Janus just stood there, silently.

"Dorian has Ares's memories. He's captured Kate—that's what Shaw's mission was. I'm sure of it now. There were rumors at the Immari base in Ceuta. Dorian brought a case out of the structure in Antarctica. It created some kind of door. He's taking Kate there. She's in danger."

"If what you say is true, Mr. Vale, we are all in danger. If they reach the portal, if she is delivered to Ares, every person on this planet, and many more, will likely perish."

89

St. Paul's Catacombs
Rabat, Malta

David stepped to within arm's length of Janus. The soft yellow light from the cube lit both their faces from below, giving the impression of two men sitting around a campfire.

"Help me save her," David said.

"No," Janus replied, his tone now sharp and urgent. "*You* will help *me* save her."

"What—"

"You have no idea what you are involved in, Mr. Vale. This is larger—"

"So tell me. Believe me, I'm ready for answers."

"First, I require your pledge that you will follow my orders—that you will do *what* I say, *when* I say."

David stared at him.

Janus continued, "I have observed that in high-stakes, high-stress situations, you prefer—or rather, *demand*—to be in charge. You have trouble taking orders and taking risks, especially when lives are on the line, particularly Kate's. This is a liability. It is not your fault. It is perhaps a result of your past—"

"I'll pass on the psychoanalysis, thanks. Look, if you promise you'll do everything you can to save her, I'll do whatever you tell me to."

"Believe me, I will do everything in my power. But I fear our chances are not good. Seconds will count, Mr. Vale. And we start now."

Janus stood, held out his hand, and the glowing cube flew from it, diving into the stone wall. A cloud of dust radiated out from the center.

David stood and watched. The cube moved deeper into the tunnel, chewing through the stone like a laser.

David touched the wall. It was smooth—just like the hollowed-out path outside the structure in Gibraltar, the darkened tunnel he had walked out of. *I really am way out of my league here*, he thought.

"So that's how you did that..."

"This little quantum cube has gotten me out of quite a few jams on my travels."

David glanced back at the dust cloud floating out of the smooth tunnel. "Yeah, well, thank goodness for... quantum cubes..."

On the ground, Milo stirred slightly. David walked over to him and knelt. "Will he be all right?"

"Yes."

David rolled Milo over. "How do you feel?"

Milo opened his eyes slowly. "Smushed." He coughed, and David helped him sit up.

"Just take it easy, we're getting out of here."

"We?" Janus asked.

"Yes. We're not leaving him here." David stopped short and shook his head. This new command paradigm would take some getting used to. "Or rather, I respectfully submit, for your consideration, that we should bring him along. He is a member of the Immaru. He found the Ark before us. His knowledge could be useful, and he could help us."

Janus walked closer and inspected the teenager. "Incredible. After all these years. How many of you are left?"

Milo looked up. "Just me."

"A shame," Janus said. "Yes, please join us..."

"Milo."

"A pleasure, Milo. My name is Arthur Janus."

Milo made the best bow he could manage from the sitting position.

At the opening to the room, the cube was cutting deeper into the new tunnel in the stone catacombs. The yellow light it emitted was fading as the cube moved farther away. David wondered how long it would take for the cube to reach the surface, and more importantly, if he could make it to Kate in time.

Kate had stopped struggling with Shaw and the guards at her side once the helicopter had lifted off. Where could she go now? She was trapped until they landed. Then what? Could she make a break for it?

They had strapped her in tight to the seat, and zip-tied her hands for good measure.

She stared at Dorian, who sat across from her. He seemed to have perfected the half-smile, half-smirk he always wore. It seemed to say: *I know something you don't. Something bad is going to happen to you, and I'll break into a full grin when it does.*

She wanted to strike him. Shaw sat beside Dorian. He stared

mildly out the helicopter's window, like a kid amused by his first plane ride.

"You killed Martin."

"*You* did," he mumbled.

"You broke his neck—"

"He was dying the moment Orchid failed. You prolonged his agony, Kate."

It was a lie. "Why, Adam?"

He tore his eyes away from the window for the first time. "I knew if he came to, he would recognize me, expose me. I'd assumed he would die without my help, but Chang's therapy, it made him better. When you left to... join David, it was the first chance I had. I did what I had to—to complete my mission. Nothing personal."

Dorian leaned forward. "Don't listen to him, Kate. We both know this is personal. Has been for, what, seventy thousand years now?" He smiled. "That's your big blind spot, isn't it? People. You never can get a read on anyone. You're clever as hell, but you never see the big betrayal coming. I just love that about you. It's hilarious."

Kate closed her eyes and willed herself not to react. She could feel the anger rising inside her. How could he always get under her skin? He manipulated her so easily. The monster seemed to know where every one of her buttons was. He pressed them with such ease, grinning the entire time, knowing exactly how she would react.

She tried to focus, tried to block him out. In the darkness, a voice called, "He betrayed us."

Kate opened her eyes. She was in a steel room that held four standing tubes. A Neanderthal stood motionless in one. She was in Gibraltar, in the chamber her father had found in 1918. This was the last memory, the one she hadn't quite been able to reach. Seeing Dorian, his words, had triggered it.

"Did you hear me?" the voice called again.

A video appeared inside Kate's helmet. A head in a helmet just like hers: Janus. He was the other member of the Atlantean science team, her partner.

"Did you—"

"I heard you," Kate said. She was leaning against a table at the center of the room. She turned around to face Janus. She had to tell him.

"I—" she stammered. "Yes, Ares has betrayed us—"

Another blast rocked the ship.

"—But I helped him." Inside her helmet, the video feed of Janus disappeared, and she stared at the mirrored reflection from his helmet. Apparently Janus didn't want Kate to see his reaction. "He told me he wanted to help. To make them safe. All of us," she added quickly.

"He used you—and our research. He must have the gene therapy he needs to build his army."

Kate watched Janus pace across the room to a control panel. He worked it quickly.

"What are you doing?" Kate asked.

"Ares will try to take the primary ship. He needs it to transport his army. I have locked it down."

Kate nodded. On her helmet display, she watched the commands scroll by. Each line seemed to bring more memories, more comprehension. The ship they stood in now was simply a local lander. They had come here on a larger science ship, capable of deep space travel. Their protocol was always minimal footprint and minimal visibility. They didn't need the ship while they were conducting experiments on the planet's surface, and they didn't want it to be seen. They had hidden it on the opposite side of the planet's only moon, burying it deep. The portal doors on the lander provided instant access to the ship if they ever needed it, but Janus's commands were locking the ship down now—it would be closed to any remote control from Gibraltar or Antarctica. They couldn't get back to the ship now and neither could Ares, at least not through a portal door.

Janus continued manipulating the controls. "I'm going to set some traps as well, in case Ares does somehow make it to the ship."

Kate watched the commands scroll by. Another explosion rocked the ship, this one much more violent than the last.

Janus paused. "The ship is breaking up. It will be ripped apart."

Kate stood there, not sure what to do.

"Has Ares administered his therapy yet? Has he transformed them?"

Kate tried to think. "I don't know. I don't think so."

Janus worked the panel feverishly. Kate saw a series of DNA sequences flash by. The computer was running simulations.

"What are you doing?" she asked.

"The ship is going to be destroyed. The primitives will find it. I am modifying the time-dilation devices at the perimeter to emit radiation that will roll back all our therapies. They will be as they were before we found them, before the first therapy."

That was it—the Bell was Janus's attempt to reverse all the Atlanteans' genetic interventions. Except, in this memory, thirteen thousand years ago, when Janus was programming the Bell, he was looking at the wrong genome. The primitives, as he called them, wouldn't find the ship until 1918, when Kate's father would dig it up under the Bay of Gibraltar. Janus wasn't counting on the time difference, the delay in finding the Bell, the genetic changes that would occur. And Kate knew there would be two very big changes—the "deltas" from Martin's chronology, the two outbreaks of plague in the sixth and thirteenth century. Yes, those must have been Ares's interventions, the administration of the therapy Kate had helped him create. Why had it come so late? Why had he waited twelve thousand years? Where had he been? And where had Janus been? He was alive here in the past, and he had been there in the future.

The ship shuddered again, throwing Kate against the wall. Her head slammed into the helmet, and her body went limp. She couldn't see anything. She heard footsteps. Janus's voice echoed in her helmet, but she couldn't make out the words. She felt him lift her up and carry her.

90

St. Paul's Catacombs
Rabat, Malta

DAVID SWITCHED on a lantern and focused on Janus. "Answers. I want to know what we're dealing with here."

Janus glanced at the rounded stone tunnel the hovering cube was slowly carving.

"Very well. We have a bit of time. Submit your first question."

Where do I start? David thought. "You saved me. How and why?"

"The how is beyond your scientific grasp—"

"Well dumb it down for my primitive hominin brain, which apparently seventy thousand years of Atlantean intervention hasn't perfected."

"Clearly. The how is somewhat related to the why. I shall start there. I will also need to give you a bit of background. I said before that you did not actually see me in Antarctica. You saw my avatar. Have you surmised why?"

"You were in Gibraltar."

"Yes. Very good, Mr. Vale. Your Dr. Grey actually figured out a great deal of the Atlantean history on this planet. It was shocking for me to read his chronology. It was quite accurate, despite the gaps in his knowledge, things he could not know."

"Such as?"

"What he described as 'A$ falls'—the fall of Atlantis, the destruction of our ship off the coast of Gibraltar. It was an attack. As you know, there were two of us. We were scientists who traveled the galaxies studying human evolution on countless human worlds."

"Incredible," David mumbled.

"This world, your species, is what is incredible. Our species is old. Long ago, we turned our focus to other worlds, and in particular, to any world that harbored human life. It became our obsession. One question in particular dominated our expeditions, the greatest question of all: where did we come from?"

"Evolution—"

"Is only the biological process. There is much more to the story; your science will reveal that one day. You already know that the universe supports the emergence of human life. In fact, the universe is strictly programmed for it. If any of the constants were even slightly different—gravity, the strength of electromagnetism, the dimensions in space-time—there would be no human life. There are only two possibilities: either human life emerged because the laws of the universe support it by random chance, or the alternative: the universe was created to foster human life."

David considered Janus's statement.

"Our first assumption was that it was merely chance; that we existed because we were simply one of an infinite number of biological possibilities in an infinite number of universes that exist in the multiverse. Our theory was that we exist, because mathematically we must exist in some universe, given that there are infinite possible universes, and we are a finite possible outcome. We exist in this universe because it is the only one our brains are capable of being aware of."

"Yeah." David had no idea what else to say to that.

"Then we made a discovery that altered our understanding, made us question our assumptions. We discovered a quantum entity, a subatomic substance pervading the universe. It was the greatest discovery in our existence. The accepted consensus was that this quantum entity was simply another universal constant, something that must exist in our universe to give rise to human life. But a group of us began to delve deeper into the mystery. Through thousands of years of practice, we learned to access this quantum entity, but we hit a wall—"

David held his hand up. "Okay, you got me. I give. I have no idea what a quantum entity is."

"Are you familiar with quantum entanglement?"

"Uh, no."

"Very well. Let me just say that we discovered that all humans are linked through the quantum entity. Some members of our society with an especially strong connection can even use the link to communicate over distances."

David's mind flashed to the dreams he'd shared with Kate.

"You find this hard to believe, Mr. Vale?"

"No. Actually, I do believe it. Go on."

"We call this quantum entity that links all humans the Origin Entity. Investigating its creation, our creation, is our great work. We call it 'The Origin Mystery.' We believe the Origin Entity exerts influence over the entire universe, that it is both the origin point and the final destination for human consciousness."

Milo nodded. "This is the creation story you gave us."

"Yes," Janus said. "Your minds had advanced so far, so quickly. You craved answers, in particular about your existence. We gave you the only answers we had, though we modified them so that you might understand them. And we gave you our code—a moral blueprint: practices that we have found bring us closer to the Origin Entity, practices we have found enhance the link, tying humans closer to each other and the harmony the Origin Entity offers. We also emphasized that every human life is valuable; every human is connected to the Origin Entity and could reveal more about the mystery." Janus paused. "Much of our message has been lost over the ages, however."

"Some still believe," Milo said.

"Yes, clearly. Ultimately, our mission here has failed, but it began with such promise. In all the years of our investigations of the Origin Mystery, we had never seen a species like yours. We monitor all the human worlds. As a historian, you will appreciate this, Mr. Vale. On this planet, a relatively minor geological event three and a half million years ago caused a cataclysm that directly led to the emergence of humanity. Three and a half million years ago, the collision of two tectonic plates elevated the seafloor of what is now the western Caribbean, forming the Isthmus of Panama. For the first time, the Atlantic and Pacific Oceans were separated, preventing the large-scale mixing of their waters. This set off a chain reaction that led to an ice age on this planet, which it's still in. In West Africa, the jungles began to shrink. A number of species of higher-order primates lived in the trees during this period. In the following years, savannas gradually replaced the lush jungles, driving those primates down from the trees and onto the grasslands. The sources of their vegetarian diet were largely gone. Many perished, but a small group took another path: they adapted. They ventured out onto the vast plains and began hunting new sources of food. For the first time, they ate meat, and it changed their brains. So did hunting. These primates, these prehistoric survivalists, grew smarter than any primates before them. They eventually made primitive stone tools and hunted in packs. This pattern—of climate disruption, of near-extinction in a rapidly changing environment, then rebound, of adapting—would come to be the hallmark pattern that repeats itself over and over again during your species' march to its current state. We came here to study you when you were still in your infancy, hoping a species with such a meteoric rise, evolutionarily speaking, could reveal something new about the Origin Mystery.

"We followed all of our usual precautions. We deployed a Beacon that followed the planet's orbit."

"A beacon?"

"A shroud—to keep anyone from seeing your development and to keep you from seeing any other human worlds. What you call the Fermi Paradox—the fact that human worlds must be abundant, yet you have found none—is actually a result of the Beacon. It filters the light you can see, and the light your world emits to anyone outside the shroud. We also followed all the other procedures. We buried our ship—"

"In Antarctica?" David asked.

"No. That's a different ship. I'll explain momentarily. We typically hide our deep-space vessel in a local asteroid belt or in this case, a moon—for added security, just in case a probe gets by the Beacon. The universe is a dangerous place, and we have no desire to call attention to our subjects or ourselves. We deployed our lander to the surface and remained here. Our routine remained the same after that, just as it was on other planets: we collected samples, analyzed our results, and hibernated, awakening only at regular intervals to repeat our process. However, one hundred thousand years ago, we were awakened early by a distress call. Our home world was under attack. Another message followed shortly after. Our world had fallen to an enemy of unimaginable strength. We were instructed to remain on a shrouded world for our own safety. We believed that our enemy would hunt any remaining Atlanteans to the end of the universe. Our fear was that the Armageddon would extend to all humans, across all human worlds. The next event you know well. Seventy thousand years ago, a supervolcano in present-day Indonesia erupted, spewing ash into the sky and causing a volcanic winter that brought your species to the brink of extinction. The population alarms awoke my partner and me from hibernation. It was our greatest fear. We thought that we could be the last of our species: two scientists who could never go home. And we were watching what could be the extinction of some of the last humans our enemy had not yet found. So my partner made a fateful decision."

"To give us the Atlantis Gene."

"Yes. She did it without my knowledge or consent. She claimed it was an experiment, to provide you with the survival gene, to see how you would fare. It was already done, and I went along.

"Approximately twenty thousand years after she administered the Atlantis Gene, another vessel from our world arrived. It landed in Antarctica, where it has remained under the ice since. The vessel contains the last of our people."

"It's a tomb?"

"Of sorts. But it is much more. It is a resurrection ship. On our world, every person is allowed a life of a hundred years. There are exceptions, such as for deep-space explorers such as myself. We have mastered medical science, but accidents happen. In those events, our citizens resurrect in these vessels."

"That's what they are?" David asked. "Dead Atlanteans?"

"Yes. Massacred when our home world was attacked. All except for one. Occasionally, our people vote to have a citizen archived. Someone of great achievement. It is a cultural honor. The person archived in that vessel was General Ares. He is a relic of our past, something we have moved on from. He was saved as a reminder. He is our most famous soldier. During the attack, he somehow got the ship off our home world. He brought it here."

"The others in the vessel in Antarctica... they can't wake up? Exit the tubes?"

"They can. However, we are now a non-violent species. The attack on our world, the brutality, the carnage... the tubes can only heal physical wounds. The people in Antarctica can awaken, but they retain their memories, down to the last agonizing second they died. It would be too cruel to awaken them. Their minds are wired a bit differently from yours. Psychologically, the trauma they endured is too great. They cannot escape the memories of what happened to them. They exist in a constant state of purgatory, unable to die permanently, unable to rise again."

David wouldn't have believed it, but he had experienced it—death and resurrection in the tube. Dorian had shot and killed him, and he had awoken, in a new body, an exact replica. "That's what happened to me, how I awoke in the tube after Dorian killed me. It was just like the people from your home world."

"Yes."

"How does it work? Resurrection?"

"The science is rather complex—"

"Dumb it down for me. I want to understand." David glanced at the cube, which still wasn't quite out of sight. "We have time."

"Very well. The piece of genetic technology you call the Atlantis Gene actually performs several functions. The most relevant, in this instance, is organizing radiation from the body into a data stream. Every human body emits radiation. The Atlantis Gene turns those isotopes into a cellular blueprint, a download of your body, including the cells in your brain, which contain your memories, up to the second you died."

"The second time Dorian killed me, I awoke in the Gibraltar ship. How?"

"That is where our stories intersect, Mr. Vale. When the resurrection ship arrived, forty thousand years ago, we had already given humans the Atlantis Gene. Ares was keenly interested. He saw in humans an opportunity, a chance to build a new army, to fight back against our enemy. He insisted that the Atlantis Gene put you in danger, made you a target for our adversary. He convinced my partner. She colluded with him behind my back, modifying the therapy, looking for a way to increase your survival abilities. I observed the changes and was suspicious. I knew your species was advancing far too rapidly, but of course we had never tampered with another species in this way. I didn't know what to expect. And I never imagined she had betrayed me. But I know why she did it: guilt, for something she did on our home world, an act that led to our demise."

"What—"

"That is a story for another time. Here on Earth, Ares had what he needed: the final gene therapy to create his army. He tried to destroy the lander and us with it—that was what happened off the coast of Gibraltar. The ship was split into pieces. We assumed his next move would be to commandeer our space vessel. He needs it to transport his army. I locked it down, preventing anyone from either the lander or Antarctica from reaching it. I also set a series of alarms and countermeasures. But our lander off the coast of Gibraltar was coming apart quickly. My partner was knocked out. I picked her up and carried her to the only place I could go."

"Antarctica."

"Yes. And Ares was waiting for me. He shot and killed her. Of course, he had disabled resurrection for both of us in Antarctica. That was his plan. He shot me too, in the chest, but I stumbled back through the portal. I emerged in a different part of the lander in Gibraltar."

David's mind raced. Yes. In the room where he had resurrected the second time, there was a damaged suit. "The suit on the floor."

Janus nodded. "It was mine. When I escaped to that section, my first move was to seal the lander off from Antarctica, to protect myself. Then I managed to reach the tube—one of the ones you resurrected in. After I was healed, I took stock. My situation was dire. The shard of the ship I found myself in was now deep underwater and far away from the coast. If I exited, I would drown long before I reached the surface, and I had no way to replicate an oxygen tank." He glanced at David. "The Immari colonel's uniform I replicated for you was much more simple."

"How did you—"

"I will come to it," Janus said, holding his hand up. "I was trapped. And alone. My partner was dead, and to my surprise, my thoughts went first to her. Resurrection is a closely regulated technology. A death sequence, sent via the radiation from the Atlantis Gene, is impossible to fake, as it must be: imagine the implications of waking to find you have a double. I tried at first to force her resurrection, to trick the system into thinking she had died. The true death sequence had been sent to the ship in Antarctica, and Ares had deleted it. My entire strategy was to fake her death to the computer in my section and have her resurrect in the part of the ship closest to the shore—so that she could escape and hopefully, stop Ares. I tried everything. I failed. However, thirteen thousand years later, I succeeded, in a way. In 1918, Patrick Pierce placed his dying wife in the tube and Kate inside her. The computer must have executed the resurrection sequence then, but the child did not mature as a normal resurrection fetus would—it was confined by the mother's body. Yet once removed from the mother, the child, Kate, began to grow, and it seems that now, her memories have returned. Those memories from my partner have lain dormant in Kate's mind all this time. Remarkable."

"How does Dorian have Ares's memories?"

Janus shook his head. "As I said, I was desperate. I tried everything. I must have authorized *any* resurrection. Ares had joined our expedition, and we had his radiation signature and memories. But... the memories would have ended thousands of—"

"Dorian also died twice in Antarctica, if the reports are true. Ares could have filled in the blanks."

"Yes... that is possible. Ares could have easily added additional memories, even shown them to Dorian during his resurrection there. As for Kate, the memories, in the recesses of her mind, they would have exerted some influence, steered her decisions, like subconscious cues." He paced away from David. "She became a geneticist, intent on studying abnormalities in brain wiring. Subconsciously, she was grasping for a way to stabilize the Atlantis Gene and complete her work. It is quite a story." Janus was deep in thought, seemingly somewhere else.

"So... what happened to you?" David asked, for lack of anything else to say.

"Nothing. For thirteen thousand years, nothing happened to me. I thought my attempts at escape and resurrecting my dead companion had failed. My last option was to kill myself in my section and program my own resurrection in the other compartment. But I was unable to do it. I had seen what had become of those from my home world who had died a violent death, the people in the tubes in Antarctica, those trapped in perpetual purgatory. So I went into the tube, and I remained there for thirteen thousand years, waiting, hoping something would change."

David knew instantly what "the change" was. In Antarctica,

David had held off Dorian and his men, allowing Kate and her father to escape. Her father had exploded two nuclear devices in Gibraltar, shattering the piece of the lander he had unearthed. "The nuclear blasts."

"Yes. They moved the section I was in closer to northern Africa. Morocco and Ceuta specifically. I immediately activated my link to the ship. I saw what had happened in Gibraltar, and then I connected to Antarctica and watched the footage there. I knew you had sacrificed your life to save a man, a woman, and two boys. The other man, whom I did not know was Dorian at the time, had been far less gallant. You observed the Human Code, our morality. You had a respect for human life. I knew Ares, and I knew what would happen next. You and Dorian were enemies. He would have you fight to the death and take the winner. I decided to download your data feed. I had to reveal my avatar, momentarily, to capture your radiation signature. The rest you know. Upon your death, you awakened in the part of the ship I had been confined to. I programmed the tubes to self-destruct—to ensure you went forward, venturing out."

"Why? What did you think I could do?"

"Save lives. I saw what kind of man you were. I knew what you would do. And you did something else, something more: you led me to a cure."

"You couldn't have known," David said.

"No. I had no idea. For the first time in thirteen thousand years, my part of the ship was near land. I could escape. The world I found horrified me, especially the Immari. I am, however, a scientist and a pragmatist. I was not aware of Continuity at that point. From what I could see, the Immari were conducting the most advanced genetic experiments. I joined them, hoping to use their knowledge, to find a cure."

"Your cure. It's a fake, isn't it?"

"It is quite real."

"What does it do?" David demanded.

Janus glanced at the stone box that lay at the edge of the soft yellow light from the cube. "It corrects a mistake, an act I failed to stop a very long time ago."

"Speak English."

Janus ignored David's order. He simply stared at the box. "The alpha was the last piece I needed. I can't believe they saved it across the ages."

"Last piece of what?"

"A therapy that will roll back all of our genetic updates—everything, including the Atlantis Gene. The remaining humans on this planet will be as they were when we found them."

91

Somewhere off the coast of Italy

DORIAN's last jab had hit Kate in the heart, he knew it. He knew her. She was so vulnerable, so easy to manipulate. He could play her like a piano.

Her eyes were closed now, but he knew she was thinking of him.

He leaned his head back against the seat cushion, and the helicopter faded away, as if he were falling down a well. He couldn't stop the memory.

He stood in a room with seven doors. He held a rifle.

A door opened, and someone wearing an environmental suit ran in carrying another person. Dorian fired at the limp body the runner was carrying. The blast ripped it to pieces and threw both of them back against the doors.

The live one squirmed, struggling to hold the dead body. Dorian closed the distance and raised his rifle. The figure rose. Dorian fired, hitting the suit dead in the middle, but his target was already through another door. He had escaped.

Dorian considered pursuing. He ran back to the control panel and worked it with his fingers. No. His enemy was in a part of the ship in Gibraltar that offered no escape. Serves him right—an eternity in a tomb below the sea.

Dorian manipulated the controls, programming one of the portal doors to take him to the scientists' deep-space vessel. He had the genetic therapy he needed to complete the transformation. Once he had the ship, he would have revenge for his people.

The control panel froze. Dorian stared at it. The scientists had locked their vessel down. Very clever. They were quite smart, but he was smarter.

He walked out of the room with the bank of doors and down the hallway. Dorian knew this hallway. He had seen it before. A door hissed open.

The same room. Three suits hung here now, and there were three cases on the small bench.

He put on a suit and took two of the cases.

He stalked out of the room, to a lab. He programmed the cases, then picked up a silver cylinder that contained the final therapy.

He exited the ship.

The area outside was an ice cathedral, just as he had seen before.

He set the case down and tapped a few places on his arm, on a control panel built into the suit. Slowly, the case changed. It seemed to flow together, and then the silver-white fluid that had been an alloy swirled at the ground and moved higher, swaying back and forth, like a cobra emerging from a basket. Two arms separated from the silver column, then clashed together. Tendrils reached across until the glowing door was complete. Instinctively, Dorian knew what it was: a wormhole. A gateway to the exact point he needed to reach.

Dorian stepped through.

He stood on a mountaintop. No, it was more than a mountain. A volcano. Tidal waves of liquid rock burned and churned below. A tropical paradise spread out across the islands that surrounded it.

He held the cylinder out, then dropped it into the soup of liquid rock.

What was this?

His mind seemed to answer. *A backup plan. If I fail—if I'm trapped on the scientists' vessel—the genetic transformation will still go forward.* It would only be a matter of time before the volcano erupted, shooting the therapy into the air and then raining it down around the world.

He set the other case down, and it formed another door. He stepped through it.

He emerged on the bridge of the scientists' vessel. It was buried of course, but he could quickly remedy that.

He accessed the controls, turning the ship's systems on one by one. He turned his head.

Did he feel...

The air... it was draining. Yes, he could feel it now.

Dorian had known that it was a risk—that the scientist could try to trap or kill him, but he had no choice but to take the risk. Waiting would have served no purpose. He tried to focus on the crisis at hand.

How long did he have?

He raced out of the bridge. His mind combed through the options.

The shuttle bay. No. He had nowhere to go. The ship was at least two hundred meters below the surface, maybe more. What was protocol?

Did they have any portal-making technology on board?

Were they allowed to carry it? Even if they did, he would never find it.

EVA suits. Yes, a suit would have oxygen.

He could feel the air growing thinner by the second. He stopped and pressed his hand against the wall, activating a ship map. EVA suits. Where would they be? Near an airlock.

His breath grew raspy.

He swallowed, but he couldn't quite get it down.

He worked the map. He needed another option. Medical. It was close.

He stumbled down the hall. The doors parted, and he collapsed inside.

A bank of six shimmering glass tubes spread out before him.

He crawled.

How fitting, he thought. To spend eternity in a tube, far below the surface. That is my fate. I cannot escape it. I will never greet death, never fulfill my destiny. My army will never rise, and I will never rest.

The tube opened.

He crawled inside.

Dorian was again in the helicopter. The wind blew across his face, and the roar of the rotor blades thumped in his ears.

For the first time, it all made sense. The pieces fit together; the entire picture was clear.

The portal in Germany. It led to the ship, to Ares. Brilliant.

Kate. She had the Atlantean scientist's memories. She could unlock the ship and free Ares. Together, Ares and Dorian could complete their work on Earth and transport their army to the final war. Victory would come soon after.

Dorian stared at Kate. She sat across from him, her eyes closed.

Ares' words echoed in his mind. *She's the key to everything. But you must wait. At some point very soon, she will acquire a piece of information—a code. That code is the key to freeing me. You must capture her after she has the code and bring her to me.*

Dorian marveled at Ares' genius. The realization, the full appreciation of the Atlantean's plan struck him. He felt... awe. Dorian finally felt as though he had an equal. No, a superior. But Ares was something more. Dorian knew it now: Ares had designed the entire process partly for him—for Dorian's own growth. The charade in Antarctica, his challenge to find Kate. It was as though Ares was... mentoring Dorian. But it was even more than that. Ares was more than a mentor to him. Dorian had a part of Ares inside of him, his memories and more—his desires, his unrealized dreams.

A father. That was the most apt term. That's what Ares was to him.

And they would be together again soon.

Dorian tried to imagine their reunion, what he would say, what Ares would say. And after... what else did Ares have left to teach him? What would Dorian learn about himself? He knew it now. That was his true desire—to finally unravel the greatest mystery of all: how he had come to be what he was.

Ares and the answers waited beyond the portal. They would reach it soon.

92

CDC
Atlanta, Georgia

Paul Brenner opened the door and walked to his nephew's bedside.

"How do you feel?"

The boy looked up at him. He started to speak, but no words came. *What's happening to him?* Paul wondered.

He checked the vitals. All normal. Physically, the boy had made a miraculous recovery.

Paul rubbed his temples. *What's wrong with me? Why can't I think straight?* His mind seemed to be in a fog, a cloud of confusion he couldn't escape.

David tried to wrap his mind around Janus's words. "You're taking us back to the stone ages? You're... *devolving* us?"

"I'm making you safe. Have you not understood a word I've

said? An enemy of unimaginable strength is hunting my people. You have some of us inside of you. Regression, devolution is the only chance you have. It will save your species."

"Assuming we're even the same species. Look, we're not going back. I don't accept this."

"I respect that, Mr. Vale. Indeed, that's why I chose you—you fight for your own kind, you sacrifice for them. You follow the Human Code. But it betrays you in this moment. You just heard the history of your world and your species. Those primates that came down from the trees and sought sustenance on the savannas, they were survivors. Ask the chimpanzees and gorillas how they feel about their choice to remain in the trees. It was easier there, but those who ventured out, who chose the hard road, actually grew stronger, adapted, and evolved—the few who survived. The tribes that marched to the sea during Toba, they were survivors too. That is the defining trait of your species. This is how you will survive this trial." Janus jerked his head toward the tunnel. "The cube is through—"

David grabbed a lantern. "This conversation isn't over."

"It has been for a very long time, Mr. Vale."

David had led Janus and Milo out of the tunnel, toward the rays of sunlight that cut across the tunnel opening. The glowing yellow cube hovered just beyond the newly carved entrance.

David crossed the threshold first. He swept the room with his assault rifle. Nothing moved. In the corner, a pool of blood spread out. David crept toward it, fearing what he would see.

Kamau. Knife wound to the chest.

David bent and pressed his fingers to his friend's neck. He felt the cold skin before the lack of a pulse. Still, he held it there, waiting, refusing to believe it.

Janus and Milo both stared at the scene. Apparently neither knew what to say.

Finally, David rose and walked over to Kate's computer. He closed it and stuffed it and the other equipment in the backpack. "Let's move out."

Outside the building, David led the group back to the square. Their helicopter was gone.

He turned to Janus. "What's the plan? We can't beat them to Germany—they're too far ahead of us."

"There is an alternative," Janus said. "If we can get there in time."

"The Knights have a plane," Milo said. "Can you fly it, Mr. David?"

"I can fly anything," David said. Landing had sometimes been an issue, but he didn't mention that. There was no need to worry them.

Dorian watched the sea below turn to land. Italy. Soon they would cross into Germany, and they would reach the portal shortly after.

The plague had crushed continental Europe. NATO had folded early, offering their resources to the humanitarian effort. Nothing could stop him now.

Kate opened her eyes. Dorian stared at her.

She didn't blink now. She wasn't scared of him anymore. She knew who he was, and she knew who she was. History wouldn't repeat itself.

"Everything okay, Kate?" Dorian asked sarcastically.

She matched his tone. "I'm good."

The helicopter touched down a half hour later, and Dorian dragged her out, onto the ground.

Humvees circled the portal, which glistened, giving off wisps of white light into the cold silent night.

They passed the Humvees, and Kate saw the dead soldiers lying on the ground. Plague victims. The German government must have dispatched troops to investigate the portal, but they had fallen sick. Those who hadn't died must have fled.

Dorian dragged her toward the glowing portal.

"Stay with me," he called behind him, to Shaw. "It closes behind us."

As Shaw pulled up even, the three of them crossed the threshold, and they were standing in a different place.

To Kate, it felt like the corridors in the tombs in Antarctica. But the hallways here were more narrow. She knew this place. It was her ship—the deep space transport that had brought her and Janus here.

Kate tried to take a breath, but she found that she couldn't inhale fully. Dorian's eyes flashed on her, but before he could say anything, air began rushing into the space. Did the ship recognize Kate? Was it coming back to life for her? Yes, that was it.

Dorian tugged at her arm, yanking her down the dimly lit hallway.

He paused at an intersection. He seemed to be trying to remember where he was going. Or had gone?

"This way," he said.

The soft beads of light from the floor and ceiling seemed to grow brighter. No, Kate realized she was just getting used to the darkness.

Another change was gradually setting in. She was adjusting. The last memory, her death in Antarctica at Ares', or Dorian's, hands had changed her.

Kate had always had trouble relating to others. She never fully "got" people. She desperately wanted to have fulfilling personal relationships, but it never happened naturally for her. It had always been work.

She had assumed that this personal desire had drawn her to autism research, to seek a cure for people who lacked the brain wiring for understanding social cues and managing language. She now knew her motivation was much deeper than that.

Dorian had been right: she wasn't great at reading people. She was easily misled. But now the game was strategy, and she knew the history. She knew the players. And she knew how it would unfold. She was smarter than he was, and she would win.

93

Outside Ceuta

David had pushed the plane to its max speed. There was no risk of exhausting its fuel.

On the horizon, Ceuta came into view. David activated the radio and began conversing with air control. The rail guns could easily blow the plane out of the sky, and he wasn't exactly sure what sort of response he would get. He didn't have any alternatives.

The response was swift. "You are cleared for landing, Mr. Vale."

David's landing was bumpy at best, but it didn't evoke a reaction from either of his passengers. They were on the ground, and they were alive. And so was Kate, as far as he knew. *One step at a time.*

As David, Janus, and Milo exited the aircraft, David spotted a convoy approaching the airfield. He subconsciously tightened his grip on his assault rifle.

The convoy stopped, and the door of the lead Humvee

swung open. The Berber chief, the same one who had branded him days earlier and helped him take the base, stepped out and sauntered over to him. A smile spread across her face.

"I thought perhaps that I would never see you again."

"Likewise."

She grew serious. "Have you returned to resume your command?"

"No. Just passing through. I need a jeep."

Fifteen minutes later, David was driving recklessly toward the hills where he had emerged, days earlier, when he'd left the Atlantean ship wearing an Immari uniform.

"I don't know where the entrance is," David called back to Janus.

"I'll direct you," Janus replied.

They drove on for what felt like an eternity to David. The slope grew steeper and the rocky terrain more treacherous. With each passing second, he imagined his chances of rescuing Kate slipping away.

Finally, Janus tapped his shoulder. "Stop here."

David pulled up next to a steep rock face. Before he'd even come to a complete stop, Janus bounded out and started striding purposefully ahead. David and Milo tried to catch up.

"What's the plan, Janus?" David shouted ahead. Janus had refused to share any real details of his plan on the plane ride, and that made David nervous.

"We'll get to that," Janus called back. He turned a corner, and when David cleared the turn, the scientist was gone. David spun around, searching. The rock face of the mountain to his left looked like the one he had emerged from, but David wasn't sure.

"Hey!" David called. He ran to the rock face and felt it. It was solid. He paced back and forth. Milo merely stood there, as if he were waiting in line for something.

"Janus!" David screamed. Janus had betrayed him. This was his plan all along— Janus emerged right out of the solid rock, and as he did so, the projection of the rock face dissolved behind him. "I had to disable the force field. Follow me."

"Oh. Well, you could have..." David shook his head and fell in behind Janus, who led them down the tunnel the cube had carved—the path David had followed out. They took the same elevator David had used.

During David's time here, all the doors had been locked. Now they opened as the three men approached.

Janus cut left, leading them into a room with four doors.

"What now?" David asked.

"Now we wait. If I'm right, Kate will know what to do. She will not only release the tube that holds Ares, she will open the entire ship. That will be our opening. It will be a very, very short window to do what we have to do."

Janus related the rest of his plan, and David merely nodded. He was out of his element; he had no choice but to trust Janus.

David turned to Milo and held out his sidearm for him to take.

Milo eyed it, then took a small step back.

"Milo, if anyone besides us comes through that door, you have to shoot them."

"I cannot, Mr. David—"

"You have to—"

"I know I must do it to survive. But it is not in me. I know if the time comes, I cannot pull the trigger. I cannot take another life. On my journey to the Ark in Malta, I learned many things. The most important thing I learned is who I truly am. I am sorry to disappoint you, Mr. David, but I also cannot lie to you, and I will not pretend to be something I am not."

David nodded. "Believe me, I'm not disappointed, Milo. And I hope the world never gives you time or reason to change." For a brief moment, he thought about himself, in his grad school days, before that building had buried him and started him on his own journey of vengeance.

Janus walked to the wall. A panel opened as he approached. He took out another yellow cube and began working his fingers in the light that emerged around it.

He returned to Milo and handed him the cube. "This is a cube similar to the one I used in the catacombs under Malta. It will not take a life, but it will incapacitate everyone within reach —you as well, Milo. It won't work on Atlanteans, obviously. But perhaps it will give you some time, time for an ally to arrive."

"Got any more high-tech weapons?" David asked.

"Nothing of use. Just follow the plan. And follow my cube." Janus inched closer to the portal door and held the cube up, ready to release it.

"I want a cure for the plague before we go through."

"I told you, Mr. Vale, that discussion is finished. You and Kate share the pure form of the Atlantis Gene. You will both survive as you are."

"Unacceptable."

"Your acceptance is not required."

Dorian brought Kate to a stop before a set of double doors.

He worked the panel, and the doors parted.

Seven tubes stood in the room. The middle one held Ares. His eyes followed them, cold and unblinking.

Dorian stared at him for a long moment. "Release him," he said without turning to face Kate.

She held her bound hands up and wiggled her fingers. "Release me first."

Dorian spun on her. "You can manage."

"I can't." She motioned to the panel. "It's impossible to work the system with my hands bound. Untie me, and I'll let him out." She paused. "What's the matter? You think both of you can't handle me? Or all three of you can't?"

Dorian nodded to Shaw, who took the assault knife out and snapped the zip tie in half.

Kate walked to the control panel. She felt Ares' eyes following her.

Her next move would determine her fate and that of many others.

The memories were clearer now, and the most vivid ones were of people, more than places. Janus. They had studied a hundred worlds over thousands of years. He had stayed the same. Somewhere along the way, she had changed. She had grown a bit more compassionate, more reflective, and more driven. And she longed to be with someone more like herself: someone with intellect *and passion*. Someone like David.

However, one thing about Janus stuck out in her mind above all else: he was the smartest person she had ever known. She was counting on that. The opening she was about to create would leave no margin for error.

She manipulated the cloud of blue light that rose from the panel.

Around her, lights snapped on, and the other control panels flickered to life.

The tube slid open, and Ares stepped out.

"Well done, Dorian."

"Now, David!"

The portal door opened, and Janus rushed through, David close on his heels.

Janus flung the cube into the hallway, and it raced away, a yellow wake of light marking its path.

The cube would find Kate, and David would lead her back to the portal. Janus had promised David that he would take care of the ship. He couldn't allow it to fall into Dorian's or Ares' hands.

David chased after the cube. From the adjacent corridor, he heard Janus's boots pounding the floor.

As soon as Ares stepped out of the tube, Kate lunged across the room at Dorian. Her attack took him by surprise. Her fist landed square on his jaw, sending him into the wall, then to the ground. She fell on top of him, and she felt Shaw's hands grip her, pulling her back. But her distraction had succeeded. Had she bought enough time? The answer came in a blinding yellow-white light that erupted throughout the room.

David pumped his legs harder, racing down the corridor. Up ahead, the glowing cube ducked into a room and flashed. David heard a scream. He pressed on.

Shaw screamed out in pain, then fell to the floor beside Kate and Dorian and began writhing back and forth.

Kate was on her feet and out the door, but hands grabbed

her. She tried to break free, but the strong hands spun her around.

David.

"Come on," he said as he sprinted down the corridor.

Dorian's ears rang, and he saw spots. Someone jerked him up. The panel on the opposite wall was exploding. What was happening?

He felt the ship shudder.

Ares slapped Dorian and held his face. "Focus, Dorian. Janus is activating the self-destruct. We have to move." He pulled Dorian up and out of the room.

Out of the corner of his eye, Dorian saw Shaw lying there, rolling in agony. Dorian gripped the doorframe. "Adam!"

Ares pulled him away, and the double doors closed. "We have to leave him. Don't be a fool, Dorian." He dragged him down the corridor.

Another blast threw them to the ground.

Dorian leapt up and started back toward the room where Shaw was still crying out.

Ares grabbed Dorian's shoulders and pinned them to the wall. "I won't leave you. If you won't leave him, you'll kill us both, and everyone down below. Choose, Dorian."

Dorian shook his head. His brother, his only family... He couldn't make that call.

The hands shook his shoulders, slamming him into the wall again. "Choose."

Dorian felt himself turn away from Shaw, away from the only person in the world he truly cared about. Then he and Ares were running. Another blast. They would never make it.

Janus keyed the final sequences into the ship and stepped back, watching the display show the ship's sections explode and decompress. The massive ship would soon be a burned out wreck.

But she would be safe.

That was all that mattered—the only reason he had come here or to any of the other hundreds of worlds.

Another shudder swept the ship. Death would come soon for him. He had finally done it—given his life to save her, something he had willed himself to do every day for thirteen thousand years in that chamber under the Bay of Gibraltar. It was so easy now, so simple. Janus knew why: he would never awaken, never resurrect. He wouldn't wake up to remember his death, would never confront the same kind of endless agony the people in Ares' resurrection vessel endured. He would die knowing he had saved the only person he had ever cared about. In that moment, he understood the stories of Kate's father. His sacrifice in Gibraltar. And Martin. Maybe subspecies 8472 had come further than he had estimated. Even so, it wouldn't matter soon. Another blast sent a shudder through the bridge, and Janus steadied himself.

How long do I have left?

Perhaps there was time to correct one last mistake. He activated the ship's deep space communications array, cleared his throat, and stood as straight as he could.

"My name is Dr. Arthur Janus. I am a scientist and a citizen of a long-since fallen civilization..."

A set of double doors opened onto a room that held three portals.

Ares worked the cloud of light from the panel. Dorian felt numb, paralyzed. Ares pulled him through the portal just as the blast broke through the walls.

Dorian stumbled into the room he had seen before, the one with seven doors. Ares was bent over, panting, his hands on his knees.

When Ares had caught his breath, he rose. "Now you see, Dorian. They make you weak. They pull at your heart. Hold you down. They try to keep you from doing what must be done to survive." He walked out of the room.

Mechanically, Dorian followed. It was as if he were looking at himself from the outside. There was no feeling now. No reaction.

Ares paused at the opening to the vast chamber that held the endless rows of tubes.

"Now you're ready, Dorian. We will save them. These are your people now."

94

Outside Ceuta

Kate flew through the archway of the portal a second before David landed beside her. The portal closed behind them.

Milo was at her side, helping her up.

"Are you all right, Dr. Kate?"

"I'm fine, Milo. Thank you." She raced to the panel beside the portal doors. Yes, the connection to the ship was closed; it had been destroyed. Janus had done well. The moment she had seen David alone, she'd known what their plan was. Janus had been brave.

Seeing David had confirmed that the fire, that little piece of herself, that small flame she had fanned, was still there. And she had to move quickly to keep it alive.

She brought up a schematic of the ship, or rather the section they were confined to. There was a medical bay, one of their labs. She could do it. She began programming the procedure—a gene therapy that would reverse the resurrection process that was rewiring her brain. She would lose the Atlantean memories, but she would be herself again. Her fingers moved quickly across the panel.

David sat up, stared at the portal door for a long moment, then ran over to Kate. "Janus should be here—"

"He's not coming."

She almost had the solution. The lab wasn't far away. A few levels.

"He gave us a false cure."

Kate made a few last modifications—

"Hey!" David took her by the arm. He held up a backpack. "The therapy he gave Continuity rolls everything back. It's going to be Flintstones reruns out there soon." He stared at her. "I brought your computer. Can you fix this?"

She looked up. "Yes. But I don't have time to fix myself if I do."

"Fix..." David searched her face. "I don't understand."

"The resurrection. The memories. I'm slipping away. In a few minutes, the final stages of the resurrection process will be complete. I will cease to be... *me*."

David let the backpack fall to his side.

"What do you want to do?" Kate's voice sounded mechanical. She waited.

"I know what I want and that's you. But I know you—the woman I love. And I know what choice you would make, the sacrifice. I know what you reminded me of a few days ago, belowdecks on a yacht in the Mediterranean. You reminded me who I really was, and now I'm reminding you who you are. I owe you that much, no matter what I want."

Kate studied him. She saw the memory in her mind's eye. His irrational bloodlust, her bringing him back, reminding him of the stakes. It was the same here, except she was all too rational, too clinical. She knew what she wanted, and she knew the stakes. But if she saved herself, if she erased the memories, she would leave this structure and return to a primitive world, populated by people she had refused to save. Countless deaths would be on her conscience. She would be the same as the people in those tubes in Antarctica, never able to be happy again, always haunted by something from the past. She would never escape this moment, this decision.

The choice was simple: her or them. Save the people suffering from the false cure Janus had submitted to Continuity —or save herself. But it wasn't that simple at all. If she chose herself, she would never be the same. But if she chose them, she might lose the last bit of herself, the last piece that held on to the person she was, had become.

In that moment, she finally understood Martin. All the hard choices he had made, the sacrifices, the sort of burden he had borne for all those years. And why he had tried so desperately to keep her far away from this world.

She felt herself take the backpack and pull the computer out. She brought up the Continuity program and typed quickly. She saw it—what Janus had done. He was very clever. He had been looking for the pure form of the Atlantis Gene the entire time. The section of the ship with their research database had been completely destroyed, and their space vessel had been locked down, making the database there inaccessible. Finding the body of the alpha had been his only choice.

It was amazing: in the genome maps, she could see all the endogenous retroviruses now—those she and Janus had administered as well as the remnants of the changes she had helped Ares/Dorian with. It was as though she was working on a puzzle she couldn't solve as a child but had returned to as an adult, with the knowledge and mental ability to finally complete it. Martin had been correct. The interventions in the Middle Ages had caused changes to the genome with radical repercussions. And those changes had compromised the rollback therapy Janus had tried to unleash with the Bell.

In her mind, for the first time, she could grasp all the changes, see them like little glowing lights in a pile of rubble. She could pick them out now, line them up and form different patterns with different outcomes. She worked the computer, running scenarios.

The Symphony database—the collection of billions of sequenced genomes that had been collected in Orchid Districts around the world—was the last piece. It was a shame that the world had to come to the brink of annihilation for such an incredible feat to occur.

The true challenge was that Kate had to stabilize all the genetic changes—both those she and Janus had made as well as Ares' interventions. In essence, she was creating a therapy that would synchronize everyone: the dying, the devolving, and the rapidly evolving, creating a unified, stable genome. An Atlantean-human hybrid genome.

After almost half an hour of work, the screen flashed a message.

One Target Therapy Identified.

Kate examined it. Yes, it would work.

She should have felt euphoria, pride, or even relief. This was the moment she had worked for her entire life: both Atlantean and human. She had finally created a therapy that would complete her life's work, a genetic therapy that would save the human race and fix all the past mistakes. Yet it felt as though she had simply completed a science experiment, arrived at a conclusion she had suspected, hypothesized, *anticipated* her entire life. Where joy should have been there was a cold, clinical interest in the outcome. Perhaps the Atlanteans didn't feel joy in the same way. Maybe joy was so four million years ago for them.

That would be her next task: fixing herself, getting back to who she was before. She wondered what sort of chance that experiment had.

She grabbed the sat phone. "We need to get aboveground."

She followed David out of the ship. On the hillside, she briefly looked down at Ceuta. Dead horses and people lay across the black, charred expanse that led to the massive wall. Beyond the wall, the ground was stained red from the carnage David had unleashed. The last remnants of the plague barge floated in the water outside the harbor, slowly drifting toward the shore.

The scene... Yes, she had made the right decision, even if it meant that she was giving up the last piece of herself. She was sure of it now.

Kate plugged the sat phone into the computer and sent the results to Continuity.

When the data had uploaded, she disconnected the phone and dialed Paul Brenner.

He answered quickly but sounded distracted, unfocused. Kate had to repeat things several times. She realized what had happened: Paul had administered Janus's false cure there—on his own cohort. Continuity was now ground zero for the radiation from Janus's regression therapy, and it had infected Paul. But Kate couldn't do anything to help him. She could only hope he found her results and could remember what to do.

She ended the call. Only time would tell now.

Dorian walked into the dark cavern. "Now what?"

"Now we fight," Ares said, not taking his eyes off the miles of glass tubes.

"We have no ship," Dorian said.

"True. We can't take the fight to them, but we can bring them to us. There's a very good reason I buried this vessel here in Antarctica, Dorian."

95

CDC

Atlanta, Georgia

Paul Brenner steadied himself against the wall. It was so hard to concentrate. Where was everyone?

The halls were empty. The offices were empty. They were hiding from him. He had to find them.

No. He had to do something else. She had sent him something. The pretty one in the movies.

A set of glass doors slid open. The screens inside blinked.

ONE RESULT

One result. Result of what? A trial. He was the head of it.

Trial for what? A cure. For the plague. He was infected. With a cure. No, that couldn't be right. How could he be infected with a cure? Something was wrong.

He surveyed the room. Empty. Coffee cups all over the floor. Stained papers on the table and chairs.

Paul sat down and pulled a keyboard closer.
A flash of clarity seized him. *One result.*
He typed until his fingers ached.
The letters on the screen changed.

Transmitting new therapy to all Orchid Districts…

96

You're listening to the BBC, the voice of human triumph on this, the first day *after* the Atlantis Plague.

The BBC has learned that the initial reports of disorientation and brain fog associated with the cure for the Atlantis Plague were only temporary side effects of the cure.

Orchid Districts across the world now report a one hundred percent cure rate with no need for further Orchid treatments.

World leaders hailed the breakthrough, citing their historical investments in medical research and steadfast commitment to staying the course in these dark times.

In related news, sources within the intelligence community have reported that citizens of nations managed by Immari International have been ordered to evacuate coastal areas. The populations of entire regions in South Africa, Chile, and Argentina are heading into their mountainous regions with only food and water.

Dr. Phillip Morneau of the think tank Western Tomorrow had this to say: "They've lost. They bet on the plague running its course, on the ruin of humanity. And we've come through it, like we always have. It's fitting: they're literally heading for the hills."

More cautious observers have speculated that the Immari move might be part of a larger pattern, possibly the beginning of a counteroffensive.

We will update this report as details emerge.

97

CDC
Atlanta, Georgia

Paul Brenner trudged through the hallways of Continuity. He felt as though he were recovering from a severe head cold. But he could think now, and he knew what he had to do. He dreaded it, dreaded the answer.

As he passed the sliding glass doors that led to the operations room, he noticed a young female analyst sitting inside, alone, staring at the screen. The tables were still arranged haphazardly and coffee cups and crumpled papers littered the scene.

Paul stepped toward the doors. When they parted, the analyst looked back at him, her eyes a mixture of surprise and hope. Or relief? It caught Paul mildly off guard.

"You can go home now," he said.

She stood. "I know... I didn't think I should... be alone."

Paul nodded. "The others?"

"Must have left. Some are... still here."

In the morgue, Paul thought, completing her sentence in his mind. He walked over and turned the large screen off. "Come on. There's nobody at my house either."

They walked together out of the ops room, and Paul asked her to wait outside his nephew's room. He pushed the door open and braced himself for what he might see...

"Uncle Paul!"

His nephew rolled over in the bed. He was bright-eyed, but when he tried to push up, his muscles failed him, and he collapsed back onto the bed.

Paul rushed to the bedside and put a hand on the boy's shoulder. "Take it easy, kiddo."

The boy smiled at him. "You fixed me up, didn't you?"

"No. It was another doctor. She's much smarter than I am. I was just the delivery man."

"Where's Mom?"

Paul leaned forward, scooped the small boy into his arms, and headed out of the room. "Just rest now."

"Where are we going?"

"We're going home."

Paul would wait until the boy was stronger to tell him.

Until they both were stronger.

Kate had long since closed the laptop and moved to the end of the rock cliff.

David was there, behind her, waiting silently.

He seemed to sense that she needed some space, but he still wouldn't let her out of his sight.

Together, from the mountaintop, they watched the sun sink beyond the Atlantic. Its last rays slid down the mountain, casting a long shadow on the bloody scene at Ceuta. Across the straits, she knew the same thing was happening in

Gibraltar, with the Rock of Gibraltar casting the shadows there.

When the night arrived, Kate finally said, "What happens now? To us?"

"Nothing changes."

"*I've* changed. I'm not the same person—"

"What you just did confirmed to me who you are. *We* are going to be just fine. I can wait." He walked to the edge of the rock cliff so that he could look her in the eyes. "I never give up on anyone I love."

As his words were spoken, Kate realized that the most important part of her was still there. She wasn't entirely herself, but there was some piece of the old Kate there, something to start from. She smiled.

David tried to read her expression. He shrugged. "What? Too much?"

She took his hand. "No. I liked it. Come on. Let's go see what Milo's doing."

At the entrance to the tunnel, she said, "I think you're right. We're going to be just fine."

EPILOGUE

Arecibo Observatory
Arecibo, Puerto Rico

Dr. Mary Caldwell moved the mouse back and forth to wake up the computer. The screen came to life and began displaying the data collected overnight. The radio telescope outside her window was a thousand feet in diameter—the largest single-aperture telescope in the world. It was sunk into the ground, looking almost like a smooth gray plate that sat on a high plateau overlooking the green forested mountains beyond.

The first rays of sunlight were peeking over the mountains, into the dish. Mary never missed watching the scene, but it wasn't the same now, mostly because of the people they had lost.

Before the plague, there had been a dozen researchers manning the observatory; now there were three. Arecibo had been losing staff for years due to budget cuts. The plague had gotten the rest.

Yet Mary returned for her shift each day, as she had done for the previous six years. She had nowhere else to go, and there was nowhere else she wanted to be. She knew the U.S. government would get around to withdrawing their power allocation any day now, but she had decided to stay to the end, until the last lights went out. Then she would venture out into the world to see what sort of work there was for an astronomer.

She would have killed for a cup of coffee, but it had run out weeks ago.

She focused on the computer. There was... She clicked one of the data feeds. Mary's throat went dry. She ran an analysis, then another. Both confirmed that the signal was organized. Not random cosmic background radiation.

It was a message.

No, it was more than that: it was the moment she had waited for her entire life.

She glanced at the phone. In her mind, she had rehearsed this scene for the last twenty years, since she had first dreamed of becoming an astronomer. Her first instinct was to call the National Science Foundation. But she had called them once a week since the outbreak. And gotten no answer. She had also called SRI International—with the same results. Who to call? The White House? Who would believe her? She needed help, someone to analyze the transmission. The SETI Institute in Mountain View, California? She hadn't tried them. She'd had no reason to... Maybe—

John Bishop, another scientist on the project, stumbled into the office. He was usually only sober for about an hour after he woke up.

"John, I found something—"

"Please tell me it's more coffee."

"It's not coffee..."

The Wait is Over!

The Atlantis World—the conclusion to this worldwide bestselling trilogy—is now available!

A MYSTERIOUS SIGNAL FROM DEEP SPACE COULD BE HUMANITY'S LAST CHANCE OF SURVIVAL. AND REVEAL THE ULTIMATE SECRET OF OUR ORIGINS.

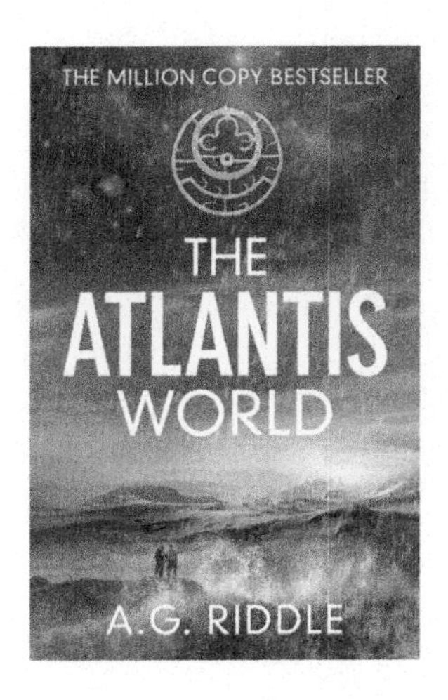

AGRiddle.com/Atlantis-World

Or turn the page... and read the first five chapters of *The Atlantis World* right now!

...

Thank you for reading *The Atlantis Plague*. If you have time, I'd appreciate a review on Amazon or GoodReads.
- Gerry (Riddle)

...

Wondering how much of *The Atlantis Plague* is fact and what's fiction?

Discover that & other bonus content at:

AGRiddle.com/plague-extras

THE ATLANTIS WORLD

A PREVIEW OF THE FINAL BOOK IN THE ORIGIN MYSTERY TRILOGY

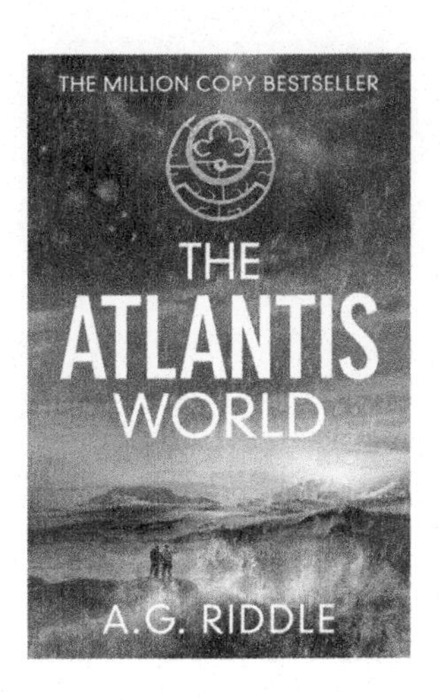

PROLOGUE

Arecibo Observatory

ARECIBO, Puerto Rico For the last forty-eight hours, Dr. Mary Caldwell had spent every waking second studying the signal the radio telescope had received. She was exhausted, exhilarated, and sure of one thing: it was organized, a sign of intelligent life.

Behind her, John Bishop, the other researcher assigned to the observatory, poured himself another drink. He had gone through the scotch, the bourbon, then the rum, and all the other booze the dead researchers had stockpiled until he was down to the peach schnapps. He drank it straight since they had nothing to mix it with. He winced as he took the first sip.

It was nine A.M., and his revulsion at the liquid would only last another twenty minutes, until his third drink.

"You're imagining it, Mare," he said as he set the empty glass down and focused on refilling it.

Mary hated when he called her "Mare." No one had ever called her that. It reminded her of a horse. But he was the only company she had, and the two of them had reached an understanding of sorts.

After the outbreak, when people across Puerto Rico were dying by the tens of thousands, they had holed up in the Observatory, and John had promptly made his first pass at her. She had brushed it off. The second followed two days later. After that, he made a move every day, each more aggressive than the last, until she had kneed him in the balls. He had been more docile after that, focusing on alcohol and snide remarks.

Mary stood and walked to the window, which looked out on the lush, green Puerto Rican hills and forests. The only hint of civilization was the satellite dish that lay recessed into a plateau in the hills, pointed straight up at the sky. The radio telescope at Arecibo Observatory was the largest radio telescope in the world, a triumph of human engineering. It was a marriage of sciences that represented the pinnacle of human achievement embedded in a primitive landscape that symbolized humanity's past. And now it had fulfilled its ultimate mission. Contact.

"It's real," Mary said.

"How do you know?"

"It has our address on it."

John stopped sipping the drink and looked up. "We should get out of here, Mare. Get back to civilization, to people. It will do you good—"

"I can prove it." Mary moved from the window back to the computer, punched a few keys and brought up the signal. "There are two sequences. I don't know what the second one is. I admit that. It's too complex. But the first sequence is composed of a simple repetition. On-Off. 0–1. Binary digits."

"Bits."

"Exactly. And there's a third code—a terminator. It appears after every eighth bit."

"Eight bits. A byte." John set the bottle aside.

"It's a code."

"For what?"

"I don't know yet." Mary walked back to the computer and checked the progress. "Less than an hour before the analysis is complete."

"It could be random chance."

"It's not. The first part, what's decoded, begins with our address."

John laughed out loud and grasped his drink again. "You had me for a minute there, Mare."

"If you were going to send a signal to another planet, what's the first thing you would put in? The address."

John nodded as he dumped more schnapps into the glass. "Uh huh, put the zip code in too."

"The first bytes represent two numbers: 27,624 and 0.00001496."

John paused.

"Think about it," Mary said. "What's the only constant across the entire universe?"

"Gravity?"

"Gravity is constant, but its measure depends on the curvature of spacetime, how close one object of mass is to another. You need a common denominator, something that any civilization, on any planet, no matter its mass or location, anywhere in the universe would know."

John looked around.

"The speed of light. It's the universal constant. It never changes, no matter where you are."

"Right..."

"The first number, 27,624, is Earth's distance from the center of our galaxy in light years."

"That distance could apply to a dozen planets—"

"The second number, 0.00001496, is the exact distance of

earth to the sun in light years."

John stared straight ahead for a long moment, then pushed the bottle and half-empty glass out of his vision. He focused on Mary. "This is our ticket."

Mary bunched her eyebrows.

John leaned back in his chair. "We sell it."

"For what? I think the malls have all closed."

"Well, I think the barter system is still in place. We demand protection, decent food, and whatever else we ever want."

"This is the greatest discovery in human history. We're not selling it."

"This is the greatest discovery in human history—at the moment of our greatest despair. This signal is hope. Distraction. Don't be a fool, Mare."

"Stop calling me Mare."

"When the plague broke out, you retreated here because you wanted to do something you loved until your time came. Me, I came here because I knew it was the biggest stockpile of booze anywhere in walking distance, and I knew you would come here. Yes, I've had a crush on you since I landed in San Juan." He held his hands up before Mary could say anything. "That's not my point. My point is that the world as you know it is over. People are desperate. They act out of self-interest. Sex and alcohol for me. For the folks you're going to call, it's about preserving their power. You're giving them the means to do that: hope. When you've delivered that, they won't need you anymore. This world isn't the one you remember. It will chew you up and spit you out, Mare."

"We're not selling it."

"You're a fool. This world slaughters idealists."

Behind her, the computer beeped. The analysis was complete.

Before she could read the results, a noise from the other side of the building echoed through the hall outside the office. Someone banging on the door? Mary and John's eyes met. They waited.

The banging grew louder, ending in the sound of glass breaking, scattering across the floor.

Footsteps, pacing slowly.

Mary stepped toward the door of the office, but John caught her arm. "Stay here," he whispered.

He picked up a baseball bat he had brought with him during the outbreak. "Lock this door. If they're here, the island's out of food."

Mary reached for the phone. She knew who she had to call now. Her hands shaking, she dialed the only person who could save them: her ex-husband.

1

Alpha Lander
1,200 Feet Below Sea Level

Off the Northern Coast of Morocco David Vale was sick of pacing in the small bedroom, wondering if, or when, Kate would return. He glanced at the bloody pillow. The pool that had started as a few drops ten days ago was now a river that stretched from her pillow half-way down the bed.

"I'm fine," Kate had said each morning.

"Where do you go every day?"

"I just need some time. And space."

"Time and space for what?" David had asked.

"To get better."

But she hadn't gotten better. Every day when Kate returned, she was worse. Each night brought more violent nightmares, sweats, and nosebleeds that David thought might not stop. He had held her, and he had been patient, waiting, hoping the woman who had saved his life, whose life he had saved two weeks ago, would somehow turn the corner and pull through.

But she slipped away a little more each day. And now she was late. She had never been late before.

He checked his watch. Three hours late.

She could be anywhere in the massive Atlantean ship, which covered sixty square miles and was buried just off the mountainous coast of Northern Morocco, directly across from Gibraltar.

David had spent the last fourteen days, while Kate was away, learning how to operate the ship's systems. He was still learning them. Kate had enabled the voice command routines to help with any commands David couldn't figure out.

"Alpha, what is Dr. Warner's location?" David asked.

The disembodied computer voice of the *Alpha Lander* boomed into the small room. "That information is classified."

"Why?"

"You are not a senior member of the research staff."

It seemed Atlantean computer systems were not immune to stating the obvious. David sat on the bed, just beside the blood stain. *What's the priority? I need to know if she's okay.* A thought occurred to him.

"Alpha, can you show me Dr. Warner's vital signs?"

A wall panel opposite the small bed lit up, and David read the numbers and chart quickly—what he could understand.

Blood Pressure: 92/47

Pulse: 31

She's hurt. Or worse—dying. What happened to her?

"Alpha, why are Dr. Warner's vitals abnormal?"

"That information is class—"

"Classified." David kicked the chair into the desk.

"Does that conclude your query?" Alpha asked.

"Not by a long shot."

David stepped to the double doors, which hissed open. He paused, then grabbed his sidearm. Just in case.

David had been marching down the dimly lit corridors for almost ten minutes when he heard a figure moving in the shadows. He halted and waited, wishing his eyes would adjust to the faint lights at the floor and ceiling. Maybe the Atlanteans could see in less light or perhaps the ship—the piece of the ship they occupied—was operating in power-saving mode. Either way, it made the alien vessel seem even more mysterious.

A figure stepped out of the shadow.

Milo.

David was surprised to see the Tibetan teenager this deep in the ship. Milo was the only other person who shared the ship with Kate and David, but he spent most of his time outside of it. He slept outside, just beyond the inclining shaft that led from the buried ship to the mountaintop, where the Berbers left food for them. Milo loved sleeping under the stars and rising with the sun. David often found him sitting cross-legged, meditating when he and Kate went to join him for dinner each night. Milo had been their morale officer for the last two weeks, but through the dim light, David now saw only concern on the young man's face.

"I haven't seen her," Milo said.

"Call me on ship's comm if you do." David resumed his rapid pace.

Milo fell in behind him, pumping his legs to keep up. David's muscular frame and six-foot three-inch height dwarfed Milo, who was a full foot shorter. Together, they looked like a giant and his young sidekick barreling through a darkened labyrinth.

"I won't need to," Milo said, panting.

David glanced back at him.

"I'll be with you."

"You should go back up top."

"You know I can't," Milo said.

"She'll be angry."

"If she's safe, I will not care."

Same here, David thought. They walked in silence, the only sound the rhythmic beating of David's boots pounding the metallic floor followed by Milo's fainter footfalls.

David stopped before a large set of double doors and activated the wall panel. The display read: Auxiliary Medical Bay 12

It was the only medical bay in their part of the ship, and it was David's best guess about where Kate went each day.

He moved his hand deeper into the green cloud of light that emerged from the wall panel, worked his fingers a few seconds, and the doors hissed open.

David crossed the room quickly.

There were four medical tables in the center. Holographic wall displays ran the length of the room—the empty room. Could she have already left?

"Alpha, can you tell me the last time this bay was used?"

"This bay was last used on mission date, 9.12.38.28, standard date 12.39.12.47.29—"

David shook his head. "How many local days ago?"

"Nine million, one hundred twenty eight thousand—"

"Okay, fine. Is there another medical bay within our section of the ship?"

"Negative."

Where else would she go? Maybe there was another way to track her.

"Alpha, can you show me which sections of the ship are currently consuming the most power?"

A wall screen lit up, and a holographic model of the ship

materialized. Three sections glowed: Arc 1701-D, Auxiliary Medical Bay 12, and Adaptive Research Lab 47.

"Alpha, what is Adaptive Research Lab 47?"

"An Adaptive Research Lab can be configured for a variety of biological and other experiments."

"How is Adaptive Research Lab 47 currently configured?" David braced for the response.

"That information is classified—"

"Classified," David muttered. "Right..."

Milo held out a protein bar. "For the walk."

David led Milo back into the corridor, where he ripped the wrapper open, bit off a large chunk of the brown bar, and chewed in silence. It seemed to help with the frustration.

David stopped in the corridor, and Milo almost slammed into the back of him.

David squatted and examined something on the floor.

"What is it?" Milo asked.

"Blood."

David walked faster after that, and the blood on the floor increased from a few drops to long stretches.

At the double doors to Adaptive Research Lab 47, David worked his fingers in the green light of the wall panel. He entered the open command six times, and each time, the display flashed the same message: Insufficient Access

"Alpha! Why can't I open this door?"

"You have insufficient access—"

"How can I get inside this door?"

"You cannot," Alpha's voice echoed through the corridor with finality.

David and Milo stood for a moment.

David spoke quietly. "Alpha, show me Dr. Warner's vital signs."

The wall display transformed, and the numbers and charts appeared.

```
Blood Pressure: 87/43
Pulse: 30
```

Milo turned to David.

"Dropping," David said.

"What now?"

"Now we wait."

Milo sat cross-legged and closed his eyes. David knew he was seeking the stillness, and in that moment, David wished he could do the same, could put everything out of his mind. Fear clouded his thoughts. He desperately wanted that door to hiss open, but he dreaded it as well, dreaded finding out what had happened to Kate, what experiment she was running, what she was doing to herself.

David had almost fallen asleep when the alarm went off. Alpha's voice thundered through the cramped corridor.

"Subject medical emergency. Condition critical. Access overrides executed."

The wide double doors to the research lab slid open.

David rushed in and rubbed his eyes, trying to understand what he saw.

Behind him, Milo spoke in awe, "Whoa."

2

Alpha Lander
1,200 Feet Below Sea Level

OFF THE NORTHERN COAST of Morocco "What is this?" Milo asked.

David scanned the research lab. "No idea."

The room was vast, at least one hundred feet long and fifty feet deep, but unlike the medical bay, there were no tables in the room. In fact, the only things on the floor were two glass vats, at least ten feet in diameter. Yellow light glowed inside, and sparkling white elements drifted from the bottom to the top. The vat on the right was empty. The other held Kate.

She floated a few feet off the ground, her arms held straight out. She wore the same plain clothes she had left their bedroom in this morning, but there was something new: a silver helmet. It covered her entire face, even the bottom of her chin. Her recently dyed brunette hair fell out of it and onto her shoulders. The small visor that covered her eyes was black, revealing no clues about what was happening to her. The only hint was a stream of blood that flowed out of the helmet, down her neck, and stained her gray t-shirt. The stain seemed to grow with each passing second.

"Alpha, what's... going on here?" David asked.

"Specify."

"What is this experiment? Procedure?"

"Resurrection memory simulation."

What does that mean? Is the simulation what's hurting her?

"How can I stop it?"

"You cannot."

"Why not?" David asked, growing impatient.

"Interrupting a resurrection memory sequence would terminate the subject."

Milo turned to David, fear in his eyes.

David searched the room. What to do? He needed some clue, somewhere to begin. He threw his head back, trying to think. On the ceiling, a single small dome of black glass stared down at him.

"Alpha, do you have video telemetry of this lab?"

"Affirmative."

"Begin playback."

"Specify date range."

"Begin the second Dr. Warner entered today."

A wave of light emanated from the left wall, slowly forming a hologram of the lab. The vats were empty. The double doors slid open, and Kate strode in. She marched to the right wall, which lit up and began flashing a series of screens full of text and symbols David couldn't make out. Kate stood still, her eyes darting slightly left and right, reading, taking in the screens, each of which remained for less than a second.

"Cool," Milo whispered.

David felt himself take a step back. In that moment, he realized some of what Kate had become, the growing gulf that existed between the power of her mind and his.

Two weeks ago, Kate had found a cure for the Atlantis Plague, a global pandemic that had claimed a billion lives in its initial outbreak and countless more during its final mutation. The plague had divided the world. The survival rate was low, but those who survived were changed at the genetic level. Some survivors benefited from the plague—they grew stronger and smarter. The remainder devolved, receding back to a primitive existence. The world's population had rallied around two opposing factions: the Orchid Alliance, which sought to slow and cure the plague, and Immari International, which had unleashed the plague and advocated letting the genetic transformation run its course. Kate, David, and a team of soldiers and scientists had stopped the plague and the Immari plan by isolating the pieces of a cure: endogenous retroviruses left by past Atlantean interventions in human evolution. The retroviruses were essentially viral fossils, the genetic breadcrumbs from instances where Atlanteans had modified the human genome.

In the final hours of the plague, with millions dying each minute, Kate had found a way to reconcile all the viral fossils and cure the plague. Her therapy had created a stable, unified Atlantean-Human genome, but she had paid a high price for the breakthrough.

That knowledge came from repressed memories within Kate's subconscious—memories from one of the Atlantean scientists who had conducted the genetic experiments on humanity over the course of thousands of years. The Atlantean memories enabled her to cure the plague, but they had also taken much of her own humanity—the part of Kate that was distinctly Kate and not the Atlantean scientist. As the clock had ticked down and the plague had spread around the globe, Kate had chosen to keep the Atlantean knowledge and cure the plague instead of ridding herself of the memories and protecting her own identity.

She had told David that she believed she could repair the damage the Atlantean memories had done, but as the days had passed, it became clear to David that Kate's experiments weren't working. She got sicker each day, and she refused to discuss her situation with David. He had felt her slipping away, and now, as he watched the playback, Kate reading the screens instantaneously, he knew that he had underestimated how drastic her transformation was.

"Is she reading that fast?" Milo asked.

"It's more than that. I think she's learning that fast," David whispered.

David felt a different kind of fear rising inside him. Was it because Kate had changed so much or because he was realizing how far over his head he was?

Start with the simple stuff, he thought.

"Alpha, how can Dr. Warner operate you without voice or tactile input?"

"Dr. Warner received a neural implant nine local days ago."

"Received? How?"

"Dr. Warner programmed me to perform the implant surgery."

Just one more thing that hadn't come up during their nightly *Honey, what did you do at work today?* discussion.

Milo cut his eyes at David, a slight grin forming on his lips. "I want one."

"That makes one of us." David focused on the holomovie. "Alpha, increase playback rate."

"Interval?"

"Five minutes per second."

The flashing screens of text morphed into solid waves, like

white water sloshing back and forth in a black fish tank. Kate didn't move a muscle.

Seconds ticked by. Then the screen was off, and Kate was floating in the glowing yellow vat.

"Stop," David said. "Replay telemetry just before Dr. Warner enters the round... whatever it is."

David held his breath as he watched. The screen with text went out, and Kate walked to the rear of the room, just beside the vats. A wall slid open, she grabbed a silver helmet, and then walked to the vat, which slid open. She stepped inside, donned the helmet, and after the glass vat sealed, lifted off the ground.

"Alpha, resume accelerated playback."

The room remained the same with a single exception: slowly, blood began trickling out of Kate's helmet.

In the last second, David and Milo entered, and then three words flashed on the screen.

`End of Telemetry`

Milo turned to David. "Now what?"

David glanced between the screen and the vat that held Kate. Then he eyed the empty one.

"Alpha, can I join Dr. Warner's experiment?"

The panel at the back of the room slid open, revealing a single silver helmet.

Milo's eyes grew wide. "This is a bad idea, Mr. David."

"Got any good ideas?"

"You don't have to do this."

"You know I do."

The glass vat rotated, its glass opening. David stepped inside, pulled the helmet on, and the research lab disappeared.

3

IT TOOK a few seconds for David's eyes to adjust to the bright light beaming into the space. Directly ahead, a rectangular display flashed text he couldn't make out yet. The place reminded him of a train station with its arrivals/departures board, except that there seemed to be no entrance or exit to the cavernous space, just a solid white floor and arched columns that let light shine through.

Alpha's booming voice echoed. "Welcome to the Resurrection Archives. State your command."

David stepped closer to the board and began reading.

```
Memory Date..Health.....Replay
=========== =========== ======
12.37.40.13..Corrupted..Complete
13.48.19.23..Intact.....Complete
13.56.64.15..Corrupted..Complete
```

A dozen rows continued—all complete. The last entry was:

`14.72.47.23..Corrupted..In-progress`

"Alpha, what are my options?"

"You may open an archived memory or join a simulation in-progress."

In-progress. Kate would be there. If she was hurt... or under attack. David glanced around. He had no weapons, nothing to defend her with. It didn't matter.

"Join simulation in progress."

"Notify existing members?"

"No," he said on instinct. The element of surprise might preserve some advantage.

The lighted train station and board faded and a much smaller, darker place took form. The bridge of a spaceship. David stood at the rear. Text, charts, and images scrolled across the walls of the oval room, covering them. At the front, two figures stood before a wide viewscreen, staring at a world that floated against the black of space. David instantly recognized both of them.

On the left stood Dr. Arthur Janus, the other member of the Atlantean research team. He had helped David save Kate from Dorian Sloane and Ares in the final hours of the Atlantis Plague, but David still had mixed feelings about Janus. The brilliant scientist had created a false cure for the Atlantis Plague that erased seventy thousand years of human evolution—reverting the human race to a point before the Atlantis Gene was administered. Janus had sworn that rolling back human evolution was the only way to save humanity from an unimaginable enemy.

David felt no such conflicting feelings for the scientist standing beside Janus. He felt only love. In the reflection of the black areas of space on the screen, David could just make out the small features of Kate's beautiful face. She concentrated hard on the image of the world. David had seen that look many times. He was almost lost in it, but a sharp voice, calling out from overhead, snapped him back.

"This area is under a military quarantine. Evacuate immediately. Repeat: this area is under a military quarantine."

Another voice interrupted. It was similar to Alpha's tone. "Evacuation course configured. Execute?"

"Negative," Kate said. "Sigma, silence notifications from military buoys and maintain geosynchronous orbit."

"This is reckless," Janus said.

"I have to know."

David stepped closer to the screen. The world was similar to earth, but the colors were different. The oceans were too green, the clouds too yellow, the land only red, brown and light tan. There were no trees. Only round, black craters interrupted the barren landscape.

"It could have been a natural occurrence," Janus said. "A series of comets or an asteroid field."

"It wasn't."

"You don't—"

"It wasn't." The viewscreen zoomed to one of the impact craters. "A series of roads lead to each crater. There were cities there. This was an attack. Maybe they carved up an asteroid field and used the pieces for the kinetic bombardment." The viewscreen changed again. A ruined city in a desert landscape took shape, its skyscrapers crumbling. "They let the environmental fallout take care of anyone outside the major cities. There could be answers there." Kate's voice was final. David knew that voice. He had *experienced it* several times himself.

Apparently Janus had as well. He lowered his head. "Take the *Beta Lander*. It will give you better maneuverability without the arcs."

He turned and walked toward the door at the rear of the bridge.

David braced. But Janus couldn't see him. *Can Kate?*

Kate fell in behind Janus but stopped and stared at David. "You shouldn't be here."

"What is this, Kate? Something is happening to you outside. You're dying."

Kate took two more long steps toward the exit. "I can't protect you here."

"Protect me from what?"

She took another step. "Don't follow me." She lunged through the exit.

David charged after her.

He stood outside. On the planet. He spun, trying—

Kate. She was ahead of him, in an EVA suit, bounding for the crumbling city. Behind them, a small black ship sat on the red rocky terrain.

"Kate!" David called, running toward her.

She stopped.

The ground shook once, then again, throwing David off his feet. The sky opened, and a red object poured through, blinding David and smothering him with its heat. He felt as though an asteroid-sized fire poker were barreling toward him.

He tried to stand, but the shaking ground pulled him down again.

He crawled, feeling the heat from above and the sizzling rocks below melting him.

Kate seemed to float over the shaking ground. She loped forward, timing her landings to the quakes that shot her up and forward, toward David.

She covered him, and David wished he could see her face through the mirrored suit visor.

He felt himself falling. His feet touched a cold floor, and his head slammed into the glass. The vat. The research lab.

The glass swiveled open, and Milo rushed forward, his eyebrows high, his mouth open. "Mr. David..."

David looked down. His body wasn't burned, but sweat covered him. Blood flowed from his nose.

Kate.

David's muscles shook as he pushed himself up and staggered to her vat. The glass opened, and she fell straight down, like a contestant in a dunking booth.

David caught her, but he wasn't strong enough to stand. They spilled onto the cold floor, her landing on his chest.

David grabbed her neck. The pulse was faint—but there.

"Alpha! Can you help her?"

"Unknown."

"Unknown why?" David shouted.

"I have no current diagnosis."

"What the hell's it going to take to get one?"

A round panel opened, and a flat table extended into the room.

"A full diagnostic scan."

Milo rushed to pick up Kate's feet, and David gripped under her armpits, straining with every last ounce of strength to lift her onto the table.

David thought the table took its sweet time gliding back into the wall. A dark piece of glass covered the round hole, and he peered inside at a line of blue light that moved from Kate's feet to her head.

The screen on the wall flickered to life, its only message:

```
DIAGNOSTIC SCAN IN PROGRESS...
```

"What happened?" Milo asked.

"I... We..." David shook his head. "I have no idea."

The screen changed.

Primary Diagnosis:
Neurodegeneration due to Resurrection Syndrome

Prognosis:
Terminal

Predicted Survival:
4–7 local days

Immediate Concerns:
Subarachnoid hemorrhage
Cerebral thrombosis

Recommended action:
Surgical intervention

Estimated Surgical Success Rate:
39%

With each word David read, more of the room disappeared. Feeling faded. He felt his hand reach out and brace the glass vat. He stared at the screen.

Alpha's words beat down upon him, smothering him like the heat from the fire poker on the ruined planet. "Perform recommended surgery?"

David heard himself say yes, and vaguely, he was aware of Milo putting his arm around him, though it barely reached the top of his shoulder.

4

Two Miles Below the Surface of Antarctica

THE SCREAMS SERVED as Dorian's only guide through the ship's dark corridors. For days, he had searched for their source. They always stopped as he drew near, and Ares would appear, forcing Dorian to leave the Atlantean structure that covered two hundred fifty square miles under the ice cap of Antarctica, making him return to the surface, back to the preparations for the final assault—grunt work that was beneath him.

If Ares was here, spending every waking hour in the room with the screams, that's where the action was. Dorian was sure of it.

The screams stopped. Dorian halted.

Another wail erupted, and he turned a corner, then another. They were coming from behind the double doors directly ahead.

Dorian leaned against the wall and waited. Answers. Ares had promised him answers, the truth about his past. Like Kate Warner, Dorian had been conceived in another time—before the

First World War, saved from the Spanish flu by an Atlantean tube, and awoken in 1978 with the memories of an Atlantean.

Dorian had Ares' memories, and those repressed recollections had driven his entire life. Dorian had seen only glimpses: battles on land, sea, air, and the largest battles of all, in space. Dorian longed to know what had happened to Ares, his history, Dorian's past, his origins. Most of all, he longed to understand himself, the *why* behind his entire life.

Dorian wiped away another bit of blood from his nose. The nose bleeds were more frequent now, as were the headaches and nightmares. Something was happening to him. He pushed that out of his mind.

The doors opened, and Ares strode out, unsurprised to see Dorian.

Dorian strained to see inside the chamber. A man hung from the wall, blood running from the straps cutting into his outstretched arms and the wounds on his chest and legs. The doors closed, and Ares stopped in the corridor. "You disappoint me, Dorian."

"Likewise. You promised me answers."

"You'll have them."

"When?"

"Soon."

Dorian closed the distance to Ares. "Now."

Ares brought his straightened hand across, striking Dorian in the throat, sending him to the ground, gasping for air.

"You will give me exactly one more order in your life, Dorian. Do you understand? If you were anyone else, I wouldn't even tolerate what you just did. But you are me. More so than you know. And I know you better than you know yourself. I haven't told you about our past because it would cloud your judgment. We have work to do. Knowing the full truth would put you at risk. I'm depending on you, Dorian. In a few short days, we will control this planet. The survivors, the remainder of the human race—a race, I remind you, that I helped create, helped save from extinction—will be the founding members of our army."

"Who are we fighting?"

"An enemy of unimaginable strength."

Dorian got to his feet but kept his distance. "I have quite an imagination."

Ares resumed his brisk pace, Dorian following at a distance. "They defeated us in a night and a day, Dorian. Imagine that. We were the most advanced race in the known universe—even more advanced than the lost civilizations we had found."

They reached the crossroads where an enormous set of doors opened onto the miles of glass tubes that held the Atlantean survivors. "They're all that's left."

"I thought you said they can never awaken, that their trauma from the attacks was too great for them to overcome."

"It is."

"You got someone out. Who is he?"

"He's not one of them. Of us. He's not your concern. Your concern is the war ahead."

"The war ahead," Dorian muttered. "We don't have the numbers."

"Stay the course, Dorian. Believe. In a few short days, we will have this world. Then we will embark on the great campaign, a war to save all the human worlds. This enemy is your enemy too. Humans share our DNA. This enemy will come for you too, sooner or later. You cannot hide. But together, we can fight. If we don't raise our army now, while the window exists, we lose everything. The fate of a thousand worlds rests in your hands."

"Right. A thousand worlds. I'd like to point out what I see as a few key challenges. *Personnel.* There are maybe a few billion humans left on earth. They're weak, sick, and starving. That's our army pool—assuming we can even take the planet, and I'm not even sure of that. So a few billion, not necessarily strong, in our 'army.' And I use that term loosely. Up against a power that rules the galaxy... Sorry, but I don't like our chances."

"You're smarter than that, Dorian. You think this war will resemble your primitive ideas about space warfare? Metal and plastic ships floating through space shooting lasers and explosives at each other? Please. You think I haven't considered our situation? Numbers aren't our key to victory. I made this plan forty thousand years ago. You've been on the case three months. Have faith, Dorian."

"Give me a reason."

Ares smiled. "You actually think you can goad me into giving you all the answers your little heart desires, Dorian? Want me to make you feel good, whole, safe? That's why you came to Antarctica originally, isn't it? To find your father? Uncover the truth about your past?"

"You treat me like this—after all I've done for you?"

"You've done for yourself, Dorian. Ask me the question you really want to ask."

Dorian shook his head.

"Go ahead."

"What's happening to me?" Dorian stared at Ares. "What did you do to me?"

"Now we're getting somewhere."

"There's something wrong with me, isn't there?"

"Of course there is. You're human."

"That's not what I mean. I'm dying. I can feel it."

"In time, Dorian. I saved your people. I have a plan. We will establish a lasting peace in this universe. You don't know how elusive that has been." Ares stepped closer to Dorian. "There are truths I can't reveal to you. You're not ready. Have patience.

Answers will come. It's important I help you understand the past. Your misinterpretation could sink us, Dorian. You're important. I can do this without you, but I don't want to. I've waited a long time to have someone like you by my side. If your faith is strong enough, there's no limit to what we can do."

Ares turned and led them out of the crossroads, away from the long hall that held the tubes, toward the portal entrance. Dorian followed in silence, a war beginning in his mind: blindly obey or rebel? They suited up without another word and crossed the ice chamber beyond, where the Bell hung.

Dorian lingered, and his eyes drifted to the ravine where he had found his father, frozen, encased in ice within the EVA suit, a victim of the Bell and his Immari lieutenant, who had betrayed him.

Ares stepped up onto the metal basket. "The future is all that matters, Dorian."

The dark vertical shaft passed in silence, and the basket stopped at the surface. The rows of pop-up habitats spread out across the flat sheet of ice like an endless flow of white caterpillars dug into the snow.

Dorian had grown up in Germany and then London. He only thought he knew cold. Antarctica was a wilderness with no equal.

As he and Ares strode toward the central ops building, Immari staffers clad in thick white parkas scurried between the habitats, some saluting, others keeping their heads down as the winds hit them.

Beyond the caterpillar habitats, along the perimeter, heavy machinery and crews were building the rest of "Fortress Antarctica" as it had become known. Two dozen rail guns sat silently, pointed north, ready for the attack the Immari knew would come.

No army on Earth was prepared to wage war here—even

before the plague. Certainly not after. Air power would mean nothing in the face of the rail guns. Even a massive ground assault, with cover from artillery from the sea, would never succeed. Dorian's mind drifted to the Nazis, his father's successors, and their foolish winter campaign in Russia. The Orchid Alliance would face the same fate if, or more likely, when, they landed here.

Soldiers greeted Dorian and Ares inside central ops and lined the hallways, standing at attention as the two leaders passed. In the situation room, Ares addressed the director of operations. "Are we ready?"

"Yes, sir. We've secured the assets around the world. Minimal casualties."

"And the search teams?"

"In place. They've all reached the specified drill depths along the perimeter. A few had trouble with pockets in the ice, but we sent follow-up teams." The director paused. "However, they haven't found anything." He punched a keyboard, and a map of Antarctica appeared. Red dots littered the map.

What's he looking for? Dorian wondered. *Another ship? No. Martin would have known, surely. Something else?*

Ares stared back at Dorian, and at that moment, Dorian felt something he hadn't in a long time, even in the corridor below, when Ares had struck him. Fear.

"Have they lowered the devices I supplied?" Ares asked.

"Yes," the director said.

Ares walked to the front of the room. "Put me on base-wide comm." The director punched a few keys and nodded to Ares.

"To the brave men and women working for our cause, who have sacrificed and labored toward our goal, know this: the day we have prepared for has arrived. In a few minutes, we will offer peace to the Orchid Alliance. I hope they accept. We seek peace here on Earth so that we can prepare for a final war with an enemy who knows no peace. That challenge is ahead. Today, I thank you for your service, and I ask you to have faith in the hours to come." Ares focused on Dorian. "And as your faith is tested, know this: if you want to build a better world, you must first have the courage to destroy the world that exists."

ALSO BY A.G. RIDDLE

The Long Winter

COMPLETED TRILOGY

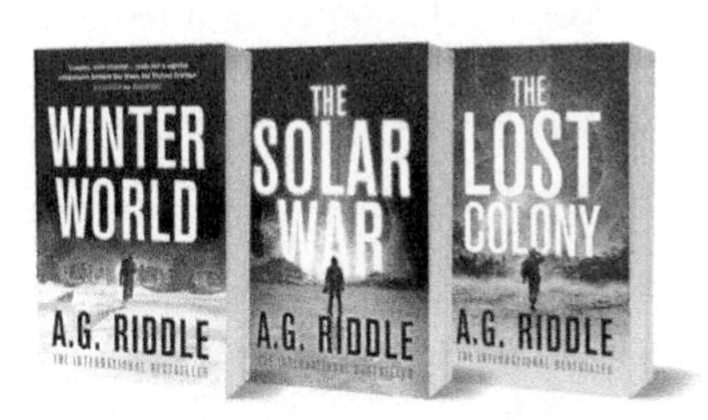

The Extinction Files

COMPLETED DUOLOGY

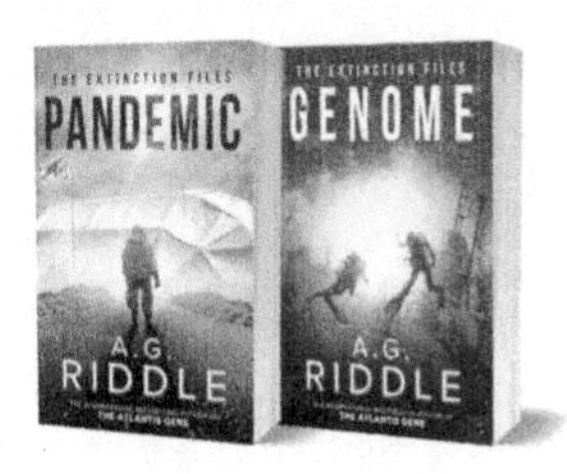

Departure

STANDALONE

SEE MORE AT: AGRiddle.com

AUTHOR'S NOTE

Thank you for reading.

The last eight months since publishing *The Atlantis Gene* have been surreal, exhausting, exhilarating, and everything in between.

I hope *The Atlantis Plague* was worth the wait. I wanted to take the time to write the best novel I could.

So many of you were kind enough to write a review of *The Atlantis Gene*, and I will be forever grateful. Those reviews helped shine a light on my work, and I've tried very hard to deserve the attention. I've also learned a great deal from those reviews, and the many words of encouragement were certainly a source of inspiration while writing this novel.

If you have time to leave a review, I would truly appreciate it, and I look forward to hearing your feedback.

Click here to write a review on Amazon: https://www.amazon.com/review/create-review?asin=B00GR5JZHQ

Update 5/5/14: *The Atlantis World*, the third and final book in The Origin Mystery trilogy is now available! Find out more at: www.AGRiddle.com/world

I hope you enjoy the last installment in the series, and thanks again for reading.

- Gerry

A.G. Riddle

PS: My web site has a "Fact vs. Fiction" section that explores the science and history in the *The Atlantis Plague*: AGRiddle.com. And, as always, feel free to email me (ag@agriddle.com) with any thoughts or feedback. Sometimes it takes me a few days, but I answer every single email.

ACKNOWLEDGMENTS

It's mind boggling how many people I need to thank.

One thing I've learned is that writing is a lot simpler when you're just writing (and not "being a writer"). I love writing, but being a writer, boy that's time-consuming!

There's a growing group of people who have helped me to focus on writing and to do my very best during those hours when I'm typing, pacing, and thinking (that's what it looks like when I'm writing).

At home, Anna ensures that I bathe regularly and maintain some social function (helpful when writing non-Atlantean characters). And now she's become involved in this riddled writing adventure, performing proofreading, marketing, and pretty much everything else except for stringing sentences together (I have to earn my keep somehow).

I also want to thank:

My mother, for her guidance and encouragement, as always.

David Gatewood, my outside editor extraordinaire, for turning this manuscript around faster than a quantum cube.

Carole Duebbert, my final review editor, for absolutely outstanding proofreading and suggestions.

Juan Carlos Barquet, for the truly brilliant original artwork for *The Atlantis Gene* (and soon to be *Plague*).

And finally, two groups I've never met.

The first: you. Readers who stick around for the Author's Note and the Acknowledgments, visit the web site, sign up for the email list, write reviews on Amazon, and sometimes, write me a note after they turn the last page.

Hearing from you all over the last eight months has been an experience I can't describe. And one I will never forget. It has truly been the most rewarding part of this entire endeavor. I simply can't thank you enough for supporting my work this early in my career.

And: to my beta readers. I'm sorry I didn't get this to you sooner, but I want to thank you from the bottom of my heart. You are: Holly Fournier, Andrea Sinclair, Annette Wilson, Christine Girtain, Dave Renison, Dr. Andrew Villamagna, Drew Allen, Jane Eileen Marconi, Joe O'Bannon, John Schmiedt, Joseph DeVous, Markel Coleman, Richard Czeck, Skip Folden, Steve Boesen, Ted Hust, Tim Rogers, Tina Weston, Doctor Liz, Amber K. O'Connor PhD of akoWriting LLC, Paula Thomas, Dustin Hermon, Dr. Tera Montgomery, Tom Vogel, Matt Fyfe, and many others.

ABOUT THE AUTHOR

A.G. Riddle spent ten years starting internet companies before retiring to pursue his true passion: writing fiction.

His debut novel, *The Atlantis Gene*, is the first book in a trilogy (*The Origin Mystery*) that has sold over three million copies worldwide, has been translated into 20 languages, and is in development to be a major motion picture.

His fourth novel, *Departure*, follows the survivors of a flight that takes off in 2015 and crash-lands in a changed world. HarperCollins published the novel in hardcover in the fall of 2015, and 20th Century Fox is developing it for a feature film.

Released in 2017, his fifth novel, *Pandemic*, focuses on a team of researchers investigating an outbreak that could alter the human race. The sequel, *Genome*, concludes the two-book series.

His most recent novel, *Winter World*, depicts a group of scientists racing to stop a global ice age.

Riddle grew up in Boiling Springs, North Carolina and graduated from UNC-Chapel Hill. During his sophomore year in college, he started his first company with a childhood friend. He currently lives in Raleigh, North Carolina with his wife, who endures his various idiosyncrasies in return for being the first to read his new novels.

No matter where he is, or what's going on, he tries his best to set aside time every day to answer emails and messages from readers. You can reach him at: ag@agriddle.com

** For a sneak peek at new novels, free stories, and more, join the email list at:

agriddle.com/email

Made in the USA
Las Vegas, NV
19 March 2021